canecutter

davide a cottone

Publicious for P.I.E. Books

Published through Publicious for P.I.E. Books
www.publicious.com.au

Legal Deposit Lodgment: (In accordance with the Copyright Act 1968)
National Library of Australia
State Library of Queensland
Parliamentary Library (Qld)

Cataloguing-in-Publication Data
National Library of Australia
Author: Cottone, D.A. (Davide A.)
Title: canecutter / Davide A Cottone
ISBN: 978-0-9873076-0-6
Dewey Number: 920.7109943

Cover design by Chelmer Office Services.
Cover Photo by Claire Elizabeth Cottone.
Book layout and design by Publicious Pty Ltd

To the Cottone Family
past
present
and future

canecutter's son

(about the author)

Dave Cottone comes from a good Sicilian immigrant family. He loved and honoured his mother and his father and the family is sacred to him. Although he was born in Australia in the bustling little sugar town of Babinda in Far North Queensland, English was in fact his second language.

He writes plays, poetry, songs, musicals, guides, short stories and novels and tells children's stories just for fun. He believes that each piece of writing has a soul with a conscience; a *sotto ego* with its writer's DNA. He insists that's why copyright is sacred. No one has the right to steal another person's soul.

If the *ego* can be defined as the 'self' and the *alter ego* as the 'other self'; the *sotto ego* is the 'secret self'— coming from the Italian word *sotto* meaning 'soft' or 'beneath', as in the expression *sotto voce* meaning 'in a soft tone'. Like a fingerprint, the *sotto ego* is unique to each individual.

Finally, he believes the *sotto ego* has a voice. It is exercised through the Arts and lingers in our hearts and minds like a kindred spirit.

Acknowledgments

A heartfelt thank you to my advisers and my proofreaders for their corrections and suggestions, my family for their memory jogs especially brother Ross and cousin Sam, my Chief-Editor Lauren Fletcher, my Sub-Editor Jennifer Lang-McIntyre and my daughter Claire for the evocative cover photo, which captures the loneliness of *canecutter* cutting cane at night by the light of a solitary hurricane lamp.

Above all, a big thanks to *Sotto*— *canecutter's* brother, the friendly little kindred spirit that you are all about to meet in this story.

Contents

COTTONE FAMILY CHART

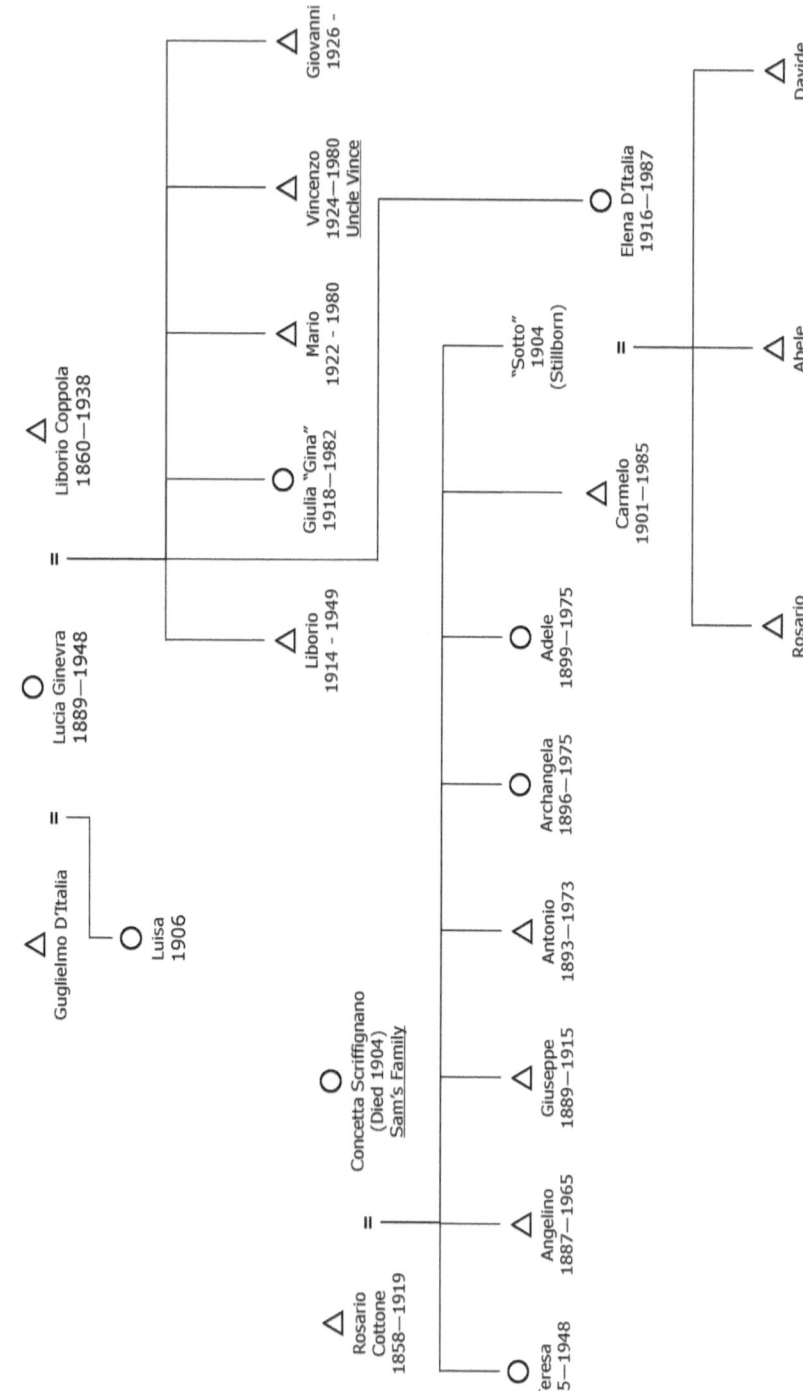

Canecutter

(by davide a cottone)

It was all shade the sugar cane was green
The work so hard their teeth were tight
In time as arms did clasp it round 'twas seen
That if 'twas burnt 'twas half the fight
How white they smiled. With song
'Tis burnt they cried
And what a sight they were
Yet were so wrong
The mighty men
That they were then.

In sweat they worked to the gong
As goodwill seemed to make it light
They slaved a day so long
To earn the pound that paid their plight
But as the time had come it moved unseen
Their backs were eased that were so tight
By arms that lift, the first machine
No longer theirs, 'twas steel 'gainst might.

They cheered poor fools who did not know its mean
Their backs grew fat it crept like night
They turned, the cut was gone, a new machine.
Now they are lean their face is quiet
All gone the smile the song the pound
All gone except the fright.

They did no wrong
These mighty men
That they were then.

The collier and the smith
Who used to spit out dust and fire
Are but the work-worn sons of him
That did the canecutter sire.

Break up their madness and scatter its fall
But mingle their ashes as greatest of all.

Chapter 1

Kindred spirit

I made a promise to Carmelo that after his departure from this world I would get his story out there. After all, I really was in the best position to do so. I knew him from when he was three years old. As a kindred spirit of the Cottone clan, I was given the grace to migrate across to his body as a sort of *sotto ego* attached to his physical being but separate from his psychological persona. When he eventually got to know me, he named me Sotto.

The transmigration happened like this. My mother was Concetta who was also Carmelo's mother. I never knew my mother as I was stillborn and she died from complications shortly after. I entered this world homeless, so I attached myself to the youngest in the family, Carmelo, who had three brothers and three sisters. He couldn't remember our mother either because he was so young when she died in 1904.

Teresa was the first-born in the family. She was crippled by polio as a child and was only mobile due to an improvised 'wheelchair', which was really a modified kitchen chair with wheels on each of the legs. She would propel herself along using anything within reach and her mobility was no handicap when it came to capturing and meting out punishment to any one of her younger siblings who misbehaved. After Concetta died, Teresa who was merely 19 years old, assumed the mantra of *matriarch*.

After Teresa came Angelino, Giuseppe, Antonio, Archangela and Adele. Their father Rosario was a huge man who had the gift of the gab and was often engaged in the heat of one discussion or another in the village square in the little Sicilian town of Agira.

At night, I slept in the spare bed near the press where the olives were crushed. It was tucked away in the lean-to attached to the house so I was privy to everything that transpired in the household. So, despite having to grow up in obscurity, it was in that spare bed and often when I was supposed to be asleep that I developed a certain wisdom; the wisdom of having to listen to others, to learn from their mistakes, meditate on their stupidity, marvel at their simplicity, empathize with their sorrows and love them for their shortcomings. Eventually, I would convince myself that despite my non-existence in their lives, I was probably their last and only hope in so far as telling his story because Carmelo spent most of his life abroad.

Anyhow, it was not long after I attached myself to Carmelo that he became very sick. In fact the whole village of Agira had been in lockdown since the first cases of smallpox were detected. Every night the conversation always returned to who had been afflicted with it, who was in hospital and what the government was doing about it. But one night, the ugliness came to our doorstep and into our very lounge room as fate would have it.

"The symptoms are not good, Don Rosario," said Dr Padrone. "If he has the disease, you are all in danger of catching it, so you have to make a decision immediately. The best place for him is in the hospital."

After the doctor left with a bottle of homemade wine tucked into his coat pocket as payment for his services, Rosario called Teresa into the kitchen.

"What are we going to do Teresa? Carmelo has contracted the disease and Dr Padrone wants me to put him in hospital."

"Not while I'm alive will our little Carmelo be going to any hospital. When smallpox comes to the village, hospitals are no longer hospitals. They become quarantine stations and they make sure nobody ever comes out again. That's how they controlled it in the past and that's how they'll control it now. No Papa, Carmelo stays with us."

"But Teresa," he protested, "what about the other children? They have to be protected."

"And so they will be Papa. Tonight we pack and tomorrow

morning, before dawn, you and I will take Carmelo up to our little sheep shack in the mountains near Assoro. There I will nurse him back to health and you will all be safe here. When he gets better, I will send word. In the meantime, arrange to deliver enough food and water up there to sustain us."

"But what about you, Teresa?"

"You don't need to worry about me, Papa. If the good Lord didn't let them take me with polio, there must be a reason for it and He's not going to let them take me now!" As Papa cast his eyes downwards, Teresa pulled herself over towards him "These are the children that I'll never have Papa... they are my children and Carmelo is my baby, Papa... you have to think of it that way."

Rosario never replied. He merely patted her on the shoulder and entered the lean-to to collect a couple of boxes, a lantern, some olive oil, flour, olives, wine, anchovies, a jar of preserved vegetables and some preserved fruit then returned to the kitchen where the sounds of packing and the secret chatter of their voices lulled me to sleep.

I was awake before they were and had already hitched myself onto Carmelo in readiness for the ride up to the sheep shack in the mountains. He was on fire and his skin was blotched all over. He could only stare at the ceiling. Rosario gathered all the siblings into the lounge room where he led the prayers. He was strong in the faith having been raised by his uncle, a Catholic priest, from when he was ten until he was married. The priest virtually adopted him and in that time Rosario not only learned the ways of the Lord but also how to read and write. This set him apart from most of the villagers in Agira. On some occasions, he would help his uncle light the candles in the Church and in the evening he would extinguish them. Today he lit a candle for Carmelo but this time it would remain lit until Carmelo returned home again.

The mules were tethered outside the house and Rosario had loaded one with all the provisions including Teresa's chair, while a second was saddled up to carry Teresa and the little boy. Rosario led the mules out through the creaky gate and glanced quickly towards the house where five little faces were peering at them through the windows. He then set off for the three-hour trek into the mountains. Nobody would look for Carmelo there.

The rugged Sicilian landscape of earthy colours during those early hours of the morning grew more and more beautiful with every slight increase in the intensity of the light. The dew sparkled on the grass. As the shadows vanished from behind the trees and huge boulders, it was as if the spirits of the night were departing as well so as not to be caught in the hysteria and hustle and bustle of the usual day in the life of mortals.

Soon the dilapidated frame of the old sheep shack came into view. It certainly was in a severe state of disrepair both inside as well as out. The shack was never meant to offer the comforts of home; rather to provide a bare essential shelter for the shepherds who cared for the sheep in the summer months. With the cooling autumn winds beginning to rustle in the trees, it would be a cold and miserable shelter in the weeks ahead.

"Papa, Carmelo is crying. Check the house for snakes and then set me up inside so that I can nurse him to sleep before you start unpacking the mule. Then you'll need to get me plenty of wood for the fire and make sure all the latches on the doors are secure."

She was good at barking out the orders and Papa was happy to oblige. He also did anything extra he could think of and set about sweeping the floor, making up the small bed for Teresa and converting the little bench against the wall into a bunk for Carmelo. I had already spotted where I was going to sleep; a cozy little nook, hard-up against the fireplace opposite the firewood stack and between Teresa's bed and the kitchen table. I would be able to observe everything from there.

Before he left, Papa explained to Teresa what Dr Padrone had told him about the disease.

"After two or three days, the rash will fade and the fever will diminish. But in one or two days after that, Teresa, the fever will return. The rash will return to the face, hands, feet, stomach, back and chest. It will turn into blisters and over ten to twelve days the clear fluid in the blisters will turn into pus, forming scabs that will take about three weeks to fall off." Teresa listened carefully and nodded as each stage of the disease was described to her. He then prepared to leave early enough to enable him to reach home by dusk; but only after Teresa had tempered his disquiet by assuring him that she had everything under control and that he was needed by the children at home.

"May God bless you, my beloved daughter and be with you and Carmelo. We will pray for you both every day, that God will have mercy on you and that the spirit of your mother Concetta will be with you every minute." He then climbed onto the mule, made the sign of the cross and dug his heels gently into its flank until it finally moved off with its mate in tow. He never looked back.

When Teresa was alone at last she took a little round hand-mirror from her purse, glanced into it and recoiled as if in horror at what she saw. She looked again and there were tears this time. She extracted the hair brush from her purse and balanced the mirror against the box on the table. With ever so gentle strokes she placed every loose strand back in place and secured it all in a bun at the back of her head. She turned to Carmelo, picked him up and hugged him.

"There my little man. You have absolutely no excuse to cry now. So go to sleep and God willing, tomorrow we will begin working on your recovery."

It happened as Dr Padrone said it would. Teresa never stopped bathing the little boy through the fevers and wrapping him against the chills. She sang to him, nursed him day and night and hardly ever slept. When he fell asleep, she prayed out loud. She rarely ate. The body fluid in the blisters turned to pus and then into scabs and day after day Teresa thanked God for His mercy. And He in turn spared them both and on the thirty-fifth day when the last scab tumbled off, Teresa sent word for Papa to fetch them both.

Rosario arrived with the two mules and all the family. There was such joy on the faces of all the children and they screamed and called out to her as Teresa came to the door with Carmelo in her arms. But then the reality of her suffering overcame them.

"You are so thin, precious sister," said Archangela.

"And pale as a ghost," said Antonio.

"Thank God for His mercy," said Angelino quietly as he took Teresa's hand and kissed it.

"You are so brave," said Adele as she threw her little arms around them both hugging them. Giuseppe just cried and Papa ushered them all into the shack.

"Come on my children, I have prepared the nicest pot of pasta sauce and brought along the best pecorino cheese you will have ever tasted. Tonino," he ordered, "boil up a big pot of water and Archangela set the table for a big plate of pasta."

Everyone went about doing some chore or another as the water boiled and the pasta was cooked and they ate. Teresa was not allowed to do one single thing for the rest of the day, except nurse Carmelo who simply refused to let anybody take him away from her anyhow.

Chapter 2

Crisis in the house of Don Rosario

Despite the deliverance of Carmelo by the grace of God, another crisis was about to be wrought upon the house of Don Rosario. Prior to the onset of winter, Rosario decided he should arrange for the clearing of some secondary growth in the wheat field, which had been left to him by his uncle on his mother's side, Padre Luigi who had passed away soon after Carmelo was born. In fact, the Padre had left him several plots of land on the outskirts of Agira and what with the land he had acquired originally in Agira through his marriage to Concetta from the Scriffignano family, Rosario was very well off in terms of financial security.

However, the land was not much value to him lying idle and he needed to fell the secondary growth so that it could dry during the winter. Some of the wood would be sold and the rest of the shrubs would be piled up and burned before spring in preparation for ploughing and subsequent sowing of wheat for the next summer harvest. Of course, Rosario himself would not be submitted to the manual labour involved as he was not accustomed to labouring work. After all, his whole youth had been spent with Padre Luigi in and around the church and he had never had to do anything more strenuous than lighting or putting out candles. So the task of clearing was left to Angelino who was 17 at the time, Giuseppe who was 15 and Antonio who was only 11.

They left the family home in Agira early one morning with two mules and a dray; the latter loaded with an array of tools, brush knives, saws, an assortment of timber and iron, some chains and a basket of food and wine that Teresa had prepared the night before. Carmelo was still weak but his father thought the day out would do him good, so Antonio hoisted him onto his shoulders and they started off for the 25-minute walk to the wheat field. I was in my usual position, so I had a particularly good 'bird's-eye view' of everything from way up there. Carmelo was so excited; wriggling around, squirming and giggling as Antonio occasionally tickled him in the ribs and jostled him from side to side.

About two hours into the job, they sat down for a bite to eat and a sip of wine. It was a beautiful day and the mules were tugging away at the last remnants of dry autumn grass hiding amongst the rocks and the palings along the fence line. An old woman was coming towards them from the neighbouring property. She had a determined stride and as she approached, the scowl on her face was easily discernible.

"Eh... Don Rosario, what are you doing here?" she snarled.

"Well, Signora Bellotta," he replied jovially, "we're having a sip of wine and a bite to eat. This is Angelino, Giuseppe, Antonio and Carmelo," he said as he pointed them out in turn, "Would you like to join us?"

"No, but I would like to know what you are doing on what was once my mother's land."

"Oh, we are just preparing it for the sowing of the next crop of summer wheat. It's been a few years now and it's time something was done with this land before it becomes all overgrown. It's had a good rest, so it should produce a bumper crop this summer."

"But this land doesn't belong to you," she insisted. "This land was given to the Church just before my mother died. You have no right to be here. It belongs to the Church."

"Oh no, Signora, you are mistaken. This land was left to me by my uncle, Padre Luigi when he died a couple of years ago. You remember, I lived with him at the Church for about ten years until I was married."

"But this land was never his to give, Don Rosario. My mother gave this land to Padre Luigi for the Church so that her soul and the souls of our ancestors would be delivered from purgatory. It was not given to him for his family. This land belongs to the Church. I don't care what he did with it when he was alive, but now that he's dead, it belongs to the Church. I suggest you pack up your things and go home as this is a matter that needs to be rectified before you do anything more on this property."

"Very well, Signora Bellotta but I can assure you all the paperwork is in order and this is only going to create unnecessary expenses for us both."

"Well, we'll see about that," she proposed as she turned her back on him and walked away. "We'll see about that. Thief!"

The suggestion that Rosario had stolen the land seemed to disturb him deeply.

"We'll soon sort this out," he assured his sons who were at a total loss as to what was happening. "Come on, let's pack up. I'll look into this as soon as we get home and we'll be back here in the morning."

That afternoon, Rosario went to the Office of the Registrar of Land Titles in Agira while the rest of the boys took the day off and went into town. The word had already gotten around that Don Rosario was trying to steal the land that Signora Bellotta had given to the Church and the boys were very uneasy about it.

That evening, I was asleep in the spare bed in the lean-to when Rosario returned. I awoke with a start when he came into the lean-to and called out to Teresa to come to him.

His daughter obeyed wondering what could warrant such an emergency consultation that it could not wait for her to finish her work. There was flour on her apron, a tea towel over her shoulder and her hands were wringing wet. Rosario helped her from her chair and she leaned on him shuffling towards the lean-to.

"Papa, what could be so important that you should summon me with such urgency?"

"Plenty, believe me daughter," he pulled up a chair for her. "Here sit... there is something very important that I need to speak to you about." He looked for a spot to sit near her and settled for the edge of the spare bed, "That business with Signora Bellotta has come as a bit of a surprise to me."

"I know," said Teresa, "the boys said it is all around Agira that the land is not legally ours. Is it, Papa?"

"Of course it is legally ours. I have just returned from checking the land titles and the land which once belonged to Signora Bellotta's mother was transferred to Uncle Luigi and all the signatures on the deed are in order. After Uncle Luigi died the land was transferred into my name in accordance with his will."

"So, there's no problem then?" She raised her hands suggesting that if there was no problem she would like to get back to her work.

"Well, there's a problem and there isn't a problem. If Signora Bellotta's mother gave the land to the Church as Signora Bellotta claims, then the Catholic Church should have been on the Title Deed as beneficiary, not Uncle Luigi."

"So, who said Signora Bellotta's mother gave the land to the Church and not to Padre Luigi? Both of them are dead and there is no proof either way," suggested Teresa. "People can leave possessions to their priest if they wish. There's no law against that is there?"

"No, not so far as I know," agreed Rosario, "but if Signora Bellotta chooses to contest the title, then it has to go to court. Who knows how that could all end up… these lawyers will keep the matter running in the courts until every last lire is sucked out of us and drained into their pockets. The problem is that Uncle Luigi left me several blocks of land and who knows what the story is with them? Once those people hear about Bellotta's complaint, they might start questioning the title deeds on those other blocks and some of them may raise a similar story to Signora Bellotta— that the lands were not left to Uncle Luigi but to the Church."

Teresa nodded her head, acknowledging there may be a problem, "So I guess we'll just have to wait and see. Now come on Papa, help me to the house and then wash quickly and have something to eat. You must be starving."

As it was, it did not take Signora Bellotta long to start the ball rolling. The next morning there was a knock on the door. It was the Court Bailiff.

"Don Rosario, I have been instructed by lawyers for Signora Bellotta to issue you with this summons to answer before the courts, questions about legal title to certain lands mentioned herein." He handed the summons to Rosario and by the time he had left, Teresa was already at her father's side.

"Not good news Papa. Now you must do what you have to do."

"Yes Teresa, this is where the blood-suckers move in. I will need to go and seek advice from Don Peppino."

"Yes and take Carmelo with you. He has to have his weekly check-up with Dr Padrone. We can't have all our good work wasted by finding he has an undetected sickness like bronchitis or something. I'll get him ready."

Of course, I got to go along for the ride. Don Peppino was very well respected in Agira and had always been a good friend and confidante of Rosario. Their fathers had fought together around the time of Giuseppe Garibaldi and the unification of Italy. Don Peppino threw his arms in the air the moment he opened his door to Rosario.

"Ah… Don Rosario, welcome my good friend," and then he shifted his gaze to Carmelo. "What a strong boy you must be Carmelo to have survived the dreaded smallpox. Terrible, terrible… come on in, come in Don Rosario."

Everybody knew everything in Agira almost the moment it happened so it was no surprise that Don Peppino knew about what had happened to Carmelo. He would also know everything about the Bellotta case as well, but pretended not to as Rosario told him his version of the events that transpired in the wheat field.

"Yes Don Rosario," he agreed, "there is no doubt now that you've been summonsed, Signora Bellotta is not going to let the matter go away. Her mother was Calabrese and you know these Calabrese as well as I do. They can be very stubborn."

Rosario nodded his head, encouraging Don Peppino to continue, "You have no choice but to go ahead with it and make sure you find a good lawyer."

"The problem, Don Peppino," added Rosario, "is that Padre

Luigi left me several blocks of land in this area when he passed away and if this case gains momentum, others may choose to contest the titles as well."

"Well, there's not much you can do about that until it happens. Remember, Don Rosario that Padre Luigi was dearly loved in this diocese. He brought great comfort to many people in his congregation. Many would have wanted to reward him personally knowing that he would have continued praying for their souls long after they had departed. I would have thought that if the land titles were transferred to his name, then those people wanted him to have the lands in question."

At this point, the Don's father entered the room and recognized Rosario immediately.

"Ah Rosario… Rosario Cottone… how good it is to see you again," and he came over and shook his hand. "Ah, you look so like your father, Giuseppe; tall, strong, determined. *'Viva l'Italia'* we always said to each other whenever we met. He was a great soldier. Tell me, how is all the family?"

"Good, Don Peppino," replied Rosario respectfully as Don Peppino Junior looked on. "We had a little bit of drama here with young Carmelo but the good Lord spared his life for which we are eternally grateful. And you'll be pleased to know my third eldest, Giuseppe who is fifteen, is talking about joining the army."

"Oh, I wouldn't recommend it… this business between the Socialists and the Nationalists is all going to come to no good. See where that young Mussolini was expelled from Switzerland last year? He's bad. There's trouble up ahead, I can feel it in my soul. They certainly don't make politicians like they used to," he laughed. "Well goodbye Rosario Cottone, Viva l'Italia and give my regards to that saint of a daughter of yours Teresa."

"He's such a character," said Don Peppino as his father ambled off.

"So, Don Rosario, I'm afraid that is where we are at."

"Can you recommend a good lawyer, Don Peppino?"

"No, because ultimately, they're only there to bleed you dry, but if it were me, I would consult with Giuseppe Sacco, of Sacco and Sacco. He is a competent lawyer."

After the usual ritual of passing on God's blessings, best wishes and the bottle of homemade wine from Rosario to Don Peppino, Rosario took his leave and headed up the hill with Carmelo for his consultation with Dr Padrone.

The consultation went well, but the aftermath from the court case in the weeks to follow could not have been worse. As feared, the worst case scenario was beginning to unfold. First one, then three and then five others decided to contest the validity of Rosario's title over the lands which they all claimed had been bequeathed to the Church and not to Padre Luigi.

"But the records do not show that the said lands were bequeathed to the Church," argued Giuseppe Sacco in his address to the presiding Magistrate. "If the records state the land belonged to Padre Luigi prior to being bequeathed to Rosario Cottone, then what is the purpose of the law, if not to protect those who abide by it? If the purpose of the law is to protect those who abide by it, then it should protect Rosario Cottone and inform the complainants that Rosario Cottone has no case to answer."

Antonio who had piggy-backed Carmelo into town this particular day to listen to the proceedings, reported this to Teresa who waited eagerly at home for snippets of news on the progress of the case.

"Well he certainly is a very competent lawyer," was her response to the news Antonio reported, but Rosario had another concern to muddy the equation when he returned home.

"Apparently, Teresa, once the Church was informed about the facts of this case, they felt there was a need to investigate this 'imbroglio' further. So they provided the complainants with a lawyer from Catania to ascertain whether or not there had been any impropriety. It seems the law is clear on this matter, but the Church made it difficult for the Magistrate to make a decision. As a result, he has been persuaded to give the complainants the benefit of the doubt and the case will now be heard in the District Court when it convenes in Agira."

Despite the fact that the law was clear, there would only be a resolution in Rosario's favour if the Church conceded and the Church was not about to concede.

"If six of God's flock have been prepared to swear on oath that each of their loved ones had told them that their lands were to go to the Church, yet instead were given to Padre Luigi, surely the Court needed to ascertain whether or not the said lands had in fact been acquired by deception. And if so, the validity of the titles must be disputed." This assertion proved to be the tipping point in the case.

"We will have to sell some of your mother's land in Agira to fund the case from here on," Rosario told his daughter one night. "According to Don Peppino it doesn't look good to challenge the Church. As well, they have unlimited funds. Our lawyer Giuseppe Sacco advises us to continue but meanwhile his fees pile up. What do you think, Teresa?"

"I'm afraid, Papa, you'll have to make the decision on this one based on the advice of people like Don Peppino."

So it came to pass that Rosario surrendered the land to the Church, who in turn agreed upon settlement, that it would not seek court costs against him out of respect for the good work Padre Luigi had done in the community throughout his forty years of service.

"The Padre will have to explain his actions to a Higher Authority," counsel for the complainants put it to the Court and in view of Rosario's acceptance that a wrong had been committed against these people, they did not wish to punish him to the extent where "the court fees of the Church would bankrupt this member of God's flock who has seven children."

Even Rosario went away believing he was lucky the Church had shown mercy, but there was no mercy shown by Giuseppe Sacco. Almost half of Rosario's land that had come to him as dowry from the Scriffignano family had to be sold to cover the expenses of the case and he now found himself facing financial ruin. The Don's fortunes had been decimated.

Chapter 3

First call to arms

Over the next few years, it soon became apparent that the fortunes of the whole community at large were in decline. The economy in Italy was on the brink of collapse. Unemployment was rampant; infrastructure was non-existent; corruption was endemic; government was completely ineffective and law and order was left in the hands of the *gabelloti*: power and money hungry overseers of the properties of the forever absent feudal landlords. In Sicily, everything was compounded by the *popolino*: a huge underclass of poverty-stricken illiterates who were abandoned by the society at large.

Throughout the countryside, peasant farmers who worked the farms and tended the livestock were being terrorized by bandits who stole their produce and their livestock. Farmers and shepherds were kidnapped for ransom and in some situations, people were being beaten and even shot. There was no respite offered by their absentee landlords or the corrupt government who failed to provide an effective system of law and order. This left the door wide open for the *Mafiosi* to fill the void, offering protection for money or anything else the *popolino* had to offer.

In the period leading up to Carmelo's eighth birthday, on the twenty-third of December 1909, Sicily's small towns like Agira had four local power centres; the Church, the local noblemen, the Mayor supported by the Town Council and the local patriarch known as the *galantuomo*, who was usually *mafioso*.

The Church was in complete denial of all the injustice engulfing the community, insisting that it was more concerned with the affairs of God than of men; a form of *give unto God that which belongs to God and give unto Caesar that which belongs to Caesar* mentality. That was until someone tried to take something that supposedly belonged to the Church as was seen in the case of Rosario's inheritance from Padre Luigi. The local noblemen were living the high life in Palermo, Catania and Caltanissetta in Sicily and in the cities on the mainland in Italy. They left their affairs in the hands of the *gabelloti* who were happy to take an agreed percentage off the top of the illicit gains made by the bandits and the *Mafiosi* exploiting the *popolino*. The Mayor and Town Council were so corrupt that everything had to be done *sotto mano* meaning bribery was the only means to get Government support and approval. The *galantuomo*, the local patriarch, ruled the roost. He ensured things got done. He offered protection to the people and despite his methods, he insisted and everybody agreed that he was a man of honour.

Meanwhile, small independent landholders like Rosario battled on as best they could. Giuseppe, who by now was twenty years old, had joined the army. Angelino and Antonio did the majority of the work on the farm, although Angelino was more of a thinker like his father. Teresa looked after the family and held the purse strings. Uncle Luigi the priest, who had had no family other than Rosario, had maintained his relationship with Rosario after he was married. He insisted that all of Rosario's children be schooled and provided money, resources and support towards their education. This education stood the whole family in good stead and Archangela and Adele would be assured of a good marriage as a result.

The twenty-third of December 1909 would be a very special day for Carmelo. Not only did he turn eight years old but Rosario and the boys would be inviting him into the world of men with the performance of a very important rite of passage.

Teresa and the girls had gone to great lengths to give Carmelo the best party he would ever have.

"So Archangela, you are going to be totally responsible for the *cannoli*. The ricotta cheese and the whipping cream are in the ice chest but you will need to fetch the pistachio nuts and the chocolate from the pantry. Adele, you can help me with the *biscotti* and you can decorate the *cassata* with the glazed fruit in that bowl." This was in addition to what Teresa had prepared the night before; mixed nut and toffee tart and hazelnut *biscotti* with a squiggle of icing on top, favourites of Rosario's; *torroni,* a favourite of Carmelo's; *tiramisu,* all the boys' favourite because it had massala in it; *chiacchiere,* a fried pastry which Don Peppino, Teresa's godfather loved and sweet cookies known as *ossi dei morti* baked in memory of their mother Concetta.

"Everybody will be here at three o'clock this afternoon so it all has to be done and the house has to be tidy well before then because we all have to get dressed to welcome the guests," she reminded them.

Carmelo was beside himself with excitement, but the biggest surprise was yet to come. The doorbell rang and Theresa told him to answer it. There at the door was Giuseppe in full army uniform with a big parcel wrapped in coloured paper under his arm.

"Carmeluzzo! Happy birthday Meluzzo!" he shouted and pushed the gift towards Carmelo.

"Giuseppe! Teresa, it's Giuseppe. He's back from the army!" yelled Carmelo and everybody in the house came running to embrace him.

At three o'clock, friends of Carmelo from school began arriving accompanied by their mothers or elder siblings. Then some of the neighbours arrived and by evening Aunty Teresa and Uncle Luigi Scriffignano, the brother-in-law of Don Rosario, arrived with all of the cousins on the Scriffignano side. They were Louisa, Antonino, Nina, Angelo, Pietro, Angelina, Maria and Gaetano the baby of the Scriffignano family. Carmelo's older siblings were so excited to see their cousins again that the whole house was buzzing with the energy and activities of the young folk.

Then the guest of honour, Don Peppino himself arrived. He was now galantuomo of the whole district and greatly respected. He was adored by his goddaughter Teresa and she would never entertain the idea of hosting an event without inviting him along. Everybody clapped when he entered.

Now that Don Peppino had arrived, it was time for the grand event of the evening.

"Dearest friends of the Cottone and Scriffignano families... As you know, Don Rosario and I went to school together and have always been like brothers. You would also know that his father and my father who passed away only last year, fought side by side in the days of Garibaldi and the unification of Italy. They are both with our Heavenly Father now. May their souls rest in peace." He turned to face Giuseppe. "I must say it is wonderful to see Giuseppe Cottone here following in their hallowed footsteps... how smart you look Giuseppe." He clapped and everybody joined with him.

"I would like to comment on the magnificent spread that the beautiful Teresa and her sisters prepared for us all and I see she has not forgotten my favourite, *ciaccchiere*. Thank you and may God bless you always, Teresa, my goddaughter." He applauded and everyone joined him again. "Now it is with great pleasure that I present this special little document to young Carmelo here on his eighth birthday. It is a licence permitting him to carry arms, so that he can take his father's shotgun into the hills to keep the bandits away when he goes to watch over the sheep." Everybody clapped as he handed the little brown hard covered licence to young Carmelo whose eyes were almost popping out of his head. "There you are, it is all officially stamped and signed by the Mayor himself. Keep it with you always and no bandits will ever be game to go near your father's sheep again, Carmelo."

"Thank you Don Peppino," Carmelo's little voice squeaked back.

Because Carmelo was too young to work in the fields, the ideal job for him and other children his age was to watch over the sheep. Straight after the morning session of school, he would set off with his dog Fido and his father's shotgun under his arm to graze the sheep on the hill pastures about one hour's walk away. Sometimes, if he was in the area, Antonio would detour to see his little brother and help him bring the sheep back to their field near the town where a share-farmer watched over them at night. They had such a close bond with each other that they would often share their most intimate thoughts and dreams.

"Do you think you would ever use that shotgun if the bandits came to steal the sheep?" asked Antonio.

"Of course I would!" exclaimed Carmelo with bravado.

"Or would you shit your pants?" continued Antonio.

"Probably," Carmelo confessed, knowing it was useless to lie to Antonio. "I'm terrified of ever having to use it. What if I killed someone?"

"Don't worry, I'm sure Don Peppino would never let anything happen to you. He gave you the licence so it's like you're his hired hand. I reckon you're as safe as a Church." Antonio's assurance put Carmelo at ease and he was glad he hadn't lied to his brother about being afraid.

"Many people are leaving Sicily and emigrating to the United States, Canada and Australia. One day I think I would like to go as well. They say the United States is the land of opportunity, if I decided to go... Carmelo, would you come with me?"

"I'm too young to leave home."

"No not now, I mean in a few years' time."

"I'll still be too young to leave home."

"I guess so. But would you come over when you are old enough, if I went over first and set everything up for us? We wouldn't have to stay there forever, just until we became rich and then we could come back and live like Don Peppino." Antonio loved to dream and Carmelo loved it when he told him about his dreams. It made him feel important.

"Maybe. It depends on whether I'm needed here. Papa may need me when he's old and if Teresa never gets married, I'll have to look after her."

"You're right, Meluzzo," Antonio conceded calling him by his pet name, "We'll have to wait until it gets closer to the time before you make such a decision."

Carmelo knew exactly what was happening with all the emigration. On weekends, because he was the youngest, he always accompanied his father to the village square and loved listening to him talk to the other men from Agira. His father seemed so wise and he loved the way everyone respected him. Many of the men had received mail from relatives who had emigrated to America, Canada and Australia and they used to ask Rosario to read the letters to them. So Carmelo was getting it *from the horse's mouth* so to speak and he would relay the information to Antonio.

"De Bruzzo's son who is working in America has just sent *twenty dollars* to his parents. Papa had to go with his father to the bank to exchange it for *lire*. Papa said twenty American dollars was a fortune in Italian Lire. You were right, Antonio; they are all rich over there! Vincenzo Favioli, who has been over there for five years now has just sent word over to his wife that he is making arrangements for her to join him in America. She has asked Papa to help her with the passport and all the paperwork that goes with emigration. People in America can even get married to someone over here and then bring them back to live in America. Papa explained to Signor Perroni (from one of his son's letters) how there is such a thing as *marriage by proxy*. His son Giovanni wanted Perroni to find him a good wife in Agira. Signor Perroni suggested that Maria Terranotte was a good woman for him to marry. Apparently, once the paperwork is done, all that has to be done is for Giovanni's brother Pietro to represent him and take the vows on his behalf in the marriage ceremony here in our Church. Giovanni will then be officially married to Maria."

"It sure is the land of opportunity," marvelled Antonio.

Any news from the political arena was also in the village square long before the newspapers reported it officially. In that same year, Mussolini was expelled from Trentino in northern Italy as a union movement troublemaker. Carmelo told Antonio what else he had heard that same day.

"They say the government is not happy with the socialist attitudes of people like Mussolini. Signor Morosi who said he is proud to be a Communist, claims Mussolini is trying to get a better deal for the workers in Italy who are being used as cheap labour by the rich."

"Yeah… no wonder people are leaving the country. They're sick of being treated like slaves. Lucky we have our own land, Carmelo, or we would be starving too."

When he returned home however, Carmelo found out Rosario was not as upbeat about the family's fortunes as Antonio was.

"We'll have to tighten our belts, Teresa." Rosario insisted. "There simply isn't any money about. Farms are not worth anything because nobody wants to buy them and much of their produce and their sheep are being stolen by bandits. Then as the young people begin to leave the country to work overseas, the land is being neglected. Who knows what will happen if Angelino or Antonio decides to go overseas? What will happen to our big family then?"

This *tête-à-tête* between Teresa and Rosario worried Carmelo.

"I've been thinking about what you were saying about going to America, Antonio. I don't think it's a good idea because Papa and Teresa need you and Angelino to help work on the farm.

"Well, you won't have to worry about that, little Meluzzo because I'm not going anywhere for a while and Angelino… well Angelino has a girlfriend and the only place he wants to be is right here in Italy," said Antonio.

"Really? Who is it Tonino?" That was Antonio's pet name and Carmelo hoped it would soften him up enough to reveal the identity of the girl.

"Not saying. You can have three guesses and I'll tell you if you're right."

"Is it Santina, that girl from Catanzaro?"

"No."

"I'll bet it's Anna Caretta. I've seen him trying to get her attention outside where she works at the bakery in Agira."

"No."

"I know, I know: Sara, that girl from Agira who went to visit our cousins Scriffignano?" He studied Antonio's reaction. "It's her, isn't it?"

"No! You lose! *Bubbo!* I'm never going to tell you now," he teased.

"So, call me *bubbo* eh! In that case I'm not going to tell you what

I heard one of the girls in town telling her friend about how much she loves you."

"Who, Meluzzo? Tell me who it is." He grabbed Carmelo and wrestled him to the ground. "Tell me or I'll tickle you to death!"

"No! No! No, Tonino, I give up. I was only kidding!" As Antonio released his grip, Carmelo ran away. Then when he thought he was at a safe distance, he called out, "You're too ugly anyway Tonino! Ha ha ha," he laughed and ran home as fast as his skinny legs could accelerate.

Chapter 4

Every which way

O ver the next six years, even as a character of no consequence in the world of mortals, I could see that nothing had improved in Italy. Her economy was in tatters while the rich got richer and the poor got poorer. Italy was a ship adrift at sea with neither sail nor rudder and there was no one of any consequence at the helm.

By the outbreak of World War One, Italy was in turmoil politically as well as economically. Every which way the country turned, there were more negatives than positives. It was a warm summer evening in early June 1915. There was excitement in the Cottone household and Teresa had invited Don Peppino to join in the celebrations as always. Don Peppino was attempting to explain his interpretation of the situation to Giuseppe who had come home on leave.

"Giuseppe, the way I see it, Italy is in a very humiliating situation. Under the agreement after Unification, Italy promised to side with Germany and Austria against France and Russia," he stated. "But instead, she has remained out of the war. In fact, the rumour is that Italy may do the opposite and join Britain, France and Russia. Italy is confused, everyone is confused and nobody knows which way to turn."

"Yes, Don Peppino— even Mussolini is confused. At first as a Socialist he was totally against the war, but this year he is openly saying that he supports the war. Now he has been branded a Nationalist and banned from the Socialist Party," Giuseppe added.

Teresa passed around the *chiacchiere* and Don Peppino took one in each hand.

"Ah my dear Teresa you spoil me with my favourite sweets. If I were a young man again, I would marry you just for the sweets. Don Rosario has been truly blessed by the good Lord with such a wonderful daughter." Teresa blushed.

"I don't understand how Mussolini could be such a turncoat against his own Party," Angelino argued. "Nothing else in Italy has changed."

"I always said that Mussolini was no good," insisted Don Peppino and everybody agreed with him.

Three days later, Giuseppe was recalled to barracks early and without notice. Italy had joined the war on the side of Britain, France and Russia just as Don Peppino had said she might. Angelino and Antonio were conscripted into the army and the whole family was haunted by what the future might hold. Every night, Rosario brought home the paper and the family discussed the progress of the war and prayed for the safety of their three beloved children. Italy was suffering heavy casualties on the Northern Italian Front in the first Battles of Isonzo where Giuseppe was serving under General Cardorna. By the Third Battle of Isonzo in October 1915, the letters from Giuseppe ceased.

"We should not give up hope," Rosario reminded the family. "Many soldiers have been wounded and many more taken prisoner. No news is not necessarily bad news. There is still hope. We should keep Giuseppe close to our hearts and in our prayers daily and never give up hope."

Letters from Angelino and Antonio continued to arrive regularly. All along the Italian Front, the postmarks on their letters would show where they had been; Gorizia, Tolmino, Caporetto, Bovec, Plezzo and Podgera and the family gave a collective sigh of relief each time they heard they were safe. The worst fears by far were held after the Battle of Caporetto, which was the twelfth Battle of Isonzo in which the Italian Army suffered major losses in terms of equipment and prisoners taken. Two hundred and seventy thousand men were captured and thirty thousand soldiers killed as General Cardorna's forces under Commander Capello were forced back to the Tagliamento River.

It took four days to cross this river, but by the grace of God, Angelino and I were spared as we retreated to the Piave River, thirty kilometres to the north of Venice, wrote Antonio in a letter to his father. *Here, the German forces of German Commander Otto von Bülow were repelled by the Allies who sent eleven divisions to the region; six French and five British. We hope the war will be over soon.*

Carmelo and Rosario worked the farm as best they could until the end of the war, but there was hardly enough to live on and nothing left over to cover the cost of repairs or re-invest in the property. Deserters from the war were also a menace and many people abandoned their properties in outlying areas for fear of them.

They never heard from Giuseppe again. Along with 600000 other Italian soldiers who never returned from that war, he was listed as 'missing in action, presumed dead'. The family never recovered from that loss and Rosario in particular was a broken man. Giuseppe was only 26 years of age and Carmelo prayed for his soul night after night and cried for his brother on many occasions, especially when he saw his face in the family photo on the mantelpiece. He would stroke the photo and often, Teresa would have to take it away from him and replace it towards the back of the mantelpiece where it was harder to reach and out of sight.

After the war, things went from bad to worse. One evening Antonio made the announcement that everyone was dreading. It was at the beginning of Spring in March 1919.

"Papa, Teresa, as you know, a lot of the young men in Sicily have emigrated to America, Canada and Australia. These are lands of opportunity and if I go over there, I'll immediately be able to provide relief for the family if things continue to get worse and it looks as if they will. I am 26 years old. I am the strongest I will ever be. I'm healthy and I'm not afraid of hard work. I have skills with farm animals and I know how to farm. I have a good education and I am quite competent as a surveyor, so these things will make me more readily acceptable in Australia. I hope to be going to Australia as soon as my application has been officially accepted." Everyone in the room gasped as the announcement was made. "Angelino and Meluzzo will be able to keep everything going here and there is definitely no longer a need for the three of us boys to work our farm. It's important that I go with your blessing; otherwise I will not go at all. But I promise you one thing I will not be staying in Australia. This is the land of my birth and this will be the land where I shall die. So your blessings are only for a time that will pass quickly. I shall be gone for a maximum of eight years, so before I reach Teresa's age, thirty-five, I shall return. This I solemnly promise."

The three girls cried as everyone gathered around Antonio and gave their blessings.

Carmelo especially felt that it was a good thing for Antonio to go, even though he knew he would miss him dreadfully.

"Tonino," he told him privately later, "I think it is a good thing that you are going because even though you will prosper in Australia, I know you would never break your promise and you will come back. We will always feel safe knowing that and we will wait for you."

"Yes Meluzzo, I shall return. But you are still young and I am hoping that in a few years' time you'll come to be with me… after I've set everything up, just like we said when we were kids. Remember?"

Carmelo nodded, then he threw his arms around Antonio and hugged him tightly until any fears he might have had simply vanished.

"We must make one other promise to each other," Carmelo insisted. "The mail to Australia takes about six weeks by ship. When you arrive in Australia and have a fixed address, you write to me. And as soon as I receive your letter, I will write to you the same night so that my letter can catch the return ship to Australia. When you receive my letter, you write back and that way we will always be looking forward to hearing from each other and our minds will be at peace."

"I promise, Meluzzo," and he thrust out his hand so that his brother could shake it.

When it came time for Antonio to leave, the whole family was buzzing around wanting to perform some small or other special act for him.

"Papa," Carmelo said to his father, "some of the people who went to Australia from around here have sent money back to their families in Australian currency and that money is kept in the Banco Nacionale in Agira. I have saved up some money and I would like to buy some Australian currency to give to Antonio as a surprise for when he arrives in Australia."

Rosario thought about it and then asked, "How much do you have Meluzzo?"

"I have enough to buy One Pound Sterling. I have been saving all of my gift money for two years for an emergency and this is an emergency because he'll need money to eat until he gets work. Now Papa, I have arranged for us to write to each other every four to six weeks so that we never lose touch and I would like to put the money in an envelope with my first letter to him, which he is not allowed to open until he gets to Australia. Then he'll get a wonderful surprise."

"What an intelligent idea, Meluzzo. Why don't we go to the bank together tomorrow in Agira and get that banknote."

When they returned from the bank, Carmelo sat down to write the letter to his brother, which he would be opening when he arrived in Australia. Rosario approached him in his room.

"Here, Carmelo," his father brandished five crisp One Pound Sterling notes and put them on the desk next to Carmelo, "put these in with yours from the rest of us. And don't forget to tell him to spend them wisely, my son."

Antonio would be leaving from the port of Naples, so they would be saying their goodbyes in Agira at the train station. It was a sad day but it was a happy day and Rosario explained why that was so as the train pulled out of the station.

"One door closes and another door opens," he said.

Chapter 5

One door closes and another door opens

Everyone was gathered around Carmelo as he sat at the kitchen table and slipped the blade of a sharp knife into the corner of the envelope from Australia. He slit it across the top. They couldn't hold back their sense of anticipation as the letter slid out.

"What beautiful handwriting."

"He has so much news to tell us."

"Thank God he's arrived safely."

"Come on Carmelo, start reading it. We can't wait."

"Maybe Papa should read it,'" said Carmelo.

Rosario took the letter, looked at it and said, "No, it's addressed to you Carmelo, you read it."

> Dear Meluzzo,
> Well here it is, my first letter to you just as I promised. I know you are all there, so hello my beloved Papa, Teresa, Angelino, Archangela and Adele. I miss you all and love you so much. Firstly, I want to reply to your letter, which I opened as soon as I arrived in Fremantle in Western Australia, which is the first port of call in Australia. I had to force myself not to open it beforehand, especially on the long voyage out here when I became so homesick I thought I would die. I think it's your fault Teresa for mothering me so well that I should still be a bit of a baby even at twenty seven years of age. I soon realized it was definitely your fault because when I saw the small fortune of money you had all enclosed with the letter, I burst

*into tears. Thank you all so much for your sacrifices as I know
you would all have had to do without a lot as a result of it.*

At this point, Teresa burst into tears followed by Archangela and
Adele. Papa was teary too. Angelino got Teresa a glass of water and
Carmelo waited until they regained their composure before continuing.

*Well, the money was certainly useful and the amount I did
spend was spent wisely Papa. In Fremantle, we had to pass
through immigration and our passports were taken from
us in exchange for a receipt and a certificate of arrival.
The passport was stamped and eventually returned to us on
the ship after we boarded again for the next leg of the trip
around the southern part of Australia and up the East Coast.
Many people disembarked in Sydney. They said there was
a lot of work there in the factories but others insisted that
the real money to be made was in the cane fields of North
Queensland. Barbagallo and Sorbello were the only two
people from our area that were on the ship with me. We all
disembarked in Brisbane and I was able to find good clean
lodgings, buy food (nothing as good as what you cook Teresa)
and secure a good berth on the train the next day to Babinda
in North Queensland. Giuseppe Barbagallo suggested
Babinda because he knew Saffiotti, Fontana and Biancotti
who were living and working there and they would be able
to find work for us cutting sugarcane. The train trip was
almost one thousand seven hundred kilometres in distance
from Brisbane to Babinda so you can imagine how large
this country is. In Townsville at about eight o'clock in the
evening, Barbagallo phoned Signor Saffiotti to tell him we
would be arriving at about three o'clock in the morning.
Saffiotti was there to meet us at the station and it was a good
thing because I cannot imagine what we would have done
without him. We carried our suitcases and climbed into the*

back of an ex-army vehicle and then travelled through the darkness into the jungle. It began to pour down with rain and the road was full of potholes but it only took about twenty minutes to arrive at the workers' barracks on Warner's farm. Warner is a very rich Englishman who owns huge plantations of sugarcane in Babinda and the surrounding areas. We all began cutting cane the very next day. Our gang comprises Saffiotti who is the 'ganger' or leader, Fontana, Biancotti, Barbagallo, Sorbello and me. My hands are so sore with blisters that I can hardly write but in no time at all, the calluses will form and it will no longer be a problem. The work is very hard, but I get it a little easier because I am the cook this week and the cook gets to finish earlier and prepare the meals. Well, you will have to wait until the next ship for more news from me. Write to me at the address on the back of the envelope. I pray God you are all well as I would never forgive myself if some harm should come to any of you and I was not there to be with you.

Your dutiful son and loving brother, Antonino.

Everyone gasped a sigh of relief that Antonio had been settled and that his move had progressed so smoothly.

"Poor Antonino has blisters," said Teresa.

"And he can hardly write," said Adele.

"The jungle sounds scary," said Archangela. "I read that there are wild Aborigines in Australia."

"Well, let's all kneel and thank God for delivering Antonio safely to Australia," said Rosario. They all kneeled except for Teresa as Rosario made the sign of the Cross.

"Dear God, we thank you for delivering our Antonio safely to Australia and we pray that You will watch over him in that foreign land across the sea and far from his family. We pray also for the departed soul of his mother Concetta and his missing brother Giuseppe and the spirits of our ancestors and that they will watch over him also and keep him from harm and return him to us safely when it is Your will that he should return."

They united with an "Amen", did the sign of the Cross and returned to the letter, passing it from one to the other.

"Look the postmark says '*Babinda*'," said Adele.

"Yes," said Archangela squinting her eyes trying to decipher the date, "But the date is illegible."

"Look at the strange address. There's no street name or number. Just *P.O. Box 155 Babinda, North Queensland, Australia*," exclaimed Carmelo.

"We must all write something back to him," said Teresa. "Carmelo, get some writing paper from the writing desk and you can start the letter off. Half a page maximum each and don't repeat what anyone else has said. Come on, off you go," and she took the letter from him and sat down to read it over and over again.

Life in Agira ground on monotonously. One day I was with Carmelo in the town square, where Rosario heard some sad news from a returned soldier who had known Giuseppe and fought with him in the Third Battle of Isonzo. It was the sixth of November 1919. Rosario collapsed immediately after hearing the news and was pronounced dead on arrival at the hospital. Carmelo was hysterical and I must confess I think that I was moved as well. After all I too had lost a father.

We were at home when Don Peppino came to the house to tell Teresa.

"I have investigated the circumstances surrounding his death, Teresa. As soon as the returned soldier confirmed that Giuseppe had died in the war, it was as if Don Rosario gave up all hope. It's as if he didn't want to go on living. I'm sure he died of a broken heart; he loved all of you children so much. I am so sorry to have to be the one to tell you this, but I want you to know that I will personally ensure that you and your family will always be looked after. You see, many years ago on the battlefield together, your grandfather Giuseppe and my father Peppino made a pact that should something ever happen to either one of them, the other would take over the responsibility for the other's family. Your father and I knew of this pact and we agreed to renew the pact to include our families. You must write to Antonio and tell him that I will watch over your family. He should stay in Australia to finish what he set out to do. Australia is truly the land of opportunity and he must not sacrifice this opportunity."

Teresa was in shock. Suddenly the whole weight of the responsibility for the family had fallen upon her. No one in the family was married and she was the eldest. Don Peppino left and she spoke not a single word until after the funeral. Everyone felt so devastated for her. Then the day after Rosario was buried, Teresa asked Carmelo to do a chore for her.

"Meluzzo," she placed a huge bowl of chiacchiere in his hands, "take this bowl of *chiacchiere* to Don Peppino. Tell him that Teresa would like to thank him for his great kindness following the death of our beloved father." Teresa was talking again and Carmelo was so happy for her that he wanted to run all the way to Don Peppino's place. However, after deciding that running with a bowl of *chiacchiere* in his hands would have appeared comical, he merely walked as quickly as he possibly could.

Don Peppino was so welcoming and courteous to him that Carmelo felt honoured by his role. Particularly since the Don so appreciated the bowl of *chiacchiere* that Teresa had sent him.

"While you're here, Carmelo, I would like to take the opportunity to discuss with you something that must always remain between us. Can you promise me this?"

"Yes of course, Don Peppino. I promise."

"It concerns the necessity for you to do your National Service in the Army. Now I'm sure you know how I feel about Mussolini. To me, he is public enemy number one. But as the leader of the Fascist Movement he is gaining power every day. Within two years, he will be running the country as a dictator and as such he will have unlimited powers. Already, his thugs, the Black Shirts are coercing people to vote for him in the elections and to obey his rules; not the rules of the parliament but his rules. This is a recipe for disaster through oppression. The King, Victor Emmanuel is afraid of him and would rather work with him to maintain some semblance of power, than against him and end up deposed. Mussolini would rather appear to be working with the King to give him some sort of credibility while knowing such an alliance would give him an enduring grasp on power in this country. Doing your National Service is compulsory, but it will also make you non-partisan and safe in the political turmoil that lies ahead for us. At the same time you can learn how the system works as well as gauge the sentiment of those within the forces towards Mussolini. In order to protect our interests in this area, I need to have someone intelligent I can trust to keep me informed about what is good for the country and what is bad for the country. In the meantime, you will receive a wage which will be handy for Teresa to manage her affairs at home."

"Yes, Don Peppino. But who will help Angelino look after the farm?"

"I will arrange for someone competent to look after the farm and I will personally make sure that Angelino stays in control without having to do all of the work. So, you won't have to worry about that. If you agree, I would like you to register for National Service as soon as possible."

"Very well, Don Peppino, but I would like to discuss the matter with Angelino and Teresa. Is that okay?" He thought about it and then added, "Not really I guess, if this conversation is to remain solely between us two."

"Exactly," reiterated Don Peppino.

"Very well, Don Peppino. As you say, it's compulsory anyhow, so I may as well have it done sooner rather than later."

"Good Carmelo, you are doing the right thing. Now go home and thank your sister for the beautiful *chiacchiere*... and Carmelo," he added most sincerely, "please accept my heartfelt condolences over the loss of your dear father."

Chapter 6

Poverty and oppression

Carmelo commenced his National Service on the mainland. He then went on to serve in the regular army. Throughout it all, I was there with him.

His decision to enlist in Army Service turned out to be a blessing after all. It did provide him with an income, security and respect at a time when none of those things were available to so many decent people who were being denied such basic human rights. The rich factory bosses who had already made their fortunes during the war, continued to tighten the screws on workers and began blaming them for Italy's woes suggesting they had no right to expect fair pay and conditions when the rest of the country was suffering.

In the north, workers had had enough. The Socialist Unions and the Anarchists urged the workers to strike and by September 1920, they had taken over many factories in Milan by force. They then moved on to Turin, Genoa, Florence, Rome and Naples. In the south, the mainly Catholic Unions incited the peasants to revolt against their landlords and they began to seize land. The workers controlled the factories, the peasants took over the fields yet the capitalists controlled the country. Neither side would yield, neither side would relent.

There was a great sense of anticipation and nervousness throughout the armed forces. The loyalties of the soldiers were becoming divided between obligation to their families and the demands of the government.

"If Prime Minister Giolitti wants us to control the workers

outside the factories across Italy, then he had better tread lightly when negotiating with the Unions who have occupied the factories," said his best friend Enzo. They had both commenced National Service at the same time and were now in the same garrison. "The country is about to implode and this could easily end up in a civil war."

Carmelo agreed, "Yes and it's not as if this impasse was not inevitable. The Unions have been working towards this for over two years, building on every success with an even greater following. The government has to negotiate or there will be blood in the streets. And what soldier wants to be fighting against his own brothers?"

"What would you do if you were asked to beat up or shoot your own brother in the street?" asked Enzo.

"Don't even talk about it, Enzo. I've already lost one brother to the Great War and I don't even want to contemplate such a horrible situation."

"Well, you better get used to it because that's what's going to happen. There will be blood in the streets. It will be brother against brother... we're on the brink of war."

But negotiate they did and no one could have imagined the outcome. Surreptitiously, over the next two years the government managed to gain the upper hand and supported by the finances of the *Confindustria*, stole the momentum from the Movement and it stalled. At the turn of the tide, the Fascist thugs were there to launch a brutal offensive against the working classes by perpetuating violent attacks and even murdering the activists.

The capitalists had triumphed after all and by the time Mussolini was appointed Prime Minister by King Victor Emmanuel in October 1922, the Fascists were deeply entrenched in power.

"So, we have been given our final marching orders," said Enzo as the friends bid each other farewell at the gates of the barracks. "*Il Duce* has demobilized the armed forces and taken full control of his elite Secret Police Force the 'ORVA'. I fear for the future of Italy, Carmelo."

"The strange thing is," marvelled Carmelo to his good friend, "that Don Peppino in our little village of Agira predicted this very outcome over two years ago. 'Within two years, he will be running the country as a dictator and as such he will have unlimited powers' were his exact words and that's where we find ourselves today my dear Enzo."

The first person Carmelo went to see after returning home to his family was Don Peppino.

"Everything you predicted about Mussolini has come to pass Don Peppino. Mussolini has demobilized the army and now relies on his Secret Police to do his dirty work for him."

"Yes, Carmelo. But what you don't know is that he has already started sending his spies here to Sicily. Sicily is the only place where he hasn't been able to gain full control; he wants power over every facet of Sicilian life. He seeks to break our spirit but the Sicilian people are a proud people. When Italy deserted us after Unification, the Sicilians would not allow themselves to be downtrodden; we stood up for our rights. My father and your grandfather fought for those rights. When the absentee landlords and the local governments failed to maintain law and order, all the families came together and looked after each other. We made sure our homes would remain safe for our wives and our children. Sicilians have been able to hold their heads high and Mussolini doesn't like that. He wants us under his feet."

"Angelino has already warned me that Fascist spies have been planted all over Sicily. He says that often Mussolini uses ex-soldiers who have returned to their homes in Sicily as spies, with the promise of positions of power under his new regime."

"That's what we are afraid of Carmelo. Every man has his price and can be bought. We have to be so careful as to who we trust. You, for example, because you come from an honourable family would never betray us but there are others who are jealous of what we have achieved in our community and they want it stripped from us. In future, when we suspect any ex-soldiers of being spies, I may need to consult with you and seek your advice on certain matters."

Carmelo was quite surprised by this statement of faith in him.

"I don't think I shall ever be able to advise you Don Peppino on any matter of importance but I am always at your service. Our families are inextricably linked."

"Thank you Carmelo, I knew I could count on you. So tell me, what do you intend to do for work now that you are unemployed?"

"I shall return to work on my father's farm, which means we will no longer be needing the hired hand you so kindly provided over the last two years."

"I was hoping you would say that. Your family misses you so much and they will want you home, at least for a while. By the way, your family will continue to receive the contribution I have been making to keep him on."

"Thank you, Don Peppino for all that you have done for us since our father died, but I cannot accept any more money. I have savings from my time spent in the army and our dear brother Antonio has been sending money home regularly from Australia. Your help allowed him to stay in Australia and now we are reaping the rewards."

"Very well, Carmelo. See what I mean when I say we are a proud people? That's what I have always said, Sicilians look after their own and that is our great strength."

Carmelo took his leave and set off home, pleased that he had been so well received by Don Peppino.

When he was in the privacy of his old room, he knelt beside his bed and thanked God for all the blessings He had bestowed upon him. He thanked God for watching over his family while he was away and for watching over Antonio in Australia. Then he thanked God for Don Peppino.

I was able to move into what was once Antonio's bed— a huge improvement on the old spare bed in the lean-to near the old olive press and light years away from the army backpack, my last place of abode. The surroundings were far more congenial as well. The walls were papered, the ceiling, quite ornate in plaster and the furniture was old but solid. There was a huge oak chest where most of his possessions had been stored, a wardrobe, a washing basin, a mirror on the wall with a framed painting on either side and a huge carpet on the floor that made the room feel snug. Carmelo sat at the writing desk, which was the most impressive piece of furniture and opened the drawer taking a blank page to write to his brother.

22nd December 1922.

My dear brother Antonino,
This is my tenth letter to you and I am replying to your ninth. It is very special because I'm writing it at the old desk in our room where we spent so many wonderful hours together. Here we laughed, joked and teased each other. Here you told me so many stories when I was young until I fell asleep. So many memories keep flooding back that I never want to leave it. Here in this room, in the top of the cupboard, I stowed away your very first letter from Australia and it's where I have kept every letter since. Greetings.

Yes, I'm back from serving my time in the army and thank God I'm still alive and in good health. So is all the family and they send you their love. Angelino's little boy Rosario is so grown up you can't imagine. He's three years old and our beautiful sister-in-law Emilia Camerata is with child so you are going to be an uncle again next year. Whenever I think of Emilia, I remember the first time you told me that Angelino wouldn't be going to Australia because he had a girlfriend and you wouldn't tell me who. To think it is the very same girl and they courted for seven years before finally getting married. Angelino said he would never marry until he had the means to support her. Times were so tough that he would never have married her if he had waited for times to improve. Then there was the war and they lost dear little

Concetta their first-born. But they are so happy now and I am Rosario's favourite uncle, ha ha because I'm the only one he knows. Just kidding, he loves you too because your name is mentioned every day! That's more attention than what I get! He knows the names of everyone in the photo on the mantelpiece and every time we ask him who his favourite is, he always says 'Seppi' and points to Giuseppe and we all laugh. He's so smart; I reckon he's figured 'Seppi' makes us laugh so he says it on purpose just to perceive our joy. Then he laughs also. Anyhow, I went to see Don Peppino. He received me like he would his own son. He has been so good to our family since our father died. He has certainly honoured his childhood promise to our Papa. What a true gentleman he is in the purest sense of the word.

The biggest concern here these days is the Fascist presence which casts a cloud of gloom all over Sicily. They say Mussolini has planted spies all over the island and that any day now, they will be arresting anyone who has any Mafiosi connections whatsoever. His Inspectors crisscross the island consistently placing fear into the hearts of all the Government officials. On the two occasions when he visited the island, everybody had to bow to him and people who didn't bow were beaten after he passed through. Can you believe it? There's no way I'll be bowing to another man. Who does he think he is, God?

Good thing you left here when you did my beloved brother. At least you will be safe if Mussolini becomes the dictator they say he is.

So to something a little more pleasant now and that is that the whole region is expecting a bumper wheat crop; the first good crop since you left. The fear is the Government will be putting on an extra tax levy this year to recover some of the revenue they missed out on during the bad years. So the news

is still bad and always will be under Fascist rule. Goodbye, dear brother. I eagerly await your tenth letter. Meluzzo.
P.S. I will now be working on the farm with Angelino and dreaming of those glorious days I rode on your shoulders as a child. You are so special to me Ninuzzo.

P.P.S. Tomorrow is my birthday.

The next day, he awoke to a most glorious sunny day, despite the fact that it was the middle of winter. He was twenty-one years old and he was home again.

Chapter 7

Uncertain times

The whole of the region was on red alert. Everyone was wary, searching for spies. Any new person entering the town was kept under constant surveillance. Paranoia reigned supreme and it seemed it had even infected emigrants overseas who were worried about their folk at home. One day, two letters arrived from Antonio simultaneously. His brother in Sicily carefully opened one.

08th February 1923,

Dear Meluzzo,
It was with great joy that I learned you were at last home again... and happy, happy 21st birthday. I hadn't forgotten you and on the 23rd of December I thanked God again for sparing you all those years ago when you were just Rosario's age. See how the wheel turns?

What does concern me is that it appeared that your letter had been tampered with. There were smudges of glue where there shouldn't have been smudges of glue. If you think that may be the case, then you should go to Don Peppino and tell him. He would want to know. Promise me you will brother. We can't have people reading our private letters.

Here in Australia, the people never cease to amaze me. They ask some of the silliest questions. For example, the other day someone asked me if we had trains in Italy. I mean Italy has been settled for thousands of years and here they just got off the ship and they ask me if we have trains in Italy! Many of the buildings are made of bamboo and many of the houses are not made from sawn timber but from slabs and corrugated iron with a dirt floor. The better houses are on poles. Tiles haven't been invented here yet. Nobody eats pasta except for the Italians and people here have never heard of capsicums. Some people actually think spaghetti grows on trees! Anyhow there are plenty of things in Australia that I find hard to understand. For example, it is considered sport for the Pacific Islanders here to hunt Aborigines on the weekend and they say that they eat them. Maybe they are joking because we are foreigners and they tell us tall tales just for fun. They do have a strange sense of humour these Australians.

At the moment it is the wet season in Babinda. It rains every day. The cutting season doesn't commence for a few months yet so we have little work to do. Two days a week we cut cord wood for the mill and two days a week we work in the fields removing the weeds from among the young cane stalks. The other three days, we relax, play cards or just talk. I am trying to learn English, so every day I get the newspaper 'The Cairns Post' and with my trusty dictionary I try to decipher what is being said in the headlines and maybe the first paragraph. It's a good way to learn and it gives me a little insight as to what is happening in the rest of the world. It seems everyone in Australia hates Mussolini.

I'm telling you this because I'm hoping you might consider coming over here to work with me for a couple of years. I miss you a lot and maybe we could even buy a farm together. We could develop it and then sell it just before we return to Italy and make a good profit. Let me know what you think.

Now I want you to burn this letter after you have read it. I have sent a second letter for the family to read. I don't want them to think I'm putting ideas into your head about coming to Australia. With much affection and kisses to the girls and little Rosario.

Your brother, Nino.

As requested, Carmelo dutifully burnt the letter and opened the second letter which excluded the disturbing parts about letter tampering and going to Australia and then passed it on to Teresa. He also carried out his brother's other request and paid a visit to Don Peppino.

Don Peppino seemed a little uneasy this time. He looked to both sides of Carmelo and beyond him into the street before ushering him inside without the usual fanfare and ceremony.

"You did well to come here and tell me this," he told him when Carmelo had related all that he had said to Antonio in the letter. "Do you recall if you mentioned my name at all in relation to any of your statements?"

"I only mentioned your name in relation to how considerate you had been towards our family since our father died. I'm certain of that Don Peppino."

"Good. Wait here Carmelo." He walked to the adjoining room and signalled to someone to come to him. He spoke quietly, nodded his head a few times and then dismissed him. Then he returned to Carmelo.

"Now, the son of the Postmaster is an ex-soldier and he works with his father I believe. Do you know him at all?"

"Yes, Don Peppino. But I don't know him very well. I think he was a corporal in the army."

"And you have destroyed your brother's letter you say?"

"Yes Don Peppino."

"Well, I think that if your brother got the letter, then even if it were tampered with and the contents noted, there is no evidence so I think for now you are reasonably safe. As your brother said, you must never do anything like that again. These are uncertain times."

Carmelo took his leave but this time he let himself out. On the way home, he stopped in at the Post Office to buy some stamps and saw the son of the Postmaster sorting mail in the back room. The ex-corporal looked up at him momentarily but didn't seem to recognize him.

Over the next few weeks, there was a buzz around town that two *Il Duce* Inspectors would be paying a visit to the Local Council to discuss matters of State. Everyone seemed fearful of these people. Word had also circulated that the ex-corporal had gone missing. When the actual date of the Inspectors' arrival was known, Don Peppino sent word to Carmelo that he should pay a visit to his cousins Scriffignano to coincide within a couple of days either side of their visit.

It proved to be a good opportunity for Carmelo to meet with them. Gaetano, the youngest of the Scriffignano cousins was four years younger than he was so he would be a young man now. Maria was his age, but all the others were older than he was.

"My, what a fine young man you have grown into Carmellino," said his Aunt Teresa as she clamped his cheek between her index and forefinger and gave it a good squeeze and a shake.

"Yes Zia." He gave her a big hug.

"So you are back from serving in the army. Ah… " She shook her hand with a limp wrist to indicate her anguish, "these are hard times for a mother. When my boys went into the army, I don't think I slept one night where I got a good rest. I was so worried about them. Of course, you lost your mother, but your older sister Teresa would have felt it. She lost Giuseppe. Ah… poor Teresa I feel for her. And your father, he died from shock. That's what we all believe. Poor Rosario… Well that's the way it is I guess. Louisa, Antonino, Nina and Angelo aren't here, but the others are. Pietro, Angelina, Maria, Gaetano come downstairs, your cousin Carmelo Cottone is here," she called out at the top of her voice. With most Italians, visits from family were a magnet to iron filings and they were down and clustered around him in seconds.

"Hello Carmelo," said Maria as she hugged him.

Angelina called out "Hello" from the other side of the room as she went into the other room to check her appearance before returning to him. "So happy to see you again," and she offered her hand to him.

"Ah... give him a hug," said Zia Teresa as she shoved poor Angelina in his direction. "He's your cousin, not a stranger."

"Good day," said Pietro. "Welcome. Have you any news from Antonino in Australia?"

"Oh yes, there's much news. I'll tell you all about it before I leave."

"Gaetano," you certainly have shot up. I'll be able to tell you all about the big cities. I've seen a lot of them now."

"Have you eaten?" came the mandatory question from Zia Teresa and then without waiting for an answer, "Come on then, let's see what we can find for you in the kitchen," and she took him by the hand like a mother leading a child and headed for the kitchen.

He spent five days there in all and it gave him a good chance to get to know them again. Individually, they were all very confident and easy going, very much like their mother except for Gaetano who was more serious. On the second day Carmelo was helping his cousins Antonino and Angelo and his Uncle Luigi pick olives in the back paddock where it was quite stony.

"Who would think," said his Uncle Luigi, "that such poor soil could yield such magnificent olives. It just proves that even when conditions are poor, you can still reap rewards if you plant the right seed. We are fortunate here Carmelo, but we worry for our country. Now with Mussolini flexing his muscles, who knows what will become of Sicily?"

"He really hates the Sicilians," said Antonino. "He thinks that by eradicating the Mafiosi in Sicily, he can stamp his authority all over Italy."

"But that's not going to happen," added Pietro. "The *Mafiosi* isn't a political party. It's a code of conduct. He has to change our behaviour as well as the way we think. That's the difference. Mussolini is a *persona non grata* here in Sicily and we hate him."

"Yes, but we can't go on pretending he doesn't exist. He is Prime Minister for God's sake," said Carmelo. "We are going to have to try a little harder than just hating him."

"And what do you suggest?" asked his Uncle.

"Well, I don't think we should be bowing to him, that's for sure."

"You obviously haven't encountered any of his Black Shirt thugs then cousin," said Angelo and he pointed to his crooked nose and a scar above his eye, "See this... and this...? Well, that's what happened to me the last time *Il Duce* walked through the streets of Agira and I refused to bow. They came down on me like a ton of bricks and they were only half serious. Two Socialists, the Cavallaro boys were shot in an altercation with the Black Shirts the next day. They were lucky they were only wounded. They could easily have been killed."

"For now at least," said Antonio, "we are going to have to bow until someone comes up with a better idea."

The next day, Pietro and Gaetano were crushing the olives and Maria and Angelina were processing the oil and placing it into bottles and a variety of other receptacles.

"So, everyone hates Mussolini," said Carmelo reintroducing the debate. "What do you think the answer to the problem is, Gaetano? What do the young people around town think?"

"They think Socialism is the answer. The rich get richer while the poor get poorer. We all only have one stomach; there should be a more equal distribution of wealth."

"So you would give up your farm so that we could have a more equal distribution of wealth, Gaetano?"

"We wouldn't have to give up our farm. There are ten of us in my family alone eating off this farm and that's not counting our children and other close relatives. But Mussolini would have us as his slaves filling his coffers in Rome with the sweat from our brows while we sit here and starve and bow when he walks past. The Socialists should have seized power in 1920 when they had the chance. It's too late now."

"We will have to go back to our old ways," added Maria, "Sicilians look after themselves. So we bow for now and strike when the time is right."

"You are quite a tactician," suggested Carmelo. "And what do you think Angelina?"

"I don't talk politics. I simply want to be a mother whose children can live in peace and not know fear. It's up to you men to figure how best to achieve that," said Angelina nonchalantly. "So, what are you going to do about it Carmelo?" she wanted to know.

"I'm going to take notice of everything you people talked about today and I'm going to have a very hard think about it."

"Great, you're going to achieve wonders with all your thinking," said Gaetano.

"Carmelo, Pietro, Angelina and Maria wash up and come in for lunch, the pasta is almost cooked," boomed Zia Teresa's voice from the kitchen. "Gaetano, go call your father, he's helping Marco shoe the horse next door. You've got five minutes, so run!"

"Ah, Zia Teresa, you make the best pasta," said Carmelo after they sat down to eat.

"Well if you think the pasta is good, you wait 'til you try my home made sausages" and she pursed her fingers together and smacked a king sized kiss onto them.

"Oh Mamma," chastised Angelina, "you boast too much. Carmelo will be expecting the world and he may be disappointed."

"Disappointed nothing!" her mother retorted, "He'll be licking his fingers along with the rest of you when he tastes my sausages." They all laughed and throughout the meal, Carmelo told them stories of the army, the big cities he had visited and that wonderful land of opportunity called Australia.

"Spaghetti growing on trees! Ha!" laughed Zia Teresa, "How on earth did the English ever win the Great War?"

"It was off the backs of the French and the Italians, that's how Teresa," said Uncle Luigi. "Ha! Do we have trains in Italy? Padre, Figlio, e Spirito Santo." He shook his head then he did the sign of the Cross and everyone laughed.

On the fourth day, word had filtered back from the town, that there had been several altercations with the Black Shirts. One person had been shot dead and several wounded; all socialists.

"Well that's it," said Carmelo, "Nobody should be allowed to get away with that. I'm going back into town."

"No you're not," said Uncle Luigi. "What are you going to do, topple Mussolini with one man?"

"I'll go, I'll go," said Gaetano. "That'll make two and there'll be others."

"Zio Luigi, these thugs need to be taught a lesson. They can't go around shooting people just because they are Socialist or *Mafiosi* or because they won't bow to Mussolini."

"Well you're not going. Don Peppino said I had to look after you and that's all there is to it. No more discussion."

The Inspectors and the Black Shirts came and went. The ex-corporal disappeared and never returned. Life settled down to a more temperate pace after that. Carmelo worked on the farm often taking little Rosario with him and on the way home he would tell him stories about 'Seppi and Tonino in Australia and his Nonno Rosario.

"And in a few years' time, we'll have to ask Don Peppino to get you a licence so you can take Nonno's shotgun up into the hills to watch the sheep and make sure the bandits don't steal them."

Often, Carmelo piggy-backed Rosario and on those occasions, I used to sneak up on little Rosario's shoulder. The view was better from up there.

Chapter 8

From Sicily to the Antipodes

Antonio was beginning to earn some very serious money cutting sugarcane. He was concerned about the political situation in Italy and tried even harder to convince Carmelo to join him in Australia. He tried to paint an enticing picture of Australia in his next letter and took great care not to make incriminating statements against the Government in the event of his letters being vetted by the Fascists.

30th March 1923

Dear Meluzzo,
I am pleased to hear that everything is fine in Agira. The wet season has passed now and the farmers are ploughing their fallow fields in preparation for planting. Meanwhile the crops are out of hand with the sugarcane already over two metres high and soon the crushing season will be upon us. A new wave of migrants— mainly from Italy and Greece has begun to arrive in the North. The Babinda area is one of the prettiest in all of North Queensland with its lush tropical rainforests and crystal clear streams. It has the highest rainfall in the whole of Australia (around 4000 mm a year) so you can imagine how quickly everything grows. I have been looking at a couple of properties around Happy Valley, about five kilometres west of Babinda. They have been partly cleared by the Hindus who have built very modest houses on them and planted a few acres of sugarcane. These are ideal

properties to buy as they are freehold and have been granted permits (called assignments) to grow a certain tonnage of sugarcane per year. These assignments are worth money once the farmer actually reaches full production.

If I knew you were coming I would consider buying a farm and we could cut our own cane while steadily clearing the land and building the farm up to full production. I hope you will think about it.

In the meantime, I hope you are enjoying the time with the family. It was good that you were able to spend those five days with the Scriffignanos— that Zia Teresa sure is a fiery one, but you have to love her.

We are of course, surrounded by jungle here and at night the sounds are so different from those in Italy. There are other distractions here as well. Some of the girls are very pretty especially in Cairns and Innisfail, which are much bigger towns than Babinda. They are mostly of British stock, whereas in Ingham, about five hours by rail-motor to the south, the population is mainly Italian. The Italian girls there are so pretty, but their fathers keep loaded shotguns beside their beds and if anyone so much as looks at them without express permission, the bullets start flying. I hope I haven't frightened you off! You can always go back to Italy like I will be doing and get married there.

Your affectionate brother,
Nino

Carmelo so much wanted to write to his brother about the ever worsening situation in Sicily under the Fascists. In Palermo on the Western side of the island, where the main crops are oranges and lemons, the Mafia had a firm hold on the economy of the area. However, with the Fascists targeting the *Mafiosi,* Mussolini decided Palermo would be a good location to establish his authority.

Using the information that had already been gathered by the Fascist's spies, under the supervision of Cesaro Mori and the Black Shirts, the Government authorities wrought havoc on the local population. Thousands were arrested during the campaign and many convicted and imprisoned. Even wives and children were taken hostage to force suspects to surrender. Wives and children are sacred in Sicilian society and the whole population was unnerved by it. This was exactly what Mussolini desired. He sought to instil fear and mistrust throughout the population so that the *Mafiosi* could no longer function as a law unto themselves.

Success in Palermo would equate to inevitable success in all other significant cities throughout Sicily and one by one the *Mafiosi* loosened their control over the economy and the people. This may have been a positive should there have been something better to replace them; but Fascist rule was cold, corrupt, merciless and unrelenting.

By the summer of 1924, Mussolini decided to determine the level of success that had been achieved in Sicily by conducting a personal tour of the island. A successful tour would guarantee his acceptance in Rome and ensure his ambitions of gaining absolute power.

Don Peppino had been identified as a prime target of the Fascists in the area centring on Agira and Assoro. It was said that he had gone into exile in France and his lands and property were expropriated by the Government. Most of the leaders in the region were stripped of their powers and Fascist pawns were placed in all the major positions of authority. This was all executed prior to Mussolini's proposed tour.

Everywhere that Mussolini went, the people were warned to obey or face the consequences. And wherever Mussolini went the people bowed. Now those who refused to bow were beaten, imprisoned or shot. It did not take the people long to become accustomed to the idea of bowing to Mussolini.

Carmelo, on the other hand maintained his steadfast attitude towards this mandate. Everyone but the infirmed was ordered into the streets when Mussolini was scheduled to parade through their town and Carmelo was there with his Scriffignano cousins, Antonino, Angelo and Pietro. Gaetano was absent in Catania, where he was studying to be a school teacher. As the Mussolini motorcade trundled through the street a never ending wave of people knelt down bowing before him until it reached Carmelo who remained erect. Before the Black Shirts could identify him and push through the crowd, his three cousins pounced on him, thrusting him to the ground. As the motorcade passed, he was obscured as the wave rose allowing his cousins time to bustle him through under the cover of the crowd.

But now he was a marked man and sooner or later his name would filter through finding its way into the Fascists' *Libro Nero*: their *Black Book*. The Secret Police kept records on everybody and on every event. Carmelo was immediately ordered into hiding. The cousins brought him to the caves in the hills on the outskirts of Agira, whilst Don Peppino's underground resistance were informed of his plight. It all happened so fast that it was a blur to Carmelo. Within a week and before any records had been updated to prohibit him leaving the country, he had his passport and a 40 pound sterling ticket on the P&O Cruiser *ORVIETO* in one hand and a suitcase in the other. Carmelo was bound for Australia.

He was unable to bid his farewells to his beloved family as the house was under surveillance twenty four hours a day. What a sad, sad journey it was to Australia. I was perched on the little porthole looking out to sea for most of the six-week journey and Carmelo never left his bed except to eat and go to the toilet and shower. He did, however, manage to write a letter to his family in Italy and one to his brother in Babinda and posted them both in Fremantle.

The voyage across the Great Australian Bight from Fremantle to Brisbane was the final straw for Carmelo. This notorious passage was at its worst and Carmelo felt that if he were going to die, it could not have been worse than this. So many passengers were seasick that the stench lingered in every room, every hall and every corridor throughout the ship. It certainly helped Carmelo realize that there were worse things than what had happened to him in Sicily prior to his departure.

On his arrival in Brisbane, it was a fine day and a cool south-easterly breeze swept across the decks of the *ORVIETO*. By the time he was on the North-bound train and heading from Brisbane to Babinda, Carmelo seemed to have recovered from the events at home that had plunged him into such a severe state of depression. Perhaps it was the realization that he would be seeing his beloved brother again soon. Or perhaps it was because it had dawned on him that he was about to embark on a great adventure in a foreign land. Anyhow it was certainly a relief to witness his change of heart.

He was soon engrossed in a conversation with a young Italian couple, the Musumecis who sat opposite him in his cabin. The colour seemed to return to his face whenever Mrs Musumeci spoke. She was pretty but a little buxom and her demeanour could almost be described as flirtatious.

"You are very fortunate Signor Musumeci, to have such a beautiful wife." This was not quite the Sicilian thing to say, but he was left unscathed and Mrs Musumeci loved it.

"Thank you Carmelo. Please call me Ernesto and my wife is Eva. So how far up the coast are you travelling?"

"I'm going as far as Babinda. I have a brother there and we'll be working together. Do you know Babinda?"

"Yes, it's a pretty town, about eight hours further north from Home Hill where we get off," said Eva. "We are only going for a short visit."

"We have family in Home Hill," explained Ernesto. "They own a sugarcane farm."

"Oh, my brother and I are looking at buying a small sugarcane farm at Happy Valley about six kilometres west of Babinda," he boasted.

"We know Happy Valley, they have a very special swimming hole there called The Boulders. So whenever you go there, I hope you will think of us," said Eva.

"I certainly will," he assured her.

The next day in the dining car, Ernesto brought up the topic of politics in Italy.

"Yes, I was in the army over there for a while and the situation was on a knife edge for most of that time," said Carmelo. The Musumecis were from the mainland and Carmelo had no way of knowing where their allegiances lay. "All I know is that a lot of people were hurt and a lot of people are still suffering. The situation is not good in Italy."

"Many of the Musumecis are anti-Fascist and Mussolini virtually drove them from the country. They had to flee for their lives."

"Tell me about it," said Carmelo. "I'm a fugitive as well. Once you have been marked, the Black Shirts hunt you down and they don't cease until they find you. Many innocent people are hurt along the way, especially family. That's why people have to leave, otherwise they will come after their families."

"Ah... we both value our freedom, Carmelo. We have much in common. Who wants to live their lives in fear? Who wants to be bound in chains? Why should we have to bow to Mussolini? People have to stand up to these dictators!"

"Yes, my dear Ernesto and Eva. Better a day as a lion than a lifetime as a lamb."

"Well spoken, Carmelo," Ernesto raised his beer glass, "Here's to Australia; the land of freedom." They all raised their glass to that.

"To Australia, the land of freedom!"

A group at the table opposite glanced over at them. They were dressed in workers' overalls.

"What'cha reckon the wogs are celebratin' now, Bert?" said the big red-faced man with a ginger moustache.

"Prob'ly toasting the rise and rise of Mussolini, Slim."

"God they're everywhere," said Slim. "A bloke won't even be able to get a job soon."

"Just a toast to good health and good friends," Ernesto informed them in English.

"Aw, awright then," said Slim, surprised that Ernesto had spoken to them in English. "Ah... yeah... well, we'll drink to that won't we fellas?" Everyone raised their glasses and drank to that.

"To good health and good friends."

Throughout the remainder of their time together, the Musumecis and Carmelo had laid the foundations of a good friendship and even exchanged addresses.

"I will write to you," Carmelo promised as the train pulled into the station at Home Hill.

"Make sure you tell us how you've settled in. We'll be thinking of you," said Eva. Then she spotted someone on the platform, stuck her head out of the window, waved and shouted, "Filippo! Filippo!"

Carmelo was studying his map and knew that the last big town before Babinda was Innisfail. As soon as the train pulled out of Innisfail, he checked his belongings. It was nine o'clock in the morning. The train was running late because there had been heavy flooding between Ingham and Cardwell. The road had been cut in several places, so the railway line had to be inspected, resulting in a six hour delay.

At ten o'clock, the train arrived in Babinda. Carmelo could see many people but there was no sign of his brother. He scanned the platform several times to double-check but Antonio was not there. He checked again that the station was Babinda before alighting the train. The bustle on the platform didn't last long. People who were there to collect freight did so and soon only Carmelo was left standing on the platform.

He was about to go to the station master when a canvas covered truck pulled up and the short, rotund, muscular driver leapt out and called to him, "Cottone?" he shouted towards Carmelo, "Is your name Cottone?"

"Yes, I am Cottone. Carmelo Cottone."

"My name is Barbagallo, Giuseppe Barbagallo. Pleased to meet you," and he thrust his hand forward to Carmelo. "All the roads around here are flooded and your brother Antonio has been unable to get into town. He phoned at four o'clock this morning to tell me he couldn't get through and asked me to meet you. Apologies, but he can't help it, eh... when the roads are flooded, they're flooded," he reiterated with a shrug of the shoulders.

"I understand," said Carmelo. "So sorry he had to trouble you at four o'clock in the morning. It's me who should be apologizing to you."

"Well, he had to phone then because your train usually arrives at three o'clock in the morning and he didn't want you to be stranded here."

He took Carmelo's suitcase and placed it in the back of the truck. "I own one of the grocery stores in town. I often pick up people, mainly canecutters and drop them off at the farms in the neighbourhood. Most of the time I find them work if they have no family here... no charge," he joked, punching Carmelo in the stomach lightly and almost winding him. "Oops, sorry. Sorry Cottone. Come on, jump in."

They pulled out of the station, passed Terranova's boarding house, crossed the railway line and headed back into town. The whole town was surrounded by mountains with ominous clouds that clung to them threatening more rain despite the break in the weather. They crossed a second railway line with a narrower gauge.

"On your right, that's the sugar mill and the railway line we just crossed is the one that the locomotives use to haul the cane to the mill. That's the Ambulance back there on your right and the Police Station."

Shops lined both sides of the main street; a garage, a haberdashery, *Arena's Bakery*.

"Ah Arena's!" He read the name above the shop. "So the baker is Italian," said Carmelo. "Then we should be assured of good bread."

"Yes, old Arena makes very good bread."

Next on the left was the Babinda State Hotel and on the right was the National Bank. Then there was the Post Office and opposite that was where Guiseppe parked the truck; outside *Barbagallo's* General Store.

"We have arrived at my store, you can buy everything Italian you want here, anchovies, olives, cheese, spaghetti. Anything you want. I don't have to worry about the competition. There isn't any. Ha, ha," He went to punch Carmelo again but he pulled it away in time as Carmelo flinched. "Ah don't worry, I only make mistakes once. Ha, ha."

Carmelo collected his suitcase and Giuseppe carried two huge ten litre tins of anchovies into the shop where a boisterous woman was working busily behind the counter.

"This is Mississa Barbagallo and this is Cottone, brother of Antonio."

"My pleasure, Signora Barbagallo. Please accept my apologies for my brother waking you up so early this morning."

"Don't mention it," she eyed him up and down. "So good looking too, just like your brother. I should have been so lucky!" she joked, leaned over and gave Giuseppe a huge kiss on the forehead. "Welcome to Australia."

"Oh yes, I forgot," said Giuseppe, "welcome to Australia."

"Cottone just phoned to say that the road is now passable, so you will be able to make your deliveries to Happy Valley," said his wife. "I told him not to come in because you would be going that way. He also ordered that box of groceries over there and you have to pick up some meat for him from the butcher's. Would you like a coffee, Cottone?" Without waiting for an answer, she poured him one and placed it on the counter. He fumbled in his pockets for some money. "What are you doing? There's no charge for the coffee. That is, unless you want a nip of whisky in it," she laughed. "Sugar is in that bowl. One thing we are never short of in this town is sugar!"

"I'll go across to the butcher to pick up the meat. I won't be long. After Cottone has finished his coffee, ask him to load those few boxes into the truck. Looks like more rain out there and we'll need to leave as soon as possible."

"Giuseppe," she called out to him when he was halfway across the road. "Don't forget to order the minced beef and the belly pork for the sausages. Remind the butcher to set the mincer on 'coarse'! She turned to Carmelo, "These Australians, they don't know how to make sausages."

Carmelo had just finished loading the boxes of groceries into the back of the truck and had gone back inside to wait when Giuseppe returned.

"Get your suitcase Cottone, it's time to go. Goodbye Mississa."

Carmelo jumped into the passenger seat and they continued up the road, due west towards Happy Valley.

"This is mainly residential area around here; mostly mill workers and business people. You can tell which houses belong to the mill workers; theirs are the least expensive looking ones. That's the hospital on the right and over there is the Doctor's surgery. Ahead of us is the road to Happy Valley. That's Mt Bellenden Ker straight ahead; the second highest mountain in Queensland."

It was covered in cloud but through the mist Carmelo could see a huge waterfall cascading down the side of the mountain.

"That waterfall you can see is what Babinda was named after. In the Aboriginal language, Babinda means *place of falling water*. These two culverts here at Stony Creek and Sandy Creek were totally under water earlier this morning. Water gets away really quickly around here. On the right there is the old tobacco barn. They soon found out it was too wet to grow tobacco here. Old Spitaro lives there— he was kicked in the stomach by a horse and he now walks at right angles to the ground."

The truck began to labour as it ascended the steep hill opposite Spitaro's place. Once he got to the top of the hill, Giuseppe pulled on the handbrake. Spitaro came outside to collect his box of groceries and he walked as Giuseppe had said.

"This is Cottone, brother of Antonio."

"Brother of who?" asked Spitaro.

"Antonio Cottone... we came on the same ship to Australia, together with Sorbello five years ago. We cut cane together on Warner's farm in our first year with Biancotti, Saffiotti and Fontana."

"Ah yes, Cottone. Antonio Cottone from Agira. So you are his brother," he said speaking to the ground. "I'm pleased to meet you."

"Pleased to meet you too, Spitaro," said Carmelo through the open driver's door of the truck. Giuseppe tucked the box of groceries under

Spitaro's arm and climbed back into the truck and they drove off.

"Now I remember your name. You and Sorbello... of course... Antonio mentioned you in his first letter back home... you phoned someone to get you at three o'clock in the morning."

"Ah yes, that was Saffiotti."

"So, what made you go into the grocery business?"

"Well I figured that everybody has to eat and all of the Italians around here couldn't even buy decent salami. So, I wrote to my paesano in Sydney who has a delicatessen and he gave me all the contacts. It's a way to make a living and it makes a lot of people happy."

They crossed the double-barrelled bridge.

"Straight ahead is the road to *The Boulders*. We go left and your brother lives in those barracks down there on the right. He will stay there until they start cutting cane again in May. Then he may stay or he may move depending on where he decides to work."

Antonio had heard the truck coming and was already halfway up the road and coming towards them. Carmelo's eyes lit up as he saw his beloved brother. He opened the door, leapt out and ran down the road to meet him. Giuseppe merely drove around them. He stopped at the barracks, carried the box inside, turned the truck around and drove past them on the way back. They were still embracing each other.

Chapter 9

Long hard summer

The evening of his very first night in Happy Valley, by the light of a hurricane lamp, Carmelo and Antonio spoke late into the night. After the rain, there was a cacophony of sound orchestrated in harmony between the cicadas, the beetles and the frogs. Intermittently, the tropical rains would sweep down again and drench the corrugated iron shelter that they were in. The orchestra would pause only to reach a new crescendo the moment it passed.

"My one regret, dear Carmelo, is that I will never see my father alive again. May God have mercy on his soul. I knew he would never recover from the shock of losing Giuseppe. I believe Don Peppino was right. As soon as Papa realized that there was no hope of Giuseppe ever returning home alive, his heart stopped."

"Yes, Antonio. The Lord giveth and the Lord taketh away. Papa died in 1919 but his grandson Rosario was born to Emilia and Angelino in that very same year. As Papa would say, 'one door shuts and another one opens'. Now young Rosario carries the spirit of his Nonno and when you return to Italy, you will find your Papa again through him. And there's a bonus for you when you arrive home; little Eloisa, Rosario's sister, will be two this year. This is the way of the world. We must have faith in God," and he cupped his brother's hand in his and kissed it.

Being a kindred spirit, I felt I had every right to stake out some territory of my own. I had just found a nice private nook above the wood stove, which I thought would be my sanctuary of solitude for the upcoming months in Australia, when Antonio scuttled the idea with his next revelation.

"I have just signed a contract to buy that small farm off the Hindus that I mentioned. I could not afford it on my own, so I have bought it in partnership with a person called Arena."

"Arena? Any relation to the Arena who owns the bakery in Babinda?"

"His brother," Antonio nodded. "There's a lot of work to be done on it, but there is a good opportunity for substantial capital gain, once the farm has been cleared and put into production. This is what a lot of migrants are doing these days; they cut cane for a few years then buy a farm with an assignment, develop it and bring it into full production."

"Congratulations Nino, I'm so proud of you. Where exactly is this farm?"

"It's about one kilometre back from the double-barrelled bridge, nestled in beneath that big hill. I'll show it to you first thing tomorrow morning and then we'll make arrangements over the next week or so to move into the lean-to that the Hindus have erected. It's not the most attractive residence you'll ever live in, but it's better than the old sheep shack we had in the mountains in Sicily."

Carmelo laughed, "Thanks for making sure I would feel quite at home here in Australia. As long as there are no rats around; you know I hate rats."

"There are no rats because there are so many snakes," he quipped.

"Snakes I can handle," and he waved away any suggestion of fear with his hand.

Or so he thought. The shelter was modest but better than Carmelo had imagined. It had a dirt floor and a recess where a new wooden stove with a chimney would provide warmth as well as cooking facilities. The windows were hinged wooden frames covered with corrugated iron that were thrust open and held in place by pieces of three by two timber with a notch cut into both ends. Carmelo then glanced up to the ceilings and there, curled around the rafters was the largest snake he had ever seen. It was roughly four metres long and about ten centimetres in diameter.

"I told you there were no rats here," reiterated Antonio as he looked up. "Don't worry, it's only a carpet snake. They're harmless... except to rats... and chickens..." Carmelo's eyes were getting larger and larger, "and the occasional dog... " Carlo took two steps backwards. "No, I'm only kidding Meluzzo... chickens yes, but dogs... no. It has come in because of the rain. Now that we're here, it will leave and it won't come back." Carmelo breathed a sigh of relief. "But the rats don't know that," Antonio laughed.

Outside on a raised platform was a small water tank that collected water from the roof. One pipe ran from the tank through the wall to the inside of the house. Another ran to a tap positioned over a slab of concrete separate from the house, which had three sheets of corrugated iron erected around it and was used for washing. About twenty metres further on, another corrugated iron construction was a pit latrine.

"About five hectares of land has been cleared and planted with sugarcane. It's out of hand now so there's nothing left to do until that crop is harvested in June or July. We have bought the crop with the farm and you and I will be cutting it ourselves. That set of discs, the plough and that scarifier behind the house go with the farm as well, but apart from that, the farm is bare. The Hindus bring their horses and their equipment down from their other farm about one kilometre back towards town on the right. The first thing we'll have to do is build stables for the horses but I will employ Garivella to organize building those and you and I can offside for him."

"So what does Arena do?" asked Carmelo.

"Well, he has put in half the money and he will pay half the expenses that go towards growing and harvesting the crop and clearing and developing the land. Apart from that, he is what we call a 'silent partner'. You and I do all the work but he only gets a quarter of all the net income generated on the farm plus a quarter of the net capital gain when we sell the farm. That's the usual arrangement that goes with silent partners."

The carpet snake never returned as Antonio had forecast and after they had furnished the house, Garivella came and they finished building the stables and a cow bale for the Jersey they had bought. It was already in calf and any day now the calf would be born and they would have fresh milk. Carmelo would be able to make their own hard cheese as well as ricotta.

"You are the horse specialist Meluzzo; a railway wagon of draught horses has just arrived for sale from Toowoomba, so we'll be going in to bid for two horses tomorrow."

Carmelo loved horses. He was quite adept at horse-riding as well, having practised the skill in the army, but his specialty was training draught horses for work. This he also learned in the army. Most Sicilians had limited experience with horses as they usually only owned mules. When he arrived at the Babinda showgrounds where the draft horses were being auctioned, he was very disappointed. The horses were in very poor condition, their coats were dull and most of them were fast approaching retirement. Still he checked every single one thoroughly, feeling them all over and looking at their teeth and hooves.

"These are not good horses, Antonio. They send them here for the migrants to buy because they don't understand what to look for. The bawly-faced one over there is mediocre but the best of the whole bunch. Anything else, I wouldn't recommend you even consider buying."

So Antonio bid for the bawly-faced one and to both their surprise it went much cheaper than many of the other horses.

"I told you these people don't know anything about horses," re-affirmed Carmelo. "Next year, you and I will go to this Toowoomba and I will buy horses for the whole district if the farmers are interested."

That afternoon, they took delivery of their horse and walked him home. He stopped every few paces to tear at the green shoots of guinea and molasses grass on the side of the road.

"They didn't even feed this poor horse, Antonio. See how starved he is," and he caressed and patted the horse as it ate. "You go on ahead. I will take him home slowly and try to bond with him. Treated properly this horse will give its heart for you. Come on Bawly, let's take it easy for a couple of days until we get to know each other." And that's where the horse got its name. When they arrived at the farm, Carmelo had a good report for Antonio.

"He's a good horse Antonio. He's quiet but he's very alert and responsive. He has a good gait and he'll work that little farm of yours better than any of those other horses today. I think you'll get by with just the one horse this year. You will need to purchase a full draught work harness so that I can begin training him as soon as possible.

Throughout the rest of the slack season, when the cane could no longer be worked, Antonio and Carmelo used axes, chains and fire to clear the vegetation and even dynamite to remove the stumps of the huge Johnstone River hardwood trees. The timber that was able to be milled was kept aside for sale to help offset the cost of clearing. Bawly did more than his share of hauling timber with Carmelo shouting commands.

"Hup there, hup there Bawly… Hold 'em boy, hold 'em… Steady there Bawly… back up…Whoa Bawly… Whoa… good boy Bawly," with a few swear words thrown in for good measure.

Carmelo also learned to use dynamite and to identify valuable timber trees. Old Fred Kruckow who owned the Mirriwinni Sawmill walked across the property with him and pointed them out.

"That's the white beech; long lasting, good for window sills. That's silver oak and that one is bull oak; good for furniture. That one is white oak; good for chamfer boards. That one is Johnstone River hardwood for building and that one is Black Bean. It's excellent for fence posts."

Carmelo didn't understand a word he was saying, but as Fred pointed them out, he just knocked a slab of bark off them with his axe. Once he knew what the valuable ones looked like, he knew which ones to keep and that was all that mattered at that point in time.

By the time the season started, they had cleared a total of five hectares of land and removed thousands of stones and tonnes of roots. The stones were placed on a sled which Bawly hauled to the boundary fence line and the roots were heaped and burned. All the land needed now was to be ploughed ready for planting in August. It had been a long hot summer and the rest of the year was still ahead of Carmelo who had yet to cut a stick of cane.

The cane was cut green. Heaps of trash, a protective covering full of very fine prickles called hairy mary, had to first be removed from the stalk. Then the cane was cut and laid in bundles on the ground. The tops of the cane were cut and then the cane was loaded by shoulder onto cane trucks; timber carriages built onto a steel undercarriage with four narrow gauge railway wheels. A steam locomotive would deliver the trucks empty to each farm and collect them full the following morning. Cutting and loading went on from dawn until dark throughout the season with a two hour break around midday.

There were three main avenues of contact and interaction with the outside world. Two times a week, Barbagallo would deliver groceries, bread, meat and *The Cairns Post*. They would hardly ever see their friend because he would leave the order at their house while they were at work and would collect the order for the next delivery at the same time. But the newspapers told them the basics of what they needed to know about what was happening in Australia and overseas. At the same time, Carmelo began to learn English by trying to read the newspapers but his progress was slow because he was too tired to concentrate and he had nobody with whom to practice his English. Occasionally they would visit other canecutters from the adjoining farms. This is where Carmelo got to know old Saffiotti, Biancotti, Fontana and a few others of Antonio's friends. He didn't get many opportunities to make friends of his own. Their third avenue was by mail. He corresponded with the family back home and decided to write a letter to the Musumecis.

25th May 1925

Dear Ernesto and Eva,
I hope you still remember me. I certainly will never forget you both because I think you rescued me from the deepest hole I have ever found myself in my whole life. I had just abandoned my family in Italy without even being able to say

goodbye and felt so guilty about it; especially for Teresa who was a mother to me.

But when I met you both and experienced your kindness and sincerity, I could feel a sense of purpose being restored to me. I have thought of you so many times and yet I have not been courteous enough to even thank you for what you did for me. Now four months later and long overdue, I am writing to you both at last.

Babinda truly is a beautiful place but very, very wet. I finally managed to visit The Boulders and it is everything you said it was. You know, The Boulders is less than six kilometres from where I live and work. Yes, my brother did buy that farm from the Hindus that I mentioned to you. Unfortunately, by the time I got here, he had already signed a contract with another partner but it doesn't matter because I am learning so much and in a couple of years' time, I hope to buy my own farm. But it must be somewhere around here because I love this little corner of the world.

The work has been hard but already I am beginning to enjoy a sense of freedom that had always been unattainable in my native country. There is no poverty or starvation surrounding me here. The people are not oppressed politically. There is no class distinction like in Italy. I sometimes feel as though I have metamorphosed into another human being; unchained, cut loose, given a second chance at life and I'm happy about that. I am already thinking about renouncing my Italian citizenship and becoming an Australian citizen. After all, this is the country that accepted me in my time of greatest need and when I had nothing. I don't think I could ever leave this country after that. Some things in life can never be repaid. I will forever be indebted to this country for the hospitality afforded to me by these strangers who have so little in common with me.

We don't even speak the same language or eat the same food. I also think it would be easier to find God here than it would be in Italy at the moment, for God is good and there is very little good happening at the moment over there and indeed in the foreseeable future.

I don't think my brother Antonio is quite ready to hear this confession yet, but I was hoping I could seek your opinions on this matter of citizenship. I sincerely wish that this letter finds you both in the best of health and that you are happy.

Warm regards to you both,
Carmelo Cottone.

From the other side of the world, another surprise was awaiting him. He and Antonio had just gone into town on one of those rare occasions one Saturday afternoon. While Antonio was settling the monthly account, Carmelo crossed the road from Barbagallo's Store to check the Post Office Box for mail. He didn't recognize the handwriting at first but as soon as he glanced at the sender on the back he knew; it was Archangela.

Archangela had married a young man from Catania called Francesco Loria in July of the same year Carmelo had fled the country. They wished to begin a new life together in America. He decided not to open it until they were home so he and Antonio could share it.

Many people were in town and it was good to see so many families out with their children. It made him homesick for little Rosario and Eloisa.

"You seem a little apprehensive Carmelo," Antonio observed as they set off for home just after dark. "You haven't found someone in town to fall in love with, have you?"

"No, it's just that Archangela has sent us a letter and she doesn't usually write. I hope everything is all right."

"You liked Francesco didn't you? For two years he courted her, didn't he?"

"Yes and it certainly wasn't easy. If I have to go through what he went through, I don't think I'll ever get married. Firstly, because he was from out of town, he had to survive the scrutiny of Don Peppino; then after receiving a lukewarm nod and warning look from Don Peppino, he had to compete with all the other suitors in the district.

"Francesco always claimed it was love at first sight, but believe me, nothing is ever that simple. In the beginning, she didn't want to know him because he was an out-of-towner. To please her, he decided to move from Catania and get a job in Agira. He couldn't get regular work, so he apprenticed himself to Enzo Scali as a hairdresser. With those qualifications, you wouldn't think he'd have a chance, but Antonio, you see, this Francesco had something special. He was a great lover of literature and so, whenever he spoke with her, he wooed her with the wisdom of the ages from an enchanting world of magic and mystique. It still took two years but by then, she was even prepared to leave her family for a foreign land as long as she could be with him for the rest of her life. Now that's romantic. I wish you and I could be so lucky." He watched as Antonio opened the barbed-wire gate to their property.

They had a dog, also called Fido, in memory of Carmelo's first dog that used to help him watch over the sheep. Their voices carried across the freshly ploughed field to the farm house where he was tied up and he started barking long before he could see them.

"Quiet Fido," Carmelo called out, "it's only us."

"It's going to have to be bread, cheese and olives tonight, Meluzzo. No time to start the fire and cook a proper meal."

"I'm not fussy and I eat like a bird anyway. You know that Antonio. Okay, are you ready for the news from Archangela?"

He took out the letter, smoothed it out carefully and then slipped the sharp point of a steak knife into the small gap in the envelope.

20th April 1925

Dearest brothers Tonino and Meluzzo,
Life in Newark New Jersey is so different from life in Sicily;
just as different as life is in Australia for you both I imagine,
my dear brothers. I wanted to tell you of how happy we
both are with our new life, so that you don't worry about
us. We have our beautiful son Orazio and he is our great
joy. Francesco, (everyone calls him Frank here in America),
is a wonderful caring man and I know he will stay true to
his promise to love me always. Never a day goes by when he
doesn't do something special for me. That means so much in a
marriage and it makes me want to reciprocate.

Meluzzo, you'll be pleased to know that I always wear the
beautiful gold medallion that you gave us on our wedding
day. It is inscribed with the date that will always be the
happiest day of my life, 12th July 1924. As I read your
name, Carmelo, on the inscription, I think of my childhood
and our beautiful family and I am happy. Then I am sad
when I realize how we have been scattered across the face of
the globe and how we lost Giuseppe and our beloved Papa.

Now we must look forward to the children of the next
generation to light up our lives and we must do for them
what our parents did for us. The latest news is that Adele is to
marry Arimondo Contessa so she too will leave the old nest to
start a new life. Teresa will remain in the family home with
Angelino and his beautiful family.

That means that my focus must turn to you two. Have you
had any thoughts about marriage, Antonio? Do you think
you will return to Italy to find a wife? You promised you
would return so I know you will. Carmelo, I'm not so sure of.

You will marry an Italian woman I hope. There are so many dangers when you marry someone from a different culture. We see it every day here in America where people are often desperately unhappy.

Anyhow, you must both check with me (after Teresa of course) for final approval! Write to me soon.

Love always,
Archangela, Francesco and Orazio. xxx

Fido entered and nestled up to Antonio.

"Ah, Fido, so you have come for your share of our humble meal have you?" and he slipped him some bread and cheese under the table. "It's nice to know Archangela is happy. Maybe we should take up reading like Francesco so we can find our own Archangela. You will have to call yourself 'Carlo' if you want to have any chance with the Australian girls," he added, "so you can be 'desperately unhappy' for the rest of your life."

"Yeah, well you know so much, maybe you can write the next letter for a change and reply to Archangela."

Chapter 10

A steep learning curve

Antonio did write the next letter to Archangela. It was on a Sunday afternoon, two weeks into the cutting season and Carmelo was in no condition to be doing anything. He had blisters on top of blisters on both hands from using the cane knife and from handling the cane itself. His body was engulfed with a rash from the *hairy-mary*. His back was so sore from climbing the ladders when loading cane onto the trucks, it felt as though he had been beaten with an iron bar. To make things worse, one of the canecutters persuaded him to drink a whole bottle of 80 Proof Rum with the assurance that it would dull the pain as well as eradicate an impending bout of the flu.

"How's your brother Nino? I heard he knocked off a whole bottle of Negrita last night in an attempt to fend off the flu and drown his sorrows," asked Sorbello who was again chosen as the ganger for their group that season. He had spent Saturday night in town with his cousin and had just returned to the barracks.

"I would say the Negrita was more the cause of his sorrows than a solution to them. About 11 P.M. after finishing off the bottle, he felt so hot he thought he'd die, so he climbed up onto the roof of the barracks where there was some sort of breeze. That's where he awoke this morning, semi-comatose and covered in frost. We hauled him down and tucked him into bed and that's where he's been all day. All he's done is groan. You can thank Biancotti for his great advice about the rum."

Sorbello went to his room and Antonio settled down to his letter to his sister.

07/06/1925

Dear Archangela and family,
The task of replying to your recent letter has fallen to me as Carmelo is quite indisposed at the moment adjusting to the backbreaking work of cane-cutting. In a few more weeks, once his muscles tone up and his skills improve all will be fine. We were overjoyed to hear how happy you all are. Carmelo and I spent the whole summer, clearing the scrub and making improvements on my own recently purchased farm. Now that the season has started, we have moved out of the farmhouse and joined the gang in Warner's barracks. With cane-cutting gangs it has to be total commitment to getting the job done. That's why they pay us such good money. Everything else is secondary. Our dog is with us, so we only go back to the farm to check on the horse. The farm is not far from here and the harvesting of my small crop has been included into our contract. We should be able to cut it out in one round, so after that Carmelo and I will work the new stool on weekends.

Warner, the man who owns half of Happy Valley also runs cattle and has offered to let Carmelo ride his horses to keep them in work and check on the cattle. He had his first ride since the army just last weekend and can't wait to get back on the horses. Each weekend, he will ride the boundary fences to carry out any repairs and keep an eye on the cattle. He actually gets paid for doing something he enjoys. You have to be a good horseman in this rugged country especially after the rains. So in reality, it will be me doing most of the work on the farm on the weekends.

Carmelo seems to be very happy in Australia. He loves the freedom and he likes the people. I tease him about marrying an Australian girl and since your letter, I told him he would have to change his name to Carlo to have a chance. It was supposed to be a joke but he already introduces himself to all the Australians as Carlo. I have a feeling he will stay in Australia and I guess, while Mussolini is in power, he doesn't have a choice.

Anyhow my dear sister, please give Orazio a thousand hugs from his uncles in Australia and tell Frank that we embrace him warmly for the way he has treated you and wish him every success and you both eternal happiness.

Your loving brothers,
Antonio and Carmelo.

The next day at 4:30 A.M. they all set out to cut cane as usual. It was cold, but they wore long-sleeved woollen shirts and long trousers to protect them from the *hairy mary* so the cold wasn't a problem. The problem for Carmelo was that he really didn't look as though he would last the day and sympathy would not be forthcoming since he had brought this all upon himself. Unless you were at death's door, you did your fair share of work in the gang or you were out. This was because everybody was paid equally. It was so much per ton of cane cut and at the end of the month, the farmer would divide the total earnings by the number of men in the gang and that's what they each received.

But Biancotti did the right thing. He worked extra hard all day to get ahead of the pack and at the end of each row, he would come back into Carmelo's row as did Antonio and between them they carried him through. Such noble gestures demanded reciprocity and created solidarity amongst the gang members.

"Thanks Biancotti, I couldn't have made it without your help today," Carmelo told him as they walked through the semi-darkness towards the barracks.

"It's okay. Felt a bit guilty about suggesting the rum, that's all."

"Nothing to feel guilty about there," Carmelo assured him. "It certainly kicked the hell out of the flu!"

Equally debilitating was the other soul-destroying task of transporting the portable rails. These were laid in the paddock and along the headland right up to the rail-head where the mill locomotive collected the trucks on the main line. Each full rail was about four metres long, was made of solid steel and very, very heavy. Two men would carry each rail and position it along the drills. Then the empty trucks would be placed along the rails in position for loading.

All the cutters took turns placing a length of line long enough to accommodate a *rake* or daily allocation of trucks.

By November, they were approaching the end of the season and the work was so much easier now that Carmelo and his body had become accustomed to it. The weather, however, was not so kind. Daily, the temperatures soared higher and higher, reaching 31 degrees Celsius. "This is the sort of weather that causes dogs to drop dead in the street," said Antonio.

"You must drink plenty of water but be careful not to allow yourself to become bloated. That's why we put vinegar in the water so that people avoid drinking just for the sake of it." The canvas waterbags kept the water cool and to keep drinking was tempting but Carmelo heeded his brother's advice.

"It's 10 o'clock," said the ganger. "Let's take a break for smoko. Carmelo, your turn to get the lunch ready. We'll be home at 11 o'clock sharp."

"Pasta with red sauce today, fellas," he called to them as they sat down, "followed by a nice juicy steak and a cool green, lettuce, tomato, onion and cucumber salad. Tin peaches for dessert... with custard." You could see the change come over their faces at the mention of good food. They would be happy to work an extra hour for that.

It was the end of the season when some cutters went south to pick fruit or tobacco; others received part-time work on the farms; whilst others went to Sydney seeking work in the factories. People like Antonio moved back to their plots and continued clearing the scrub and working the stool for the next season's crop.

When the rains came in mid-January, the majority of work ceased, except for Carmelo who kept on boundary riding, rain, hail or shine. He carried the tools of his trade with him in a homemade billycan cut out of an olive oil tin, which he hung off the side of the saddle. In it was a pair of fence pliers, a hammer, a spike for removing stubborn staples and some tie-wire and fence staples. He also carried a short-handled cane knife. It was invaluable in situations where a tree had fallen onto the fence or to clear away the vegetation when he was mending fences. Apart from that, he would monitor the progress of cows which were heavily in calf and would help with the delivery if the mother was showing signs of distress or exhaustion.

"Babinda Creek is in flood," Antonio remarked as the rain pounded the walls of their tin shack at the farm. "The level-crossing into Warner's farm is going to keep rising and you may not be able to get back tonight Meluzzo. What do you think?"

"I have to go, Tonino. There's a Hereford cow heavily in calf. If she's fallen down in this wet, she may not be able to get up. I'll go up and check then I'll return early."

The rain was not going to relent and sheets of water enveloped man and horse as they pushed against the mist that swirled above the swollen waters of the double-barrelled bridge. Carmelo huddled under his broad-brimmed safari helmet and held the reigns tightly watching every puddle and hole in the road for signs of danger. Nothing would wish to follow a man through this avalanche of water, but Fido did.

At the level-crossing, just past Saffiotti's barracks where Carmelo first reunited with Antonino, the waters of Babinda Creek were lapping around the roots of the giant blue quandong tree. This meant that the crossing would be about seventy centimetres deep; shallow enough for a horse to cross but still dangerous. Carmelo dismounted and scooped Fido into his arms before placing him across the horse's mane and then remounting. Carefully under a very tight reign, as if he could feel the river rocks under the horse's feet, he guided the horse through the fifty metres of crossing. On the other side, Carmelo relaxed his grip on the reigns to allow Fido to jump off. In that split second, the horse leapt against the slope of the creek bank to commence the ascent and its hind legs collapsed as the hooves lost traction on the slippery clay. Dog and horse went in separate directions but Carmelo's foot was still hopelessly trapped in the stirrup and you could hear the bone snap as the full weight of the horse came down upon his leg. At first, the horse couldn't find the traction to raise itself and in its panic, bounced and wriggled as Carmelo clenched his teeth against the pain. Fido began barking furiously and the horse gave an almighty shove and heaved itself to its feet. The steed hobbled and limped to one side looking remorseful as Carmelo grabbed his own leg, which was broken just below the right knee and at right-angles to the rest of his body.

"Go Fido... go home!" He growled at the dog, but to no avail as Fido licked him all over the face. "Go home Fido... go home...Get Antonio!" and this time there was no misunderstanding. The dog leapt back into the water and paddled towards the blue quandong tree. Carmelo watched him lose momentum against the weight of water and vanish downstream with the current.

"There boy, steady boy," he called to the horse. "We should have listened to Antonio."

An hour passed. Carmelo was calm but I knew he was thinking of his family in Sicily. He began to slip in and out of consciousness. There was barking from the direction of the quandong tree. Carmelo was unconscious but when Antonio's voice boomed out, Carmelo came to and hoisted himself onto his elbows. He could see Antonio but Antonio could only see the horse, which had remained at Carmelo's side.

"Meluzzo, can you hear me?" Antonio shouted in our direction through the rain.

"Yes! I'm here. I'm alright. But my leg is broken!" He screamed back.

"Is your leg broken?"

"Yes!"

"Anything else?"

"No!"

"I will contact the ambulance. Can you wait?"

"Yes!"

An hour later, an ambulance brought along a horse drawn wagon large enough to accommodate a stretcher and two ambulance officers. When they arrived, the rain had abated. They forded the stream and Jack Johnston, the chief ambulance bearer, knelt beside Carmelo, checking him all over as he spoke.

"Well, made a real mess of yourself this time didn't you, Carlo?" He began preparing his leg for a splint.

"Ah Mr Johnston... grazie... grazie!" He had met Mr Johnston before to have cane trash particles removed from his eye.

"The real hero is Fido. Antonio said he saw him coming up the railway track from Agis' farm which means he was washed right down to the second crossing before he made it across. Then Fido had to convince him not to go searching for you there."

"Fido. Si si. OK Fido?"

"Yeah Fido's OK."

"Ah grazie Dio."

"Now this is Mick. We thought we may have been able to use the horse but it looks like he's dislocated his shoulder. He's not going anywhere until we can get a vet here. So we're going to put you on Mick's shoulders and he's going to carry you across the creek."

Carmelo allowed them do whatever they wanted with him. He had no idea what Jack was saying.

"Here Mick, I'll tie this rope to you and I'll lead the way. If I lose my footing, I'll let go and you keep going across. Don't worry about me. Now if you lose your footing hang on to Carlo like all hell and I'll come in after you both. We'll go with the current to the next crossing where Fido came out."

"Okay Jack, hoist him up."

They were halfway across when Antonio couldn't bear it any longer and pushed forward into the crossing.

"Wait there Tony!" Jack screamed. "It's all good here."

Fido went berserk when they finally reached the other side and jumped all over Mick in an attempt to get to Carlo.

"Ah Fido... good dog," said Carlo as he reached for Antonio's hand. "Thank you Mr Mick. You very strong man," he said carefully in his broken English.

"No worries mate," said Mick.

Carlo was loaded onto the stretcher and placed in the wagon. They began the slow seven kilometre journey into town.

Doctor Carrol from the Babinda Hospital took one look at the break and decided Carmelo should go on to the Cairns Base Hospital for treatment. Carlo was loaded back into the wagon and taken down to the station. As the goods train was coming through from Innisfail to Cairns at 2:30 P.M. they booked a berth for him and Mick and Antonio. It was obvious Carmelo was in a lot of pain but he kept quiet not wanting to distress Antonio.

When the goods train arrived, they simply pushed open the sliding door and Carlo was placed on the floor on the stretcher where he remained with Fido beside him for the two hour trip to Cairns. An ambulance vehicle was waiting at the station to transport Carlo to hospital.

Upon their arrival, the Superintendent did little to hide his unhappiness at the state of Carlo's leg.

"This leg hasn't been set properly or it has shifted while the patient was being transported to hospital. This doesn't leave us a lot of choices because the break is very severe and I'm concerned that if we try to reset it, the chance of infection will increase dramatically," he commented to the Nurse. "Let's admit him to a ward and see how things pan out over the next few days. I would like to try to avoid breaking the leg again. He'll have a bit of a bowed leg but that's a better option than a massive infection where there's a chance of losing the leg." He looked at Fido, "What's that dog doing in here, Nurse?"

"Sorry, Mr Cottone, but no dogs are allowed in the ward," she informed Antonio.

Antonio, Mick and the dog left. About two hours later, Antonio and the dog returned to find Carmelo had been assigned a bed on the verandah.

"Mick's gone back to Babinda on the rail-motor," he told his brother. "Here, I've bought you The Cairns Post so you can pretend you can read English and here is a small dictionary so you can compose poetry for the nurses, Carlo," he teased. He then handed Carmelo some money with a caution, "Don't spend it all on the nurses and here, I've bought you a box of chocolates to share with them. Archangela would be proud of me! Now I must go, but I will keep in touch with the hospital to find out when you're being released. Otherwise, I'll see you next Saturday afternoon. Ciao eh... " and he hugged his brother and disappeared.

As he did so, Nurse Walters approached him to place a thermometer in his mouth, which worked in his favour as he didn't have to talk. Having read his chart, she then took his pulse. His heartbeat must have been rapid but the nurse didn't notice.

"So what's new Carlo?" she asked glancing at the paper. She took out the thermometer and without waiting for an answer, read it and placed it straight back in. "Temperature is good, pulse is good, now it's time to take your blood pressure," she said as she wrapped the pressure bandage around his arm and pumped on the little rubber inflator.

"So do you cut cane then, Carlo?" asked Nurse Walters as she removed the pressure bandage from his arm. When he didn't reply, she bent over and made the action of grasping cane, pulling it to one side and cutting it with an imaginary cane knife in the other. "Cut cane?" she repeated.

"Si, si," Carmelo nodded.

"Yes, yes" repeated Nurse Walters. "I can see we're going to have to teach you some English while you're in here," and she tapped him on the nose twice like a child.

Just then, the bandage and plaster-of-Paris team of two nurses arrived to work on the plaster cast.

"You wouldn't be offering to do that if he were old, fat or ugly," said Nurse Williams.

"Would so."

"Would not," said the nurse with no name tag. "He certainly is a looker, this one. Blue eyes, brown hair, fair complexion; must be from the north. You from Italy, Carmelo?" she asked wanting to confirm it.

"Sicily," he replied. "Me, Carlo."

"Pleased to meet you, Carlo," said the nurse with no name tag.

"This is Nurse Walters, Nurse Williams and I'm Mary."

"Mary, Mother of God, Maria" said Carlo and they all laughed. They carefully washed the limb, shaved it and then began applying the cast.

During his stay in hospital, Carlo was kept busy rolling up newly washed bandages, folding laundry and reading the paper with his dictionary. The nurses would read small passages to him when he asked and he would practise his pronunciation which always got a giggle out of them and a broad smile out of Carlo. Then he would reward them with a chocolate. Soon more nurses came to help Carlo with his English and receive a chocolate for their services and on the third day, he had to send one of the nurses to buy more chocolates with Antonio's money.

On Friday, the Doctor decided Carlo should stay another week.

"I'm not happy with the residual swelling in the toes Nurse. We'll keep him in for another week but I want him walking every day to help get the blood circulating."

So Carlo graduated to making beds, ironing sheets and practising his spoken English with the nurses. *Bed, sheets, pillow, pillow-slip. bandages,* were just the beginning of an ever expanding vocabulary and an ever shrinking supply of chocolates.

Then he thought he would try to impress the girls by writing a postcard to Antonio in English. Using his dictionary, he began composing his rough draft.

November 16 1925

Most loved brother Antonino,
I am learn English with much beautiful womans in hospital who eating all chocolates give me you and more. Are all much kind person toward me and I given many work them help do bed, bandage, sheet iron and bend laundry. Doctor say collecting me Saturday one week forward November 24. You embracing Carlo.

For the price of two chocolates, he negotiated with Nurse Walters to polish his rough draft. The final draft with a picture of Ellis Beach just outside Cairns was addressed to Antonino Cottone, P.O.Box 155 Babinda N.Q. and read:

16th November 1925

Dear Tony,
I am learning English from the most beautiful woman in the hospital. She is sweeter than all the chocolates you gave me. The kind of person you always wanted me to meet is working right here making beds, ironing and folding laundry. She will be so sad when you come to collect me next Saturday 24th November to go home. I think she loves me. Carlo.

Carlo had trouble seeing how the dictionary could get it so wrong but he figured it was more important to impress Antonio by showing him how his time had not been wasted in hospital. The letter was stamped and posted by Nurse Walters herself and it gave Carlo great joy.

Antonio came to collect him on the 24th of November as arranged and kept insisting he wanted to meet the someone so special Carlo had mentioned in his postcard.

"So where is this *most beautiful woman?*" asked Antonio. "The one who loves you so much."

"What are you talking about Antonio? They are all beautiful women and I'm sure they all love me very much but I would never choose only one as special. They are all special."

"Yeah yeah, how come I'm Antonio all of a sudden? And what happened to *Dear Tony?*"

As Nurse Walters, Nurse Williams and Maria came to farewell Carmelo, he handed a large box of chocolates for all of them to the nurse with no name tag and Antonio guessed she must be the one.

Chapter 11

People come and people go

Incapacitated as he was, Carmelo was little use on the farm so he conscientiously applied himself to his study of English. He continued using *The Cairns Post* in conjunction with his dictionary. As a diversion, he also ensured the best meals were awaiting Antonio at lunch and dinner each day. That Saturday, Antonio returned from town with some groceries, two large bottles of *North Queensland Lager* and a letter.

"There's a letter from Teresa. It will be wonderful to receive word on what's happening at home. Ready for a beer, Meluzzo?"

"Yes please, Nino. Here pass me the letter. I'll read it aloud while you're pouring the beer." Antonio passed him the letter and Carlo opened the envelope carefully without cutting it.

16th February 1926.

Dearest brothers Antonino and Carmeluzzo,
It was with such sadness that we heard about your accident with the horse Carmeluzzo. It must have been such a worrying time for you both. Thank God everything was resolved and we pray you are on the way to a full recovery. Everyone here is well and little Eloisa never stops talking. She is such a joy and Rosario is seven years old this year. How fast time flies; your elder sister is forty-one years old this year! Now, some very exciting news for you both: you know the Malaponte family who live just across the road from us?

Remember the father Filippo died of the Spanish Flu just after the war? As if the war wasn't bad enough, but losing the head of the family was so tragic for a family of eight children… fortunately the two eldest boys were old enough to work and earn some money for the family. After resisting the temptation to emigrate for so long, Giuseppe decided to go first and now he is being followed by Natale— the third eldest. Soon most of the family hopes to move also. They have a relative on the mother Maria's side in the town of Home Hill in Australia. We understand it is in the same state of Australia as Babinda so I gave him your address and he promised to write to you both. Angelino has been receiving a lot of work surveying, which is such a blessing as a supplement to our farm income. We could never have survived the last few years without your help dearest brothers but things are now stabilizing for us. God has been so good.

Angelino and Emilia send their love and Rosario and Eloisa send hundreds of hugs across the sea to you both.
I embrace you both my beloved brothers,
Teresa xxxx

P.S. Rosario wants to know when Don Peppino is going to give him his licence to use Nonno Rosario's shotgun to save the sheep from the bandits. I guess that must be you talking Meluzzo. I told him we can't do anything until Don Peppino returns to Agira. But I worry for our noble benefactor Peppino; nobody has heard from him. T xx

"Well, I was in Giuseppe's class in Agira," said Antonio, pushing a cool glass of lager towards Carmelo. "His oldest brother Antonio was only two years ahead of us at school. We were so naughty, putting little notes on the back of our mathematics teacher Zappa. He was old and half asleep most of the time. As soon as he found out, he would yell and scream about how disrespectful we were and everyone would be dying to laugh but far too afraid to do so."

"See, now you're paying for your sins, cutting timbers in the forest, sugar-cane in the fields and sharing a house with pythons."

"Natale was about twelve or thirteen when I left Sicily."

"Yes, he's five years younger than me. Home Hill eh… I remember Home Hill well. That's where Ernesto and Eva Musumeci had family— you know, the people I met on the train on the way up here? It's only about eight hours away from here."

"Bit of a worry as to what has happened to Don Peppino," said Antonio as he topped up Carmelo's glass and then his own. "What do you think the story is?"

"He's not communicating because he doesn't wish the Black Shirts to take revenge upon his family. In Mussolini's Italy, he's an outcast and an outlaw now… just like me."

Antonio continued to work from dawn to dusk clearing the scrub on his farm but he found it difficult on his own. He was not as adept at working with horses as Carmelo, so he only utilized Bawly for the very taxing work and attempted to do the rest himself. Week after week of this backbreaking work was taking its toll on his brother and Carmelo worried for him. As the work continued, he became lethargic, walked with a stoop and had been complaining of headaches.

"Antonio, you can't continue like this. It's harming your health. You will need to hire help, especially in your case where you're trying to do much of the work the horse should be doing."

"Yes Carmelo, but it's not worth hiring someone. Maybe we should go on a short holiday somewhere and take a break from all this work. It's too hot to work anyway and the wet season will be upon us soon. We could go to Cairns by train and visit one of the beaches or we could go south to Home Hill and Ayr. The sugarcane farms there are irrigated. It would be good to explore down there."

"What a great idea! I was beginning to think the only way to see anything around here was to break a leg. Maybe we can go to Cairns and be Tony and Carlo for a while and meet a few girls. I've got contacts there you know."

Antonio laughed, "Well, you make a list of things we need and I'll go into town to sort out something with the bank and with Arena. We leave the day after tomorrow."

"Okay. Now make sure you bring back a loaf of fresh Vienna bread from Arena's Bakery for tonight. I'll have a surprise waiting for you."

It was as if Carmelo had discovered a new lease on life. He juggled all the ingredients needed to make Antonio's favourite *bully beef stew*; potatoes, onions, garlic, black olives, a tin of *Edgell* green peas, a tin of corned beef and a few sprigs of mint. He leaned against the wall, sautéed the onions and garlic, added enough water to cover the potatoes which had been cut into cubes and brought it to the boil. Then he added the tin of corned beef, stirred it and left it on the wood stove to simmer under a slow heat adding salt and pepper to taste. After about twenty minutes he stirred in the tin of green peas, the black olives and the mint and took the stew off the hotplate ready for the evening meal.

When his task had been accomplished, Carmelo sat on a cane chair outside the front door with his foot propped up on a stump. Taking some flakes of tobacco from the yellow packet of *Log Cabin Medium* he rolled it out in the palms of his hand. The sweet aroma of the crushed tobacco wafted around his nostrils. He paused to enjoy the moment, then rolled it into a perfectly symmetrical cigarette, admired it, licked the end, put it in his mouth and ignited it. The first scent of a freshly lit cigarette is when it is at its most tantalizing. He drew deeply down into his lungs and then slowly exhaled, extracting every ounce of enjoyment from it.

He was daydreaming when Fido suddenly caught a glimpse of Antonio at the gate, barked and ran down to meet him. It was evident that Antonio could barely open it and had even more trouble closing it again. The short distance was painstakingly long. Then as he began to walk towards Carmelo with a small bag of groceries in one hand and a loaf of bread under his arm, he developed a swagger. He halted two or three times as if to draw breath and when he finally reached Carmelo, he was deathly pale.

"What happened at the gate, Tonino? You took a long time; is it broken or something?"

"No Meluzzo... I don't feel too well. I have a splitting headache, my eyes are sore... my muscles ache and I think I have a temperature."

He entered the house and by the time Carmelo was mobile, he found his brother sitting at the kitchen table with a thermometer in his mouth. Having waited a minute Carmelo reached over to take the thermometer.

"You do have a temperature, Tonino. It's very high, 105 degrees. The muscle pain I can understand but the eye pain and the temperature; that would have to be something more serious."

"I hope it's not Weil's disease. That would be two weeks of hell."

"Oh no, what is this Weil's disease, Nino?"

"It's a disease carried by rats and canecutters usually contract it from handling cane that has been urinated on by them. But we haven't been cutting cane so I can't imagine it would be that. Anyhow, we'll see how I feel tomorrow. For now, I'm going to take two *Aspros* and go to bed."

"But Tonino, you should have something to eat. I've made bully beef stew and it will go well with some of that bread you bought."

"Thanks, Meluzzo but I'm too tired and I have no appetite. Maybe tomorrow." Antonio stood up, went to the medicine cabinet, took two tablets and headed for his bed.

"Good night, Meluzzo. We'll talk in the morning."

When all was quiet, Carmelo limped to the stove, scooped a small portion of stew into a bowl and sat with a slice of fresh bread; but he too had lost his appetite. Fido was blessed with more than simply the scraps that evening.

Throughout the night, Carmelo looked in on his brother who was delirious and burnt with fever. He sponged him down, whispering softly to him, but nothing seemed to ease the pain. Carmelo had that same look of care, concern and love that I had witnessed so many years ago in Teresa as she stooped over him in that old sheep shack in the mountains in Sicily.

"It's my eyes and muscles. The headaches are killing me and I can't hear properly. You will need to walk to Agis' house and phone the ambulance first thing in the morning, Tonino. I need to go to hospital."

"Hospital, no need to go to hospital Nino… I can look after you here."

"This isn't Italy, Nino and I haven't got smallpox. The hospital is the only place for me, trust me."

The ambulance arrived with the horse-drawn wagon at 9 A.M. It was once again that Jack Johnston found himself checking a Cottone's pulse and temperature. He could all but shake his head.

"You guys have certainly been in the wars, Carlo. This is definitely a hospital job."

Carmelo understood *wars* and *hospital* but couldn't determine how his brother's illness and the war were related. With Carmelo still perplexed, they loaded Antonio onto the wagon and soon Johnston's intentions were clear.

"Thank you Mr Johnston. Go hospital?"

"Yes Carlo, he's going to need a doctor."

"Doctor, I understand. Carlo come too." Carlo climbed up beside his brother in the wagon, talking to him every step of the way as Fido followed faithfully behind.

Dr Carrol's eyebrow furrowed as he read the clipboard attached to the foot of Antonio's bed. Matron Rasmussen stood ramrod straight beside him.

"High fever, myalgia, headache, ocular pain, lethargy; not good signs, Antonio. How long has this been going on?"

"Five or six days… maybe little more. You think might be Weil's Disease, Doctor?" asked Antonio.

"How is your hearing? Any hearing loss?"

"Yes, a little bit like wax in ear."

"What work have you been doing?"

"Very heavy work doctor, clear the scrub."

He turned to address Matron Rasmussen, "I hope not, but early symptoms suggest it could possibly be Scrub Typhus, Matron. We'll need to put him under strict observation over the next few days to see if any further symptoms develop. For now we'll just work on keeping the temperature down with stronger medication to manage the pain. Any signs of a rash or other symptoms and we'll need to look at other options. Let me know as soon as there's any change either way."

"Yes Doctor," she replied as she jotted down some notes of her own.

Carmelo sat with his brother until ten o'clock that evening and Fido sat under the bed.

"You'll have to go now Mr Cottone," said a young nurse who entered weilding a wash bowl and sponge. "I'm Nurse Patty and I'm going to give Antonio a sponge down now."

Carmelo simply sat there.

"You'll have to go," she repeated, "It's ten o'clock… " she tapped her watch, "come back tomorrow. Vene domane," she tried in Italian.

"Ah domane. Yes tomorrow come back Nurse," he repeated.

Antonio opened his eyes, "Yes Meluzzo, come back tomorrow and remember to bring the photo of Rosario from beside my bed."

"Yes Nino, I'll be back early," he turned to exit and then swivelled around giving a short whistle, "Come on Fido." His devoted dog leapt out from under the bed and was right upon Carmelo's heels, but no sooner were they out of sight when Fido looked back, looked up at Carmelo and then slunk back into the ward and back under Antonio's bed.

The following day, his condition had worsened. There was a visible rash on the trunk of his body, his speech was slurred and his deafness had increased.

Dr Carrol was quite explicit, "We'll have to increase the medication to reduce his temperature, Matron. He needs cold compacts on the forehead and tepid sponge every four hours. I'd say it's Scrub Typhus and that's about all we can do. I expect he'll experience tremors and nervousness as the disease takes hold. Keep his fluids up. We're just going to have to ride this one out."

Carmelo placed the photo of Rosario on the bedside cabinet. Antonio smiled and thanked him through slurred speech. Nothing he could say would fool me. Antonio was gravely ill.

"Meluzzo, the doctor thinks I have Scrub Typhus. It's a serious disease but I'm young and strong. I have known one other person who got this and he survived, so I'm not worried. Yesterday, I went to the bank because I knew I wasn't well and I wanted to take precautions. I had to think of you and be sure that if anything happened to me, you would not be abandoned here in a strange land. I should have done it a long time ago but we put these things off when we are strong and healthy."

"What are you talking about, Nino?" gasped Carmelo distraught from his insinuations. "What did the doctor tell you? You should have done what a long time ago?"

"Nothing Meluzzo… it's just that I should have taken precautions to safeguard your future, that's all. Now look behind the photo of Rosario, in there you'll find a bank passbook. It's a trust account in your name. If something happens to me, I have six hundred pounds sterling saved and this will become immediately available to you. The farm will also be yours once the usual procedures are carried out. That will take some time."

"No Tonino! What are you talking about? Nothing is going to happen to you!"

"Pray God, nothing will happen to me. But this way I can set my mind at ease and not have to worry about you. Today, before three o'clock, you must go down to the bank and record your signature on this account with the Manager Mr Geyle. He will look after all your affairs."

Carmelo was in a state of shock as Antonio lapsed in and out of consciousness. Then, to make things worse, the Catholic priest came to his bedside and introduced himself.

"I'm Father Cavallaro," he said to Carmelo in Italian. "I am told your brother is very sick. But have faith my son, I will pray for him, the Church will pray for him. We will pray for God's mercy." He did the sign of the Cross over Antonio. "God bless you my son. God be with you during these next few days and give you strength." Then he did the sign of the Cross over Carmelo. "And God bless you too my son. Keep the faith that your brother will be restored to health and it will come to pass."

"Thank you Padre. Thank you for your prayers. We come from a very religious family."

"But I don't remember seeing you at Mass on Sundays."

"No Padre, it was very remiss of us. Our great-uncle was a priest. My name is Carmelo."

"I will call on your brother each day, Carmelo and pray for him."

Over the next two days, Antonio's battle between this life and the next intensified. On both days, Father Cavallaro stayed true to his promise and prayed to God while Carmelo sat and wrestled with God.

"Dear God… what has this poor soul done? What has he ever done but love and honour his family? Please do not forsake him now. Please God, only you can help him now."

On the third day, Father Cavallaro offered Antonio his last rites, blessed him and absolved him of his sins. Carmelo remained calm. It was as if he was trying to bask in the time that they had remaining together. After Father Cavallaro left, he sat close to Antonio and prayed aloud.

"Dear God… you did not forsake me in my hour of need, you gave me Teresa. Please God, send someone who can do for my brother what my sister did for me," he begged.

"Don't worry," soothed Nurse Patty as she rested her hand on Carmelo's shoulder, "priests often give the last rites as a precaution. It doesn't mean the patient is going to die."

Not recognising a word, Carmelo reached for the hand on his shoulder as if his prayers had been answered.

On the fourth day the rash on Antonio's body transformed into sores and on the fifth day they began to ulcerate. Carmelo remained steadfast in his faith. He was calm and no longer felt anguish. Every time Antonio opened his eyes, Nurse Patty was there; bathing him, turning him, administering his medication, combing his hair, offering him sips of water. Carmelo loved her more deeply than he had ever loved anyone outside of his family before.

"The fever has broken, Mr Cottone," she tapped the thermometer and pointed to the floor. Carmelo instantly recognised that the news was good. "I must report this to the sister. I think he's going to be all right, Mr Cottone." She was so excited that he was certain the news was good.

That evening, Antonio was fully conscious and sipping water from a glass with a straw. Occasionally his hand would shake and the straw would shoot off at a tangent, but would eventually settle to find the glass again.

"How is your hearing?" asked Dr Carrol. "Is it improving?"

"Yes Dr Carrol, but a little bit like wax in ear. But no headache and no sore muscle. Only itch, very itch."

"Okay, all good signs Matron. Hit those little nasties with the Calamine Lotion and pump as much water into him until his urine is crystal clear. Want him up and walking tomorrow." He patted Antonio on the shoulder. "Well done Tony, you've beaten this one— providing no complications arise."

After the doctor, the matron and Nurse Patty left, Carmelo placed the empty glass on the bedside cabinet and took away Antonio's straw. They just looked at each other and then Antonio broke the silence.

"I'm hungry. I think I'm ready for that *bully beef stew*, Meluzzo."

"Yeah, well Fido got both our shares so you're just going to have to wait until lunchtime tomorrow now, aren't you? You know that dog has not left your side for the whole time that you've been in here— except to eat our *bully beef stew* that is! "

"Good dog Fido," Antonio called and Fido acknowledged the compliment with a little whine that didn't even necessitate him raising his head off the floor, followed by a few thumps on the wooden floor with his tail.

A week later, the two brothers found themselves on the rail-motor to Cairns; one with a leg in plaster, the other still covered in Calamine Lotion, but they did have their day at the beach and a cold beer or two. Only one thing was obvious and that was the fact that not one single girl showed the slightest interest in either of them. Surprisingly, they didn't give a damn.

It was not long before their talk returned to their plans for the future. This next season was to be Antonio's last. His eight years were drawing to a close and he would return to Sicily as he had promised. He and Carmelo discussed selling his share of the farm to Arena.

"I wish I could offer you my share of the farm, Meluzzo, but I am going to need some capital to set up a business in Sicily when I return."

"Of course you must sell the farm. I'll be fine here and as soon as I get some capital together, I'll be doing exactly the same as you did."

"Well not quite, Meluzzo. You see, all the money that I earn from the cut this year will be going to you. Just a long term loan, mind you. That means, with a loan from the bank you'll be able to buy that small farm up the road where the Hindus stable their horses. It's a good farm and a lot of it's cleared. There's no house on it but it's under cane. They only want nine hundred pounds. It'll be a good start for you. You can secure it with a deposit of one hundred pounds. The Hindus take this crop and when it's yours after giving them the balance owing, you get the crop. What do you say?"

"Thank you, Ninuzzo. I would love that farm. We must negotiate for Bawly to come with me. And if I can find a work harness for Fido and the cow, I should be able to put them to work as well."

So they put down the deposit, finished the cut and the bank gave Carmelo the loan to buy the Hindus' farm up the road for only nine hundred pounds. Bawly, Fido and Jersey the cow remained with Carmelo and Antonio returned to Sicily as he had pledged so many years ago. If it was possible for a spirit to have feelings, I guess I would have felt all warm inside.

Chapter 12

A great leap forward

All of Carmelo's money was now dedicated to his recently acquired property, which was mortgaged to the National Bank of Australia. The property had stables for four draught horses, which included a separate workshop space with a bench, a "chop-chop" engine and a storage area for molasses and bran for the horses, as well as an entire wall reserved for the draught work harnesses. Carmelo modified one of the draught horse bays into a bail for the Jersey cow. The only other building was a small corrugated iron storage shed for fertilizer erected on stumps to provide easier access for loading and transporting the bags. As there was no house on the property, Carmelo remained in Saffiotti's barracks at the end of the cut and went to his farm each day as it was only a fifteen minute walk away.

When Carmelo arrived to deposit his final pay for the season including Antonio's as well, Mr Geyle, the bank manager asked him into his office.

"Hello, Mr Cottone. Would you like me to call in Nellie to interpret for you?"

"No need, Mr Geyle. My English improved lot but you be patient with me."

"So, your brother Antonio has left Australia for good. He made me promise to look after you, so if you have anything you want to talk to me about regarding your finances, please feel free to do so."

"Thank you, Mr Geyle. My brother love too much me. He still thinks looking after me."

"So, where are you living now that the season is over?"

"I live Saffiotti barracks and walk farm each day."

"And what will you do when the next season starts. Where will you live?"

"I live barracks and work farm on weekenda."

"Have you thought about building a house on your farm during the slack season? It would add a lot of value to the property."

He nodded, "…but I need cut cane one more season for money."

"Maybe we can lend you the money now if you wish. The Bank thinks you are a good customer and we would like to help you. Also, have you considered cutting your own cane next year? You are an excellent worker and it will allow you more time to work the farm properly. If you develop that farm you can make a good capital gain in just a few years."

He thought for a moment, "What you suggesta?"

"That's what I suggest. There are some good carpenters out of work in town at the moment. They would be happy to take on the job and the bank will look after the finance of it all. Now I want you to think about it and if you agree, we can arrange to meet here at the bank next week with the builder. He also has an account with this bank."

"Thank you, Mr Geyle. No need think. We meet next week and start soon possible. Thank you for looking me, Mr Geyle. See, Antonio was right, I still need looking me."

On the way home, Carmelo stopped by the Post Office to check Box 155. In it was a letter with handwriting that was unfamiliar. He turned it over and saw that it was from Natale Malaponte. This time, he sat down on the steps of the Post Office and opened the letter carefully.

P.O. Box 136
Home Hill.
26th November 1926.

Dear Antonio and Carmelo,
I am writing to you under strict instructions from my mother Maria Malaponte. I'm sure you remember me and I understand your sister informed you that I would be coming

to Australia to join my brother Giuseppe in Home Hill. Mamma's sister, Sara and her family have a farm there and Giuseppe and I will be living with them until our two brothers, Antonio and Orazio arrive in early December.

I have mentioned you both to Zia Sara and she has asked me to invite you to our place for Christmas. Maybe we could spend a week together and we could all be reunited with my brothers. Zia Sara knew your mother when they were children, so they go back a long way.

I have just finished my first season cutting cane and Giuseppe and I will be encouraging our two brothers to organise our own place as soon as possible. That way, we will be able to bring the whole family out here and start a new life together. Of course, that will be a few years away at least. Antonio has two children; one and two years old, so leaving them behind is a great sacrifice for him. Orazio our other brother, is still young. He is only seventeen.

I hope this letter finds you both in the best of health. Please inform me whether you will be able to spend Christmas with us. It would be a great pleasure to have you here.

Your close family friend,
Natale Malaponte.

P.S. You can write to me at the Post Office address above and if you can come, I will immediately send you the details regarding how to find us and a contact phone number as well.

I await your early reply with great anticipation,
Natale

Carmelo resolved to reply immediately, so he hurried to Barbagallo's store for a pen and some paper. He would write the letter and post it before returning home.

"Ah Cottone, good to see you. Giuseppe, Giuseppe, Cottone is here! Sit down, sit down. I'll bring you a cup of coffee. Have you heard from Antonino yet?"

"No Signora, he is still on the ship to Sicily. He won't arrive until after Christmas."

"Of course, Sicily is a long way away and I forget. But in my mind and in my heart it is just across the street. If I didn't think this way, my heart would break for all the loved ones I left behind." She brought the cup over to him as he sat at the little table in the corner. Then Giuseppe entered, his hands covered in salt from the anchovies.

"Ah Carmelo, how are you? Give me one minute while I wash my hands. I have anchovies all over them." He wiped them before shaking hands with Carmelo.

"I haven't had a chance to have a talk to you for a long time. You've been so busy with the season. How's the farm? Are you happy with it? Will you stay in the barracks at Saffiottis' place?"

"Give him a chance to drink his coffee, Giuseppe. Questions, questions, questions. Here, have your coffee."

"Thank you, Mississa."

"Yes Giuseppe, very happy. If it weren't for my brother, Nino, I would never have been able to buy it so early."

"Nine hundred pounds is a great price. It was nine hundred pounds, wasn't it? With the crop too, eh? You can't go wrong, Carmelo."

"I'm thinking of building a house on it this slack season and maybe cutting my own cane instead of staying with the gang. That way, I'll be able to work the farm better. What do you think?"

"Ah... spoken like a real farmer, Carmelo. That is the only way to do it. A man can only serve one master. Build a house, cut your own cane and work the farm like it should be worked; not in your spare time on weekends. You can't go wrong." Then he thought about it. "But the money, what about the money? Will the bank agree to it?"

"I think so. I'll know next week."

"Well, the bank doesn't lend money unless there is no risk. They would sell their own mother rather than take a loss. If they give you the money, you know it's a good thing."

"That's a good way of looking at it," said Carmelo. "Thanks for that, Giuseppe," and he raised his coffee cup to him. "Now, I just got a letter from a family friend who comes from my home town Agira."

"Ah, Paesano! Where is he? In Australia?" asked Mrs Barbagallo.

"Yes, he's in Home Hill. Can I have a pen and some writing paper to respond to him? Save me coming back tomorrow to post it." Then he reached into his bag and brought out a box of chocolates. "This box of chocolates is for you because I don't have a girlfriend and you're the nicest lady I know."

Mrs Barbagallo was overcome with emotion. "Oh thank you, Cottone. My husband never gives me chocolates. I've got to wait for my customers to give them to me. You should be ashamed, Giuseppe."

"Come on, you've got a whole shelf full of chocolates here in the shop and you want me to give you more?"

"That's not the same is it, Cottone? Anyhow forget about that. You haven't got a girlfriend, I'll make some inquiries back in Sicily for you."

"Thanks Signora, but I'm too young to get married. Not until I reach the age of Christ. Then I'll get married."

"Wise man Carmelo! See my hair," said Giuseppe, "all gone. That's from getting married too early!"

"It's good for you to go to Home Hill. Plenty of good Italian women there. Maybe you'll change your mind," she laughed.

"And Signora can I get 200 grams of anchovies, a loaf of bread and some olives and cheese for an easy meal tonight?"

"Ah, bad sign, Cottone," she shook her finger at him, "you need a wife or you will die of starvation before you get to the age of Christ."

Carmelo wrote the letter and posted it. Then he walked home. It was so lonely without Antonio. Carmelo had spent so many nights just smoking and staring at the wall since Antonio left. Christmas would be something to look forward to.

Everything went to plan and the following Tuesday, Carmelo met the builders and they decided on a house and a price. The bank clerk drafted the papers and as a bonus, the builder agreed to build a pit latrine if Carmelo was prepared to dig the hole.

A team of carpenters would commence on the house as soon as the plans were approved by Council and they were confident it would be ready for Carmelo before the January rains. Immediately, I noticed a huge change come over Carmelo. It was as if all of the barriers he imagined before him in his adopted country had been lifted. He didn't have time to stare at the wall anymore. Pity he had to express his joy by trying to whistle and sing, because he was no good at either.

Chapter 13

New horizons

By the time Carmelo had dug the pit for the latrine at the farm, Natale had replied to his letter, excited about Carmelo's acceptance of Zia Sara's invitation to spend Christmas with them. His brothers would be arriving in Brisbane on the fifteenth of December and he was going to meet them there and return with them on the rail-motor to Home Hill. He invited Carmelo to come early and go down to Brisbane with him.

Carmelo accepted, thinking it would be a good opportunity to detour to Toowoomba to visit the Harristown Area Saleyards Work Horse Auction that was advertised in *The Cairns Post* for the sixteenth of December. The brothers could return without him to Home Hill and that would offer them a chance to settle in before Carmelo returned a couple of days later.

With the trip south arranged, Carmelo harnessed up Bawly and did a final scarify of the twenty-five acres of land under cane. It was a monumental job, but scarifying was not hard on the horse and every three rows, Carmelo would let the horse spell while he chipped away the grass at the end of each row with a hoe. A second horse was a high priority now if the farm was going to be worked properly.

"Good boy, Bawly. You'll get an extra ration of bran and molasses tonight," he promised as he rattled the chains on the horse's flank with the long leather reigns. The horse's ears would twitch back and forth any time Carmelo spoke, listening for commands and encouragement. "Good boy, Bawly. Giddy-up there, Bawly."

The builder's name was Michael McIntosh.

"Just call me Mick," the builder insisted after several attempts and several mispronunciations of his last name. "You did a good job with that pit. We'll build the outhouse first so the boys can test it out for you. So, you're going away for a few weeks? We'll have the frame up before Christmas and the roof on before you get back. Reckon you'll be able to move in at the end of January. She'll be spic and span, painted and ready to go."

"Thank you, Micka. I leave two cases of *North Queensland Lager* in fertilizer shed for all to share for Christmas."

Carmelo packed his port for Home Hill. In a towel, he wrapped a bottle of McWilliams Sherry, a bottle of Cinzano Extra Dry White Wine and a bottle of brandy. He bought the biggest box of chocolates from Mrs Barbagallo's store.

"Ah Cottone, you found another woman to give chocolates to, eh? You forget about this old girl as soon as someone else comes along, eh? Doesn't matter, I forgive you... the quality of the chocolates from Barbagallo's store are nowhere near the quality of the chocolates you bought me from Cairns, eh?"

"You're still my favourite, Mrs. Barbagallo. Can I have a large tin of those Spanish anchovies in salt, a kilo of your best green olives, a kilo of your best black olives, a Veneto salami, a Lismore salami, a slab of pancetta, and a wheel of pepper cheese?"

"Hey, maybe you should come to our place for Christmas, Cottone."

"Well it just goes to show, you've got to get in early if you want to invite the most eligible bachelor in town to your Christmas party," he joked.

With all that food squeezed into his suitcase along with the wine and his clothing, it was a good thing Mick was able to take him to the station the following afternoon.

"You should get down to Home Hill about ten o'clock tonight, Carlo. Have a good holiday. We'll have a nice surprise for you when you get back."

"Thank you, Micka," he shook hands. "Merry Christmas, Micka."

"Yeah, merry Christmas, Carlo. Thanks again for the beer."

Carmelo was very excited at the prospect of seeing familiar faces from the old country, as well as receiving some first-hand reports on life back home from the two brothers Malaponte. The monotonous rattle of the steel wheels hammering at rail-length intervals and the sharp dry squeak of the springs on wood as the train trundled south, mesmerized him. He quite enjoyed a light meal in the dining car and then returned to his seat for the last leg of the journey.

Natale was at the station walking beside his carriage and tapping on the window as the train applied its brakes, grinding to a halt. He then entered the carriage.

"Welcome, Carmelo. Here let me embrace you. Good to see you again."

"Thank you, Natale. Thank you for your kind invitation." They threw their arms around each other and there was much shoulder slapping.

"Quickly, your suitcase... if we hurry, we can catch the bus that goes right past our place."

Zia Sara was not unlike his own Zia Teresa Scriffignano; extroverted and most welcoming.

"Ah, Carmeluzzo. You are all Cottone. I see your father Rosario in you. Welcome, welcome. Natale, take his suitcase up to his room. Now tell me, have you eaten? Come, I have kept a large plate of pasta for you because I know the food on the train is inedible. And keep some room for the stewed fruit I've prepared especially for you and Natale's brothers."

"What do you have in that suitcase, Carmelo? It weighs a ton," said Natale as he prepared to take it to his room.

"Just a few things for your lovely Zia Sara. Here, let me empty some of it before you go."

"Carmelo, why did you bring all those things? No need to bring anything. We have everything here."

"I know Zia Sara, but I wasn't sure if you had this brand of chocolates. A special brand for a special lady." She liked that.

She gave him a hug, "Thank you, but you shouldn't have. Ah, pepper cheese— my favourite and Venito salami. Anchovies, it's so hard to buy good anchovies. Zio Umberto will be ecstatic. My God you've brought half of Babinda here with you. Thank you, Carmelo."

Natale prepared a small suitcase of his own and the following night they both took the rail-motor to Brisbane to meet his brothers. They berthed at the Hamilton Wharf and because their passports had already been processed in Fremantle there was no delay at Customs and Immigration. They stayed overnight in Fortitude Valley and the four boys were able experience a late night exploring the streets, shops and several entertainment venues in Brisbane. Early the next morning, a quick romp through the Botanic Gardens would be their last adventure in the capital city before Carmelo boarded a train heading west through Ipswich to Toowoomba.

"We'll meet again in a few days' time," Carmelo called to them. "Safe trip."

The train trip to Toowoomba was quite spectacular. The rich black soil of the salad-bowl farmlands around Gatton contrasted with the sparsely vegetated grazing land in the hills. A patchwork of textures and colours covered the whole farming landscape. Lettuce, tomatoes, cabbage, onions and potatoes were cultivated intensely and there were broad acre plantings of corn, millet and lucerne. Everywhere, armies of synchronised sprinklers squirted and sprayed sheets of water onto the crops reflecting momentarily a kaleidoscope of colours. Then as the train climbed into the terrain leading to the Great Divide, all was stark and foreboding; closed in and hostile after the plains.

Toowoomba was a bustling hub. Grain from the Darling Downs and livestock were the principal products that sustained the economy of the town, which provided stores, tools, implements and mechanical and transport services. Feeding off these were the banks and insurance companies who provided financial services. Hotels with their broad open verandahs offered accommodation for hordes of itinerant workers and Carmelo chose to spend two nights in one situated close to the Harristown Area Sale Yards on the outskirts of Toowoomba.

This was a fact-finding mission and Carmelo needed to learn the basic procedures for participation in the auction, taking possession of the livestock, transport to the railhead and care of the animals during transport. Most importantly, he considered acquiring an agent who could provide language support; but the main European ethnic group was German and he did not meet one Italian in the whole two days that he stayed there.

"I see you've got a dictionary there. That's all you need. No rocket science needed here. Even at the auction. You notice most of them use hand signals and these are people who were born here," said Klaus a huge bald-headed native German with a red beard whose accent was heavy, yet he spoke with surprising clarity.

Carmelo laughed, "Yes, that's true, hand signals are international language."

"Not quite, you make the wrong hand signal and you might find yourself with a huge bill and a whole lot of horses you didn't want. You come with me today and watch and I'll teach you the trade, okay?"

"Thank you very much, Klaus," and they shook hands on it.

"Find me at the yards around 11 o'clock and I'll show you the ropes. What do you know about horses anyway?"

"I work with them in time in army and had some good teacher there." Probably not a good idea to mention the army, considering the Italians had just fought the Germans in a World War just ten years ago. I think he realised this when it was too late.

"Well, as long as your teachers were better than your troops," quipped Klaus.

Carmelo was happy to leave it at that. Klaus with his square jaw, resembled the classic stereotype straight from the war posters.

Klaus was true to his word. For the rest of the day, Carmelo shadowed his Aryan tutor and was convinced that there was nothing he could do that the Aryan could not do better. So he let Klaus know.

"Well Klaus, I pick the good horses, but you must do the bid and paperwork. When I come down, I like you be my agent."

"You sure you don't want to give it a try?" smiled Klaus.

"Me sure, thanks for show me how difficult it is."

"If you're looking at a wagonload of horses, I can contact you when I know there's a good selection coming up for auction. You don't want to be making the trip for nothing, eh?"

"Yes right, Klaus, very good idea." He and Klaus certainly seemed to understand each other well.

The next day, Klaus invited him to go to the Downs to look around. At 8 A.M. Klaus picked him up from his hotel in his 1920s Armstrong Siddeley utility and they headed south to Warwick.

"This is where most of your draught horses come from. Many farmers breed their own as a sideline and others might want to sell a horse for some reason. Before a scheduled sale in Toowoomba, drovers come along and pick up a whole lot of horses along the way and walk them to the saleyards. Then after the sales, they walk them back and deliver them to their new owners. It's a good business and it provides a valuable service."

Klaus pulled over beside a wheat-field where a *Buckeye* mechanical reaper was being pulled by three Clydesdales. As it spat out clumps of wheat every ten metres or so, men would scramble to pile them into larger stacks. The foreman, with a dog at his heels, was barking orders urging the men on.

"I not imagine the size of these wheat-fields. Fields in Italy so small in compare to this. Harvesters very impressive. So beautiful horses," he marvelled.

They returned through Clifton and Ma Ma Creek where Carmelo spied his other great passion, cattle.

"What beautiful stock. One day I come down here and settle on large property and run cattle. This is such excellent place for cattle."

"Well, anytime you want to buy property down here, write to me and I'll pick you up at the station and show you around. I sell a lot of property down here and have a pretty good idea about the prices."

As they drove up the range to Toowoomba, Carmelo could feel the change in temperature and inhaled deep breaths. Klaus was amused by this.

"If you like the air so much, maybe you should move down here,

Carmelo. I'll take you to the lookout so you can get a glimpse of the whole valley looking east. That might help you decide."

As he looked east across to the Lockyer Valley, Carmelo gasped.

"What a country my Australia," was all Carmelo needed to say.

That afternoon just before closing, Carmelo walked across to Klaus' office from his hotel with a carton of cold beer over his shoulder.

"I no can leave without give appreciation in some way. Thank you very much again for your hospitality Klaus."

Chapter 14

Seasons

The word 'season' had taken on a whole new meaning for Carmelo: 'the wet season', 'the cutting season', 'the slack season', 'the festive season' and finally 'the duck season'. All were very important periods of time that Carmelo had experienced in Australia. It was now 'the festive season' and what better family to share it with than Umberto, Sara and their family and the four Malaponte brothers. All the special things inherent to his childhood at Christmas were here in Home Hill with this wonderful family: the *tagliatelle* home-made pasta, the ham encased in dough and roasted to perfection in the baker's oven, the *Rami di Miele, Ricotta Torte, Trionfo di Gola, Dolci di Natale, Torta di Pistacchio* and old favourites like *cannoli with cream* were all on the menu along with scrumptious locally grown watermelon, pawpaw and mangoes. Hence 'the mango season' and 'the watermelon season' was added to the list of his new experiences.

The most exciting of all was a totally new experience; it was 'duck season' and Umberto took all the men, with the exception of Giuseppe who was out of town, to a huge lagoon where ducks flocked to in their hundreds at that time of the year. Umberto took aim with his double barrelled shotgun and released both barrels. Three ducks hurtled to the ground as he reloaded it for Carmelo. The visitor took aim and fired the first shot. Two ducks fell and he passed the gun to Antonio who took aim and brought another two ducks down with the second shot. Umberto loaded the gun again and handed it to Natale who boasted by nominating the duck he was aiming for.

"The one on the right about thirty metres away." He fired and passed the gun to Orazio.

"I'll take those two about fifty metres away."

"Don't like your chances at that distance," said Antonio. In this instant, when Orazio failed to bring even one of the ducks down, Antonio proved wiser.

"That's enough," said Umberto. "There'll be no ducks left if I leave you four here for much longer. Eight ducks in all is more than enough for us to pluck."

"Carmelo, Antonio, Orazio... you haven't tasted duck until you taste the duck that Sara cooks," added Natale.

Soon the exploits of the day were overshadowed by a conversation that returned to their beloved Sicily and respective families. Carmelo loved hearing that Angelino brought Rosario and Eloisa to the village square in Agira every Sunday always buying them a giant gelato each.

"He had to do that so they wouldn't annoy him as he chatted with the other men in the village," said Antonio. "You know he loves to talk. He's so like your father— always helping everyone whenever he can and offering his opinions on anything and everything."

"My mother Maria spends a lot of time with your sister Teresa," said Orazio. "They are both without partners so they enjoy each other's company. Teresa is less mobile these days but she is very high spirited and the two little ones keep her busy. As we left she was saying how nice it would be to see Antonio again and to our surprise he was already on his way. How long was he in Australia?"

"Eight years," said Carmelo.

"Do you think he will come back?"

"No, Antonio loves Sicily too much. I don't think he'll return. I'm hoping he'll meet a nice girl and settle down."

"Well my mother and Teresa already have plans for him. They work their magic in mysterious ways these old women," said Antonio Malaponte.

"Adele has moved away from Agira. We don't see her much but she seems happily married. How is Archangela finding America?"

"I had a letter from her a few months ago and they seem very happy. They have a little son called Orazio... same as you Orazio. So, I guess he'll grow up to be a wild one."

"Who me? I'm quiet as a lamb," insisted Orazio.

As they talked about his family, Carmelo could sense them right there beside him in the living room and he felt a strong yearning to be nearer to them. "I'll certainly miss my beloved Antonio in Australia."

"We will always be here for you," Antonio assured him. With those words, Carmelo was able to quell any feelings of melancholy. This place and these people would always be a home away from home for him.

He did return to a pleasant surprise in Babinda. The house was at lock-up stage and the wet season was late.

"If the rains hold off, we'll have you in here in the next couple of weeks," Mick assured him. "Old Warner dropped in to see if you were here. He wanted you to contact him when you got back."

Carmelo had to go into town and stopped in to see Warner while he was there.

"Happy New Year Carlo," said Warner, visibly pleased to see his boundary rider back.

"Thank you, Mr Warner. Happy New Year to you too."

Warner looked at his leg, "Looks like you've been left with a bit of a bow in that leg, Carlo."

"Yes, they no set it too good so that's the way it will stay. It feel strong and it no affect my work."

"Do you feel up to doing a bit of boundary riding for me again? I hear you've decided to take on farming fulltime and I thought the extra money might come in handy."

"I very much like that and like the same horse too. Is a good horse that one."

"Well that's not going to be possible, the mug rider who took your place couldn't tell the back of a horse from its front. Tried to get him to jump a barbed wire fence, would you believe? The horse nicked the top strand and fell breaking its femur. We had to put her down. I fired the guy, but that's not going to bring the horse back."

"I very sad to hear that Mr Warner."

"Anyhow, there's a couple of riding horses I'd like you to look at.

You can choose one and I'll buy it. You would have to be as good a judge of horseflesh as anyone I know."

"I like to Mr Warner. In fact, I been down to Toowoomba to Draught Horse Auctions. See how they operate. Some beautiful horses for sale down there and cheap to the prices up here. The Clydesdales are magnificent. I made good friends with agent down there. He say if I can get enough people interest in wagonload horses, I tell my friend, then go there bring a load back."

"How many horses to a wagonload, Carlo?"

"Fourteen maximum, but with Clydesdales, big. Better buy for one dozen. It a long journey and little bit of extra room make big difference."

"Well, I reckon I might be interested. If you can get me good horses at the right price, I'll take ten and another two for you for your work. As well, I'll cover your transport costs and your accommodation in Toowoomba. Think about it and get back to me as soon as your agent fellow gets in contact with you."

"When you want me to look at these riding horses?"

"Tomorrow morning at 10 o'clock would be good. Can you make it then?"

"Sure Mr Warner. See you then."

Carmelo fenced in an area of land beside the house and dug and fertilized the soil for a vegetable garden. He arranged for Mick to send a carpenter for two days to build a small chicken coop and added a run himself. Around the house he planted, mandarin, orange and lemon trees, a peach tree, a granadilla vine beside a timber trellis, a passionfruit vine, a mango tree and a grove of bananas down beside the stables but away from the horses. It rained so regularly in Babinda that there was no need to water the plants. As it was the slack season, there was no other work to do on the farm other than keep the headlands clear of grass with a scythe. The boundary riding work was enjoyable and provided a small but welcome income.

In April, Carmelo received a letter from Klaus informing him of an upcoming sale in Toowoomba.

7th April 1927

Dear Carlo,
I want to tell you about a big sale of work horses to be auctioned on the 25th of April. This is usually one of the biggest sales of the year and there will be a great variety of good quality horses available. I thought if you were interested you might want to come down and if the prices are right and the animals are suitable, you could take a wagonload back up north with you. The horses are available for viewing in lots and individually the day before the auction. I could book a room at the hotel for you if you want.

Regards,
Klaus.

Carmelo relayed the message to Warner.

"Perfect Carlo. We really need some good horses for this season as it looks like being a bumper crop. As well, the industry is expanding rapidly and good horses will be hard to come by locally. Count me in. You know the deal. I'll arrange to have six hundred pounds in cash ready for you a couple of days before. Anything else you need, just let me know."

On the 22nd of April, Carmelo collected the money from Warner and left on the rail-motor to Brisbane. From Brisbane he took the train to Toowoomba and was met by Klaus in his Armstrong Siddeley utility at the station.

"Thank you Klaus for meet me at station. Do you book hotel room for me?"

"Yep, same hotel, different room, same price. Just in time too as there are a lot of buyers and itinerant workers in town at the moment."

As Klaus drove down towards the hotel he was dying to ask the question, "Tell me Carlo, how did you manage to get such a large order together? "

"I boundary riding for one of the huge plantation owners. He trust me with horses and want me to select them."

"Well, I can guarantee he'll be pleased with what we can buy here."

"What the arrangement is for payment for your service?"

"Standard. All auction prices are in guineas. The agent takes one shilling in every guinea. That covers all the paperwork and organization at the auction and at the railhead and I do all your bidding for you. You pay your accommodation of course, all transport costs to the railhead and to Babinda via Brisbane. When will you be going back?"

"With the horses I go back. Same train. I must look after them."

"No need to look after them, the railway staff will do that. But you will need to be on the same train if there's no one in Babinda to claim them."

Carmelo spent the entire day inspecting the horses. That night, he discussed his observations with Klaus.

"The horses I like you bid for are very quality horses. Now all we have do is get them at right price."

"That's my job. You tell me what you think they're worth and I'll do my best to better it. If we can buy them by lot, it's much more likely that we can get a better price."

The following day the Harristown Saleyards were a hive of activity. The auctioneer gathered everybody together and in a polished display, as would never be seen in Italy or Sicily, established his utter dominance. Of special note was his reference to God.

"As far as everyone here is concerned, you need to know there's only one God. And for today at this auction, that God is me. We've got a lot of horses to get through today and we need to get everything right. All bids are in cash. When the hammer falls, that decision is final. You make your way over here to my clerks and get the paperwork done. Any problems— you sort it out with them."

The auction was under way, but the horses were going for prices higher than Carmelo had hoped.

"Don't worry," said Klaus. "There are always the people who are in a hurry or don't know much about prices. We let them spend their money first and then we move in for the bargains when the money runs out."

"I no worry, Klaus; I have you."

One lot of six quality Clydesdales appeared and Carmelo wanted them.

"You can go to maximum on this lot, Klaus. Up to forty guineas each if you must."

Klaus was cool under pressure. Twice Carmelo thought he would lose them and the bid hadn't even got to thirty guineas each. He could feel his heart racing and he was a wreck just listening to the bidding. Then finally the hammer came down.

"One hundred and eighty-six guineas! Sold to Klaus up the back there for one hundred and eighty-six guineas. Congratulations Klaus… top lot that one!" thundered the auctioneer. Carmelo could hardly believe his luck. They were a gift at that price. He'd paid more than that for Bawly and he was only a Clydesdale cross. These were purebred giants.

About twenty minutes later, Klaus clinched the second lot of six. They were draught horses, shorter and stockier than the Clydesdales but quality working horses nevertheless— especially for ploughing. The lot was sold to Klaus for only one hundred and fifty guineas and Carmelo was ecstatic.

"Yes!" He punched the air as the hammer fell. "Klaus, you mighty agent."

That evening, the horses were loaded onto the K Wagon ready for their 5 A.M. departure to the coast. When Klaus arrived to collect Carmelo from the hotel, he had the customary carton of beer over his shoulder ready for him.

"Ah, Carlo, you're too generous. You don't have to do that."

"I must, I must. The only thing I sorry is that you deserve the best and they no sell NQ Lager here. Next time I come, I bring a carton down with me." He rummaged in his bag. "Oh, this box chocolates for girl in office, Klaus."

At Ipswich, the goods train spent about an hour shunting carriages back and forth. The K wagons with the horses usually remained at the back and there were four wagons with over fifty horses in this train. Some railway workers watered the horses. After that, Carmelo checked his purchases every couple of hours. It would be a long journey and Carmelo knew that the horses' muscles would be tense after hours of travel attempting to maintain their balance on the moving floor of the wagons. Thus the shunting with the other wagons at the sidings was a Godsend as it enabled the horses to relax. He had a good supply of sugar cubes and he fed one to each of his horses at each stop. The wait in Brisbane was a long one. Carmelo waited beside his wagon and talked to his horses. Nobody came to water the horses.

Once the goods train chugged out of the Brisbane station, Carmelo was content. It would only be a matter of time before his mission would be accomplished. However, it was a particularly hot day for mid-autumn and by Bundaberg, the horses were restless. Carmelo took the opportunity to find some water and brought it over to his horses. A railway worker appeared suddenly behind him.

"Hey you! What'cha think ya doin', Mister?" He shouted, "no one is allowed near the horses."

"These yes my horses and I giving them drink. They have thirsty."

"Thirsty... rubbish! They won't need a drink 'til they get to Cairns. Show me your paperwork."

Carmelo produced his wagon receipts.

"All right, you do what you want with your horses. I'm in charge here and you stay away from those other horses, you hear?"

Carmelo didn't answer.

The next long stop was at Rockhampton and the horses had spent a whole day in the blistering sun. His horses looked fine but some of the horses in the other wagons had their tongues hanging out. Carmelo went looking for the railway worker. He was nowhere to be found so he took one of the buckets and gave his horses another watering. When they had finished, he started on the second wagon and gave each horse a third of a bucket each. They were scrambling for the water. He had hardly emptied the third bucket when the railway worker appeared.

"I thought I told you not to water the bloody horses. Can't you understand English?"

"Yes I understanda English but these animals thirsty. I help you water them."

"I don't need your help and they ain't getting any water. Why don't you mind your own business!"

Carmelo ignored him, collected another bucket and returned.

"I told you to mind your own business, smart arse," said the irate worker.

"This my business. My business horses and this horses need drink."

"Well I will bloody-well report you to the station-master! Bloody know-all!" He stomped off in the direction of the station master.

Carmelo was watering the horses in the third carriage when the worker returned with the station master in tow.

"See he's still doing it, even after I told him not to, Mr Dwyer."

"Why are you watering the horses when the guard told you not to?" asked the station master.

"They have no water from Ipswich. Thatsa ten hours in the hot sun in a crowded wagon. It's cruel not to give water. He no do it, I do it. He no can to stop me. It's only water."

"How do you know they're thirsty?"

"Well, one in every three has tongue hang out." He pointed to one horse.

"Sounds fair enough to me." The station master turned to face the worker, "now get a bloody bucket and help him for Christ's sake, you bloody idiot. The train will be pulling out of the station in fifteen minutes." He patted Carmelo on the shoulder and sauntered back towards his office.

Warner was also a good judge of horseflesh and when he set eyes on the animals at Babinda station he was very pleased.

"You've got a good bunch here, Carlo and they've arrived in tip top condition. Well done."

"Yes," Carmelo handed over the paperwork. "Toowoomba the place to buy work horses. They work them hard on the Downs." He handed Warner an envelope.

"All the receipts and the unspent money in envelope, Mr Warner."

"You tell me which two horses you want and I'll take the rest," suggested Warner.

"They all good horses. You to take your ten first and I take the other two."

"Look, I'll get these over to the farm across the creek from Saffiotti's barracks. How about you drop over tomorrow morning and you can walk two back to your new farm."

"Okay, see you tomorrow. I happy you like the horses."

Next morning, Warner had left two horses out for Carmelo. One was a fine purebred Clydesdale and the other, a smaller draught horse mare.

"Hope you're happy with these two, Carlo. They should work well together." Then he handed him an envelope. "And here's a little bonus for doing such a good job."

In it was a crispy ten pound note, which was about one week's wage cutting cane.

He placed two halters on the horses, "Come on Bully. Come on Mini. I'll show you your new home and introduce you to my old workmate Bawly. He's going into semi-retirement and it's thanks to you two."

Chapter 15

Itchy feet

Carmelo and Antonio never relinquished their practice of remaining in communication via mail. As Carmelo received a letter from Antonio, he would immediately write back so that every two to three months letters would have been exchanged. When Carmelo read his brother's letters he could imagine himself walking the streets in Agira with him, talking to his old friends and acquaintances and even sharing the warmth, the chatter and the food around the dinner table. He could imagine Angelino's kids hanging onto Teresa's skirt awaiting the delectable sweets she was preparing for their salivating tongues, their laughter and the noise. It was so evident that Angelino was ecstatic upon the return of Antonio that Carmelo was happy for him. He felt Angelino had always assumed the burden of responsibility to be there for the rest of the family while he and Antonio had abandoned ship and cast their lots in search of a more promising life abroad.

Antonio on the other hand was able to appreciate the softer side to his working life in Sicily. With the money he had saved in Australia he was able to buy himself a far more comfortable existence as a liaison officer between the Government and the townspeople. Carmelo's reminders of the pre-dawn to dusk days in the field cutting cane, chipping weeds and living day to day in a virtual cultural desert, devoid of music, song and festivity were enough to ensure he would not yearn to return to Australia hastily. Through the pages of Carmelo's letters, Antonio could revisit the "place of falling water" as the tropical rains played drum rolls on the corrugated iron, overflowed the guttering and filled the tanks. From the safety and comfort of his lounge room, he could ride the boundaries of Warner's cattle properties, deliver calves, fish for eels in Babinda Creek, buy draught horses in Toowoomba and go duck-hunting with the Malaponte brothers in Home Hill.

For Carmelo and for Antonio it was as if they had remained united, living the dream they had always desired, whilst still dreaming of the life they no longer had. Time stood still for them both as it always would, at least while they remained single. Footloose and fancy free, they would always be boys, forever young, with only themselves to be concerned about. Yet it seemed as though the years had flown.

16/05/1929.

My dear and beloved brother Nino,
It is as if it were yesterday that I bought my first little farm with God's grace, some of your money, my meagre savings and the loan from the National Bank. Since then I have built a house on the property, cut and carried more loads than many people carry in a lifetime and ridden more kilometres than you can even imagine now that you have become sedentary... ha ha... I joke.

On a more serious note, Australia's export prices have been falling continuously and I have read in the papers how our burden of debt has become enormous. This means that the country's reliance on international credit has increased dramatically. People employed on public works projects are losing their jobs as the foreign loans used by the Government to finance these projects become too expensive.

Because of our total dependence on these export prices, there is the danger that our economy may be crippled. So, just as times in Europe are going from bad to worse, these are not good times in Australia either. Up to 200 000 people are employed in Public Works Projects.

Consequently, I have decided to accept an offer on the farm for three thousand five hundred pounds from a Piedmont person Ugo Biondi who has a young family. Although this represents a good capital gain for me, the bank is only prepared to lend him one thousand pounds on top of his five hundred pounds deposit. The rest of the money needed; a sum of two thousand pounds, I will have to carry myself, which I have done at the standard bank rate of six per cent. I hold second mortgage after the bank on the property.

He is a good hardworking man and I have no fear that he will honour his debt. Because I am single and still young, I will be able to return to cutting cane for a couple of years to earn some guaranteed cash while work is still available.

I have found the land that I would really like to own. It is on the banks of Babinda Creek on the other side of the level-crossing where I broke my leg. About two kilometres of the property fronts onto the creek and extends across a large area of rich river flats. Some undulating land beyond that is still arable and I would like to run cattle of my own up into the mountains that cradle Mt Bellenden Ker one day. But these are only dreams for now.

I have sent some money by telegraphic transfer to Angelino's bank account for Teresa. Dear sister, please buy something special for Rosario and Eloisa, so they don't forget their favourite person in all of Australia. Inform me by return mail that the money has arrived safely.

I embrace you all my dear family. Never a day goes by that I do not thank our good Lord for you all and ask that He bless and watch over you.

Your loving brother and uncle,
Carmelo.

Carmelo was right about the oncoming economic depression. He was again cutting cane for Warner on his Happy Valley plantation and was now ganger. The ganger was not selected by the farmer; he had to earn the position on merit. He had to be the best and he enjoyed the respect of his men for that reason. The fact that he spoke English was a bonus for Warner as well as for Carmelo. He used every opportunity and every moment of his spare time to practise his oral English with native English speakers. Consequently the improvement in his use of English over the last three years was quite impressive.

"You did the right thing to sell your farm when you did, Carlo. We are well into the season and the price of sugar has collapsed and even the Government is in trouble."

"Yes, but I do not want my gain to be someone else's loss. Ugo Biondi is a good man and he has a young family. This is a great sadness for me."

"Hopefully, this newly elected Country Progressive National Party can get the economy back on track. They are selling a lot of the State owned enterprises." He knew Carmelo was interested in current affairs.

"I read where they have passed a special bill in parliament, The Babinda State Hotel Act, which allows the sale of the Babinda State Hotel."

"Yes and the word 'State' will be removed. The new owner will have a monopoly for five years. That means no competition."

"Do you think you might be interested in buying it, Mr Warner?"

"Might be, depends on how much they want for it. Anyhow, if Forgan-Smith, the new Opposition Leader of the Labor Party gets his way, the sale won't go ahead. He's worried that your mob might form a syndicate and take over the pub."

"Doesn't he like Italians?" asked Carmelo.

"I think it's just politics talking. He's taking advantage of the fear circulating in the electorate and covertly trying to get the Britishers onside. That's all it is."

"Well, if you buy the hotel, you can give me the job as manager... eh?"

"I think you'd better stick to boundary riding, Carlo. You'd probably take up drinking and swallow all my profits."

The sale did go ahead despite Forgan-Smith's concerns and the hotel was not bought by a syndicate of Italians or by Warner. It was purchased by John O'Hagen of Brisbane for fifty thousand pounds.

However, Forgan-Smith's brand of fear was circulating in the Anglo-Australian community. Italians were being discriminated against mainly through ignorance and Carmelo would read of more incidents of racism and even violence against non-British people in The Cairns Post. Employment predominantly was the root cause, but there were also concerns about Italians moving out of the lowly paid strata of society and buying farms, property and businesses of their own.

This fear was compounded by the Fascism dilemma, which took front stage in Australia as Mussolini cemented his authority in Europe. By 1929, the main topic of conversation of ethnic Italians in the fields and on the streets was Fascism.

"Mussolini has made peace with the Vatican. Even the Catholic Church now agrees that Fascism is the best course for Italy," said the Fascists.

"Who can forget the Fascist violence throughout Italy in 1922 with the March on Rome and who can forgive the actions of Mussolini's Black Shirt thugs?" asked the anti-Fascists.

To all the Italians involved in the global Diaspora, but mainly to America, Canada and Australia, Mussolini's Italian Fascist Party's (PNF) policy reiterated that Italian communities abroad should see themselves as Italians first.

"Do not forget, Italians, the country which has given us our common birth. Keep in touch with the ideals of the mother country. Foster the interests of Italy in the land where you reside," Mussolini dictated.

The Dante Alighieri Italian Club in Babinda, which was fiercely anti-Fascist and was established as a support group for victims of Fascist violence at home was suddenly confronted by a sudden surge of support for the Fascist regime. Roman Catholic Bishop McGuire in Townsville and Archbishop Duhig in Brisbane openly claimed that being Italian was a patriotic feeling inseparable from a belief in Fascism and the practice of the Catholic faith. Carmelo could not believe what he was hearing and reading.

"How could the Church stoop so low?" argued Carmelo. "Where was the Catholic church when the peasants were being beaten and their freedom usurped by Mussolini's Secret Police?"

No one offered the answer to that question because it was anti-Fascist; but Carmelo could sense the same murmuring in the crowd now in Australia that he had once heard from Fascist sympathizers in Italy. The Babinda, Brisbane and Innisfail Fascios were the three strongest Fascist clubs in Queensland at that time and within a short time most of the Italian communities embraced these clubs with the first official Fascio in Queensland being established in 1929.

"Let's go and listen to what they have to say in Innisfail," others in his gang would suggest to him. It was usual that gang members had so much respect for the ganger they would virtually seek his permission in this manner. "Aldo Signorini, the head of the Innisfail Fascio will be addressing hundreds of Italians this Saturday."

"No, I won't be going. We were invited to this country to work, not play politics for Mussolini. What loyalty did Mussolini offer returned soldiers who fought for Italy on the Western Front in World War One where hundreds of thousands of lives were lost? He abandoned them leaving them to fend for themselves. Instead he set up his own Secret Police to make sure everyone obeyed him."

Italian farmers and field labourers were being approached by Fascio members to declare their allegiance to the cause.

"Do this and you will gain the respect of all Italians and the protection of *Il Duce* through his representatives here in Australia," they were promised. Some were even offered money, purportedly to have come from *Il Duce* himself. Farmers were put under duress with threats.

"If you awake one morning to find your tractor shed has been blown up, don't say we didn't warn you."

Field labourers were often taunted and provoked so that non-conformists became involved in scuffles in the street. This division in the Italian community between the Fascists and the anti-Fascists, which included Communists and Anarchists created a considerable degree of friction that only served to increase the phobia of Anglo-Australians.

Especially during the Depression, these individuals relied on support groups to survive increasingly harsh times as the traditional network of family was unavailable to them in Australia. The clubs, with their sense of community, were often misconstrued by individuals as sanctuaries of last resort guaranteeing a 'safe passage' through the socio-cultural and political divide threatening to engulf them.

Carmelo knew the time had arrived when he would have to make one of the most important decisions of his life. On the 20th of May 1930, he dressed himself in a suit and tie and swore allegiance to *His Majesty King George V* and received his *Certificate of Naturalization* whereby he became entitled to all political and other rights, powers and privileges and became subject to the obligations, duties and liabilities to which a natural-born British Subject was entitled.

For the first time in his life he felt irrevocably free and he thanked God for that.

Chapter 16

Putting down roots

All of the old gang that Carmelo started off with had gone the way of Antonio and moved on from cutting cane except that they didn't go back to Italy. In fact they all stayed in Babinda and around Happy Valley. Antonio had finally taken the plunge. In 1931, he married the beautiful Grazia Sinopoli, but whether Teresa and Mrs Malaponte had anything to do with it, Carmelo would never know.

In the period to 1933, Carmelo cut cane but also entered into an entrepreneurial adventure with Sorbello. They repurchased Antonio's old farm, expanded it further and resold it to Zannoletti for six thousand pounds. After that, he made the decision to risk everything to purchase that dream property on the banks of Babinda Creek. He paid twelve thousand five hundred pounds to Bisunta Singh for one hundred and twenty nine acres with a house, stables and sheds and a crop of eleven hundred tons of cane.

The dwelling was a well-built regular two bedroom farmhouse with a large lounge, a dining room and a kitchen area with a split-level lean-to attached for the bathroom and laundry area. The house was partly furnished with a double bed and a spare bed and a wardrobe in the main bedroom and two beds in the second bedroom. There was a cane lounge with a matching cane bookcase and a wireless. In the dining room was a heavy wooden table with six chairs and in the kitchen were a kerosene fridge and a wood stove. The inside walls were not sealed and the building had a cement floor. A four metre by three metre covered deck faced north-east and overlooked the entire property with the creek on the left and the farm framed by a ring of green mountains.

He wrote to his brother to give him the news.

25th October 1933

My dear brother Antonio, Grazia and precious little baby Cettina,

What a joy it must be for you both and for Teresa as well, to have little Cettina to cherish for the rest of your lives. Now Rosario and Eloisa have a cousin to play with. I am so happy for you all and miss you all so much. Now that I have been naturalized, I am a British citizen and as such, Mussolini will have no hold over me and the Consul here in Australia has assured me that it would be safe for me to return to Sicily for a holiday without fear of being detained. So I am planning to come back for a visit in three or four years' time.

I have finally purchased the property that I have always dreamed of. It is truly a paradise on earth, nestled into the evergreen mountains and drained by the crystal-clear Babinda Creek and two of its tributaries. I share boundaries with old man Saffiotti, Cristiano, Loiaconi and Accatino on this side of the creek. What was part of Warner's plantation, on the Boulders' side of the double-barrelled bridge has been purchased by Saffiotti, Biancotti and Fontana in partnership.

The soil on my new farm is a rich well-drained sandy loam but there are some stones on the hilly areas. At the back, a huge volcanic crater which I call 'la buka' will serve as an excellent horse paddock and a dry paddock for the cow. The farm is presently under a variety of cane called Badilla and the sugar content is a bit above mill average.

There is much that needs to be done. I will need to build a tractor shed and a bale for the cow. Ploughing is too cruel on the horses and I will be buying a Caterpillar D2 crawler tractor to do that heavy work. This slack season I will probably cut some cord wood for the mill for extra cash. There is a lot of land that needs to be cleared so I will have plenty to occupy my time. I will need about 500 cases of dynamite to completely clear this farm. La buka has to be fenced in so that I can plant more cane in the hills and I need to fence in an area near the house for the cow.

Banks have tightened up on all lending, and I have had to borrow money privately. The bulk of it, I have borrowed from Accountant Jim Davies and I have had to borrow smaller amounts from the Secretary of the Mill Mr. Kelly, Ferraro Brothers and Sorbello.

So, my dear family, you can see I will certainly have no time to contemplate marriage for the next few years. Tell Teresa and Mrs Malaponte to keep an eye out for me but not to be in too big a hurry.

A thousand kisses for my three precious gems Rosario, Eloisa and baby Cettina.

May God bless you always and watch over you.
With much love Carmelo.

Carmelo worked hard to set the farm up as a place to bring up his future family as well as provide him with an adequate income to allow him to live comfortably in his tropical paradise. He did use up 500 cases of dynamite and cleared eighty of the one hundred and twenty nine acres. Sixty acres he kept under cane and every year, twenty were left fallow after four years of producing cane. Each year he would plant beans to return nitrogen to the soil and sometimes a patch of watermelons for a small cash crop on the fallow land. The other forty-nine acres comprised horse paddocks in and around *la buka* and about four acres opposite the house for buildings and a house paddock for the work horses and another for the cow. Also opposite the house block on the other side of the road and the locomotive railway-track, were an implement shed, living quarters for the farm labourers, a tractor shed with attached cow bale and calf pen. Two water tanks collected water from the farm buildings. Attached to that group of buildings was a corn shed butting up against the stables which could accommodate five horses. A chop-chop engine was housed in a workshop area where all the work harnesses were kept. Molasses and bags of bran and other food supplements for the horses were kept under cover beside a forage shed. A small shed was built beside the line for the jigger which was a motorized vehicle about two metres square on steel wheels, used for transport to town via the locomotive railway line.

The last building well downwind from the house was a chicken pen and run made snake-proof with galvanized iron and chicken wire. All these buildings were a stone's throw from the creek bank at the confluence of Babinda Creek and one of its small tributaries.

Carmelo would often walk down to the creek to bathe and wash his clothes just to enjoy the serenity of it all. He often set steel fish traps in the creek and at night would fish for freshwater eels which were a delicacy. He made his own cheese, butter and ricotta. He had a vegetable garden, a pineapple grove, a clump of banana trees two orange trees a mandarin tree and a peach tree. Once a week, Giuseppe Barbagallo would deliver fresh bread, meat and other stores along with one week's supply of *The Cairns Post*.

His next job was to cut forty poles which he planted in the soil beside the railway track to carry a telephone line to the farmhouse from old Saffiotti's place. The first time he tested it out and heard, *Good afternoon, Babinda Telephone Exchange, number please*, he was ecstatic. He now had a link to the outside world and his own phone number; *128 Babinda*.

Beside the house, Carmelo planted a granadilla vine and built a trellis. Along the back fence, he planted a passion-fruit vine and placed an extra water tank off the lean-to attached to the laundry and shower room. He had the inside of the house sealed with masonite by Jerry Sieber, a German immigrant, who also built a wooden floor over the existing cement slab. The house was almost ready for a wife except that he still needed to save for a couple more years to be able to afford to go back to Sicily to find one.

He cut his own cane and worked the farm with the help of an Albanian called Cedric and two Sikhs, Rashim and his father Bagh Singh, who lived in the workers' quarters across the road. The Sikhs wore turbans in accordance with their religious beliefs and were the most incredibly noble human beings Carmelo had ever known. They were peaceful, dignified, hard-working and wise. They were compassionate, generous, caring and humble. They were respectful and commanded respect. They were everyman's equal.

Every two weeks, Carmelo would go into town with the jigger to do business and collect the mail. A letter from Antonio was in the box as Carmelo had expected and he couldn't wait to go home and read it.

16th May 1935.

My dear dear brother Meluzzo,
By the time you receive this letter, our beloved daughter Cettina will be two years old. Her eyes are as blue as the sky and she chirps like a mountain parrot as she walks around the house. Even when the shutters are closed, she brings sunlight into the room. We love her so much my dear Carmeluzzo and I can't wait for you to see her.

We are all well although Teresa is less comfortable these days. She misses you too.

Rosario is sixteen years old and this year he enters the seminary. Eloisa is a young lady now. At twelve, she is mature for her age. The extended family is growing quickly and the next generation is flowering. Our cousins, the Scriffignanos, are all busy with their young families and we see a lot less of each other these days.

My business has taken a turn for the worse. My partner has absconded with a large part of our liquid assets and he has left me with a mountain of debts that I must honour for the sake of the family name. Much of the money I slaved for in Australia has been lost and if it was not for the surveying work that Angelino gets I would be in dire straits. I offside for him and it puts bread on the table. The farm is small but it provides us with olives, wheat, fruit, vegetables and nuts which is a blessing.

I am so sad to have to bring you such bad tidings but we have never kept anything from each other and I don't want to start now. The good news which far outweighs the bad is that we are well and lack nothing so do not be preoccupied with this. The Police have been unable to locate this vagabond and we fear that he has squandered the money anyhow.

I often think of your little farm and sometimes in the serenity of the early morning or around dusk, my spirit seems to take time out to walk with yours hand in hand across the cane fields, through the creek and into the forest. It gives me such joy that I never want it to end but it does pass and I know that you will come soon so I accept it passing with joy and not disappointment.

Know that we think of you every day and look forward to your return in the near future.
We embrace you a thousand times.
Your loving brother Nino and family.

The news moved Carmelo to tears. He wrote back immediately.

14th July 1935,

Dear Ninuzzo,
I received your letter today and was so sad to hear of your misfortune. You must be strong and remember our father's words; "One door closes and another one opens".

Tomorrow I will send a telegraphic transfer immediately to your account to tide you over. Every month, I will send you more money but do not be embarrassed by this. In your words, it's just a long term loan. You have repaid it so many times already, having carried me on your shoulders all those years as a child. Please, do not even make mention of it in your letters unless for some reason the money does not arrive.

I will leave after the harvest next year and my workers will look after the farm. Tell Teresa and Angelino that I will stay for at least four months and we can all be together again just like old times.

I look forward to holding you all in my arms and to meeting the beautiful Eloisa and precious Cettina for the first time. Keep the faith dearly beloved brother. Where there is life, there is hope.

Your loving brother
Carmelo.

Chapter 17

Revelation

Carmelo had just been in town having sent the first promised telegraphic transfer to Antonio. I had never seen him so depressed since the trip over on the boat from Italy. His mind seemed totally preoccupied by the tragic events surrounding his brother. Throughout the whole ride back from town on the jigger he just stared straight ahead at the track. His eyes were glazed and his spirit was inconsolable.

As he pulled up at the farmhouse, a young family of five was walking down from the house with Fido shepherding them towards him. There was no sign of any vehicle or mode of transport so they must have walked. They were immaculately dressed and came across to him as he was lifting the jigger off the line. The father two-stepped across to help him shove the jigger into the shed near the chicken pen.

"My name is Dellacosta," he said, after Carmelo thanked him for lending a hand. "And this is my wife Mrs Dellacosta, my eldest daughter Nellie and my two young sons Albert and Edmond."

"Pleased to meet you. You have such a beautiful family Mr. and Mrs. Dellacosta. My name is Carlo Cottone. I see you have no means of transport. Are you staying close by here?"

"No, we are from Edmonton near Cairns. We have a house-meeting in Babinda this weekend and people are coming from all over the place from Cairns to Innisfail."

Carmelo took one step backwards, "Do you belong to one of those political clubs. If you do and you have any link to one of the Fascios, I must respectfully ask you to leave my property," he insisted.

"No Mr. Cottone, I can assure you we have no political

connections. We are in Babinda for a religious gathering to meet with other people of our faith."

"Oh, in that case, welcome. People who uphold the faith are always welcome in my home. Would you like to come up to the house for a cup of tea or a cold drink?"

"That's very kind but we don't want to trouble you Mr. Cottone," said Mrs. Dellacosta.

"No trouble at all, I insist. You have travelled so far. You can't leave without accepting my hospitality and it would be lovely to have someone to talk to."

"Thank you then, Mr. Cottone. It would be nice to take a short rest before we set off back to Babinda," said Mr.Dellacosta.

"Call me Carlo, please. Come, follow me." He turned to address the three children, "I'm sure the young lady here and the two soldiers would love a cold drink. Or you can have some fresh cow's milk if you prefer." He pointed to the cow in the paddock. "That's Jersey over there. I milk her every day. Maybe we can take you over to see her little calf before you go." The two little ones accepted immediately with their eyes opening up widely and with a slight shy nod of the head.

The family sat down in the lounge room and Carmelo lit the primus and put a saucepan of water on to boil for the tea. "What would you like to drink children?"

"Milk please," replied Albert and Edmond.

"What would you like to drink Nellie? There's lemonade and there's orange soft drink."

"Lemonade would be nice," responded Nellie to which her mother gave one of those stares that suggested she should have replied, "Water will be fine thanks."

Carmelo returned with the cold drinks and a plate of *Arnotts Assorted Biscuits*. Albert and Edmond took a biscuit each and their milk and moved out onto the deck. Nellie smiled ever so sweetly as she accepted the cold glass of lemonade. She was tall and statuesque, with blue-black hair and she was so pretty. She was about eighteen years old.

"The tea won't be long," said Carmelo as he sat down opposite them. "So I take it you walked across the creek to get here. It's quite a distance from town. What made you decide to come out this way?"

"It's a beautiful day for a walk," said Mr. Dellacosta. "But the main reason, is that wherever we go, we want to spread God's message and for people who are already committed to God we love to share His goodwill and build friendships. We minister to people in the hope that it will help fulfill the Creator's promise of a peaceful and secure new world."

"What an admirable goal that is. But do you really think that such a world is possible?"

"Everything is possible to those who believe. In our faith, we believe it is possible because the Creator promised it."

"How refreshing it is to hear you speak of such a paradise. Yet so many things in history have conspired against it. It seems to me, that man, by virtue of his nature will only be content when he can dominate everything around him. He wants to subjugate others and have control over everything including the environment."

"Yes, Carlo and that is why my people believe we must not let that happen. Those who want what the Creator promised must go out into the world and make it happen. If you want to have wheat then you must plant seed."

"Yes." Carmelo excused himself. "A moment while I make the tea."

He went back into the kitchen, made the tea and returned with a pot and three cups, some milk in a jar and some sugar in a bowl.

"But how many faiths have said and done just that Mr. and Mrs. Dellacosta? People have even died for what they believe in and all to no avail. In many cases, we have ended up worse than when we started. Religious wars are a good example of this." He poured their tea and passed each a cup. "Please help yourself with the milk and the sugar."

He continued, "How many times must people say to others what you have just said to me? How many times must we keep doing what you do?"

"As many times as it takes, my dear Carlo. As many times as it takes. Are you a religious person Carlo?"

"I come from a very religious family. My father's uncle was

a Catholic priest and my father lived with him for many years. But the Church has not been fair with us. My father lost almost all of his assets because of the Church. Yes, I am and will always be a devout Christian, but my heart is not with the Catholic Church."

"Yes, many people have become disillusioned with the mainstream churches. It's sad, but for a variety of reasons, many Churches have let God down. They haven't fulfilled their purpose we believe according to God's will."

"What exactly do you believe? How, for example does your faith differ from the Roman Catholic Religion?"

"For a start, the way we go about ministering to the people is different. We do not believe in negative protest. We believe in positive instruction. According to *2 Timothy 2:24,25 : a servant of the lord is not to engage in quarrels, but has to be kind to everyone, a good teacher and patient.*

Secondly, we can tolerate no division in the Church. We accept that there will be differences but these must not be divisive. We carry our weak if we think they are weak. We do not cast them off. Together we get on with our work for the greater good which is the Creator's promise of a peaceful and secure world.

Finally, it's more about what we do not believe in that makes us different from the mainstream Christian religions. We call them *the six myths.* We do not believe that the soul is immortal, that the wicked suffer in Hell, that all good people go to Heaven, that God is a trinity, that Mary is the Mother of God and we do not believe in the use of images and icons in worship."

"So what do you believe happens to the soul when we die?"

"A person is a living soul. At death, a person simply ceases to exist."

"If you don't believe in Hell, what do you believe?"

"God is a loving God. God does not punish people in Hell."

"Don't you believe in Heaven either?"

"We simply believe that not all good people go to Heaven. The majority of good people will live on Earth not in Heaven."

"So what is the trinity?"

"The trinity can only be traced back to late fourth century dogma."

"Surely Mary is the Mother of God."

"No. Mary is the Mother of the Son of God."

"There should be no statues of God and Jesus and Mary and the like?"

"No, we believe God does not approve of the use of images and icons."

"Nothing too major, I would imagine in those differences," suggested Carmelo.

"I guess that depends on the extent of your imagination. That is, how much we want to read into those differences and how much importance we attach to those differences."

They drank their tea and Carmelo thanked them for their commitment to God and for coming to visit him. He also accepted some reading material in English and Italian and promised he would read it.

"Now I would like to do something for you and offer you a lift into town. That is if you have the courage to ride on the jigger."

Mr. Dellacosta declined but Nellie wasn't going to let the offer go that easily.

"Come on Pa. That would be such fun. Please Pa?" Then the soldiers made a chorus of it.

"Come on Pa. It would be such fun. Please Pa? Come on Pa. That would be such fun!"

And the chorus won out.

"Well, now look what you've let yourself into Carlo. Maybe for the children's sake."

"I don't know," said Mrs. Dellacosta, "I wouldn't want to miss out on it either. Looks like fun to me too."

"But first, I promised to show the calf to the children." Carmelo reminded them. They went down to the cow-bales and Carlo put some chaff into the food trough. He then sprinkled on some bran.

"This bran Jersey is from Alberto and Edmomdo, because you are special for bringing this little calf into their world." Then he added some molasses, "And this molasses is from Nellie because you're going to let them cuddle your little calf."

Jersey put her head through the bale to eat and Carmelo pushed the bar across to lock her in. He then brought the calf in and let her go to the mother.

"There, now you can pat her. While mother and daughter are feeding, they won't be worried about strangers."

"She's so beautiful," said Nellie, "What's her name?"

"Jersey," said Carmelo.

"But that's the mother's name."

"I call all my female cows Jersey so I don't get confused. This is Jersey the Third."

Nellie laughed. "You may not get confused but I'm sure the cows do."

Mr Dellacosta and Carmelo lifted the jigger onto the line and Carmelo filled the tank up with fuel. "Okay, everyone jump onto the jigger; ladies first. Now Alberto and Edmondo. Mr Dellacosta, there's a good spot for you. Hang on while I push-start it."

Carmelo engaged the decompression lever and started pushing. As soon as the jigger reached walking speed, he released the decompression lever and the motor began to chug over. Two chugs later and it was firing. Carmelo jumped onto the back of the jigger and reached over to open the throttle and they were on their way. Mrs Dellacosta and Nellie hung onto their hats as the two little ones screamed with excitement.

About one kilometre along the track Carmelo pointed to a cutaway in the creek-bank.

"That's where you came up this morning. We will be going further on to the crossing where the locomotive passes to collect the cane trucks. That will be fun boys."

And it was. The line was submerged about five centimeters under the water and as the jigger entered the crossing, water sprayed everywhere. There was about forty metres of crossing and the girls were pleased when they finally got to the other side and didn't have to worry about the spray.

The jigger got to a speed of about ten kilometers per hour as it chugged along down the track and around the bends.

"What happens if we meet a locomotive?" asked Mr. Dellacosta. "There's only one line."

"You pray, and we jump, Mr. Dellacosta," laughed Carmelo and the girls laughed with him.

When they got into town, the Dellacostas alighted near Arena's bakery opposite the Ambulance.

"Thanks for the lift Carlo," said Dellacosta. "Thanks for the lift Mr Cottone," said the others. Mr. Dellacosta helped Carmelo lift the jigger off the line and turn it around for the return trip. Carmelo then gave them his phone number.

"Next time you come into town, give me a call on 128 Babinda and we'll arrange for me to pick you up. You can stay for lunch and maybe we can have a swim."

This trip back to the farm was so different from that morning's. It was the old Carmelo back in charge of his own destiny and he thanked God for the Dellacostas.

He started working twelve hours a day in the field and at least another two hours a day looking after the animals, the vegetable garden and doing the bookwork. Rashim and Bagh Singh helped work the farm with hoes while Carmelo and Cedric did all the heavy cultivating and soil preparation with five draught horses. He also had a live-in housekeeper who cooked his meals and looked after the house.

It was back-breaking work at a break-neck pace but the thought of returning to his family after so many years sustained him. The one slack season in between the two cuts, gave him a breather, but most of it went into catching up on all the work that had been neglected during the season such as mending the harnesses, repairs to implements and general maintenance. By the time he was ready to leave, the farm was in pristine condition. All that needed to be done was for Cedric to scarify the crop twice before it was out of hand and for Rashim and Bagh to keep the headlands clean and distribute the rat-baits.

Chapter 18

The Prodigal Son

In late November 1936, Carmelo found himself on the deck of the HMS *Orford*; a twenty thousand ton, one hundred and thirty metre long ocean vessel that had led the line of merchant ships at the ceremonial opening of the Sydney Harbour Bridge. He was in the purser's office.

Whilst waiting to be paged regarding an enquiry he had, he took the opportunity to read the noticeboard and study the pictures and photos on the walls. One photo in particular caught his attention.

"Do you follow cricket?" asked the lady beside him who was peering at the same photo. "Some photo that one; the mighty Donald Bradman with his team travelling on this very ship to England in their quest for *The Ashes* in 1934."

"No, I don't, but they certainly do look determined," said Carmelo.

"Yes, that's Donald Bradman there and the photo next to it is the Australian Davis Cup tennis team. They also went over on this ship. Do you follow tennis?"

"No, but they look determined too."

She laughed, "I'm Gertrude, my friends call me Trudy. I'm going as far as Colombo." She offered her hand for Carmelo to shake.

"What a pleasure it is to meet such a beautiful woman. Hello Truda, my name is Carmelo but my Australian friends call me Carlo. So you are interested in cricket and tennis… you must be English."

"I come from Wales actually. My name is Trudy not Truda."

"Yes Truda, such a captivating name for such a graceful lady." He was still having trouble pronouncing some words, especially names.

"Well Truda, is fine I guess. You can call me Truda if you like."

"Would you like a coffee in the lounge, Truda? I presume you are waiting to be called up too?"

"No, I was merely looking around. I would love to have a coffee with you, Carlo." There was something about the way she accepted the invitation that deserves special mention because the tone suggested she was interested in more than just the coffee.

Just then, the purser called out his name.

"One minute, this won't take long." Carmelo hurried over to the purser.

"Eh… I'm Cottone. My matter is not urgent, so I'll return to you later. Thank you."

He abandoned the bewildered purser to again meet with Truda.

"The matter was not urgent, but having a coffee with you certainly is Truda." She gave him a very special sort of a look which I read this time as some definite sign of positive connectivity and so did Carmelo. "Come, let me escort you to the bistro then. I think the one on the upper deck has a much better ambience than the one on this deck."

The HMS *Orford* was leaving the harbour and as they looked towards Sydney, the impressive structure of the Sydney Harbour Bridge seemed to crown the city for all its beauty.

"Isn't it beautiful, Carlo?" A comfortable silence sat with them as they watched and sipped their coffee. Then Truda turned to him, "So where are you off to, Carlo?"

"I'm returning home to Sicily to see my family. I haven't been home for twelve years."

"So, quite the prodigal son, eh?"

"Well, my parents are no longer alive, but yes, my brothers, my sisters and my nephews and nieces will be preparing to 'kill the fatted calf' I'm sure."

Over the next few weeks, I pondered as I had never known Carmelo to be so different; so happy and so totally engaged with a woman. From my vantage point on the lip of the porthole, I came to the conclusion that these two people were deeply in love. They were inseparable. All he desired was to be with her. They shared every meal, attended the ship's countless functions, danced only with each other and even frequented the ship's casino. The experience was captured forever in their memories, but also through the numerous photos taken together and separately.

To be more specific, Trudy was a few centimetres shorter than Carmelo. She was of fair complexion, had light auburn hair and was a little on the buxom side. Her light brown eyes contrasted with the blue-grey of his. His fair skin had a golden tan and she would run her fingers all over his body.

"Do you know who Adonis was?" she asked him one day.

"No. Should I? Was he a cricketer or a tennis player?"

"No, silly." She punched him playfully. "He was a Phonecian God and he was tanned and had strong muscles just like you. All the girls loved him."

"I see. That is quite a compliment." He pulled her towards him and gazed deeply into her eyes.

"What? What are you thinking?" she queried.

"If I'm Adonis, then you must be Aphrodite the Greek goddess."

"You knew all the time," she punched him again. "Was he a cricketer or a tennis player!" she scoffed in retaliation to his previous question.

They laughed as they basked in the breezes that the HMS *Orford* created as it carved its way through the Indian Ocean.

First the island of Ceylon, then the city of Colombo appeared like a jewel in the ocean. But to them, it was a dark cloud on the horizon. This was where his beloved Truda would disembark. The HMS *Orford* would berth in Colombo for two days and that was all the time they would have remaining to be together.

"A car from Foreign Affairs will be coming to pick me up. I will be debriefing all morning but we can meet again this afternoon if you wish. I could show you around and we can spend the night and tomorrow in a hotel until it is time for you to leave."

"Come with me to Italy, Truda. Meet my family and tour Sicily with me."

"That's not going to be possible at this point in time. Maybe in the future."

Carmelo was love-struck and irrational. He knew they both needed time to think.

"Okay Colombo Queen, let's meet this afternoon. What time?"

"The Colombo Queen meets the Australian Adonis at three o'clock dockside. Okay?" She gave him a peck on the cheek. "There's my car, Carlo. I love you!" She called as she strolled down the gangplank.

Carmelo waved as he was speechless. Still, he watched as she walked across to the car. The chauffeur opened the door and with the briefest of waves she entered the car and was gone. He was suddenly overcome by the fear that he might never see her again and he momentarily panicked that something might have been left unsaid. At three o'clock he would know.

At three o'clock, Trudy did return with a female companion. She ran to him and enveloped him in her arms. Any doubts he might have had, vanished in that instant.

"This is Bess. She's a good friend of mine who works with me. She wanted to meet my bronzed Adonis. Bess this is Carlo."

They shook hands. "Pleased to meet you, Carlo. Sorry I can't stay, some of us have got to work." She climbed into the car and drove off leaving Carmelo and Trudy hand in hand.

Carmelo had arranged for a man with a rickshaw to show them the sights of the city. He signalled for him to approach.

"Voila, this is our transport for the afternoon. Romantic, don't you think?"

"Very."

"Okay. It's over to you Aphrodite. Do with me what you will."

It was the third of January 1937.

Chapter 19

A rendezvous with Mussolini

From Colombo to the Red Sea and through the Suez Canal, Carmelo was not someone anyone on the ship would desire to know or even have the chance to for that matter. His face was as long as the pyramids were wide. Nothing could capture his sense of wonder. Nothing could reinstate his *joie-de-vivre*. He moped around and only toyed with his food. He no longer went to the movies nor attended social functions on the ship. He even failed to ascend onto the deck. In short he was terrible company and a complete bore.

He attempted to write letters to Trudy but they all ended up in the bin. She had captured his heart and mind and when he slept, he woke with nightmares. He missed her so dreadfully he no longer knew which way to turn.

As the HMS *Orford* broke waters into the Mediterranean Sea, it must have suddenly occurred to him that there was absolutely nothing he could do to prevail over this situation; he should move on with his life. The overwhelming excitement of twelve years of separation from his family coming to an end was also ample motivation.

When the ship entered the Straits of Messina and he could see his beloved Sicily, he knew he was home. He was full of anticipation and remained on deck for the rest of the journey to Naples, revelling in the maritime activity surrounding the ship from the racing sloops, to the sailing boats, catamarans, trawlers, fishing boats, ferries and the pleasure craft. Each vessel they encountered was alive with waving crew; the atmosphere throughout the ship was eclectic as the passengers rose to the realization that their journey was nearing its end.

They were in Italian waters and the Port of Naples beckoned the ship to berth by its shores.

Onshore in Naples, however, Carmelo soon felt as though the blood had been drained from those happy faces. The excitement was dead, swallowed up under the stern gaze of the military personnel who stood sentry at every twenty paces; armed and foreboding. As soon as Carmelo presented his passport to immigration, the officer cross-checked his name against a list and he was asked to stand aside.

He soon found himself flanked by two *carabinieri*.

"Cottone, Carmelo?" asked one police officer.

"Yes," answered Carmelo.

"We have been instructed to ask you to come quietly as there are some questions that need to be answered in private."

"What if I refuse?"

"Then we shall have to arrest you and that will involve a lot of paperwork and a lot of time wasted, Mr Cottone."

"Very well, so be it. Arrest me and I wish to remind you of my rights as a British Subject and ask that the British Consul be advised immediately that I seek representation."

Carmelo was arrested and placed in custody. That night, he was taunted by his jailers.

"So, you renounced your citizenship? Being Italian, not good enough for you, eh? So you're a Britisher now? Big deal. Traitor!"

Anytime he requested anything, even a drink of water, he was subjected to further taunts.

"No British water here scumbag. Italian water isn't good enough for you, so you'll just have to do without, won't you?"

"Very well," Carmelo replied quietly. "I will mention your concerns to the British Consul and we'll see if something can be done about it so that in future, international travellers won't have to remain in custody without charge and without water as well."

That was enough to get him a glass of water but it didn't stop the taunts.

"You have been charged and you will have to answer the charges," the guard assured him. "Looks like you want to be a troublemaker as well... Hope they lock you up and throw away the key. Why do you come back to Italy if you don't want to be Italian? With a bit of luck, they'll take you out and shoot you."

Carmelo asked that he be allowed to speak to the Officer-in-Charge, saying that he had a letter from the British Consul in Canberra, which he would like to personally hand over.

The guard disappeared and failed to return, thus Carmelo remained in solitude all night.

In the morning hours, two guards returned to collect Carmelo from his cell.

"You have a visitor, Mr Cottone. Come with us please." They seemed much more polite than the previous day. He was led along a narrow corridor that opened into a large reception area. "Sit at that table over there, please."

Warily, Carmelo took a seat at the table as one of the guards sauntered over to a well-dressed official in the Visitors' section. The official returned with the guard and introduced himself.

"Hello Mr Cottone. I'm Ian Jacobs from the British Consul's Office. I understand you are being held here without charge and have come to ask the police to release you forthwith. It's a simple procedural thing from here on, old chap and you should be out of here before you know it. I trust he is being treated well?" he asked the guard.

"Yes Mr Jacobs. I am being treated well." The guard seemed relieved by that comment.

"Good, then I'll organize the paperwork while they return your possessions to you and we'll be done then. I have a car outside and would be happy to drop you off at the Consulate so that they can assist you with the next leg of your journey. Welcome to Italy, Mr Cottone." He shook hands and left with the guard. Carmelo was immediately treated with the greatest courtesy after that and while he waited for the paperwork to be completed he was brought bottled British water and offered a packet of British cigarettes.

At the Consulate, Carmelo was asked to wait outside the Consul's office. A secretary opened the door and ushered Carmelo in.

"Please come in, Mr Cottone, the Consul will see you now."

As he entered, the Consul lifted his eyes from whatever he was reading and addressed Carmelo.

"Welcome Mr Cottone. We do so deeply regret the treatment afforded to you at Immigration upon your arrival. Things seem to be getting very unfriendly towards Italians returning from overseas. They seem to have very long memories or a very efficient recording system in the Public sector and I do suspect it is the latter. Is everything in order?"

"Yes sir and I would like to take this opportunity to thank you for being so prompt in gaining my release. Mr Ian Jacobs in particular was very kind."

"That's our job here and we are pleased to have been able to be of assistance. I simply wanted to meet you and wish you well during your stay. Know that we are available twenty-four hours a day. We strongly recommend that if you wish to avoid unnecessary hassles during your stay in Italy, you apply for a *tessera*. It is simply an identification document that is 'Mussolini compatible' should we say for want of a better word. They can prepare the application for you and it would be available tomorrow."

"Thank you again, sir." Carmelo stood to leave.

"Oh and there is one more thing Mr Cottone. This letter was flown in and delivered to our office a few days ago. It has your name on it and the name of your ship HMS *Orford*. By coming here, you have saved us the trouble of having to find you." He handed Carmelo the letter and they shook hands.

Carmelo was left wondering who the letter could possibly be from.

Upon his arrival at his hotel, Carmelo turned the letter over and over, again and again. His name and the name of the ship were typed on the envelope, so there were no clues there and no sender's name on the back. It was a Foreign Affairs envelope, however, and he figured it had to be his Trudy. He opened the letter revealing nine photographs and a short note.

5th January 1937,

My dear Carlo,
What a wonderful time we were able to spend together from
Sydney to Colombo on the HMS Orford. I thank you for that
and I shall never forget it. I am sending some snapshots of you
and me on the ship and in Colombo. There is also an earlier
photo of me in my bathing suit on a beach in Wales.

On my return, I was informed that I had been transferred to
London on promotion. I promised you I would think about a
possible future for us and the answer is yes, but it would have
to be in London and I understand if you consider this out of
the question for you.

You can write to me C/- Foreign Affairs Office in London,
but if you decide to terminate all communication between us
I understand.

Whatever happens, I will always remember what a wonderful
gentleman you were and will think of you always as my
Adonis from Down Under.

Much much love,
Aphrodite xxx

It was sad, but it did bring closure to what Carmelo had already
accepted was something memorable that occurred on the HMS *Orford*
and one that would always remain on the HMS *Orford*. Yet, by the
way he kept looking at the photos and re-reading the letter, I suspected
those nine photos and that letter would be cherished by Carmelo for
the rest of his life.

Chapter 20

The homecoming

Antonio was at the station to meet Carmelo in Agira. They embraced as Antonio offered some apologies.

"You must forgive the rest of the family for not being here to meet you as well. Teresa is far more incapacitated now than when you left. Everyone decided to stay with her so that they could all meet you at once. Welcome, welcome home my dear, Meluzzo," and he hugged him once again.

When they were within sight of the house, the family was hanging over the fence and cluttering the front doorway, screaming and waving to him. There was quite a slope declining to the house so Carmelo had reached a half-trot by the front gate. Everyone was there, except for Archangela who was in America. They hugged and kissed him and little Cettina the youngest, stood bewildered with her big bright blue eyes wondering what the commotion was for. Then there were people he was yet to meet. Arimondo Contessa was Adele's husband, Grazia Sinopoli was Antonio's wife and Emilia Camarata had married Angelino and their two beautiful children were Rosario, now eighteen years old and Eloisa, fourteen. Carmelo scooped Cettina into his arms, hugging her tightly.

"Hello, Cettina. Do you know who I am?" He asked her.

"Yes, you're Meluzzo, our favourite uncle in Australia," she called out confidently to which everyone laughed. Still carrying Cettina, he rushed to Rosario and Eloisa and the three of them clung together.

"So Rosario, Don Peppino didn't come back and you never did get that gun licence."

"No need Zio. I'm studying to be a man of the cloth. I have chosen to be a 'fisher of men'. I don't need to shoot them."

"Eloisa, you are so grown up. A couple of more years and you can come visit me in Australia." She liked that. You could tell it made her feel adult as she drew in a deep breath and stood tall.

"Now, where's the most important woman in the whole world?" He said it particularly loudly because he wanted Teresa to be able to hear it from her bed. Then he entered into her room. She extended her arms towards him. Another one of her children that she couldn't have was home again and in her arms. Nobody could have known more than I did about what this homecoming meant to Teresa. Sotto to sotto, I was getting vibes from Teresa that only spirits could transmit.

"Now your beloved sister can die happy, Carmeluzzo," she sobbed. "I am so so happy you came back to be with me one more time."

"Of course Teresa. You are the only mother I ever knew. Of course I would return to see you. If it weren't for Mussolini, I would have been back long ago."

"Well, it's not too late. Angelino, Antonio, get my wheelchair. No, it's not too late, Carmeluzzo. Mrs Malaponte and I have been scouring the whole district trying to find a suitable wife for you. That's the one last thing, I forgot, that I want before I can die happy; for you to find a good wife."

Angelino brought over the wheelchair and he lifted her carefully into it.

"I've made all your favourite sweets and you are going to have the best dinner since you last left Italy. The only difference is that I have had to leave all that to the new mistresses of the house, Emilia, Grazia and Adele. I am so fortunate to have my dear Emilia. She lives here and has to tolerate all my grumbling. She deserves a gold medal."

"I'm sure she does, Teresa." He took the handles of the chair and moved her slowly into the dining room. "Emilia, please put on the water for the pasta. Today, we made the same sauce that our father, God bless his soul, brought up to the summer shack in the mountains when you recovered from that dreaded smallpox disease. It was pork spare ribs fried with garlic and onion in sauce from home-grown tomatoes, garnished with lots of basil."

"That's my favourite Teresa! Thanks Emilia, Grazia, Adele."

And all his favourite sweets were revealed as well, including *chiaccere*.

"I never celebrate an event in this house without making some *chiaccere* to remember our benefactor Don Peppino. Nobody has heard from him since he left our village. Who knows what evil deeds were perpetrated against that great man. We pray for him, for your father and for your brother Giuseppe every day, Carmeluzzo."

"Yes Teresa. He certainly was a very special person to us and a great man in our community."

Carmelo emptied his suitcase of presents and there was much excitement in the Cottone household that evening.

Then they feasted and in the afternoon they were joined by Mrs Malaponte from across the road and members of the Scriffignano family. Mrs Malaponte had a thousand questions regarding her boys and Carmelo uttered every form of assurance to put her mind at ease. That night, he slept in the spare bed as his old room had been taken over by Angelino and his wife while the spare room now belonged to Eloisa and Rosario prior to his leaving for the seminary.

The next morning, the two brothers were supposed to complete a surveying job on the outskirts of Enna City proper. Angelino left early and Antonio was to collect some surveyors' pegs and be there by mid-morning. He decided to drop in to see Carmelo on the way and invited him along for company. Looking forward to a cross-country hike through the Province to revive some memories, Carmelo was enthused.

"Don't forget to bring along your *tessera*. All strangers are vetted in Sicily these days."

After collecting the pegs, they embarked upon a bus.

"So, this place you're surveying, who does it belong to?" asked Carmelo, simply to make conversation.

"It belongs to Liborio Coppola. He was once a wealthy landowner with many share-farmers and thousands of sheep. In the late twenties, bandits cleaned him out bit by bit. They stole all his sheep and terrorized his share-farmers. He has survived by selling off parts of his estate and that is why we are surveying his property now. He is preparing to sell off another two-fifths of the property."

"So, is there still no law and order around here? I thought Mussolini was supposed to have cleaned up all the *Mafiosi* in Sicily."

"These days, there's only one sort of *Mafiosi* around here and they all wear black shirts. Mussolini is bleeding Sicily dry and he won't stop until we're all on our knees."

"Hey, you are going to have to save me from Mrs Malaponte and Teresa. They are determined to find me a wife. I'm not too sure that I want to marry an Italian woman despite the warning our Archangela sent us both when we were in Australia."

"So what sort of woman are you thinking of marrying?"

"Well, I think British women are adorable. They have the most tantalizing accent and they have sex appeal."

"Is that so? Have you ever courted a British woman?"

"Well, on the way over, I fell in love with this English woman and I must confess I told her I was prepared to marry her."

"Are you dreaming or did they give you electric-shock treatment in Naples?"

"No, I'm serious." He took out his wallet and showed Nino the nine photos. Nino studied them carefully.

"Maybe they should have given you electric-shock treatment in Naples. She's a pretty girl but marriage is a big step. What did she say to your proposal of marriage?"

"She said if I were prepared to join her in London, she would be happy to marry me."

"So, she's not prepared to live on a cane farm in the middle of nowhere and live with someone who comes home black as the ace of spades and smelling of horse manure after working all day from dawn until dusk. She's not prepared to cook your meals and raise your kids and go nowhere because you don't have any money. I'd say she's smart going for the London option."

"So what do you think I should do? Sign up to Teresa and Mrs Malaponte and leave it all to their better judgment?"

"Well, I wouldn't necessarily go that far. But there are plenty of beautiful women around here."

"Yeah, show me one."

"Okay, if it's beauty you want, I'll show you the most beautiful woman you have ever seen. But mind, you only get to look. This woman is all class. She wouldn't even consider talking to a bum like you dressed like that. You have a look and if you like her, you sneak away and come back another day looking respectable. Deal?"

"Yeah, yeah, sure, Nino... the most beautiful woman I've ever seen. As if. It's you who's dreaming, Ninuzzo."

The bus pulled up and they walked the short distance to where Angelino was operating a theodolite.

"Did you get the pegs, Nino?" he asked. "You weren't wrong about that Coppola girl. She is a stunner." He motioned to Carmelo, "Here Meluzzo, come and have a look through the telescope on the theodolite. Give me your considered opinion."

"You're not serious I hope. Looking at someone through a telescope? Isn't that an invasion of privacy?"

"Not when she's just hanging clothes on the line. Here take a look... whoa," he shook his right hand as if he had just picked up something that was too hot to handle.

Carmelo put his eye to the scope. "Hey, how do you focus this machine?"

"Focus, what do you mean focus? That's just your eyes turning to water. Here move over, let me have a look," said Antonio. He shook both his hands.

"I told you she was a stunner. It's focused. Here have another look and tell me if she's the most beautiful woman you have ever seen."

Carmelo put his eye back to the lens, "She's gone."

"Well, what do you think?"

"I told you she's gone. You guys are just playing games with me. So this is the sort of work you grown-up guys do, eh? No wonder Antonio never came back to Australia."

While Antonio and Angelino positioned the pegs, Carmelo strolled around the property. Eventually, he arrived at the gate leading to the Coppola residence. He continued and witnessed a girl playing the violin under a huge cork tree. He was carrying a surveyors' peg in his hand. When she saw him out of the corner of her eye, she recoiled momentarily. He quickly introduced himself.

"Oh, excuse me. I'm with the surveyors who are surveying your father's land." He showed her the surveyors' peg. "Sorry to disturb you, but I heard you playing and it quite captivated me. I'm Carmelo, originally from Agira but presently from Australia." He dared not risk speaking in the Sicilian dialect for fear of offending her. She smiled and offered him her hand. He kissed it gently and took two steps backwards. He was starry-eyed and caught for words; mesmerized in her presence. "Please forgive me for intruding on your music session but allow me to say you play like an angel, Signorina."

"How does an angel play, Carmelo?"

"An angel plays to soothe the soul, Signorina."

"Do angels in Australia play to soothe the soul, Carmelo?"

"I have never heard an angel play in Australia."

"Oh I see, only in Italy."

"No, not even in Italy, only you Signorina."

She giggled. "That's quite a compliment Carmelo. So what are you doing in Australia? Are you digging for gold or do you hunt kangaroos?"

"Neither Signorina, I have a small property."

"Are you a surveyor too?"

"No, my two brothers are surveyors." He showed her the peg again, "I just carry the pegs."

Someone called from the house, "Elena! Elena!"

"Mother is calling me. Nice to have met you Carmelo from Agira and presently from Australia."

"Nice to have met you too Signorina… Elena… Signorina," stuttered Carmelo.

He walked trance-like all the way back to his two brothers who were busily driving in wooden pegs all around the property

"Meluzzo, where have you been?" asked Angelino.

"Listening to an angel playing a violin. I have never known a sound so sweet."

Nino looked at Angelino and shook his head. "I think they gave him electric-shock treatment in Naples and he has no recollection of it."

"Well that's it for today. Nino forgot to bring the marker paint so we'll have to come tomorrow to mark the pegs. Then it's all done."

The next morning, Carmelo dressed casually in long trousers and a coat with an open necked shirt. He wore a shooters' cap. In his hand he held a package tied with a pink bow, which Eloisa had helped him wrap after he had sworn her to secrecy. Angelino and Antonio simply stared at him. They asked no questions all the way to Enna and Carmelo told no lies.

When they arrived at the worksite, Carmelo walked towards the residence.

"Looking for angels again today, Carmeluzzo?" asked Antonio jovially. Carmelo ignored him.

"We'll see you down at the residence then, Meluzzo," said Angelino. Carmelo ignored him as well and walked on. Antonio and Angelino could only look at each other, shaking hands furiously as they marvelled at the feats of their kid brother.

Carmelo approached the door of the residence, cap in hand. When he knocked softly, nobody answered. He knocked a little louder and after a while, he knocked quite loudly. An old lady, a servant in uniform, answered the door.

"Yes, can I help you, sir?"

"Yes, I would like to speak to the Signorina Elena, if I may."

"Do you have an invitation, sir?"

"No."

"Do you have an appointment, sir?"

"No."

"Then I'm afraid you can't speak to her. Can I take a message, sir?"

"Yes, could you please give her these chocolates from Australia."

"Of course, sir. Who should I say they are from?"

"Just from Australia. Thank you."

"My pleasure," and she closed the door quietly in his face.

Carmelo was now entrenched in a dilemma. He couldn't return to his brothers unrequited as he would lose face. He should not have been so cock-sure of himself. His alternative, to remain near the house was impossible for fear of being thought of as a 'lazarone' lay-about. He shouldn't have been so presumptive in his treatment of the seductive signorina. He settled for situating himself just out of sight of both the house and his brothers until such time as his brothers arrived. He would join them at the gate and stroll casually along with them to the front door; thus nobody would be the wiser.

He did exactly that and when they reached the door and knocked gently, the old lady opened it almost instantaneously.

"Good morning sirs. Have you finished your work?"

"Yes Madam," said Angelino. "Here is the completed paperwork."

"Fine," she handed him an envelope. "Here is your payment. Signor Coppola thanks you for your work Signor Cottone."

"Thank you Signora," said Angelino and as he and Antonio turned to leave, the old woman passed a small envelope to Carmelo; placing a finger to her lips, signalling to remain silent.

Chapter 21

Love story

Elena's mother, Lucia Ginevra married Guglielmo D'Italia and gave birth to their child Luisa in 1906. Guglielmo departed for America soon after and Lucia waited and waited for his return to no avail. He was never heard from again. After seven years, Lucia was courted by the suave and sophisticated Liborio Coppola who was twenty-nine years her elder. He was a prosperous landowner, who after his wife died in 1913 fell hopelessly in love with the twenty-four year old Lucia. However, there were obstacles in the way of legitimizing the relationship. Firstly, Lucia's first marriage was in the process of being annulled and secondly, the family of Coppola's deceased wife had concerns relating to inheritance considering she had borne seven children to him.

Coppola's younger lover's child Liborio was born in 1914 and was named after his father who acknowledged paternity and gave him the Coppola name even though they were unmarried. But when Lucia fell pregnant with a second child to him in 1915, the family decided to take action. At that time, it was imperative that a newborn be registered within three days of birth so that the birth certificate, the *atto di nascita* could be issued.

The day Elena was born on the 11th of January 1916, Liborio's two eldest sons, Pietro who was twenty-six and Eduardo who was twenty-one, took it upon themselves to deprive their father of liberty for three days until the mandatory period had expired. Because Liborio was trussed up and being guarded by his sons in a disused barn in the countryside, he was unable to sign the papers acknowledging he was indeed Elena's father.

Lucia was distraught, for without a signature, her daughter Elena would forever be branded illegitimate and there was no greater shame for any young girl in Italy. As the marriage annulment to Guglielmo had not yet been processed, Lucia took the only course available to her and on the third day gave Elena the legitimate name D'Italia.

In 1917, the annulment became official and Liborio married Lucia and fathered another four children to her. So, of the six Coppola children, Liborio, Elena, Giulia, Mario, Vincenzo and Giovanni, only Elena lacked the Coppola name.

Carmelo was fifteen years older than Elena, a common equation for the time. He was from a respected and well-educated family of independent means so there was no barrier there. The fact that he was living in Australia was a double-edged sword though; on the one hand, they would probably never see their daughter again but on the other it was widely believed throughout Italy that there was a bright future to be forged in such overseas countries. It was only perchance and by good luck if there happened to be some sort of chemistry going on for the two people involved.

Carmelo was about to test the water for the chemistry. He was seated on the bus to Agira with his brothers and had just read the contents of the scented envelope.

To Carmelo from Agira and presently of Australia,

Thank you for the lovely box of Australian chocolates. They're certainly much sweeter than those in Italy and the shapes are different from Italian made chocolates as well. My favourite is the pineapple shape. Sorry you were turned away today but my mother would never allow you to see me in such an informal manner. Your request would be considered quite brash and so the maid had no choice but to turn you away.
You may, however, write to me and I would dearly love to know about life in Australia.

Regards,
Elena

"What's the matter?" asked Antonio slapping him playfully on the face. "You look like you're about to faint." Carmelo hopelessly stared at the roof of the bus. "Meluzzo, are you okay?"

Carmelo handed the note across to Antonio, "I think she loves me."

Antonio scanned the note again and again with Angelino peering over his shoulder; both were flicking their hands furiously in disbelief.

"Meluzzo, what do you have that your brother and I don't have? 'Out of focus', 'There's no one there', you pretended. You knew you were on a good thing the moment you laid eyes on her through the theodolite," said Angelino.

"Yeah… we're proud of you, Meluzzo. You sure they didn't give you electric shock treatment in Naples?" Antonio joked.

"He still might need it to come back to earth if this thing backfires," suggested Angelino. "We need to give him the right advice. He's obviously not too good on protocol; 'Your request would be considered quite brash'," he mimicked as he read the sentence from her pen.

Carmelo snapped the paper back from him. "That's enough of that… now, if you want to help me, tell me what I should do next." They both rattled out hundreds of possible scenarios, actions and procedures.

"Good, now I know what not to do. Thanks brothers." The bus halted and he bolted through the door and ascended the street as Angelino and Antonio picked up any object they could find to hurl at him.

The next day, Carmelo sent flowers. The day after that he sent more flowers. On the third day, on dusk, he sent a small bouquet of big red roses with a brief note.

A message from the gods at 8 o'clock tonight outside the gates.
Something for you to soothe the soul.

As promised, a string quartet materialized outside the gates and played for Elena until ten o'clock. Now, I know about souls and believe me, I was there with Carmelo hiding in the bushes and after hearing them play, I figured there could well have been a lot of soothing going on.

Chapter 22

A night at the opera

On the other side of the envelope containing the message from the gods, Carmelo left a contact address hoping Elena would write to him. She wrote to thank him for the flowers and the 'two hours of absolute bliss created by the string quartet'.

She continued:

I am sure now that mother would not think you brash anymore, but it would still be impossible for you to visit me here at the villa. Next week, my mother and I will be returning to Catania. Our family has an apartment there and my mother owns a millinery shop in the main street. I work there as well, so there would be nothing to stop you visiting to browse. You may be interested to know that the opera Aida *by Giuseppe Verdi is presently playing in Catania at the Teatro Bellini di Catania. We are planning to go there with my sister Luisa and her husband Giovanni Gravina who is a Lieutenant in the army.*

Best regards,
Elena

Carmelo required help and he knew just the person to enlist in his aid. "How would you like to visit your Zia Adele in Catania?" he asked Eloisa. "I love going to her place. When can we go Zio Meluzzo?"

"I was thinking maybe tomorrow but I have to check first with your mother and with Zia."

The pair soon found themselves on the train to Catania.

"Do you like hats?" he asked Eloisa.

"Sometimes. Are we going shopping?"

"Yes and I am going to buy you a nice hat and a pair of pretty shoes."

Adele and Arimondo were so excited to see them both. She had no children and at thirty-eight years of age the likelihood was slim.

"Isn't Eloisa quite the young lady, Meluzzo?"

"Well, she's going to be even more so when we buy her a hat and a pair of shoes to dress her up for the opera."

"Opera, what opera?"

"Well, since we are here, it would be a good opportunity for Eloisa to see the opera. *Aida* is performing at the Teatro Bellini di Catania and the four of us are going."

"When?" asked Adele.

"I'm not sure yet. I'll tell you tomorrow after we go to the milliner's to buy Eloisa a new hat... and you too if you want one. Now I'm paying for the tickets, so you can't say 'no'. What's more, Eloisa and I would never talk to you again if you did." He gave her a kiss on the cheek and Adele gave Arimondo a look, which suggested she suspected something.

After a restless night, the morning came and they found the millinery shop where Elena worked with her mother. Carmelo introduced Adele and Eloisa to Elena who in turn introduced the trio to her mother. The interaction was very proper as if they were merely customers.

"Will you be staying long in Catania?" asked Lucia.

"Oh we live here Signora, my husband and I. My brother Carmelo lives in Australia and young Eloisa here lives with her parents in Agira."

"Australia... the land of opportunity I hear. Is it true, Signor Cottone?"

"I think so but you have to forgo much when you go to Australia. I haven't been to an opera in the whole of the twelve years I've been in Australia. There, it's mostly work and sleep with the occasional outing on weekends."

"Well, *Aida* is in town at the moment," said Lucia.

"Yes, in fact we are hoping to see it but we haven't arranged tickets as yet. That's why we're here… to buy a hat and some pretty shoes for Eloisa."

"Well what a coincidence, we have a box for tomorrow night. Maybe you would like to join us? I would like to know more about Australia."

"That would be wonderful. Is tomorrow night suitable for you, Adele?"

Elena dressed Eloisa to look like a true princess and Adele indulged herself, buying a daring creation that made her appear sophisticated. Carmelo was clad in a charcoal suit, black tie and white shirt. Elena was stunning in a floor-length sweep train chiffon evening dress. She even caught the imagination of a photographer who offered her a bouquet of white roses and photographed them both in a classic pose.

It was certainly a night to remember for Eloisa who revelled in the action on stage while Carmelo seemed more interested in admiring Elena. Adele, Lucia and Eloisa allowed themselves to be overwhelmed by the tragic storyline, whilst Arimondo and Giovanni discussed the army for the duration of the evening.

With all members of the party thoroughly satisfied, Lucia invited them to lunch at the villa that weekend.

"You should meet Signor Coppola in consideration of the fact that you have accompanied his daughter to the opera, Signor Cottone. I have not had a chance to talk to you about Australia. Signora Contessa, you must promise to accompany your husband. The men can amuse themselves and we may enjoy a game of cards perhaps."

"Would you care to shoot some pheasants, Arimondo?" asked Giovanni.

"That would be different," answered Arimondo.

"What do you shoot in Australia, Carmelo?"

"Ducks mainly and occasionally wild pigs, but I'm not such a good shot. I prefer riding."

"Then we will ride and shoot this weekend," said Giovanni.

Chapter 23

The truth matters

As it was, Liborio Coppola looked much older than Carmelo imagined. He was, after all, seventy-seven years old but he seemed drained of all energy.

"My daughter seems to have shown a more than casual interest in you, Carmelo and I worry for her because she is so young. She has just now on the eleventh of January turned twenty-one. She is still a child and has no experience of the world."

"Please be assured Signor Coppola that my intentions are honourable and I would never take advantage of your daughter."

"A woman so young can often become infatuated with the glamorous notion of living in faraway places in the arms of a heroic character, but as you know, reality is never like that. In fact it is quite the contrary. Faraway places tend to fester and the further they are away from civilization, the more lawless they become. Lawlessness fosters abuse, exploitation and a sense of hopelessness. A room without walls is not a room and a land without laws is not for a woman as delicate and sensitive as my precious Elena."

"Let me assure you Signor Coppola, Australia is in no way what you seem to imagine in terms of lawlessness. It may have been unsafe as a penal colony, but today everyone is safe in Australia. There are no bandits, no deserters, no secret police, no Mafiosi, no Black Shirts. There is discrimination but mainly because of ignorance on the part of a few. Australia is truly the land of the free and although immigrants have to sacrifice a lot, they can rest assured their children will be free from the scourge of class distinction, arrogance, poverty, hunger and political oppression."

"I believe you Carmelo and all I want you to understand and accept is that the truth matters— especially if you truly love someone."

"I promise to bear that in mind when speaking with your daughter. In fact I will ensure she understands how hard life can become in Australia."

"Secondly, I wish to make you aware of something that no young person has had enough time to learn. This is the influence of family. If one comes from a good family, then the individual becomes like a fish out of water when removed from that family environment. Love that is not platonic, plateaus quickly and as children enter the equation, it falls away and is replaced by bitterness and disappointment. This is because the heart yearns for the life it left behind. The love of a wife can never measure up to the love of a mother. They have not one element in common. A wife does not become a mother to your child and remain a wife to you. A wife metamorphoses into a mother when her first child is born and remains a mother the rest of her life. This process is irreversible. Men have trouble coming to terms with this fact of life but after having fathered thirteen children to two wives, I'm certain of this fact. I tell you this Carmelo because for you as well as for Elena, the truth matters. If Elena were to follow you to Australia, it is almost certain she will not see her father alive again. It is highly likely she will not see her mother alive either. When that time comes, she will reflect upon it and lay the blame squarely on your shoulders for taking her from them. As time passes she will long to be with her siblings and her children will not know their grandparents, their uncles and aunts nor their cousins.

In a foreign land they become becalmed at sea and they look at you as if it was all your doing. These are the things I have told Elena to consider before she makes any decision because it was my duty as a good father to tell her that. You might want to consider telling her the same if you believe that what I say may be true."

They could hear Arimondo and Giovanni's approach.

"The warriors are coming. Will you be participating in the ride and the hunt, Carmelo?"

"I think not Signor Coppola. Perhaps I should start telling Elena the truth about Australia."

"Then you must excuse me. This old man needs his rest in the afternoon or he will not be present at dinner. And what a shame that would be, as I believe we will be having pheasant tonight. Is that not correct, Giovanni?"

"Depends on how good a shot Arimondo here is."

Lucia, Eloisa and Adele retired to the pergola beside the pond to play cards and Elena told them she was taking her violin to the cork tree to practise her scales.

"Do you mind if I come along to hear an angel play scales?" he asked her. She smiled and he followed in her footsteps. "Your father shared some interesting points of view with me, Elena. He is quite a philosopher."

"Did he explain to you how a wife metamorphoses into a mother after she has her first child?"

"As a matter of fact he did, Elena. Interesting hypothesis that. You don't agree, I take it?"

"Too deep and meaningful at my age. I'll leave that thinking for when I reach his age."

"Tell me, Carmelo, what is life really like in Australia?"

"Well, to tell you the truth you cannot begin to imagine how terrible it can get."

Nobody knew Elena better than her father. That wise old man knew that nothing would change her mind but he still told her because it was his duty as a good father.

"He says I'm a city girl and I should marry someone from the city so that I may live the life to which I am accustomed," she told Carmelo.

"He is right on this, Elena. After all, he only wants the best for you."

"Why, why do you say this? Don't you love me?"

"Of course I do. That's why I want you to make the right decision."

"It's never the right decision. Something always goes wrong."

"What do you mean?"

"Six months ago I was courted by a young prince, would you believe?"

"A prince... yes, I do believe it Elena."

"He was studying at the University of Catania and was an attaché to the Court of Emperor Haile Selassie 1. Apparently, he must have seen me in the millinery shop. Anyhow, I began receiving huge bouquets of flowers from 'A Devoted Admirer'. Then I received gifts daily. One day, a huge basket of fruit, the next it was nuts and this was followed by flowers, then silks, then objects of art. Finally an invitation was delivered to our apartment;

Prince Alberto, attaché to the Court of Emperor Haile Salassie 1, requests the pleasure of the company of Elena and Luisa D'Italia at the upcoming production of Giuseppe Verdi's Opera, 'La Battaglia di Legnano' at the Teatro Bellini di Catania.

"So, what happened?" asked Carmelo in a muted tone.

"The whole world of the Coppola household descended into chaos. No one knew what to do. Can you imagine the excitement, the preparations, the soul-searching that occurred in anticipation of such an event? Anyhow, I thank God for my sister Luisa. She carried me through it all. She was so calm and courageous throughout the whole event."

"What happened?"

"I told you, something always goes wrong. Anyhow, we arrived at the Teatro with the invitation and we were immediately ushered to the premier box in the theatro. There were several young people; boys and girls, sipping champagne and conversing. We curtsied and offered our hands as we were introduced. I cannot explain how exciting it was to be the centre of all those interesting people's attention... until I was introduced to Prince Alberto." She paused to draw breath.

"Why, what was it?"

"He was black, Carmelo. The Court of Emperor Haile Selassi 1, don't you understand? He was Ethiopian. I nearly fainted. Luisa saved me. She was so calm, so sweet. I don't remember one single act of that play. I was so embarrassed. I knew my family would be so disappointed. They would never understand. You see there is always something wrong with everyone. With him it was because he was black. With you, it's because you live in Australia and not even in the city— on the frontiers as you describe it. If we love each other, what does it matter?"

Carmelo attempted to lighten the situation.

"So tell me Elena, how did my humble flowers compare with his bouquets and baskets of fruit and nuts and silks and objects of art? I feel very humbled."

"Ah… but you sent the quartet to sing at my gate. That was the coup de grâce my dear Carmelo."

When it was announced that they would be married, Teresa approached Carmelo regarding a matter with Mrs Malaponte.

"All of Mary Malaponte's children are in Australia except Vito and Rosa who live in Genoa. She has no one remaining in Agira to stay with. She wants to know if she could go to Australia on the same ship as you and Elena. She won't be any trouble. She's afraid to go on such a long journey on her own."

"How old is she, Teresa?" asked Carmelo.

"She's sixty-six but never had a sick day in her life. She will take her own cabin and she will be good company for Elena. I think you should say 'yes' to her."

"Then I shall say 'yes', my dear Teresa and that's all that needs to be said about it. You can tell her. She will need to acquire a passport and have her affairs in order over here. Tell her if there is anything she needs, I am at her service."

It was a morose day for all when the time came for Carmelo and Elena to return to Australia. Eloisa could not halt her tears and Cettina sobbed because Eloisa was crying. Only Teresa remained strong.

"You are doing the right thing, Carmelo. Search and you will find. Ask and you shall receive. I may not be here the next time you return, but return you must for your wife's sake at least. She is such a beauty. I am so happy for you. You were always my baby. Go now with all my blessings." Carmelo bent down to kiss her and took a long look at those loving eyes in the crippled body that had watched over him all his life.

Elena knew she may never see her father again, but her mother was still young at forty-eight. There was every chance of reuniting, thus the parting was bearable. But the one who was most distressed was the youngest, Giovanni. He was eleven years old. His love was for horses and each time she had told him a story, his greatest love would be somewhere in it.

"Wipe those tears, Giannino. Elena is travelling to Australia and when she returns she's going to buy you the most beautiful horse you have ever seen. You wait and see. Now you study hard and be good for Mamma and Papa... promise?"

After his solemn promise she hugged him and then embraced Vincenzo, Mario and Giulia.

"Ah Giulia, how can I live without my Gina? Everybody's Gina? The light of our lives? I will miss you so much."

Then she hugged Liborio and he patted her on the head, "Our family will miss the music you bring us. When you are gone, you can imagine what it will be like here. The birds will have stopped singing and I fear they may never sing until your return. Please come soon, Elena."

Finally and the moment that brought tears to her eyes was when she faced Luisa.

"Don't cry, Elena, there are too many things to celebrate, such as not abandoning us for Prince Alberto for example," to which they both burst into laughter through their tears.

"May God be with you always and bless you both. You are always here in my heart. You will never be far away."

Elena held Luisa's three children, Armando who was ten, Enzo who was eight and Mario who was three.

"You are the only nephews I have. You will always be so special to me." Then she hugged Luisa again, then Giulia, her mother and finally her father, holding him tightly for that additional moment that was ever so poignant.

The final farewell was to Italian shores as Carmelo, Elena and Mrs Malaponte boarded the HMS *ORONSAY* on the twenty-fourth of April 1937, bound for Australia.

Chapter 24
The nightmare

The nightmare ensued for Elena from the very first night on the Mediterranean Sea. The HMS *ORONSAY* bucked and lurched from side to side so violently that Elena was afraid to get out of her bed, which only worsened her situation. By the second day, she was dry-retching and unable to hold any food whatsoever in her stomach. The doctor on board explained to Carmelo what he needed to do.

"Food is not important, Mr Cottone. It is crucial, however, that she receives her fluids. Even if she brings it up, you must ensure she keeps trying to drink water. As well, try to give her flat lemonade. That will offer her energy. Hopefully after a few days Elena will become accustomed to the movement of the boat and the nausea will subside."

Carmelo was pleased to have Mrs Malaponte with him on the ship. He had no idea of what he should do to console his wife or what he could do to help her. Alternatively, Mrs Malaponte was a true veteran having raised eight children of her own, virtually on her own as her husband had passed away nineteen years ago.

"Signora Malaponte, you are an angel from heaven. What would we do without you?"

"Ah, don't mention it. You and Elena are like my children to me. I am so happy not to be a burden to you both."

Carmelo immediately suggested that Mrs Malaponte relocate into their room so she could be with Elena all of the time.

"I can sleep in your room if that is okay... only at night mind you and only until Elena feels she can cope without you."

For five days, not a morsel of food passed her lips but at least she was able to hold water and was enjoying the lemonade. On the sixth day, she asked for some fruit. Carmelo went immediately to fetch her some.

"What is this strange fruit, Meluzzo?" she asked as she surveyed the yellow mass of pulp encased in soft skin and the size of a small watermelon.

"It is papaya and it is so sweet, you will never believe it possible until you try it." He scooped a teaspoonful into her mouth. The smell alone was enough to prompt her dry-retching all over again.

"No wonder," said Mrs Malaponte. "That smell would be enough to make anyone vomit. It smells like soap."

"But it tastes like something from another world."

"Precisely and at this moment that's exactly what she doesn't want; food from another world. She's suffering with food that is of this world let alone 'another' world."

"Here, try some and you'll see what I mean," insisted Carmelo.

"No thanks, Carmelo. You have it and please, would you eat it outside; the smell will have me dry-retching soon."

Carmelo felt completely useless. He had spent twelve years living in a world of men and this scenario was utterly foreign to him. Fortunately, she was in the loving care of Mrs Malaponte and by the middle of the second week she was able to dress and move to the dining room. She would happily have eaten in her room, but she was met with strict doctor's orders that she obediently observed.

"It will do her good to get some fresh air and enjoy the social life on the ship," he suggested. "When we arrive in Colombo, Carmelo you must take her ashore to experience the sensation of dry land." He smiled at her, "perhaps you could do a little bit of shopping. Good therapy that." Carmelo quickly translated and she returned the doctor's smile.

"Grazie molto," she called after him as he disappeared from the room.

The thought of shopping did elevate her spirits and by the time they landed in Colombo she and Mrs Malaponte were ready to search for exotic artefacts. The first object she fell in love with was a pair of elephants carved from rich ebony timber. With ivory tusks and ivory toenails, they stood at thirteen centimetres high, complementing each other perfectly. The piece of artwork she found most irresistible was a raw silk tapestry featuring a wild tiger; this piece would prove an essential acquisition. She also purchased an array of knickknacks— ideal gifts for people in Australia— and bundled some small items of jewellery into packets and posted them back for each of the women and girls in both families back in Italy.

They arrived in Fremantle on the twenty-fifth of May 1937 and Elena was able to set her feet on *terra firma* for the second time but this time it was something truly special. She had arrived in Australia.

The last leg of the journey, the train trip from Brisbane to Babinda was special also; Carmelo had arranged for them to stay with the Malapontes in Home Hill for a few days so Elena could meet Mrs Malaponte's family. Antonio was the eldest and married to Lucia Nascone; together they had two children, Philip 13 and Mary 12— named after Mrs Malaponte. Next was Giuseppe, then Santa, Natale, Orazio and Concetta, all siblings of Antonio Malaponte. Concetta was the youngest at 23. Young Mary was Elena's favourite from the first instant; she was forever smiling and Elena adored her.

The great attraction of course was firstly the reunion with their mother and secondly the arrival of Carmelo's new bride. There was much to celebrate and the festivities lived on for three days. It was as if they were in Italy; thus it served as the best counter measure for culture shock that Elena could have hoped for. But it came to pass and they were soon on the train en route to Babinda. In the silence of the cabin, Elena had time to reflect and was suddenly overwhelmed by tears.

"What is it Elena? Why are you crying? Is everything alright? What's wrong?"

"Nothing… I don't know why I'm crying. I feel okay. I just can't help it. I guess I just need to get whatever it is that's bothering me out of my system."

"Please don't lose hope now, Elena. I don't have Mrs Malaponte to save me."

To which she laughed, "Mrs Malaponte is so sweet. She was like a mother throughout that voyage. That's probably what it is. Leaving her reminded me of having to leave my mother."

They arrived in Babinda and the late autumn rains were poised to welcome her. Giuseppe Barbagallo was at the station to collect some goods and his eyes protruded from his head when he saw Elena alight from the train.

"Cottone… Cottone…welcome back," as he approached he shook his hands without once taking his eyes off Elena.

"Elena, this is Mr Barbagallo. He was the first man to meet me in Babinda and now he is the first man to meet you."

"Ah Signora, you are so attractive. Did he win you in a lottery? Otherwise, how could he be so lucky?" He looked at the sky, "Curse this rain… take care… it's blowing in onto the platform. Watch you don't get wet." He looked at Carlo, "If you don't have a ride, I can take you to the shop. You can meet Mississa there Signora and have a warm cup of coffee. Then I can run you out to the farm if you wish."

"That would be so nice Giuseppe. This is the only part of the journey I didn't plan. We will need to get some stores as well," answered Carmelo.

Mrs Barbagallo was full of praise for Carmelo's choice of wife.

"Cottone… what a prize specimen you have brought back to this wilderness," she said as she circled Elena twice. "He's a very lucky man, Signora. If he'd left it to me, I would have found him a packhorse. That's what you need to survive in this place."

"Come on, Mississa. You are only frightening her." He addressed Elena directly, "don't you listen to her. She just woke up with a headache this morning and even a description of heaven would sound like hell."

Giuseppe loaded their substantial order of stores into his delivery truck and drove them to Happy Valley. They passed the hospital, skirted the hill past Gee Kee's place, drove down and crossed Stony Creek and Sandy Creek and then up Spitaro's hill past the tobacco barn that he lived in and along the flats past Carmelo's first farm.

"That's the first farm that I bought Elena, there on your left. I sold it to Biondi. They have a young family with two children. Across there, on your right, that's the farm that Antonio bought with Arena and that's where I lived for a year when I first came here; in that shack, tucked in at the base of that little knoll you can see."

They crossed the double-barrelled bridge and turned left.

"That other road goes to *The Boulders*, the pristine waterhole I told you about, surrounded by dense tropical jungle and fed by cold mountain streams. Just ahead, on the right are Saffiotti's barracks where I met up again with Antonio on my arrival in Australia and where I lived when I cut cane."

Barbagallo shifted his truck back into first gear as they entered the shallow causeway crossing at Babinda Creek. "Right here, on this bank, this is where I broke my leg when the stream was in flood and my horse fell on top of me." Up the bank to the other side and the road opened out onto the home farm.

"This is the home farm, Elena. Everything on your left and to your right is our property." A sense of pride echoed in the way he spoke. "… all those river flats, those undulating hills and right up into the mountains."

Carmelo was so thrilled to have returned to his tropical paradise tucked into the corner of Happy Valley on the banks of Babinda Creek. He was ecstatic as he introduced his workers, the Singhs and Cedric to his wife.

Elena on the other hand was far from ecstatic. She seemed bewildered much to Carmelo's surprise and disappointment.

"What do you think, Giuseppe?" he asked as Barbagallo unloaded the last of the stores from the truck. "Do you think she likes the place?"

"She will need time to appreciate these beautiful surroundings the way you do, Cottone. She'll be going into shock anytime now, but she'll come out of it soon enough. After all, look at it through her eyes and think, what can a sophisticated city girl really see here?" He looked around shaking his head. "She can see a corrugated iron clump of buildings about to be devoured by the encroaching jungle. She's stuck here with two Indians, an Albanian, five draught horses, a decrepit old dog and a cow and a calf with the same name. She hasn't even met the neighbours yet! She's going to need time, Cottone and a pair of rose-coloured glasses would help."

His parting statement left Carmelo flat, but he appreciated the wake-up call Barbagallo had dealt him.

"Elena," he promised her, "you'll get used to this. Just give yourself time to become accustomed to it all. We won't meet the neighbours for a few days. What do you say?"

Elena simply burst into a torrent of tears. She was inconsolable. The sounds of the crickets and frogs croaking at night and the incessant rain pounding on the roof deprived her of sleep. She cried for her mother and her sisters. She was so lonely.

"How do you feel?" Carmelo would ask her every morning and every morning the enormity and the hopelessness of her situation compounded.

"I'm so lonely. I miss my family, Meluzzo. This is like being sentenced to solitary confinement. I can feel the jungle suffocating me. I miss the sounds of the city."

Carmelo secretly consulted many of the wise women of the town for advice.

"She has been crying virtually without fail for six weeks. Nobody can cry for that long unless they are genuinely unhappy."

They all agreed with him. "It goes further than that," they added, "nobody can cry for that long unless they are genuinely unhappy about virtually everything. If she was happy about something, she would stop crying for some of the time." Their logic was not lost on him.

He purchased a gramophone and some records of the famous arias and that improved her mood. He brought her to visit Mrs Biondi and her two little children and that helped. He took her to town to the movies and that helped, but she was unimpressed with the inconvenience of getting dressed, having to travel into town on the jigger and return at night in the cold air or worse, being drenched by a sudden shower of rain.

Three months after their arrival, Carmelo felt so hopeless about the state of unhappiness he had brought upon his wife. She tried to disguise her tears, but Carmelo knew she had cried every day. When he came home at lunchtime or after work, Elena's spirits would rise and she often willed him not to return to work. But it was the middle of the season and he had no choice.

"I should have heeded the advice of her father before we were married," he confided in a phone call to Mrs Malaponte. "He predicted this would happen. It's not really her fault. I was being selfish in not realizing how bad it could be for her here."

"I think you're being a bit hard on yourself, Carmelo. It's quite reasonable that Elena would take some time to get used to the isolation here in Australia. She doesn't speak English and she has no young friends. I'm here with my family and I still pine for my friends. You said yourself that she's happy when you come home so it's not you she is unhappy about. I think she's just lonely. Leave it with me, Carmelo. I will talk to Antonio about allowing his daughter, Mary to stay with you for a few months. You could both stay here for a couple of days and return with Mary."

When he spoke with his wife, he was mysterious, "I'm planning a very special surprise for you this weekend."

She sat upright in her chair, "Surprise? This weekend? How exciting!"

"Yes, so don't you go planning anything for this weekend, okay?"

"Yeah sure, you mean like organizing a 'Johnny Cake Cooking Party' with Rasshim or a 'Happy Valley Draught Horse Race Meeting' or a game of 'Guess the name of the next calf'," she laughed.

Carmelo was oblivious to the humour but grateful for her laughter, thus he forced himself to smile as she offered him her lips.

"When will you tell me so I can do what I have to do?"

"How about Friday?"

"Thursday would be better."

'Okay, Thursday. But you have to promise to cheer up in the meantime."

As soon as Elena heard they were going to the Malaponte's she lit the wooden stove and set upon baking cakes and biscuits. That night, the next morning and for the duration of the train ride, Elena was her effervescent self again.

"How long do you think Mary will stay with us? She is such a delightful girl. I love her. Meluzzo, I have been praying so hard for something like this to happen. Do you think there might be a chance that her parents will let her stay for a couple of weeks?"

"We'll have to wait and see, my dear. I certainly hope so."

Elena could not believe her ears when Mary told her. "Three months!" she exclaimed.

"Yes, my parents asked me a couple of days ago. I couldn't believe it either. I've been praying too but I never imagined it would be anything like this. I needed to get away. They treat me so like a child, except for Nonna. She knows I'm grown up."

They returned to the farm with Mary on Monday night after a glorious day of song on the train and even on the way to the farm on the jigger. Carmelo was enveloped by his sister Teresa's presence. "Ah Teresa, thank you Teresa for Mrs Malaponte," I heard him uttering as he heard them giggling on the little verandah out front. After his prayers that night he told Teresa he was certain it was her working through Mrs Malaponte that had brought about this good fortune and thanked her.

Chapter 25
The home farm

During the three months the twelve year old child spent with Elena, she helped her develop a sense of belonging and ownership in this new land. She guided her to recognise the farm as a sanctuary in itself where they were their own master and to lose her fears in this hostile land and ward off the fretting for her family overseas.

In that short period, Mary and Elena travelled alone to town and back on the jigger many times. They swam in the creek and went for walks in the rainforest and across the cane paddocks to bring Carmelo company and his smoko as he worked the farm with his horses. They cooked special meals, listened to records and never missed one episode of Blue Hills on the wireless. They played cards and Elena played the violin and mandolin and with Mary's help, she began to explore the intricacies of the English language.

Mary returned home leaving behind a contented Elena. All she and Carmelo longed for now was the patter of little feet. But 1938 brought only the scourge of the cane grubs, which chewed off the plant roots and stunted the plant's growth reducing sugar yields. By 1939, Carmelo's crop yield was reduced by forty per cent. Urgent meetings were held in the Babinda Community Hall attended by politicians, millers and officers of the Sugar Experiment Station.

Bull Simmonds, nicknamed thus because of the shape of his head and because of the way 'he always threw his weight around', spoke on behalf of the farmers and millers, "we'll all be ruined," he said, "if you people at the Sugar Experiment Station don't get off your behinds and find some chemical that can get rid of these grubs."

"There is hope on the horizon," said Mr Jenkins from the Sugar Experiment Station. "Scientists have come up with a chemical called, gammaxene, which has proved to be lethal to the grubs."

"Well, why aren't we putting it on our crops?" yelled Charlie Agis who was so short he had to stand on a chair in order to be seen by the Mill Committee Chairman.

"Please let Mr Jenkins finish first Mr Agis. Then you can all ask your questions. No more interjections please!" The Mill Committee Chairman retorted.

"In answer to that question, we're not putting it on our crops because it is so lethal it may kill humans as well. So, we have to conduct further tests to determine if it's safe enough to use. Any questions?"

"How long might it take to do that and what are we supposed to do in the meantime?" asked Bull once the Committee Chairman had given him the nod.

"In a couple of years we hope and in the meantime, we'll just have to learn to roll with the punches."

Not only did the grubs multiply by fifty per cent in 1939, but so too did Carlo and Elena's little family. On the seventeenth of September 1939, Elena gave birth to a son Rosario Giuseppe. Nothing else mattered as far as they were concerned; except that war had once again engulfed Europe.

As far as his creditors were concerned, the situation with the grubs was problematic as well. For the first time, these creditors were in danger of losing their money so the purse-strings were tightened to breaking point. Carmelo's income was significantly reduced yet his financial commitments remained unchanged. He had only one course open to him. He would have to cut cane an act he had not performed since 1935. He tried to explain it to Elena.

"In 1934, there was an outbreak of Weil's disease killing several cutters. The only way to get rid of the bacteria was to burn the cane before cutting it. The sugar millers and the farmers opposed this because it reduced the sugar content and caused the cane to deteriorate very quickly. The powerful Australian Workers Union who represented the mainly migrant workforce wanted laws passed making it compulsory to burn the cane so that the health of the workers would be protected."

"So what happened?"

"Hundreds of canecutters from Ingham, Mourilyan and Hambledon mill areas decided to strike and refused to cut cane that was not burnt. Other mills followed and soon the Australian Workers Union was able to get a law passed requiring cane to be burnt before it was cut."

"That was good news."

"Yes it was. But because burnt cane deteriorated quickly, large gangs of men were required at any one time to cut the burnt cane on individual farms. That's when I had to stop cutting my own cane because the mill would not accept one truck of cane here and one truck of cane there. They would accept only a rake of ten to fifteen trucks per day from individual farmers. So, we had to join with other farmers in order to have our cane cut."

"So, how are you going to cut your own cane?"

"I have to do it secretly without the union knowing or else they will black-ban my cane and it will be left in the field to rot. When I explain my financial situation to the canecutters, they won't care if I join the gang but they are not permitted to cut with me. So, I will have to cut my share of cane at night. For example, if there are thirty rows of burnt cane and there are six cutters including me, then I must cut my share, that is, five rows at night. Then when it comes to pay them, I keep one sixth of the total earnings."

"Poor Carmelo, is there no other way to make ends meet?"

"No Elena, at least we can live off that money and our creditors will not be able to get their hands on it."

So Carmelo would take his hurricane lamp into the night and cut his share before the rest of the gang arrived the following day to cut the remaining allocation. This allowed him enough money to live and a little extra, which he saved in case of an emergency. He would usually work five hours and return at one o'clock in the morning, all covered in soot from the burnt cane. Embarrassed to be seen so soiled by Elena, he would go to the creek to wash before taking a hot shower at home. He would also rinse his dirty clothes before placing them in the laundry pile.

By 1940, the situation with the grubs had worsened for Carmelo. The gammaxene remained unavailable and the grubs claimed another ten per cent of his crop. But for many other Italian farmers, their situation had become completely devastating. Not only were their farms decimated but hundreds were 'randomly captured'— the term used on their arrest papers and then interned as 'enemy aliens' following Mussolini's entry into the war against the allies on the tenth of June 1940. Carmelo followed the progress closely in *The Cairns Post* and kept Elena informed of any issues of particular relevance to them. "Under the 'National Security Act' passed on the ninth of September 1939, severe restrictions have been placed on work and travel for all Italians and it is an offence to speak a language other than English on the telephone." He quoted, "these orders apply equally to all British Subjects of Enemy Extraction whether naturalized or Australian born."

"So, what was the purpose of naturalization if you are still treated as Italian in times of war? According to that statement, even our son Rosario who was born here is considered Italian and has lost his rights as an Australian citizen," Elena quipped.

"That's what it says, Elena. There are bad times ahead I fear, for as long as this war persists."

They soon discovered that the entire male contingent of the Australian Malaponte family comprising five men, were interned in that year, including Mrs Malaponte's grandson Philip who was only sixteen years old. That left Mrs Malaponte, her two daughters Santa and Concetta, her two daughters-in-law Lucia and Signorella and her granddaughter Mary at the farmhouse unprotected and without means of support.

The news about the Malapontes caused Carmelo to become distraught. If he were to be interned, who would look after Elena and his young child? And how long would it be before his creditors repossessed his farm and threw his wife onto the street? She was alone. She knew nobody excluding the Malapontes. He decided to keep his head low. He remained on the farm and saved as much money as he could, keeping it hidden in the event of his being condemned to the Malapontes' fate.

The general procedure for being interned was that someone in the community—Anglo-Australian or otherwise could report any Italian or German suspected of collaborating or individually jeopardizing the security of the country. They would immediately be captured and interned as enemy aliens. Who could believe that a person who was naturalized, a British Citizen or even born in Australia, could still be interned if the finger were pointed at them?

"Today I heard that Lennie Omodei was interned. He was born in Australia. Nobody is safe anymore," he told his wife. "If they come for me, there won't be much time so we have to be prepared. You know where the money is hidden. Keep some on you at all times and keep the rest hidden. Maybe, you can go to the Malaponte's if the creditors take the farm. Give Mrs Malaponte all the money and she will look after you like her own daughter. That's all that I can suggest."

"You have done nothing wrong. You do not belong to the Dante Alighieri Club, the Italian Returned Soldiers Club or the Babinda Fascio. You are not an Anarchist or a Communist. You have no contact with the Italian community at all. You do not attend secret meetings. You are always here with your wife and family. How can you be plotting against the security of Australia?"

"There are rumours that creditors are using this policy to capitalize on the hard work done by the migrants in developing their farms. Once the farmers are interned, the creditors move in and repossess the farms, put in a manager and later on, they resell the property and make all the capital gain."

"Do you think our main creditor, Mr Davies would turn you in and destroy a young family just for capital gain?"

"I certainly hope not, Elena. The people of this country have always been good to me. For every bad person who has done me wrong, there has always been a better person to set it right again. We have to keep the faith. What more can I say?"

"Meluzzo, you worry too much about us and soon it will affect your health. Already you have lost a lot of weight since our marriage. I want you to know that I am not afraid of the future. Since we were blessed with our little Saruzzo, I feel I am strong enough to cope with any hardship. As long as we are alive and healthy, that is all that matters."

"I'm pleased to hear you say that and I believe you. There is only one more thing I would ask of you before I can let the matter lie."

"What is it, Meluzzo?"

"You have progressed so well with your English using The Cairns Post and your dictionary, but it's not enough. I want to employ a live-in housekeeper who can speak in English to you all day. Only this way can you ever hope to master the language. Saruzzo will go to school in a few years and he too needs to be exposed to the language. After all, this is his country now. Australia is a lucky country, Elena and with God's will, he will never have to suffer the poverty and political oppression that has passed over Europe in waves for centuries."

The first person Carmelo approached was his old housekeeper Annie.

"I'd love to help Carlo but me husband has just got a job in Cairns. But there's a middle-aged English woman who's a widow. Her husband was killed while dynamiting fish near the mouth of the Russell River. He was a nice bloke, an Aussie who left her with two children. They're now married and left home. Sue's a lovely lady. We went to school together; only difference is she speaks a lot better English than me being Pommy and all. At least your wife will learn proper English and won't speak strine like me." She laughed. It was hard to get a word in when Annie was wound up. "So how's that pretty wife of yours, Carlo? I see you got a kid."

"Yes his name is Rosario Giuseppe. I named him after my father Rosario and after my brother and grandfather Giuseppe."

"Ah, ya can't call him Rosario. Call him Ross. And forget about the Giuseppe bit or he'll get the crap beat out of him at school."

"How can I find this Sue lady?"

"She's secretary of the Country Women's Association. I could take you down to meet her if you want. I know she's looking for a job. Don't know if she'd be interested in living in but."

They went down to the CWA Hall which was opposite the Police Station and the women were engrossed in their afternoon tea. The people there didn't seem too friendly; perhaps because they were all women and a man had just entered their midst.

"Just wanted to talk to Sue for a minute if I could please Mrs. Jensen. It's about a job."

"Hello Annie, what's happening?"

"Not much. This is Carlo… You still looking for a job? Wants someone who can teach his wife English mainly and to do some other light duties."

"He's Italian isn't he?"

"Yeah, but he's different from the rest of 'em… he's a good bloke, Carlo. Worked for him myself in the past. I can vouch for him… real gentleman."

"What's his wife like?"

"She's a real cutie. I never spoke to her but she ain't no old battle-axe or nothing."

"I'll have to think about it."

Annie relayed the message to Carmelo who was standing right beside them.

"She'll ring you back."

"Does he speak English?" she asked Annie.

"Yes, I do. I've been in Australia for sixteen years. My wife can read and write a little English but her spoken English is poor. She needs a native speaker to practise with, that's all."

"Oh… oh sorry, I didn't know you could speak English. Ah look… well probably no need to think about it. I'll do it but I won't live in. I'll come every day. Is that okay?"

"I'll pay you the basic wage."

"Good, Mr Cottone. I can start next Monday if you wish. I can ride out to Happy Valley on my bicycle."

"What a good idea, I must buy a bicycle for Elena too."

Trevor's Bicycle Shop was only thirty metres from the CWA Hall next to Arena's Bakery. Richie Trevor was busy burning a patch onto a bicycle tube.

"Can I help you, Carlo?"

"Yes, I would like to buy a bicycle for my wife."

"Well, it'll certainly be a lot easier for her than pushing that damn jigger. I got just the bicycle for her. Here it is, the famous Malvern Star; the bicycle made famous by Hubert Opperman in 1921 and the Australian Company that sponsored teams in the Tour de France of 1928 and 1931. It's on special."

"I'll take it," said Carmelo to the super-salesman who couldn't believe his luck.

"I'd do business with you anytime, Carlo. Anything goes wrong, you tell Mrs Cottone to bring it to me and I'll fix it free for one year."

Carmelo loaded it onto the jigger and for the entirety of the trip home worried whether Elena might be too prim and proper to ride it.

He could never have been more wrong. Elena absolutely loved it.

Chapter 26

Captured

As the war raged in Europe, Anglo-Australians in Babinda and all over Australia became more and more xenophobic towards the Italian community. The war propaganda machine had ignited and inflamed matters via the media. After only six months, Sue the housekeeper explained that there was a lot of pressure on her to resign from her job with them and she left.

It was early Thursday morning on the fifth of March 1942. Carmelo was on the front deck when he saw the police van approaching the house. He feared the worst and called to his wife who was bathing Rosario in the tub; he had a temperature and was crying.

"I'm coming," she said. "The baby is crying, what is it?"

She turned around to find him standing beside her. "The police are here. We have to remain calm. Are you okay?"

Stunned, she nodded.

By the time Elena had dressed Rosario, there was a loud thumping on the back door.

"Carmelo Cottone, Babinda Police. Can you come to the door please?"

"Sergeant Peters, come in. You are early enough to have a cup of coffee," said Carmelo.

"Sorry, Carlo. We have come here to place you under arrest as a suspected enemy alien. You must come with us. You will need to take identification papers and some essential items only."

Carmelo had readied himself for this moment. So many Italians had already been interned and he knew the procedure. He had a small port packed and his passport and other important papers were inside. He took a small pillow and blanket as well and halted at the door to embrace his wife and son who was still crying.

"I'll phone you as soon as I know what's happening. If Rosario gets worse, you phone the police station. Is that okay, Sergeant Peters?"

"Yes, that's fine. Just ask for me, Mrs Cottone."

Carmelo held his son until the boy stopped crying and then regretfully handed him back to his mother. "Goodbye my big son. Look after your mother while I'm gone."

The sergeant waited for Carmelo to sit in the police van before handcuffing him.

"This is not necessary, Sergeant Peters."

"I know, Carlo. It's standard police procedure."

The two Hindus and the Albanian appeared to lend a sort of muted support as a light shower of rain swept across the Bellenden Ker Ranges to the west and washed over everyone. Carmelo acknowledged them and then looked to the house where Elena stood on the front deck, her actions like the windscreen wipers of the van as she wiped her son's eyes and her own simultaneously with a white handkerchief, again and again and again. Carmelo was heartbroken.

At the station, a young constable was helping a scribe process Carmelo's internment documents.

"Let's see," said the scribe. "Place and date of capture: The fifth of March 1942.

"*Weight?*"

"Eleven stone," said the constable.

"*Height?*"

"Five foot six inches."

"*Eye colour?*"

"Blue."

"*Personal effects?*"

"One port, one rug, one pillow and a sum of five pounds seventeen shillings and four pence... toiletry, clothes, a passport and some documents."

"*Reason for Internment:* Sarge, what do I put for 'Reason for Internment'?"

"Just put 'master warrant'," said Sergeant Peters.

"*Date of Entry:* When did you come to Australia, Mr Cottone?"

"I arrived in Fremantle on the tenth of December 1924 on the HMS *ORVIETO* from Naples in Italy," said Carmelo.

"That's the year I was born, Mr Cottone. That's a long time ago," commented the scribe.

"Not long enough it seems."

"*Property in Australia:* please describe any property you own in Australia, Mr Cottone.

"I own one hundred and twenty-nine acres of land with a house on it."

"*Statement of Service:* did you serve in the defence forces in Italy?"

"Yes, I served in the Italian Army from 1920–1922."

"*Visits to country of origin:* have you been back to Italy, Mr Cottone?

"Yes, in 1936–1937 to get married."

"Okay, that's all. Could you sign here please, Mr Cottone?"

Carmelo signed.

"Now Mr Cottone, you'll be placed in a cell until we're told what to do with you," the young constable informed him.

"So, what is the reason for my internment?"

"Let's see," he read the form, "reason for internment… master warrant, Mr Cottone. That's what."

"What is a master warrant?"

"Good question. What's a master warrant, Sarge?"

"A master warrant is a list of a couple of hundred people to be arrested for suspicion, in this case, of being enemy aliens. Came through from Brisbane."

"Can I make a phone call Sergeant Peters? I need to call my solicitor and my wife to tell them what's happening."

"Let him use the phone, Constable. You'll have to speak to your wife in English, Carlo."

Carmelo first spoke to his solicitor, Jim Davies who was also his main creditor on the farm.

"Hello Mr Davies, Carlo here. I am at the police station and now I too have been arrested on suspicion of being an enemy alien. Is there anything I should know or do?" He listened for a reply.

"Okay, so you'll come down to the station and talk to me here? I would appreciate that. Thank you."

Then he phoned his wife.

"Hello Elena. Is Rosario feeling a little better? Good. Mr Davies is coming down to talk to me at the police station. Don't worry. I'll phone you when I know something new."

Carmelo was taken to a cell at the rear of the station and was allowed to carry his port, his rug and his pillow with him.

"I'm one of the last to go, Constable. They have taken just about all of the Italians in town now. Barbagallo, Sorbello, Fontana, Saffiotti, Catalano, Zucco, Scuderi, Arena, Nucifora, Costa, Zappala, Poppi, Pennisi and Cantarino. I guess it just had to be a matter of time before they arrested me as well. Who will protect our wives and our children?"

"The police will protect them, Mr Cottone. I guess it's better to be safe than sorry," replied the young constable.

When Mr Davies arrived an hour later, he had more surprises in store for Carmelo.

"There's no knowing how long you will be away for; probably the duration of the war. I am going to have to appoint a manager to run your farm.'

"But why, Mr Davies? I have three workers on the farm. They looked after it well enough while I was in Italy. There's no need for a manager."

"As soon as the season starts, they won't be able to organize the harvesting, the pay sheets, the purchasing of fertilizers and chemicals and do the planting as well as look after the farm. We'll still keep them on, but as your creditors we have to look after our own interests as well as yours. We will be putting in a fulltime manager and he'll need somewhere to live. Now the best we can do is find a small house in town for your wife and your boy. They'll be safer there and it will be easier to live in town anyhow. They'll have to get out of the farmhouse by early May to give the manager a chance to get organized."

Carmelo remained silent; he would not have a say in the matter.

"I'm sorry, Carlo, but that's the way it's going to have to be."

"Tell me, Mr Davies, what rights do I really have as a Naturalized Citizen and a British Subject with a British Passport?"

"Unfortunately, not many at all because you're still an ethnic Italian and classified as a British Subject of Italian extraction. However, at the internment camp, you will be given the opportunity to lodge an appeal and present your case before the Advisory Committee. That is the only body who can recommend your release to the Minister. I'm sorry Carlo, there's nothing more I can do for you."

Later that afternoon when Sergeant Peters came to see him, Carmelo requested to make another phone call to his wife.

"I need to tell her that our creditors are going to appoint a manager for the farm and please, Sergeant Peters… just this once… it will be best if I speak to her in Italian as there is so much she needs to understand."

Carmelo was transported to Brisbane and interned in the Gaythorne Camp where he was read his rights under The Geneva Convention and The International Red Cross. At the very first opportunity he had, he wrote a letter to his wife.

12th March 1942.

My dearest Elena,
A week has passed and I find myself here in Brisbane at the Gaythorne Internment Camp. My first thoughts are for you and Saruzzo. How are you both?

This is the same camp where the Malaponte men are being held. However, I have not seen them as they are in a different compound. They have treated me well except that the food is inedible. They actually feed us sandwiches made with spaghetti from a tin. I guess they are trying to do the right thing by feeding us spaghetti but if only they knew how repulsive tinned spaghetti is to us— they would be embarrassed.

They have told us our rights under The Geneva Convention and The International Red Cross and it is comforting to know that they abide by international rules of war. We actually had to sign a document saying we understood our rights. We also had to sign a paper listing any property that we owned and its value. I have recorded the values below for your information.

- *129 acres*   *12 500 pounds*
- *House*   *260 pounds*
- *Furniture*   *305 pounds*
- *Barracks*   *350 pounds*
- *Men's quarters*   *150 pounds*
- *D2 Caterpillar Tractor* *900 pounds*
- *Farm Implements*   *500 pounds*

On the way down, we were jeered by the locals every time the train pulled into the station. It shows that there is a lot of anti-Italian sentiment in the community. You need to be aware of this, but I don't think you need to be afraid as there are too many good people with principles who will not stand for any form of impropriety.

I intend to lodge an appeal against the internment orders and present a case before the Advisory Committee as soon as possible after arriving at the camp.

I would like you to write a letter to my brother, Nino and explain our situation to him. Tell him and the family not to worry as we are in Australia and this is the land of the free. Tell him that I believe all will turn out well in the end. This is what happens in war and we pray for God's intervention in these unpleasant times. I will only communicate with you, my dear. Be brave.

May God bless you and Saruzzo and watch over you both. Nothing else matters.

Your loving husband,
Carmelo

Elena wrote immediately; a fortunate act as on the very day he received her letter, he was informed that he was being transferred to Southern Command; he would be interned in the Loveday Camp in South Australia.

15th March 1942

My dearest Carmelo,
Rest assured that we are both well and that I have no fear although that is not quite true. Yesterday, the jigger ran out of petrol near the double-barrelled bridge on the way back from town where I had bought four gallons of home kerosene for the fridge. It was almost dark so I had to lift the jigger off the line and leave it there. I walked towards home carrying Saruzzo on my hip and as we approached Saffiotti's barracks, I saw this black man walking towards us. It was dark and at that moment, I felt so frightened, I thought I would die. Then I thought of our dear son, Saruzzo in my arms and it gave me such courage as I have never known before. Well, just as the man was almost upon us, he called out.

'Don't be afraid, Signora Cottone. It's me Cantrato.'
It was such a relief. Poor Mr Cantrato, he is so black and he
must have sensed I was afraid.

Cedric went to collect the jigger next day. That will make me
remember to check the fuel before I go out. Anyhow, I mostly
ride everywhere on my bicycle with Saruzzo strapped onto the
carry-seat at the back.

The situation regarding Mr Davies is not so good. He has broken
his promise and now wants me gone by the end of March. That's
merely two weeks away. He has a house for me in town and
when I am packed, he will send a truck to collect me.

I thought about it carefully, Meluzzo and I know you want me
to go into town with Saruzzo because you are concerned about
us; but I am concerned about the farm and I don't trust Mr
Davies. My father, gone four years now, may his soul rest in
peace, always said 'possession is nine-tenths of the law' and I
presume this is so here in Australia too. So I've decided that as
long as I remain on the farm, I will remain in possession. That
way he wouldn't be able to swindle us out of the farm. What
if it were him who had you interned? You have worked too
hard for it all to be lost by the unfortunate circumstance you
find yourself in. So, I approached Cedric and Rasshim and his
father and they have agreed to give me one room in the workers'
quarters. They are good men and we will be safe with them.
Please do not feel bad about my actions as I have chosen to do
them of my own free will. You have always been so considerate
of my needs and I am here for you now."

Your loving wife,
Elena

The barbed-wire, the guard towers, the tents, the wet straw bedding and the horrific food awaiting Carmelo at Loveday Internment Camp 14A in Barmera, South Australia, would dissolve into insignificance each time Carmelo read Elena's letter. And every time it brought tears to his eyes. But they were tears of comfort; not tears borne of sadness.

In Loveday Camp 14A, Carmelo reunited with several other Italians from Babinda; the most notable being his great friend Giuseppe Barbagallo.

"Giuseppe, it gives me great joy to know that at least throughout these trying times, we are together. How are conditions here in the camp?"

"It's wartime, Cottone. What can you expect? The worst of it is not the treatment by our captors but the friction between the Fascists and the Anti-Fascists. Italians are always their own worst enemy. The Anarchists and the Communists are causing a lot of trouble. It's best to be non-partisan and stay away from any of the organized groups in here. Anyhow, how is everything back in Babinda? How was the Mississa the last time you saw her?"

"She's fine but she's missing you terribly. She runs the shop like a proper business now that you're away," joked Carmelo. "So are there any stories about people being released from here?"

"The only hope people can have of being released is to lodge an appeal and you have to be naturalized and a British Subject to lodge an appeal. As you know, I was never naturalized, so I'm in here for the duration of the war. As for those who have lodged an appeal, I know of no one who has been successful and I have been here for more than a year now."

"Well, I shall be lodging an appeal as soon as possible. Mr Davies, our main creditor on the farm has appointed a manager to run the farm. He will be living in the house and Elena and Rosario will have to go down to live in the workers' quarters. Elena has got it inside her head that Davies might try to take possession of the farm, so she refuses to leave even though he has offered to get her a house in town.

I have to get back to the farm as soon as possible and I need to be with my wife and son."

"She's got a lot of courage for a woman of her privileged background. You must be very proud of her Carmelo, just like I am of my Mississa. Now regarding appeals, there's a Mario Di Martino in here who is trying to organize a barrister to defend him and several others. Maybe, you can ask to join that group and he can put your case forward for you."

"Thanks Giuseppe, I'll make some enquiries."

Carmelo submitted his application to have his case heard. He did not ask for the services of the barrister who defended Mario Di Martino. When it was time for his case to be heard, he refused the prosecution's offer of help from the Greek interpreter who had been a liaison officer between the administration and the Italians who could not speak English.

The court case was set for the seventeenth of September. Rosario would turn three years old on that very day and Carmelo uttered his prayers to God as he entered the court room.

"Dear God, you are the way and the light. I ask for no special privileges from this court; just that Your will be done. Please help me to say what needs to be said to gain my freedom if You believe I am innocent of these charges and deserve to be free."

The Advisory Committee consisted of a triumvirate of three government personnel chaired by Major Millhouse, a barrister from the Government Intelligence Unit. The prosecuting officer was Lieutenant Cross.

Cross outlined the prosecution's case and presented every minute recorded detail of Carmelo's past in Italy and his history of almost eighteen years in Australia. Apart from the fact that he was of Italian extraction, there seemed to be little evidence or likelihood of his being classified as a threat to the security of Australia. So Cross hammered the fact that Carmelo had served in the Italian Army from 1920 to 1922, which tragically coincided with the rise to power of Benito Mussolini.

"What do you have to say to these charges of being a Mussolini sympathizer?" asked Major Millhouse.

"Mussolini was the reason I left Italy your Honour. Because I refused to bow to him in the streets of Agira during his tour of the island, I was relentlessly pursued by his secret police The Black Shirts and had to flee Italy so that my family would not be persecuted. That's what Mussolini did; he would imprison the women and children or kidnap family members and refuse to free them until the fugitive surrendered."

"So why did you join the army in the first place?"

"After World War One, it was difficult to get work and the economy was in tatters. There was revolution in the streets and in the factories with the unions, the Communists and the Anarchists all wanting to take control and the Nationalists and the Fascists trying to maintain their control. National Service in the army was compulsory at that time, so I was advised to join the army and at least be paid for my services and have money to help support my family. My father died in 1919. My three brothers had all fought in World War One on the side of the Allies and my brother Giuseppe was killed in the Battle of Isonzo on the Italian Front in 1915."

Lieutenant Cross started prodding trying to find a chink in his armour.

"But you do love Italy, don't you, Mr Cottone? After all it is the country of your birth."

"If I loved Italy, I wouldn't have come to Australia. Yes I loved Italy once but that was before Mussolini came to power. I detest the Italy that stands with Mussolini."

"So if Mussolini was deposed, you could easily find it in your heart to love Italy again. Would it be correct to assume that?"

"No, I made my choice. I brought my wife back to Australia because Australia is my home. I renounced my Italian citizenship under oath. God is my witness."

"But you renounced your Italian citizenship. What would stop you renouncing your Australian citizenship? You would simply take another oath and God would still be your witness. Can you see anything wrong with that logic?"

"Two things: this is the country which extended its hand to me when my own country wished me dead. This is the country which offers my son, who was born in Australia and is three years old today, the chance to be truly free. I could never waiver my allegiance from the country that gave me a second chance at life. I would have to be a vile person to do that. I have no malice in me. When I give my word, I remain true to it. Secondly, why would I bring my son who has a chance to be truly free in Australia to Italy, which never has and never will be free? Italy has soiled its own nest and now the generations that follow must sleep in it."

"Your two brothers... you have two brothers, Angelino and Antonio. Do you love them?"

"Of course I do. They are my flesh and blood."

"Why didn't Angelino come to Australia?"

"Angelino remained in Italy to care for the family. Apart from both our parents having been deceased, our eldest sister is a cripple. As head of the family, it was expected of him that he should stay behind."

"Why did Antonio go back to Italy? Why did he not remain loyal to Australia as you claim to be?"

"Antonio did not run away from Italy, he ran away from hunger. Before he left he promised my father and the family that within eight years, he would return to Italy to be with the family. At the age of thirty-six despite a very bright future in Australia, he sold everything and returned to Italy as he promised he would. Antonio would never break a promise made to his father and his family."

At this point, Major Millhouse stood and addressed Lieutenant Cross.

"Lieutenant, could I please ask Mr Cottone a couple of questions?"

Lieutenant Cross sat and gestured to Major Millhouse.

"Mr Cottone, tell me, what do you want more than anything else in this world?"

"I want to be allowed to go home to my wife and my little child so that I can be the husband and father that God expects me to be."

"I have no doubt that you are a God-fearing person and that you love your brothers. I also believe you are a man of your word. Am I correct?"

Carmelo thought for a few moments. "I do not fear God. I love God and yes, I love my brothers. And yes, I am a man of my word."

"Very well Mr Cottone, answer this single question carefully and honestly. From your answer, we will decide whether or not you should be allowed to go home to your wife and your young son." He gave Carmelo time to compose himself.

"Imagine yourself in this situation: Australia has been invaded by Italy and the Axis powers. You have sworn allegiance to Australia and as you say, God is your witness. Australia calls upon you to defend your country. Carmelo, Australia really needs you now. You have your double-barrelled shotgun you use for shooting wild ducks and wild pigs. You agree to join your fellow Australians and fight the enemy. The enemy attacks and from their flag you see they are Italian. You raise your gun to shoot and in your sights you see your two beloved brothers, Angelino and Antonio. What would you do? Would you shoot them to save your country? We want a simple 'yes' or 'no' answer."

Carmelo's eyes moistened as he pondered the question.

"Think about it carefully. Take your time and answer honestly."

Finally Carmelo spoke, "I cannot answer it with a 'yes' or 'no'. I would appreciate, if instead, I could ask Your Honour a question and let your answer to my question be my answer also."

Lieutenant Cross leapt from his chair.

"Who do you think you are, Mr Cottone that you think you can play games with this court?"

"I am a nobody, a prisoner of war behind a barbed-wire fence, guarded by soldiers in towers with machine-guns. Why would a man with no voice want to play games with this court? No, I give my voice, my proxy, to His Honour to answer on my behalf through my question to him; a simple 'yes' or 'no' answer."

"Answer the question Mr Cottone or your appeal will be dismissed and you will remain in this camp for the duration of the war," warned Lieutenant Cross.

"I would rather be machine-gunned by your guards and let God be my judge. If men must judge me now and I hope that you can, having afforded me the privilege of this appeal, then ask not from a man who has no voice. Take instead my answer from His Honour when he says 'yes' or 'no' to my question."

"Very well Mr Cottone, you have been warned," said the Lieutenant about to orchestrate his ultimatum.

"No wait, Lieutenant Cross," interjected Mr Millhouse, "allow Mr Cottone his question. After all, we did offer him the privilege of this appeal as he said and we should see it through. I am happy to be his proxy if he truly feels he has no voice. Ask your question, Mr Cottone."

"Thank you, Your Honour. Now I know, whatever the outcome I have been granted justice and I thank the court. Your Honour, imagine yourself in this situation. Australia is in the grip of civil war between the east and the west. You have sworn allegiance to the east because you are from the east and your property, your wife and your young son are in the east. The east calls upon you to defend what you value with your life. The west attacks and you know that all your wife and your little child have to protect them is you. You have your double-barrelled shotgun that you use for shooting wild ducks and wild pigs. You raise your gun to shoot and in your sights you see your two own brothers bearing down on you with loaded guns and fixed bayonets. What would you do? Would you shoot them to save your wife and child? Your Honour, as men who are all equal in the sight of God, there can be but one answer to that question. Your answer is my answer."

Major Millhouse returned to the bench as one of the triumvirate of judges to discuss Carmelo's fate. After substantial head shaking and nodding the panel of judges came to a decision and Major Millhouse stood to deliver the decision of the court.

"In this appeal against Mr Carmelo Cottone of Happy Valley,

Babinda being classified as an 'enemy alien' it is the unanimous opinion of this court that the appeal should be upheld and that Mr Cottone is to be released immediately. Could you please see to it, Lieutenant?"

The Lieutenant was shocked at the decision. He struggled to regain his composure. "It will take some time for the paperwork to go through Your Honour. Then there is the recommendation to the Minister."

"Oh poppycock, that can all be done as a matter of course. I want Mr Cottone to be put on the first available train back to his wife and child. He's already missed his son's birthday. To put him on a train tomorrow would be the least we could do. Now see to it, will you?"

It was there in that courtroom that I came to understand what Carmelo meant when he told Elena that for every bad person who had done him wrong, in Australia, there had always been a better person to set it right again.

Chapter 27

Debt and devastation

Carmelo was one of the last of the Italians to be interned and one of the first to be released. Elena arranged a special party to celebrate Carmelo's return and to thank Cedric, Rasshim and Bagh Singh for their support whilst Carmelo was away.

"We think you have lost your little son to us Mr Cottone," said Bagh. He now refuses to eat his dinner because we feed him fresh 'johnny cakes' every afternoon. Isn't that right, Rosario?" Rosario simply smiled and twisted his body on one leg.

"You were so fortunate to have been released," said Cedric.

"I was fortunate that the man from Military Intelligence was a good man, Cedric. He listened to what I had to say and even told me privately that I should never have been interned in the first place."

"And we think your wife is a special woman, Mr Cottone," said Rasshim. "She's a fighter just like you. We know things about her that you will never guess."

"Like what, Rasshim?"

"Like we think she should go into training as a runner in the 1944 Olympic Games if there is one. Did you know she could run?"

"Hardly," said Carmelo, "look at those feet, they're so tiny. No, I can't accept that she's a runner at all."

"Go on, Mrs Cottone. Tell him about the incident with the jigger. We were in the field working with our hoes and we saw it all happen."

"Saw what happen? What incident with the jigger, Elena?'

"Tell him in Italian, Mrs Cottone."

"It was every mother's nightmare, Meluzzo. I had strapped Saruzzo on the jigger so that he could not fall off while I pushed it to start it. I was pushing the jigger with the decompression lever out and just as I released it and the motor started, I tripped on one of the sleepers of the railway line. The jigger kept accelerating because it was on full throttle and I was still on the ground when I realized that the barbed-wire gate across the railway line near the fertilizer shed was closed.

Meluzzo, it could have decapitated our son. I got back up on my feet and ran the whole six hundred metres after the jigger, which kept going faster and faster. When I saw the barbed-wire only about one hundred metres away, I suddenly felt as though I was running twice as fast and with fifty metres still to go, I leaped onto the jigger, pushed back the throttle, pulled the decompression lever and pulled as hard as I could on the brake lever. Thank God, the jigger stopped with only twenty metres to spare. I was utterly winded and I fell to the ground crying until Cedric and Rasshim came running down from the paddock to see if I was hurt."

"Yes, we saw it all Mr Cottone. She almost flew in that last fifty metres," said Cedric in Italian.

"Oh my God!" was all Carmelo could mutter.

He had only been away from his farm six months and in that short time, he returned to a farm that was mired in debt and plagued by cane grubs. Under the manager appointed by Davies, the farm output had been reduced to only five hundred tons; in stark contrast to the two thousand three hundred and fifty tons under Carmelo's control.

"No amount of hard work can combat the grubs, Carlo. Effectively, the best we can do is put the farm on a care and maintenance basis until we find out if the gammaxene can keep the grubs under control," suggested Mr Davies.

"Well, why haven't you put gammaxene on this year's crop, Mr Davies?"

"There is not enough gammaxene being produced. At this stage, it is only being rationed out and to be honest with you, Carlo, none has been apportioned to any farmer of foreign extraction. That's the way it is at the moment, I'm sorry."

"So, what am I supposed to do, pack up and leave? What do you mean by putting the farm on a care and maintenance basis?"

"You're an excellent farmer and your creditors don't want to lose out on their investment. We would like you to stay on and run your farm because you are the best man for the job. However, we want to be in control of the finances. We will pay you four pounds ten shillings per week and the rest of the farm income must go to the creditors. The only other option is to put the farm into receivership. We don't want to have to do that to you. You have a young family and a home here on the farm."

"So, when will control of the farm income revert to me?"

"Only when your debt is repaid under the present arrangement or you are able to organize alternative finance."

Carlo was devastated by that news. He had no choice but to accept their offer.

In the meantime, Carmelo had some other bad news to contend with. He had received notice that his crawler Caterpillar D2 tractor was to be impounded by the Government for the war effort. If he didn't have the D2 to plough his fields for next year's plant, it would mean he would have to go back to using horses and he would have to modify the plough in order to attach it to the horses' harnesses.

The Cairns Post brought daily news on the Japanese forces in the Pacific. By October 1942, the Japanese had conducted forty-six bombing raids on Darwin, which had originally been devastated by Japan's Pearl Harbour veterans on 19th February 1942. Darwin was a major port for the navy, a home base for the army and an air force base for long range bombers. General Iven Mackay's view was that the northern coastline of Australia was indefensible with existing troop numbers. The Minister for Labour and National Service, Mr Eddie Ward alleged that the Liberals, under Robert Menzies had a plan for a Brisbane Line to abandon, in the event of an enemy attack, the entire northern part of Australia. There were American Servicemen and women in the streets and in bases all over the north. According to the newspaper, air-raid shelters were being built at railway stations from

Brisbane to Cairns for the protection of the travelling public.

"Saw the air-raid shelter myself in Cairns," the local ambulance bearer Jack Kapor told Carlo while he was having a piece of grit removed from his eye. "The shelters are forty-two foot by twelve foot wide and the walls are twelve inches thick. There's no doubt the Japanese are coming, Carlo. It's just a matter of time."

Kapor's statement set Carmelo thinking about building a shelter on the farm. Part of the dining room had been partitioned off for an office and Carmelo thought it an ideal place underneath that section as it was above ground and only about one and a half metres of soil would need to be excavated. Together with Cedric, Rasshim and Bagh, Carmelo built a ten foot by ten foot air-raid shelter with twelve inch thick walls in accordance with the specifications Kapor had given him.

As far as I could gauge, there was no great fear of the north being abandoned to the Japanese and *The Cairns Post* played its part in allaying any fears the locals may have had. Carmelo relayed any relevant information he read on the matter to Elena.

"The paper says that the 503rd Parachute Infantry Regiment arrived from the United States of America just a few days ago on the 2nd of December and has been transferred to a camp at Gordonvale; 'Further strengthening the commitment the Allies have given to defending every inch of our soil'," Carlo quoted. "So much for abandoning the north to the Japanese, especially now that we have a US Air Force base close by as well."

The concentration of US and Australian troops continued in the north.

"You must tell me if you have any concerns about being so isolated from the town, Elena. We can always make some arrangements for you and Saruzzo to stay in town."

"It's probably safer here, Meluzzo. Anyhow, I'm not leaving our air-raid shelter. We could hide in there. The trapdoor is covered by a mat and table. Nobody is going to be looking for us there."

It was early February before the cane crop recovered from the retarding effect of the grubs. Carmelo was passing the scarifier for the last time in the paddock near the Buka, which meant "hole" in Italian. It was in fact the remnants of a volcanic crater. Cedric and the Hindus hoed the weeds at the ends of each row. It was the paddock furthest from the house and enveloped by dense tropical rainforest. Elena was hanging out clothes when she heard the roar of a solitary plane flying overhead. As it passed, it left behind white mushroom-like shapes that floated carefully towards the earth. She was sure it must be the Japanese. Elena panicked. First she ran to Rosario, then with him in her arms she ran into the bedroom and placed him in the cot. She had to tell Carmelo. At the front of the house, when Elena was pregnant with Rosario, Carmelo had erected a long bamboo pole so that in the event of an emergency, she could hoist a bed sheet up the pole and Carmelo would see it from any position on the farm.

Carmelo reached the end of the row and glanced towards the house in the distance. To his surprise he recognized the bed sheet and he knew there was something wrong and that it must have been urgent.

"Rasshim, something is wrong down at the house. See that bed sheet? When I get down to the farmhouse, I'll lower the flag if I want you to return. Otherwise, I'll be back as soon as I can."

Carmelo took the shortcut through the fields and he was at the house in twenty minutes. Elena came running towards him with Rosario in her arms.

"The Japanese... I'm worried the Japanese have attacked. Many soldiers jumped out of a plane into the mountains over there." She pointed in the direction of Mt Bellenden Ker.

"Planes you say? How many?"

"Only one."

"And how many soldiers?"

"I don't know."

"Estimate... ten... twenty?"

"About twenty. I've put food, water, some blankets and pillows and a lantern in the air-raid shelter. What about the others?"

"They'll be safer up there. I told them not to come down until I lower the flag."

It was about 11:30 in the morning and Elena had made a magnificent pot of pasta sauce ready for bottling. Carmelo immediately phoned the Babinda exchange and told them about the sighting.

"I'll pass the information on to Sergeant Peters. Suspect Japanese paratroopers landed in the mountains behind Cottone's place at Happy Valley around 11:00 A.M... is that correct?"

"Yes, hurry please and phone me back when you know something."

After about twenty minutes, the phone rang.

"Hello, Cottone here. Who's speaking? Ah... Sergeant Peters. You got my message. No, nobody has come out of the mountains yet... Only my wife and I and my son Rosario... The three workers are up in the paddock. You are trying to get in contact with the Defence Forces? Okay, you want us to go into the air-raid shelter. You think you will be here in about half an hour? Okay Sergeant. Yes, I have a double-barrelled shotgun. Yes, I'll bring it down into the shelter with me." He smashed the phone back onto its hook.

"He said to wait in the shelter."

They descended into the shelter and replaced the rug under the table and waited.

After a short while, they heard noises outside and people talking. Carmelo looked at his pocket watch. It was 12:15A.M. The police wouldn't be there for another quarter of an hour. Soon the sound of heavy vehicles could be heard on the road towards the house. There was quiet as the vehicles came to a halt just outside the shelter. This was followed by chatter and a series of commands. Then there was quiet again. Footsteps walked the length and breadth of the house and finally they could hear the heavy boots on the floor above them. Their hearts were racing and Elena held her hand over Rosario's mouth.

"You can come out now, Mr and Mrs Cottone. It's Sergeant Peters here."

"It's safe, Elena. Thank God."

The sergeant tapped on the trapdoor as Carmelo raised it upwards and to one side.

"It's okay, Carlo. They're American paratroopers on a training exercise. Come on up and meet the Allies."

Sergeant Peters looked inside the shelter and saw the gun.

"Reckon you could take on a whole battalion with that blunderbuss. Here let me introduce you to Sergeant Robert Eugene Hofer from Indiana and lately of the United States 503rd PRCT Parachute Infantry Regiment. Sergeant Hofer, this is Carlo Cottone, Mrs Cottone and their son, Ross."

"Pleased to meet you folks. Hope we didn't give you a fright." He leaned over to look inside the shelter and then towards the kitchen. "Mmmmm... something smells good in the kitchen. Reminds me of home."

"Sergeant Hofer is conducting jump-master training with a single twenty member squad. That's why there was only one plane."

"That jungle out there is as close as it gets to the conditions in New Guinea with its high mountains, hot temperatures and rugged terrain." Hofer reached down in his socks and exposed a huge blood-filled leech. Carefully he used his army knife to remove it from his skin. "Right down to the leeches," he added.

"Our personnel carriers have arrived but we are still waiting for Major Wilkes to begin a debriefing session. Thought the men might like to have a swim in the creek so if you don't mind, we'll be around for a little while. Love the white sheet on the bamboo pole."

"That was my signal for Carmelo to come home."

"You've trained him well Mrs Cottone."

"Sergeant Hofer," she continued, "while your men are having their swim, how about I put on a huge saucepan of pasta and you can sample my home cooking? Your men must be starving," said Elena.

"Are you serious? There are twenty-one special troops and eight transport personnel."

"There's no trouble at all, Sergeant Hofer. If I can feed five, I can feed thirty. It's all the same when you're eating pasta and there's plenty of sauce prepared. And you too, Sergeant Peters, is anyone with you?"

"Just Constable Harris."

"Well, Constable Harris too."

"Thanks very much, that'd be nice," said Hofer.

"Likewise," said Sergeant Peters.

The men headed off to the creek and Elena filled the clothes copper with water— it held ten gallons. She added a quarter of a pound of salt and stoked the fire with some dry Johnstone River hardwood. Carmelo lowered the bed sheet from the top of the bamboo pole. He wanted to be able to share this event with his workmates. Then he placed twelve bottles of North Queensland Lager in the fridge and prepared the table. There were two loaves of bread, a round of homemade cheese, black and green olives and anchovies. He sauntered to the garden, picking several lettuce, five cucumbers and some tomatoes, which were soon made into a huge salad with finely chopped onion and plenty of olive oil and vinegar. Finally it was time to put the homemade sauce on the wood stove to heat.

"The only problem is we don't have enough plates and cutlery," said Elena trying to consider a solution.

"No need," said Carmelo, "Soldiers always come prepared. They'll have their own cans, cups and cutlery. We only need some for the two policemen and maybe, the drivers."

When she saw the men approaching the creek bank, she placed eight kilos of No 29 spaghetti into the copper.

"Okay, you guys, listen up! Now the lovely lady in there has gone to a lot of trouble to make you a nice homemade meal. So watch your manners," snarled Sergeant Hofer. "All I want to hear outta you guys is 'yes please ma'am and thank you ma'am'. Now take out your canteens and cutlery and line up near the door."

Elena filled their plates with spaghetti and topped each one up with her special sauce.

"When you've finished, there's more. Come back as many times as you like and take what you want from the table."

Carmelo stood at the door and filled their mugs with NQ Lager as they abandoned the house to eat in the yard, which was filled with conversation of "Sure beats tinned spaghetti," or "I thought spaghetti only came in tins," or "What brand of tin spaghetti was that?"

And there were certainly plenty of 'thank you ma'ams' from all and sundry.

By the time Major Wilkes arrived, they appeared as though they were ready for an afternoon nap. Sergeant Hofer's call soon put an end to any of those dreams.

"Okay you great bunch of neanderthal street-loungers and bums... On your feet, the party's over! Have you forgotten there's a war on out there that we are supposed to be trying to win? You've got five minutes to hit your straps and look like soldiers again." Hofer turned to face his Corporal. "Carry on, Corporal."

"Yes Sir!" The corporal saluted. He turned and shouted his orders at the assembled men.

"Attention. Full battle dress in three minutes and ready to afford Major Wilkes the respect he deserves. On the spot... Hup... Hup... Hup two three. Quick march!"

Chapter 28

The awakening

The American presence in the Far North was a resounding wake-up call to the Anglo-Australian community. Here suddenly, was a whole nation of people with a similar ethnic background yet a totally different perspective on life. Americans were fun, they had loads of money and they spent it. They were suave and the Australian women went mad over them. These guys danced, they drove fast cars and did silly things like race draught horses up the main street. Best of all, they knew how to treat women. They made them feel special and they respected them.

Carmelo was outside *Joe Barbagallo's Store* when he saw two Americans pay one lucky farmer one pound each, just to borrow his two horses and race them down the main street while the rest of their *buddies* laid bets.

"Who ever heard of riding draught horses in a race? These Yanks have got shit for brains and too much dough for their own good," said Joe Garden, a mill worker, to his mate.

"Yeah, they all think they're cowboys. Bet they couldn't rope a horse if their life depended on it. They think they can just take our women."

"Yeah. Go home Yanks!" Joe cupped his mouth with both hands and yelled as the two horsemen came lumbering past.

"Who's going to save your skinny little arses if we all go home?" asked a tall, burly American soldier as he collected bets after the race. "The Brits didn't want to know you. They just drew a line through Brisbane and said, *you're on your own now mate.* So you went on bended knee to ask Uncle Sam for help."

"We didn't do nothing," said Joe's mate.

"Precisely," said the soldier as two Australian girls went up and threw their arms around him. He dealt them each a couple of ten shilling notes.

"Leave our women alone, Yank!" said Joe.

"Wooor…I'm really scared. Please don't hit me Matilda," teased the soldier holding his hands up in mock awe. The girls giggled and poked their tongue at Joe.

Joe thrust a foot forward as if he was about to leap on him but his mate was quick to step between them and avoid a confrontation.

"Come on Joe. You might hurt him. He can have the girls. They're not worth fighting for."

Australians also tried to treat the Negros with the disdain that they treated Aborigines which was a big mistake and meant that the Military Police were forever breaking up fights in bars and at dance halls.

The Americans were quick to upgrade the infrastructure as well. They built a cement road between Gordonvale and Cairns and built quality bridges over causeways. A steel demountable girder bridge was also built across one of the small creeks near Carmelo's farm so that heavy army vehicles could have easy access when they conducted army exercises in the rugged mountains behind his farm.

"Another plane went down on the range today," Rasshim informed Carmelo as he fed huge handfuls of cane-tops through the chop-chop machine for the horses.

"That means they've lost two planes there now," said Carmelo. "According to the papers, they are preparing for a landing in New Guinea to intercept the Japanese."

On the 22nd May 1943, Carmelo and Elena were listening to the 6:00 P.M. ABC news on the radio.

General Douglas MacArthur arrived in Cairns yesterday and went immediately to Gordonvale to witness a jump-master training exercise involving five C47 planes and one hundred paratroopers. Sadly, one paratrooper was badly injured and he died on his way to hospital. At a cocktail reception last night General MacArthur awarded the dead soldier a medal posthumously. He pronounced the soldiers of the 503rd Parachute Infantry Regiment ready for battle and congratulated Major Wilkes on a tremendous job well done.

"That's the same Regiment that Sergeant Hofer belonged to and Major Wilkes is the man who came here to debrief them after the jump," said Elena as she turned the volume up a little.

"It certainly is a small world," Carmelo acknowledged with a slight nodding of his head.

The elite 503rd Parachute Infantry Regiment is expected to be deployed in New Guinea where the Japanese have been advancing south towards Port Moresby.

"I will pray that God will watch over Sergeant Hofer and those poor men who had lunch here with us. It is so sad to think those young men are all risking their lives to save us and they are not even Australian."

A regiment of Australian soldiers have been training alongside the Americans in preparation for an assault.

"I remember how our family prayed for our three brothers every night when they fought in the Battles of Isonzo on the Italian Front in World War 1. Poor Giuseppe never returned from the Front and our dear father died of a broken heart when he heard the news."

In a separate incident, an Australian ship carrying a cargo of impounded machinery on its way to New Guinea to contribute to the war effort, was sunk by a Japanese submarine late this afternoon. The Japanese peril is on our doorstep, said General MacArthur, and repeated Winston Churchill's words that we would fight them on the land and on the sea and in the air and we would defeat them.

"So much for my beautiful Caterpillar D2," said Carmelo. "Gone to the bottom of the sea."

Things in Europe began to unfold quickly and each evening they both listened intently to the news for any inkling that the war might soon come to an end. With Italy, the first was on 25th July 1943 when the spectre of Mussolini began to fade with his arrest. The second was on the 8th September when the Allies accepted Italy's unconditional surrender and the third was on the 6th October when Italy actually declared war on Germany.

Mussolini put himself back into the equation when he was freed by a German Commando and regrouped his loyal followers under the umbrella of the German Commanders.

With Germany, they both knew that the end was near when they heard about the bombing of Dresden on 13th and 14th of February 1945. Thirty-five thousand civilians were killed and hundreds of thousands were injured. On 20th April, US President Roosevelt died and Harry S Truman was elected President. Before anybody had time to worry about the ramifications of that leadership change, the news was out that on the 28th April, Benito Mussolini, his mistress, Clara Petracci and thirteen Fascist Leaders were captured and shot by partisans. Two days later, Adolf Hitler and his wife Eva Braunn committed suicide. On the 7th May 1945, their little three valve *Mendelssohn Shortwave Music Masters Radio* was tuned to 4CA Cairns when it blurted out the news:

> *We interrupt this programme to bring you the news that Germany has surrendered unconditionally to the Allied Forces.*

Elena heard it first and ran down to the Caterpillar shed and out the back where Carmelo was milking the cow.

"Germany has surrendered! Germany has surrendered. The war in Europe is over!" she screamed over and over again. Rasshim and Bagh and Cedric came running out of their quarters and as soon as the news sank in, the five of them just kept hugging each other.

The bombing of Hiroshima on 6th August 1945 and Nagasaki

three days later brought Japan to its knees and an end to the war in the Pacific with the official surrender signed on the USS Missouri on 15th August 1945.

The world was at peace at last but everyone knew that the road to recovery would be long and hard for Europe, Asia, America and Australia and right down to their own back yard on the family farm at Happy Valley. After all, Elena and Carmelo had another mouth to feed. Their second son Abele Liborio was born on 31st July 1945 and was just over two weeks old.

Chapter 29

Off to school

Elena felt as if she were walking beside herself with worry at the thought of Rosario travelling over five kilometres to school by horse on his own.

"Elena, the horse is twenty years old. She is so old; the fastest she can go is a walking pace. Don't worry, Rosario will be fine. Talk to the horse and pat her Rosario. 'Good girl, Betty'. Come on, you say it."

Rosario patted the horse.

"Good girl, Betty. Good girl, Betty. Good girl, Betty," he repeated as he patted her.

Carmelo had a beautiful white saddle horse called Dolly. She was young and frisky and nobody rode Dolly but Carmelo.

"I will be riding into town with him on Dolly every day this week, so by the time he has to go on his own, he'll be an expert horseman, won't you Rosario?"

"Si Papa."

"Yes Papa. You must speak in English at school, otherwise nobody will understand you."

"Yes Papa," he repeated.

They embarked upon their journey, father and son, up the road and beside the bamboo Carmelo had planted to stop the creek eroding the bank away. Elena was waving a white nappy and each time Rosario turned she was frozen in place, but for the waving.

They reached the barbed-wire gate across the railway line near the fertilizer shed and the moment they turned down to where Carmelo had broken his leg, she was invisible. The horses reached the shallow causeway, which was strewn with smooth fist-sized river rocks. Their hooves would wobble as they secured a footing but it wasn't a problem for them. In fact they seemed to enjoy the cool water.

"Hold the reigns tightly, Rosario otherwise Betty will want to drink and as she puts her head down, you will slide down her neck and into the water."

When they reached the other side, Carmelo pulled gently on the reigns. "Whoa Dolly… whoa. You do the same with Betty. Hold the reigns firmly and say 'Whoa Betty… whoa'."

Rosario tugged firmly on the reigns and half-whispered as his father had ordered. The horse stopped.

"Now squeeze your legs into the saddle so you don't fall off and let the reigns go loose. You'll see, she will drop her head and have a drink."

He squeezed his legs into the saddle, loosened the reigns and immediately Betty dropped her head for a drink. She had three long slurps as did Dolly and that was enough for them.

"Okay, pull the reigns again and give her a nudge in the ribs. 'Come on Betty… giddy up'. You say it. That's all there is to it," Carmelo told him. "Betty will follow the road until you tell her to stop."

They passed Saffiotti's barracks and crossed the double-barrelled bridge. The horses clip-clopped over the bridges and the sound insinuated that they were travelling faster. "Now, when people ask you your name, you should say Ross. That's the English word for Rosario. So, at school you are Ross and at home you are Rosario or Saro or Saruzzo."

Rosario loved Saruzzo because it was his pet name and he beamed with satisfaction each time his father uttered it. In fact, he had hardly used the word since Abele was born and he was increasingly worried his father didn't love him as much anymore.

Carmelo hoped he had been sensible in sending Rosario to the state school. Not one other Italian parent had taken their children through the gates of the state school; preferring the Catholic Convent School instead. His good friend and real estate agent Tom Carr had warned him.

"I don't think it's a good idea, Carlo. He'll be the only Italian and the only Catholic at the school. What with the war and all, it's probably not a good idea. His English is almost nil and he has no friends because your neighbours don't have any young children. At the Catholic school, there'll be many children in the same situation as him and he would find it much easier there."

"But Rosario is an Australian, Tom. It's no good hiding him away in a convent with the nuns. At home he can have plenty of practice at being Italian but at school, he has to practise being an Australian," Carmelo insisted.

"Well, don't say I didn't warn you. I suppose you can take him out if it doesn't work."

They reached Spitaro's steep hill.

"You'll have to squeeze your legs into the saddle and keep the reigns really tight, otherwise the horse will want to go faster down the hill to take the weight off its knees."

Rosario did as instructed. They passed through Sandy Creek and Stony Creek and up the hill past Gee Kee's and the hospital and finally to Mrs Ling's corner store.

Carmelo had arranged with Mrs Ling, to leave the horse in her backyard during the day. There was a huge mango tree there for shade and Carmelo had provided half a forty-four gallon drum for water during the day.

"You will need to help him off the horse when he gets here please, Mrs Ling— for a while at least. And you will need to put him on the horse in the afternoon to come home… again, only until he works out a way to get on by himself. I'll leave my horse here and walk him to school for this week. I'll talk to you when I return."

The school was about four hundred metres from the corner store and Rosario was pale and trembling by the time he arrived. Carmelo pretended to be oblivious and joked about how much fun he would have at school. They went up to the office where Carmelo waited to meet Mr Kaski, the principal.

"Mr Cottone… so this is young Ross here, is it?"

"Yes Mr Kaski."

"Does he speak any English?"

"Very little, but he understands. He's very shy. Shake hands with Mr Kaski and say 'hello'."

After much coaxing from his father, Rosario extended a limp hand but remained mute with eyes fixed on the ground.

Fortuitously Mrs Savage happened to be walking by.

"Excuse me, Mrs Savage, could you take Ross Cottone down to Mr Rouge in Prep One, please?"

"Yes Mr Kaski." Mrs Savage was a formidable woman who wore suffocating corsets and appeared efficient and in control. Rosario hopelessly allowed her to drag him along as he frettingly looked back at his father hoping this nightmare would soon be over.

It was then that I made the momentous decision to abandon Carmelo for the day and attach myself to Rosario. The poor boy was so pathetic; I felt it would offer me comfort if nothing else.

When he and Mrs Savage reached the door, every eye in the class burned into him as soon as they realised he was Italian. Even Mr Rouge failed to remain composed.

"What's he doing here? Why aren't you over at the convent? You don't belong here... all Dagos go to the convent school over the road." The class erupted with laughter.

"That'll be enough of that talk Mr Rouge. The war's over and it's a fresh start for everyone. This is Ross Cottone." This met with murmurs.

"Cottone the pony... bony Cottone... Cottone macaroni," and the class roared again.

True to her name, she glared as the class froze in mid-laughter. "We'll have none of that, do you hear?"

"Yes Mrs Savage," the class responded in unison as Ross's ardent defender hurried off.

"You can sit with Mick... no?... or Johnny... no? What about you, Peter? No? Looks like nobody wants to sit with you and I can't say I blame them. Mick, you sit with Johnny and you sit on your own, Cottone."

Rosario obviously didn't understand and even after Mick

begrudgingly moved next to Johnny, he stood where he was. Rouge finally grabbed him by the arm and shoved him behind the empty desk.

"You'd think you could learn English before coming to this school. Sit there you little scumbag!"

Rosario simply froze in his seat; he didn't even remove his school bag from his shoulders. As soon as Rouge's back was turned the crowd launched bits of paper at him and pulled faces.

When the bell pealed for little lunch Rosario remained seated.

"You can't stay in here, Cottone. Go on... go on... go outside," Rouge said to him as he lifted him by the arm and ushered him out. "Tell your father tonight you don't belong here. Tell him to put you with all your *compadres* over the road. Go on, go downstairs with the others."

Rosario must have registered the body language because he did stumble downstairs. All the other students were eating sandwiches as he opened his bag and took out his lunch tin. His mother had prepared him some salami sandwiches; his favourite.

"Ouuuuuuuuu... yuk...salami sandwiches... ouuuuuuu... smelly yuk! He's got salami sandwiches!" two girls sang as they danced around him laughing.

"What else you got, Cottone macaroni?" said a porky child with chubby fingers as he rummaged around in his lunch box, "Ouuuuu... smelly cheese sandwiches. Yuk... you stink." He knocked the lunch box from little Rosario's hand and its contents splattered to the cement floor. Several children drew near to stamp on them and kick them around. Rosario remained still, shaking and wondering what was happening to him.

The bell tolled again and everyone milled towards class; with no hand to guide him Rosario followed. On his desk, he found a new school slate with a neat wooden frame bordering it and a new slate pencil on the end of a tin pencil holder. Beside the slate were three books.

"They're yours to keep, Cottone. Make sure you look after them or you'll have to pay for them if they are lost or damaged," warned Mr

Rouge. Rosario stared but was too afraid to lift the pencil, even though he was obviously dying to do so. At that moment, another teacher entered the room and the students stood.

"Good morning students. Thank you. You may sit down." They sat in chorus and Rosario did the same again.

The teacher spoke to Mr Rouge who disappeared soon after.

"Mr Rouge will be back after lunch," he informed the class. I'll be looking after you until then." He had a kind face.

"You must be Ross, I'm Mr O'Rourke," he said and offered his hand. Rosario timidly took it and Mr O'Rourke shook it firmly. "Now class, take out your copybook." He leaned over and took the copybook from Rosario's pile and opened it for him. Rosario could smell the strong smell of tobacco as Mr O'Rourke stood close to him. It reminded him of his father and he felt safe. "Now, I'd like you to copy the sentences on page three onto your slates in your neatest handwriting." He then dragged the teacher's chair and sat beside Rosario. He put the pencil into his right hand and positioned the slate so that it was just right for him. Then he placed his hand over the little boy's hand and started shaping the first few letters.

"There you are. Easy isn't it? Now you try." Rosario looked at this kind stranger sheepishly and then at the students beside him and then at his slate. "Go on, give it a try," the teacher urged.

Rosario copied the first few letters and looked at O'Rourke for approval.

"Good boy, Ross. That is so neat," he said as a couple of other students craned their necks to inspect his work. "What are you kids gawking at? Go on, get on with your work!" he ordered as they snapped back on task. He gave Rosario a gentle smile, "Well done Ross... keep up the good work."

The bell rang. "Okay, pack up your things and put your hands behind your backs," ordered Mr O'Rourke. "Stand up and go out in single file starting from Mary in the front row." They all acted accordingly with Rosario following suit. Outside, all the other students were opening their lunch boxes and Rosario could only look on; there was no food remaining in his lunch tin. One boy came to him. He was tall and very thin.

"Hello Ross, I'm Eddie Grant." He revealed a sandwich and offered it to Rosario. "Would you like one of my sandwiches? It's got vegemite on it."

Rosario took the sandwich but lacked the courage to eat it so he simply held it and stared at Eddie.

"That boy who threw your sandwiches on the ground is Norm Williams. He's a big bully. He's the best fighter in our class."

At that point, Norm strolled over and shoved Eddie out of the way.

"What are you doing feeding the enemy? It's his mob who killed lots of Australians during the war. The Ities are our enemies." He pushed Rosario backwards, "Aren't you? Aren't you?" he persisted. All the other boys began to gather as Rosario stumbled, his foot dropped into the shallow waste water drain at the edge of the cement floor and he went sprawling onto the ground, landing on his back. As he raised his eyes upwards, he saw Mr Rouge on the verandah, leaning over to see what the commotion was.

"Come on boys... haystack!" and Norm threw himself onto Rosario. The others soon followed yelling "Haystack... haystack!" and piled on top of the two boys.

Rosario could hear Rouge calling from the verandah, "Good on you boys! Get into him. Get him around the neck... make him squeal." Rosario hoped Rouge was telling them to stop. Eventually, someone did come to his rescue.

"You boys break it up!" he heard a female teacher shouting. She started dragging the boys by their hair. "You Williams... you Tobler... Patrick...Get to the office!"

And suddenly, the remainder dispersed. Rosario had a bleeding nose and his finger was sore from someone standing on it, but he was still holding Eddie's vegemite sandwich in his other hand. "What's this all about, Frank?" she demanded of the boy nearest her.

"Nothing, Mrs Sieger. It was an accident I think."

She dusted Rosario off, took his sandwich from him and wiped the blood from his nose with a small floral handkerchief. "They're just bullies. They should be ashamed of themselves. What's your name?"

Rosario didn't answer.

"His name's Ross, Miss," said Frank.

"Ross Cottone," added Eddie.

"Well, Ross Cottone you come with me and we'll see what we can do about the mess you're in."

As Mrs Sieger and Rosario appeared at the office, Mr Kaski was finishing the process of caning the three boys. Rosario thought he would be next and he attempted to wriggle away from her.

"No, you're not in trouble," she assured him by patting his head.

Norm slunk past muttering, "I'll get you for this you little Itie. You just wait."

"What did you say, Norm Williams?" asked Mrs Sieger placing her hands on her hips.

"Nothing, Mrs Sieger. Sorry, Mrs Sieger," and he raced off before she could say anything else.

"Something is going to have to be done about this bullying Mr Kaski. It's not this little boy's fault he's Italian. What are we supposed to be educating these boys for if we can't even teach them that?"

"Well, I did warn his father that he should have thought about enrolling him in the convent school across the road. I know you mean well Mrs Sieger but he is Italian and he is Catholic. Wouldn't it be better if he went to the school across the road? He can't even speak English."

"Well, I'm happy to help him with his English, so if we can stop the bullying, maybe we can do our bit to bring everyone in our community together. You have to give it to Mr Cottone; he's got guts sending his little kid into this hornet's nest. Mr Cottone's a good man. He's been in Babinda for over twenty years and never done anything but work hard and stay out of everyone's way. I'll talk to the boy's father and I'll start teaching him English for half an hour every day after school. He'll be fine in a couple of months."

That afternoon when Rosario returned to his desk, he saw that someone had taken his new slate and replaced it with a dirty chipped one. He said nothing as Mr Rouge taught the rest of the class. When the bell rang out for the final time that day, Mr Rouge presented him another new slate and took the chipped one away. The boy smiled and promised himself he would never let it out of his sight again.

Mrs Sieger waited with Rosario outside the school gate and his heart leapt when he saw his father approaching on Dolly.

He dismounted from his horse and raised his hat to Mrs Sieger, "Good afternoon good teacher."

"Good afternoon, Mr Cottone. I just wanted to talk to you about Ross here. Do you have a moment?"

"Pleased to meet you, Mrs Sieger. Is everything okay?" He sensed an altercation.

"Yes, I'm sure everything will be fine. I just wanted to ask your permission to keep Ross back for half an hour after school each day to give him special classes in English."

"Of course, Mrs Sieger. I would appreciate that very much. I've been a bit neglectful in that area. How long do you wish to do that for?"

"Probably a couple of months. Maybe less."

"That's fine and I'm happy to pay you. Just tell me how much you think it will cost."

"Nothing at all, that's my job. I'm happy to do it. Maybe we can start next Monday."

"You are too kind Mrs Sieger." He turned to Rosario, "how was your first day at school, Rosario?" There was no reply.

"A bit overwhelming, I would imagine…" answered the teacher on his behalf, "first day of school and all."

During the trip home, it was the same. Rosario was unusually quiet. His father looked at him but could not catch his eye.

"Did something happen at school today?" No answer.

"Were the teachers good to you, Rosario?" Still no answer.

"Rosario, look at me! What's the problem? Why aren't you talking to me?"

The tears welled in his eyes. Carmelo caught Betty's bridle and pulled on the reigns of his own horse.

"Whoa Dolly… whoa there girl," and both horses came to a halt. "Now, we're not going any further until you talk to me," he said in a stern voice as they dismounted. Rosario burst into tears. "What's the matter son? Tell me why you are crying."

"You… you… you," he sobbed.

"I what?"

"You never call me Saruzzo anymore. Ever since Abele was born, you always call me Rosario. Don't you love me anymore, Papa?"

Carmelo gave him the warmest embrace he could and lifted him high into the air, "of course I love you, Saruzzo. Is that why you've been so quiet? Of course I still love you… more than ever. Maybe I haven't called you Saruzzo because you're a big boy now and Saruzzo is a bit of a baby's name and you're no longer the baby."

"Mamma still calls you, Meluzzo and you're not a baby."

"That's because I was the baby in my family and so all my brothers and sisters call me Meluzzo. That's why."

"So Abele should be, Abeluzzo?"

"That's right and so he will be when he's old enough to understand us. Until the next baby comes along and then he will no longer be Abeluzzo." Rosario hugged his father tightly.

"Okay, back on your horse. Mamma will worry if we are not home soon. She'll be dying to know how you went at school today. After that and until they rode the two horses into the house paddock adjacent to the stables Rosario didn't stop talking. He told Carmelo about the nice slate and his new books and the nice male teacher and how Eddie was his friend. Carmelo pretended not to notice the band-aid on his finger and the redness around his nose.

Elena swept across the horse paddock and scooped Rosario into her arms, kissing him all over.

"I'm a big boy now, Mamma. I go to school. Abeluzzo is the baby now."

"Yes, Abeluzzo is the baby now, but you're still my baby too, Saruzzo."

"Mamma, can you make me Vegemite sandwiches tomorrow, just like Eddie?"

The next morning Elena waved Rosario farewell as he and Carmelo trotted off to school.

"Papa will buy some Vegemite today and tomorrow you can have sandwiches just like Eddie," she called after him.

At the creek crossing, Rosario did everything right. He was confident and he was careful.

"Don't forget that if the creek is ever in flood, you wait for me on the other side to lead the horse across. Never try to cross on your own. It's too dangerous." At Mrs Ling's store, they left the horse and Carmelo brought him the rest of the way to school on Dolly. "Have a nice day and I'll see you after school this afternoon." He looked at the note Elena had put in his pocket, "Vegemite is that how you say it?"

"Si Papa, Vegemite, Vegemite."

At the first break on the second day, Rosario's lunch tin remained hidden. He was too frightened Norm and the other boys would tease him again. But by lunch he was ravenous. He sneaked away from the others and sat near the sand pit to open his lunch tin. Elena had stowed something special in there. Apart from his favourite salami sandwich, she added two freshly baked biscuits and two tantalizing Minties wrapped in their white and green paper with the red writing. He saw Eddie playing near the swings so he motioned to him to come over.

"*Biscotti, dolce?*" he asked as he offered him sweets. "*Prende, prende.*" He insisted Eddie take one.

As Eddie reached for the sweet five boys ran from behind the toilet block and pounced on Rosario. "Haystack... haystack!" they yelled as they piled on top of him, pushing him to the ground. But this time, they didn't linger long enough to be caught. As he retreated, Norm took a handful of sand from the sandpit and threw it onto the lunch tin's contents.

"That's for being an Itie," he yelled as he scurried away.

On the third day, Rosario couldn't wait to try the Vegemite sandwiches his mother had prepared for him.

"Are you sure you like these Vegemite sandwiches?" she cross-examined to ensure he hadn't changed his mind.

"Si Mamma, they are my favourite," he insisted, even though he had never tasted one.

Again, he didn't eat anything at little lunch. At lunch, he slipped away from school and walked to Mrs Ling's to eat under the tree with Betty. He opened the tin and saw the sandwich, almost salivating with anticipation; but the very first bite almost made him vomit. It had such a strange salty taste that made all his saliva come rushing into his mouth. He swiftly spat out the remains. It tasted terrible. Betty came to investigate what he was eating and recognized the bread. She snorted as the little boy offered her half the sandwich. Betty chomped on the lunch and as soon as it had dissolved, nuzzled him for more. He gladly surrendered the second half as well. Rosario was so pleased that his Mamma had put another two *biscotti* and two *dolce* in the tin otherwise he would have missed out on lunch for the third day in a row.

On Thursday, Rosario requested salami and cheese sandwiches again. He told his mother he had changed his mind about the Vegemite sandwiches and wanted his previous favourite.

"I didn't think he could possibly like them," she remarked to Carmelo. "You should try them. They taste like hospital food."

That day, he again sneaked to Mrs Ling's and the salami and cheese sandwiches were received like old friends. That afternoon, instead of collecting him from school, his father had arranged to meet him at Mrs Ling's.

But as he initiated the walk from school, he saw a gang of boys gathering around Norm Williams. He fled as fast as he could, but they chased him all the way to Mrs Ling's. Fortunately when he reached the haven of her shop, Mrs Ling was hanging out some clothes in the backyard and as soon as the boys saw her they turned and walked away.

"We'll get you tomorrow, you lousy Itie and then I'm going to kill you," shouted Norm as he turned to leave. Rosario understood the word 'kill' and he was terrified.

Next day was Friday and Rosario refused to go to school; he

aired every excuse but his father would accept none of them. Finally, Carmelo convinced him because he had found a very special surprise and it needed to be bought by Friday or the man would sell it to some other little boy. That was the saving grace for Rosario.

"The next two days are holidays… you won't have to go to school and you can play with your surprise all weekend."

Rosario couldn't wait.

That afternoon after his last lesson with Mrs Sieger, there was no sign of Norm Williams or his gang. Rosario looked all around and he knew that if they were nowhere in sight, he would be too fast for their hefty frames and Norm would never catch him before he reached Mrs Ling's. He set off at a brisk pace scanning ahead and behind him to ensure they were nowhere in sight. I sensed a feeling of relief as he turned the last corner and Ling's Corner Store was but a block away when suddenly, the whole gang was there waiting for him. They appeared from in front and from behind. They had lain in wait. Now they would kill him and Norm Williams confirmed it.

"I'm going to kill you, you little Dago," he hissed as he strode towards him spurred on by his pack.

Rosario was paralysed as the fear overtook him, but just as Norm reached him, he witnessed his father round the corner on Dolly. Rosario bellowed out in Italian.

"You can't kill me because my Papa is behind you and he'll save me!"

The bully catapulted himself onto Rosario to the cheers and taunts of the whole gang. But the smaller of the two grabbed him by the throat, smashed his head into his nose continued to pummel him with clenched fists until his assailant screamed to his mates to help, but they had all run away. Carmelo had to physically detach his son from the boy and before Carmelo could say anything, Norm waddled off all bloodied and bruised and with his tubby little knock-kneed legs bouncing off one another.

"Saruzzo, what have you done to that poor little boy?" asked his father.

"He said that he and his mates were going to kill me, Papa," he yelled.

"Well his mates certainly weren't much help to him, were they? So… is this why you didn't want to go to school today? I don't think he'll be giving you any more trouble for a while. Come on, have I got a surprise for you! "

When they got to Mrs Ling's place, Carmelo handed a petite package to his son.

"Here it is. This is the special surprise I have for my special grown-up boy for finishing his first week of school. Come on open it." Carmelo was as excited as the boy was.

Rosario opened the packet and inside was the best fighting weapon he had ever seen. It was an Olympic shanghai with a steel fork, long stretchy rubbers and a soft leather pouch.

"Wow, Papa. This is the best present in the whole world. It's just like the one Dave has in the 'Dad and Dave' movies." He hung it proudly around his neck and rode tall all the way home with the shanghai swinging from side to side.

"I can't wait to show Eddie on Monday," he informed his father.

"Maybe you can tell Eddie about it on Monday and show him some time when he visits you at the farm. I don't think shanghais are allowed at school," said Carmelo not realising Monday would be a very different scenario for Rosario. Norm was sitting all alone with a severely bruised nose and not a friend in sight. He never troubled Rosario again and I returned to Carmelo, content in the knowledge that Rosario was now in complete control of his own destiny as far as bullying was concerned.

Chapter 30

Two letters

Carmelo was determined to claw his way into control of his own affairs at the farm. He could not accept the idea of working as a slave for Davies and the collective of creditors on a weekly allowance of four pounds ten shillings per week as had been the case over the past two years. Gammexane was now freely available and he had already doubled the output of the farm. But most importantly, he had to think of his family and a future for his three sons; Davide Antonio was born on the 4th of September 1947 and he needed a father who could offer him and his brothers some sort of a start in life.

He approached the National Bank of Australia about taking over his debt and was pleasantly surprised.

"You have come to me at a very fortunate time, Mr Cottone," said Mr Hammond. "I have only been manager at this branch for six months and I find myself in the wonderful position of having quite a large sum of money at the bank to lend out to worthy and of course trustworthy customers. I consider, after having perused your past history with this bank that you would fall comfortably into that category."

"So, how much do you think I could have?"

"How much do you want? Let's start from there, shall we?"

"Ideally, I would like to consolidate all my loans. In the four years from 1944 to 1948, I have reduced my debt with them from nine thousand six hundred pounds to seven thousand one hundred pounds. I also need to purchase an ex-army truck at the sales in Cairns next week so that I can transport cord wood to the mill and have something a bit more respectable and practical in which to transport my family. That's another five hundred pounds."

"So, you're asking me for seven thousand six hundred pounds? What is the condition of your farm implements and machinery?"

"The Government has made reparation for seizing my D2 Caterpillar tractor for the war effort. They have replaced it with another, which is not as good but it's satisfactory. All my implements are in good condition and my horses are all well, thank God."

"So, seven thousand six hundred pounds then?"

"Yes please."

"Very well, I'll get my staff to draw up the documents. We'll need to bring the mortgage back over to the bank," he extended his hand to Carmelo.

Carmelo could not wait to bring the good news to Elena.

"I'm so pleased that the farm will be out of the hands of that Judas, Davies. He tried his best to take this farm from us. At least the banks don't have a personal interest in the farm," Elena emphasized.

"Soon you will be able to travel to town, to Innisfail and Cairns in style my dear Elena," he added. But, it wasn't quite the style Elena had been previously accustomed to in Sicily.

Carmelo said as much and more in his next letter to Antonio a couple of weeks later.

16th June 1948.

My beloved Nino,
It is with great joy that I can report to you that God has delivered me from the clutches of my debtors Jim Davies and the others. I am no longer dependent on their handouts. Without one single proviso, the bank reviewed my case and granted me the money to repay them. As well, he approved a sum for the purchase of a truck. I was able to purchase an old ex-army Dodge at the sales for only three hundred and fifty pounds so I will have a little bit of money in reserve for an emergency.

Now Elena doesn't have to suffer the humiliation of riding into town on the jigger anymore. Although, I must admit she's not too happy about having to operate the windscreen wipers manually when it rains.

Only three weeks ago, we were all on the jigger. Elena had Abele on one knee and Davide who is only nine months old, on the other. We were sitting on the slatted seat with Rosario hanging on for dear life at the back. Around the bend at Agis' farm, the cane was so high we couldn't see anything ahead of us. At the last moment, a locomotive hurtled around the bend on its way to deliver several bogeys of rails to the farmers in Happy Valley. Elena screamed and we had no time to do anything but jump for our lives. We ended up all over the place. The loco driver was as white as a ghost. He thought he had killed us. Fortunately we survived with just a few scratches and it was then I decided we would need a truck. But I could never have imagined how I could afford it.

Now I am focused on paying off the debt. Rosario is in his third year at school and he has made some good friends. His English is very good and he speaks with no accent whatsoever. When his friends are around, he always speaks to me in English and I go along with it. But at home we have a rule that he must speak to me in Italian. When he is alone with his mother, they often speak in English but at the dinner table, we only speak Italian. Elena has insisted that the children should not speak the dialect, which is probably a good idea as Italian is spoken and understood all over Italy.

Abele is such a placid boy. He has long blonde curly hair. He loves his food and you can tell Teresa that we feed him his full-cream milk from the cow in a one litre beer bottle. "Mook, mook" (milk) is still his favourite word. Daviduzza

has a very happy disposition. Rosario spoils him; a little bit like you did me, Nino. Actually, we all spoil him a bit.
With three children now, I feel very driven to working hard and paying off the debt.

You asked about coming back so that Elena's mother and Teresa could see the children. It breaks our heart to have to inform you that it is too early yet but with God's grace, we hope to be able to do so in a few years' time. Please explain it to Teresa and give her a special hug from all five of us. We hope to get a studio photo of the family next time we go to Cairns and I will send copies to both families.

I embrace you all, my brothers, my sisters, nephews, nieces and in-laws,
Carmelo

P.S Elena sends her love.

Carmelo posted the letters and then checked the post box for mail. There were two aerogrammes; both postmarked Rome. Letters could be sent from the capital by airmail so that they arrived in a matter of days after posting. One was addressed to Elena from Luisa and one was addressed to Carmelo from Antonio. Carmelo sensed that the news in both letters would not be trivial and decided to leave them so that he and Elena could peruse them together. He placed them on the dashboard and his glance continued to return to them all the way home.

"I'm afraid to open the letter, Meluzzo," said Elena as she shied from it. "Will you open and read it to me, please?"

Carmelo nodded and slit the letter carefully with a sharp knife and read the contents aloud to Elena.

My dearest sister Elena,
I am so sad to inform you that you will never see our mother
again. She passed away silently in her sleep and rests now
with God. She was so young, only fifty-nine years old and
we needed her so much. She has always been the rock in our
family, especially after our father died— may God bless his
soul. My heart bleeds for you so far away. Rest assured my
dear Elena, that not one day passed when she did not speak of
you. She wanted so much to hug you and hold your children
in her arms but it was not God's will. We must be grateful
that we have all reached adulthood. Oh how I miss you my
sister.

I will send a letter with photos and other things soon.

I love you, I love you, I love you,
Luisa xxxxxxxxxxxxxxx

Elena stood reaching her hand out to receive the letter when she
fainted. Carmelo placed her on the sofa and began fanning her with
a newspaper. As she began to stir, the only words that came out of her
mouth were 'Mamma, Mamma' and she swiftly burst into tears. She
was inconsolable. Carmelo carried her into the bedroom and returned
to the kitchen to get some water for her. The babies were asleep but
Rosario had just ascended the stairs with a 'johnny cake' from Rashim
in his hands.

"Mamma is not well Rosario. She has heard some bad news. Best
you wait in the kitchen and I'll talk to you in a minute."

Carmelo made some pasta and added the sauce Elena had made
earlier and prepared three plates; one for Rosario, one for himself and
one for Elena, which he covered with another plate and placed in the
safe. He then heated some milk and put it in a beer bottle with a teat
for Abele and propped it against a pillow beside him. The baby was
still asleep so he let him be.

That night when he slipped into bed, Elena asked about the contents of the other letter. He lied, telling her he hadn't read it. He hadn't wanted to tell her that he too had lost the only mother he ever knew. Teresa had passed away in her sleep. She was only sixty-three. The one who had always been the rock in their family was now gone too. Carmelo would never see her alive again and she would never hold his children in her arms.

Carmelo had to console his wife. She was his prime concern. He had taken her away from her family and he was all she had. Elena was so young and so heartbroken that he could not come to terms with her loss. As for Teresa, he consoled himself as he prayed for her.

"You are with our beloved parents now my dear sister and with God. For me you will always be God's messenger here on earth. Because of you, I will never lose my faith in God and I will pray for you every day as I do for the good souls of our beloved parents and our brother Giuseppe. Watch over us my sister and until we meet again we will always be together in my thoughts."

The next morning, Elena appeared quite composed and Carmelo was so relieved. He certainly didn't expect her to be and he believed she had every right not to be. She didn't seem angry with him either and she had every right to be.

"Meluzzo, I've been thinking about the family in Sicily."

"Yes Elena, I'm so sorry I took you away from them. I asked too much of you and I'm sorry. You've lost your mother, your father... you have no siblings here... you do not know your nephews and nieces... you even left your friends behind. If I could do it again, I never would have brought you here. I wish we could go back but we can't at the moment."

"Maybe we don't need to, Meluzzo. My brother, Vincenzo for example... he has no work. He's married and he has no real future in Sicily. He could come here and start a new life with us. Then when he has been here a couple of years, he could bring his wife and they could raise a family in Australia."

Carmelo thought about it, "Now that you mention it, Cedric has already said this will be his last season with us. He'll be returning to Albania. Maybe your brother would be interested in taking his place."

"Meluzzo, that would make me so happy if I could have my brother here."

"But this is heavy manual work, Elena. Do you think he would be prepared to do manual work? Your family are landlords not farmers."

"Everything is changing in today's world. I'm sure he would learn very quickly. He's very intelligent as well. It wouldn't be long before he'd have his own business. We just have to give him a start and then he can go his own way. What do you think, Meluzzo?"

"Well, no harm in asking him I guess. Why don't you write a letter to him at once and see what he says?"

When she received confirmation from Vincenzo, Elena could hardly contain her enthusiasm. "He wants to come, Meluzzo. This is going to make me so happy."

"So, if he leaves in early November by ship, he could be here for Christmas."

"The ship is too slow Meluzzo and he only wants to come by plane. He said he will pay us back," Elena implored him.

"We could convert the office above the air-raid shelter into a bedroom for him."

"Yes! Let's do it. Our children are going to have an uncle after all."

Chapter 31

Uncle Vince

With Uncle Vince came all the trappings of a new world. He was suave, sophisticated, and fashion-conscious. He had a *joie de vivre,* which was contagious and even pretended he could speak several European languages. He was well educated, had an incredible general knowledge and a sense of wonder that could captivate any listener. Above all, he commanded a presence that lingered and a smile that was unforgettable. Elena was keen to present her brother to her friends and the first family to meet him were the Biondis who now lived at Fishery Falls.

"He is such a handsome gentleman, Elena," commented Mrs Biondi. "They certainly know how to make them in Italy."

"It's so refreshing to have him around. He has so many stories to tell and he's always happy and looking for some new adventure."

"I love his white explorer's helmet," said Fedora, Mrs Biondi's daughter. "He looks like something out of darkest Africa about to conquer Australia."

"I heard that," said Uncle Vince who was sauntering in from the kitchen with some orange juice for the ladies. Fedora blushed as Elena came to her rescue.

"Well, you shouldn't be listening to ladies' conversation, Vincenzo. What happened to the manners our mother taught you?"

"It was an accident. Is that the thanks I receive for bringing you all a lovely cold drink? That's good manners isn't it, Fedora?" Fedora was twenty-two and unused to conversation with men. She could feel her face glowing a bright red.

"Well, we have to give Vincenzo credit where credit is due, Fedora.

Which other man in North Queensland would treat women so nobly as to bring them a cold drink when they could merely hang around and wait for the women to bring it to them?" answered Mrs Biondi.

"See, big sister. Why can't you appreciate me like Mrs Biondi does? After all, there's a limit to how much a city dweller can hear of talk about cane grubs, the nails used to attach shoes to horses' hooves and the price of chemical fertilizers." The ladies laughed.

"Yes, I would imagine this would be culture shock to you, Vincenzo. Thank you for the drinks," said Mrs Biondi in a conciliatory tone. He passed a drink to each of the ladies but not without teasing Fedora first by withdrawing her drink as she was about to take it.

"Don't be so mean, Vincenzo," snapped Elena as she took the drink and passed it to Fedora herself. "Now, go back to the boys and stop flirting with the ladies."

He issued Elena with a peck on the cheek. "You'll be sorry when I'm gone, big sister. I was just about to tell Fedora here about the wave of feminist supremacy sweeping across Europe. Now she's going to be left in the backwater and it's all your fault."

"Why did you send him away, Elena?" sulked Fedora after he was gone.

"That's enough of that, Fedora," said Mrs Biondi with a light tap to Fedora's wrist. "He's a married man." The three women laughed but it was only Fedora who blushed.

Young Rosario's nose was a bit out of joint because Fedora's brother Ron was not paying him the attention that was usual. Even though Ron was eight years older than Rosario, he always treated him as an equal. They could talk for hours about fishing or hunting but what Rosario loved most was talking to Ron about machinery.

"When are you going to show me your new Massey Ferguson tractor, Ron?" Rosario begged of him. But Ron ignored him. He was more interested in Vincenzo's opinion of his recent flight from Italy.

"Did you get a chance to go into the cockpit and chat to the pilots?"

"I certainly did. I asked one of the hostesses to organize it for me. I have never seen so many gauges in my whole life. The view from up there, you simply can't imagine it. Unless you can imagine what it might be like in Heaven. Fluffy clouds float in an eternally peaceful blue sky streaked with flashes of golden sunlight, which at dusk smears the horizon blood-red. It's so quiet up there but for the hum of the engines and the whir of the propellers."

"I'm looking around at the moment for a light plane. I'm dying to learn to fly," said Ron.

"You should build your own," said Vincenzo. "They have these kit planes that they ship to you in a crate and you build it yourself. You have all the equipment you need here on the farm and it is so much more affordable. As for learning to fly, the pilots told me it's almost as easy as driving a car. You should do it, Ron. I'll make some enquiries for you."

"Thanks Vince, I'd appreciate that."

"Don't mention it. It's nice to know we have similar interests."

Rosario seized the opportunity to usurp the adults' conversation.

"You know Uncle Vince, Ron and I went up into the mountains behind the farm to look for one of the US C47s that crashed into Mt Bellenden Ker during the war."

"Really, Saro? I didn't know there were planes flying around there during the war."

"They were paratroopers on jump-training missions just before the Australian landing in New Guinea. Two planes were lost in a period of just a few months," Ron explained.

"Anyhow, Ron and I went right up into the scrub in search of them."

"We found one just in behind the falls," said Ron.

"Yes, we were able to bring back a few things; a few gauges and a couple of magnets," added Rosario.

"Were there any bodies in the fuselage of the plane or scattered around the area?"

"No," said Ron. "The plane had already made the drop and the crew was able to parachute to safety."

"Incredible. You must show me the magnets, Saro, when I am home. I can show you some interesting experiments with magnets."

Elena was craving for Vincenzo to meet their dear friends the Malapontes from Home Hill. As soon as the five Malaponte men were released from the internment camp in 1943, the yearly visits resumed. Carmelo and Elena would go to Home Hill for Christmas and stay for a couple of weeks and then Mary would return with them for anything up to a month. It was becoming more and more difficult now that Elena had three children but the Malapontes were so welcoming that they refused to halt the visits. Rosario was now allowed to accompany the men on their duck-shooting sprees and Uncle Vince proved quite adept at shooting.

"He's lucky he wasn't born ten years earlier," Giuseppe Malaponte told everyone at the dinner table after the day's hunt was over. "Mussolini would have used him as a sniper for sure. Vincenzo took six ducks today and he only stopped because he didn't want to take out our whole quota on his own."

"It's not about being born lucky, Mr Malaponte. It was more about being lucky on the day. Beginner's luck, I would call it."

Now Mary was only one year younger than Vincenzo. Elena warned him to watch his behaviour as Mary was her dearest friend. She issued very strict behavioural guidelines to Vincenzo prior to developing their acquaintance after the Fedora experience.

"Don't you even dream about getting any ideas of turning Mary's head with your sweet talk. First of all, you're married. Secondly, Mary has met a lovely man in Brisbane. Thirdly, Mary is family. You treat her like a sister."

"Wow Elena, anyone would think I was a Casanova. I'm simply a friendly fun-loving person. Sure, I love women but it's never anything more than friendship. Don't be a silly sister and stop worrying. Okay?" He wrapped her in a hug.

"I'm sorry, Enzo. It's just that I know the girls find you irresistible. I don't want you causing any trouble, that's all."

"I understand. You have nothing to worry about."

He was true to his word. Throughout his stay in Home Hill, he was utterly charming but his conduct remained exemplary on every occasion. He left, loved by all and with his reputation as a gentleman intact. However, Mary did not return with them to Babinda for the first time in years.

"There simply isn't enough room for you in Babinda now that Vincenzo is there," her grandmother explained. Whatever the reason, nobody argued with Nonna.

In a very different arena, Vince did not show the same enthusiasm when it came to working in the field.

"Elena, how is he ever going to survive the harvesting season? This is only the slack season and he can't even get out of bed until ten o'clock. He has no interest whatsoever in farming."

"He needs time to adjust to this type of work, Meluzzo. You said yourself, he's a gentleman not a farmer. He's more interested in business and the arts."

"Well, at least he could make an effort to pull his weight. His output is less than half of what Cedric used to do. You'll have to talk to him, Elena. A fair day's work for a fair day's pay; that's all I ask."

Vincenzo was fiery and indignant about Carmelo's attitude towards him.

"He treats me like a peasant yet I'm the one who is supposed to be educated, Elena. His only interests are the farm, politics and the Bible. He has no interest in art, in culture or in learning. He is restricted to working from dawn to dark. He reads nothing but that newspaper *The Cairns Post* and *The Canegrower* and those religious magazines. I'm a man of the world, Elena, I like going out, I like music, song, theatre and opera. I like people and here I am stuck in this solitary confinement where I'm only allowed out to chip cane for exercise with two Hindu holy-men."

"Enzo, Carmelo has to work hard for our family to survive. It's not fair to criticize him because he works hard and doesn't have time to go out and have fun. He has different priorities from you."

"I'm not saying that he doesn't work hard, I'm simply suggesting he should work smarter."

"How?" asked Elena.

"By going into business."

"What sort of business, Enzo?"

"We could start a soap factory. I've shown him the plans and his response was to tell me that we were running out of toilet paper and I should hang onto them in case I need them for something more practical."

Elena giggled, "I thought you said he didn't have a sense of humour?"

"He doesn't and you know that, Elena. You don't really believe he could think of something as witty as that, do you? His response was more like, 'Come on, come on, just get rid of the weeds in the cane before I call you Soap Factory'. He's become cold and colourless and he's dragging you down there with him."

"Thanks, Vincenzo. That's a cruel thing to say about your sister. Cold and colourless?"

"It's true, I haven't heard you play the violin or the mandolin since I arrived from Italy. What is the piano in your lounge room for? I've never heard you play it."

"You're very ungrateful, Vincenzo." She heard the baby crying and abandoned him to hold the baby. When she returned, Vincenzo was waiting with a magnificent painting of a cane field in full flower.

"What do you think of it, big sister? I've been painting it in secret... just for you. The paint isn't dry yet. I think of you every day and of what you have tried to do for me. Farming simply isn't in my nature. This is me, Elena." He offered her the painting.

"It's so beautiful. I love the colour of the mauve and you have made those flowers leap towards the sky imploring the world to come to them."

"Exactly, as in life, we have to reach out to be seen and to be heard."

Elena became very defensive of Vincenzo after that and began to squabble with Carmelo as a result.

"Why do you always defend your brother, Elena? He has made no effort to repay the money he owes us for the plane flight. I have never placed any pressure on him because I assumed he was sending the money home to his wife. Then I received a letter from your brother Liborio saying that in all the time he has been here, he has only sent one pound to his wife. That's disgraceful. What's more, did he tell you his wife was pregnant? Of course not. He doesn't want anything to upset any secret little romance he might be trying to get going or any secret little agenda he might have."

"What letter? What pregnancy, what little romance? Carmelo, show me the letter."

"The letter was addressed to me and I burnt it. I didn't want to upset you. But Elena, now he is trying to come between us as well. These are all things that shouldn't happen and we shouldn't allow them to happen."

"Well, what are we supposed to do?"

"I have already taken some action. It was my duty to write back to Liborio and I did. I told him to make arrangements to send Marianna to her husband here in Australia as soon as the child is born and is old enough to travel. For your part, I think you should tell any woman he meets what I have told you. That way we will remove the danger that he poses with her falling in love with him and creating a scandal and a tragedy that no parent or woman should ever have to endure."

"Where will they stay when she arrives?"

"Initially she will have to stay with us. Vincenzo will need to find another job in Innisfail or Cairns as soon as possible and rent a place for them to stay. We can't carry him anymore. There are several jobs advertised in *The Cairns Post* for trades people, carpenters, painters and assistants. What do you think?"

"I'll talk to him."

Vincenzo redeemed himself from that point forward. A little boy, Liborio Ermete, was born to Marianna Panvini and they arrived in Australia soon after. By the time she arrived, Vincenzo had a job in Cairns as a house painter and with his entrepreneurial flair managed to establish his own painting business under the trade name of *Flying Brushes Company.*

Chapter 32

Soul searching

Carmelo received a surprise phone call one evening from Mr Dellacosta.

"Carlo, it's me Frank from Edmonton. It's been many years and I don't suppose you would remember us. My wife and I and our three children visited you at the farm about fifteen years ago. Do you remember us?"

"Yes I do Mr Dellacosta. Tell me how is your good wife and your three beautiful children?"

"We are all well thank you and the children are all grown up now. Please accept my apologies for leaving it so long to contact you again. I am so ashamed. Please forgive me."

"Of course, Mr Dellacosta. What is important is that you are all well. I was hoping you would come and visit again one day."

"Well, that's what I wanted to talk to you about. This weekend we are having a National Convention for the faithful in Cairns and I wanted to invite you along to hear some of our people talk about their experiences."

"I see, that would be interesting but I have a wife and three children now."

"Please try to come along. If you wish you can stay with us on Saturday night, we have plenty of beds here. That way we could go together."

"Very well, let me discuss it with my wife and I'll contact you tomorrow." Carmelo hung up the phone.

"Who was that, Meluzzo?" asked Elena.

"They are a very devoted religious family. I met them here on the farm before returning to Italy. They are such nice people."

"What did they want?"

"He has invited us attend their national convention for the Christian faithful in Cairns. Would you like to go?"

"To Cairns? Certainly, as long as I have the chance to go shopping."

"But this group is not Catholic. In fact it isn't a mainstream church; they are an evangelist group who spread God's Word by going out amongst the people."

"Are they gypsies?"

"No Elena, they are ordinary devoted followers of Christ. In fact, their doctrine is not that much different from the mainstream Christian religions. They just do things differently. That's all, I guess."

"Maybe we could visit Vincenzo if we are going to Cairns."

"It's a two day gathering, so maybe we could go to Cairns on Saturday morning and you can do your shopping. You could phone Vincenzo and Marianna and ask them if it would be okay for us to stay the night. Then on Sunday we could arrange to meet the Dellacostas at the venue."

Elena was excited about the meeting. "It's so long since I've been to worship and I'm looking forward to saying some special prayers for my mother."

That Sunday, Mr and Mrs Dellacosta and their grown-up family were waiting outside the Cairns Showgrounds for Carmelo and his family to arrive. The men were immaculately dressed in long-sleeved shirts and ties and they wore coats despite the warm weather. Carmelo was casually dressed in long trousers and a short-sleeved shirt but Elena and the children were dressed for church.

"So pleased to see you, Carmelo. You remember my wife Angela and my three children Nellie, Albert and Edmond?"

"Yes Mr Dellacosta. This is my wife Elena and my three children, Rosario, Abele and Davide."

"Ross," said Rosario as he shook hands.

"Please call us Ben and Angie. No need to be so formal," said Mr. Dellacosta.

Inside the venue, everyone was exceedingly welcoming. There were well over one thousand people and it was evident that it had been well planned. Ben and Angie introduced them to many people from the Edmonton group.

"This is Ted Putt, an elder in our church and his wife Pearl. This is my father Albuino. And this is Alf Pennisi and his wife Margaret; from Babinda would you believe."

Pearl handed her white cane to Ted and immediately reached out to take Davide from Elena's arms.

"Who's this little fellow?" she asked Rosario.

"That's my baby brother David and this is my other brother Abel. I'm Ross."

People were beginning to deliver their testimonials.

Everyone was in awe of some of the incredible stories those people divulged and all rejoiced as they heard how God's intervention rescued their desperate souls. Stories of pain and suffering, of remorse and retribution, of deceit and dishonesty, of hopelessness and heartlessness, of shame and abuse, of jealousy and greed, of anger and lust and of pride, all rang true and humbled them.

"There is a saying in Italian that everyone has their own cross to bear," Carmelo commented to Ted Putt.

To which his new friend replied, "hallelujah".

"My mother used to tell me about the penitent who confessed 'I used to cry because I had no shoes until I saw someone who had no feet'," said Elena. Pearl with her white cane simply nodded knowingly.

The entire assembly personified commitment to the faith and exuded love and compassion for one another and for humankind. Carmelo and Elena were deeply moved by what they heard and saw at that Convention of the Faithful.

"My spirit feels as though it has been cleansed," was Elena's response to Angie's request for feedback.

Carlo's was unequivocally complimentary. "Among these people

I can find peace," he said to Ben, "I have tried so hard for so long without success."

When they returned to Uncle Vince's place that afternoon, he was sceptical about what Elena was telling him.

"It's human nature, Elena. People get ensnared in the excitement of the moment."

"But I have never known such a sense of exhilaration and of being set free from whatever it is in this world that makes us feel trapped, unhappy, afraid and insecure," insisted Elena. "How do you explain that?"

"It's a psychological phenomenon, big sister." Uncle Vince went over to the bookcase and took out the index volume of the 'Encyclopedia Britannica' and shuffled through the pages. "Karl Marx … in his Communist Manifesto of 1848… Now he had something to say about it. Let me see." He placed the index volume back on the shelf and removed another. The shuffling resumed as he read snippets of the text, audible only to himself.

"Ah, here it is Elena. 'Religion is the opiate of the people'." He placed the book down and peered at her over his thick-rimmed glasses. "You see Elena, it's like a drug. You get hooked on it and you never want to lose that feeling of exhilaration you are talking about. But reality rules and as the ecstasy wears off, the agony of the real world returns."

Carmelo was listening intently, "I don't agree. They are not pompous and pious like the people in the church I know. They are caring and forgiving and compassionate. It is as if they are God's messengers sent to bring goodwill into the world. It's different with these people, Vincenzo."

"It's always different, Carmelo. I hope they don't disappoint you." He placed the book in the collection and started ruffling through magazines on the bottom shelf. "Here Elena," he offered her a magazine entitled 'Psychology Magazine'. "You should subscribe to this. It's the sort you'd enjoy. It explores the realms of the mind, what makes us tick and why we are the way we are. There's a whole new world of scientific thought out there. We have to begin to embrace it for our children's sake. The world is changing and if we refuse to change then we will be left behind."

His statement left them deflated. "Come on, I can see that my negativity is depressing you. I want to show you something very different. I have been doing some experiments with hypnosis." He went over to the reel to reel tape recorder on the desk in the lounge. "On this tape I have recorded something that will make your hair stand on end."

Rosario's interest was suddenly aroused by his statement. "Come here, Rosario and listen to this." Rosario moved closer to the machine, looking at it intently. "I hypnotized this elderly man who works with me," explained Uncle Vince. "He's sixty-three years old. As I bring him back in time to his youth, listen to how his voice changes." He pressed the play button.

What they all witnessed astounded them. At fifty, the man's voice seemed much clearer. At forty, it seemed much brighter. At thirty it was crisp. At twenty it was effervescent. At ten, shrill. At five the sentences were short. At four they were broken. At three he only uttered words and phrases. At two he spoke nonsense words and at one, he only gargled." Uncle Vince stopped the tape.

"Now, it's what happens next that will absolutely amaze you." He pressed the play button and the machine spoke.

"I want you to go back further into the past, further, further... to before you were in your mother's womb. Relax... " There was a pause, "Where are you? What can you see?" asked Uncle Vince's voice.

"It's dark, it's cold, I don't know where I am," said a voice, but it wasn't a child's voice anymore. It was a woman's voice; mature, distinct and clear.

"Whoa... ?" Rosario gasped as his jaw dropped in amazement.

"What on earth is happening?" exclaimed Elena. "It's a woman's voice. He was a woman in his previous life? Oh my God!"

"Come on, Elena, it's late. We need to go back home now," was all Carmelo could muster on the matter. "Thank you for having us

Marianna and Vincenzo. Come on kids, kiss your Zio and Zia and embrace your little cousin. It's time to go."

"Here Elena, take this copy of the magazine. Read it and let me know what you think," said Uncle Vince as a parting gesture.

For the duration of the trip home, their discussion was centred on the Convention of the Faithful.

"Angie offered visits with Nellie for a Bible study session and I accepted," she told Carmelo.

"That's nice of them. I see they have a car now. So Angie must drive, eh?"

"No, I believe Nellie does. I've got a whole pile of reading material from them that they asked me to read."

"Alf and Margaret Pennisi asked if we would be interested in fellowshipping with the Babinda group. I think it might be a good idea. What do you think?"

"Babinda might be a bit of a worry. You know what the Catholics think of parishioners who break away from the church and join these evangelist groups."

"Who cares what the Catholics think?" said Carmelo.

"Well not just yet. We'll see how it goes with Angie and Nellie first."

"When I listened to those testimonials, it made me think about how cruel this world can be. In the 'Myth of Sisyphus', Sisyphus was condemned by the Gods to a life whereby he had to roll a huge boulder to the top of a hill and just as he almost had it up there, he would lose his footing and the rock would tumble back to the bottom again. I'm beginning to feel as though I have been condemned to a similar fate. I escaped Mussolini as an enemy of the state, then I'm interned in Australia as an enemy alien, then the grubs, then the debtors and then just as the National Bank offers me a lifeline, the price of sugar collapses so that we're not even covering the cost of production. Now I have to cut our own cane just to cover the interest on our debt and put food on the table. I will always keep the faith but how long can a man go on, Elena?"

"We have our health, Carmelo? We should be grateful for that at least." Carmelo had to agree.

It was only when Elena became very ill a short time later that Carmelo felt he had truly been abandoned.

"The news is not good, Mr Cottone," said Dr Spooner the specialist physician in Cairns. "Your wife has a grossly enlarged heart and it seems to be some sort of virus that we know nothing about. We have given her drugs to stabilize her but she will need to go to Brisbane for further tests. When can she leave?"

"Immediately, if you say so, Doctor. Can she travel by train?"

"Train is probably best but she will need someone to accompany her."

As soon as they returned to the farm, Carmelo phoned the Malaponte's in Home Hill and relayed the Doctor's report to Antonio.

"Antonio, as a special favour, is there any way you could ask your daughter Mary to accompany her to Brisbane? I could book her seat from here and Mary could catch the train in Home Hill. The tests can only be done in Brisbane and they should be back in three or four days."

"Of course, Carmelo. When you have the exact details, phone me and Mary will be ready."

Somehow, the Catholic priest from Babinda had heard the news and he travelled to Happy Valley to minister the Last Rites to Elena.

"I don't believe I am going to die, Father," said Elena.

"Well, it's best to do it just in case." He read her the Last Rites and blessed the house and he left. In fact, Elena seemed quite relaxed about her predicament; she was more worried about Carmelo and the children. Carmelo would have to care for the children and she had important things to get done and organize before she left for Brisbane.

Her most pleasant surprise was the sudden arrival of Angie and Nellie the following morning.

"Carmelo phoned us about the concerns with your health. We have come to comfort you, be with you and provide whatever you feel you need dear, Elena," said Angie. But it was Nellie whose heart leapt out to Elena as she threw her arms around her, hugging her tightly.

"Please be strong, Elena, my darling. God will watch over you for your sake and for the sake of your family. Be strong for you will not be forsaken. In my heart of hearts, I know you will get well. My God is a good God and I will pray to him for you for every moment you are away. When you feel weak, my strength will come to you and when we are both weak, our Lord will carry us both. He will not forsake us. You must believe it."

"My dear, dear, Nellie, you are so sweet. How could I ever give up, knowing you are with me? I promise you I have no fear and I have faith in God. I am so appreciative of your kind thoughts. As well, I have my dear friend Mary accompanying me and with her, there won't be time to feel sorry for myself. She is so full of laughter and laughter is the best medicine."

They spent the day praying and preparing for the journey south the next morning. Carmelo was so touched by the compassion shown towards his wife by them both and before they left, he filled a box with some of his best homemade cheese and home-grown vegetables.

That evening, Carmelo lit many candles and the household was so peaceful it was as if a protective shroud had been cast over the entire valley and it had become their sanctuary. In two day's time, Elena and Mary would be witnessing the city lights of Brisbane.

"Well look at that poster," said Elena as she and Mary Malaponte stood down from the train in Brisbane at Roma St Station. She read, "*Madame Butterfly* the ballet is being performed at 'His Majesty's Theatre' in Brisbane on Wednesday evening, June 15, 1949. Mary, you and I are going to enjoy some good old-fashioned Old World culture together at last."

Mary was so excited; she clapped her hands and jumped for joy as she scrutinized the poster.

"See, my dear Mary, something good can always come out of even the worst of situations."

Chapter 33

A closer walk

Elena and Carmelo had always maintained their faith but events were beginning to unfold whereby their journey became an even closer walk with God. Elena improved as Nellie had promised and her miraculous recovery was the last of a whole series of events in their lives, which led them to believe that they had never had to walk alone. In Home Hill that Christmas, Carmelo shared his feelings with the men of the Malaponte family and Elena shared hers with the women.

"The time has come my dear, Mary, when we feel we need to give something back," she explained to her. "Carmelo and I have committed ourselves to spreading the Word of God as well as knowing it and respecting it. For my part, I will try to learn through Fellowship and Bible study. Carmelo has taken a more courageous path to bring God's Word directly to the people. Already this week he has visited many, many people around Home Hill on his bicycle and he has discovered what it takes to really believe."

"I do it," explained Carmelo to Antonio, "so that people who feel they have very little in this life can have the opportunity to know the Lord and be uplifted and walk with Him. I do it so that people who already have enough in life can have the opportunity to share what they have and the privilege they enjoy with others."

"But the backlash from other Christians of other denominations is horrendous," Antonio reminded him. 'Bible bashing' as they call it is universally despised. Why would you put yourself through this? Life is hard enough as it is."

"True Antonio, true. I guess in the end, we all make choices and we must take responsibility for those choices."

"But the interesting thing about both you and Elena is that you don't actually bible-bash. You don't preach fire and brimstone."

"If only people could love one another and follow God's commandments and be shown His Word, I believe this world would become the paradise it was always meant to be."

"Ah, so you want the world to be perfect, Carmelo?"

"Yes."

With the price of sugar plummeting and interest rates skyrocketing, farmers were being squeezed financially every which way. It was 1952 and the dreaded letter informing Carmelo and Elena that the bank was going to foreclose on their property arrived. All those years of work, all their struggles amounted to nothing.

Carmelo contacted the Country Party Member for Mulgrave in the Queensland Legislative Assembly, Robert Watson.

"The bank has written me a letter advising me of a pending foreclosure on our farm at Happy Valley. Mr Watson, I have no other recourse but to appeal to the Premier himself for assistance. I need an appointment with him."

"It doesn't work that way, Mr Cottone. You can't have every Tom, Dick and Harry requesting an appointment with the Premier of Queensland. There simply aren't enough hours in the day. The process is that I take up your matter on your behalf with the relevant Minister, which in this case is Harold Collins, the Secretary for Agriculture and Stock."

"So, you're telling me that private individuals cannot get appointments with the Premier because there aren't enough hours in the day to deal with them."

"That's right."

"So, no private individuals have any appointments including Tom, Dick and Harry?"

"Correct... if you want to be funny."

"Then I would be the only individual asking for an appointment with the Premier and there would be plenty of times in one day to squeeze in one individual for an appointment with the Premier."

"Look, Mr Cottone, I'm not particularly interested in word games. I explained the process and that's all I can do for you."

"Mr Watson, I'm not interested in games either. My farm is in jeopardy and I need help. When you asked me for help, I put your sign up on my property. I supported you right through the election. Now I'm asking you to please help me." He paused, "what about you? Can you get an appointment with the Premier?"

"Of course I can."

"Then can you arrange an appointment with the Premier and I'll accompany you?"

"Look, Parliament sits again next week. If you want to go to Brisbane, I guess I can arrange for a very brief meeting with the Premier. What exactly do you suggest I tell him you want to talk about?"

"Tell him I want to talk to him about losing my farm and all the work I put into this country as a pioneer since 1924."

Carmelo packed some cheese sandwiches and boarded the rail motor for his trip to Brisbane. He explained to Elena how he had followed the career of Premier Vince Gair and admired him. He believed he was a very capable politician. Gair was appointed Premier in January, so he had plenty of time to become familiar with the job. Carmelo prepared some brief notes in a small pocket-sized spiral notebook so that he could make maximum use of the time allotted to him.

Premier Gair introduced himself, "Vince Gair, Mr Cottone. Mr Watson here states you are one of the pioneers of the sugar industry and that has always been an industry close to my heart. It's a pleasure to meet you."

Carmelo took his hand, "It's an honour for me to meet you Mr Premier. People like you are the salt of the earth. From nothing you have achieved everything in your political career and I congratulate you."

"Thank you, Mr Cottone. It certainly hasn't been easy. At fifteen years of age in 1916, I started off in the Railways on forty-eight pounds per year and from that time to now, the salary may have gone up, but the work has certainly got a heck of a lot harder."

"So, we were born in the same year Premier Gair. That means we have two things in common and the second thing is that we have both worked hard. I arrived in this country in 1924."

Robert Watson couldn't believe his ears. Carmelo started with that sentence and then simply proceeded to give the Premier in great detail a full description of his whole life in Australia from the day he landed in Fremantle. Twice he tried to intercede and twice Premier Gair signalled him not to interrupt. The Secretary for Agriculture and Stock made it painfully obvious as well that he was a very busy man by continually looking at his watch and glaring at Watson. But Carmelo continued on and on and Premier Gair listened intently until his final sentence, which was over twenty minutes later.

"… and Premier Gair, I have always kept the faith. I have always believed that the Lord only places upon a man's shoulders as much of a load as he can carry and I have carried it willingly. I have cut and loaded cane by hurricane lamp at night and worked the farm by day to make ends meet and I did it willingly. I have never claimed one day of unemployment handouts from the government and I will always be indebted to this country for the hospitality afforded me and my family by its people. But I can't carry this extra load that the banks have thrust upon me with the threat of foreclosure. You are my last hope in this blessed democracy that we live in."

There was silence in the room as Premier Gair stared at his desk deep in thought. Both Watson MLA and Secretary Collins stood bolt upright at attention like soldiers ready to leap into battle on the orders of their commander.

"There are provisions under the Rural Assistance Scheme that were set up especially to address similar incidents of distressed family farming businesses, Secretary Collins. Kindly look into the matter and arrange for an immediate stay of proceedings on the foreclosure issue and set in motion the necessary processes to ensure a hasty resolution to the crisis."

Premier Gair stood and walked to Carmelo, shaking his hand. "You did the right thing coming to me, Mr Cottone. You have nothing to worry about anymore. Secretary Collins will look into the matter and it will be resolved as soon as possible. You will receive official notification in the mail."

The Premier then went to Watson MLA and shook his hand, "Thank you, Mr Watson for bringing Mr Cottone to me. This is what good governance is all about. The Minister will arrange through his office for Mr Cottone's farm and affairs to be inspected by the Agricultural Bank. I expect that Mr Cottone is eligible for a fifteen year interest free loan to help him get over the protracted effect of the grub infestation on the industry as well as other market and financial stress factors."

As soon as they exited the office, Watson MLA punched the air.

"Yes. You did it, Carlo. Man I could do with a cold beer."

"You helped make it happen, Mr Watson, so the beer is on me. Where's the nearest hotel?"

"What do you mean, hotel? We have our own bar right here at Parliament House. So let's celebrate this with a cold beer and a free lunch in the Mess."

"Okay, but I pay," insisted Carmelo.

"You don't pay here. It's one of the lurks and perks of being in government. Come on Carlo, it's my shout."

Chapter 34

Back on track

Carmelo and Elena now had three children at school and moving into town was rapidly becoming a priority. They were fortuitous enough to come to a financial arrangement with the Jackson brothers to move into their stately weatherboard home in Munro Street opposite the Babinda hospital. The main reason for this was that Davide who was quite a delicate child, suffered from severe stomach cramps after riding to and from school each day on the horse.

With the support from the Government through the Agricultural bank, Carmelo's life, which had been derailed, was now back on track. Within the short space of one year so much had changed. Carmelo was about to harvest a bumper crop, the sugar prices for home consumption had increased dramatically and Premier Gair had been successful in important sugar industry negotiations in England while attending the coronation of Queen Elizabeth II.

Charlie Baldwin, the North Queensland Area Representative for the Agricultural Bank, who had inspected Carmelo's farm and approved the fifteen year interest free loan had become a good friend.

"That's the difference between someone like the Premier and ordinary blokes like you and me, Carlo," said Charlie. "Can you believe, Vince actually had the chairs that had been allocated to him and his wife Nell for the coronation in Westminster Abbey shipped home to Australia?"

"Well, I'm sure it was all legal, Charlie. If he chose to do something that might seem strange to you and me that doesn't mean he can't still be in tune with the electorate. Premier Gair is a great man, Charlie because on his way to the top he never forgot his roots, his values and his commitment to the people of this state. When my world was collapsing all around me and the banks were threatening to bury me completely, he was the man who rolled up his sleeves, picked up a shovel and helped dig me out. How can you ever repay a man like that?"

"Sure Carlo, but you have to wonder what makes him tick when you come across such a staunch monarchist. As you know Australians don't like getting too carried away when it comes to being friendly with the Poms and that includes the Queen."

"It's simple, Charlie, he has a big heart; that's what makes him tick."

"Yeah… there's no doubt about that," agreed Charlie. "Anyhow, I've finally made the big move. I've resigned from the Bank and bought a dairy farm in Millaa Millaa."

"What? Are you serious? You gave up a good paying secure job with the Agricultural Bank just to become a dairy farmer?"

"You sound surprised. I thought if anyone would understand, you would. It's all about working for yourself, about being your own boss. Farming is in my blood and it's all about lifestyle. For the first time in a long time, I feel free again."

"Yes, I do understand but you have a young family and a good education. You don't have to work on a farm like me. I certainly don't want my three boys to be farmers. I want them to get a good education and have an easier life."

"Well, you're right about giving them a good education because they will have that forever and no one will be able to take that away from them. But as to what they want to do with their lives, you might find out you will have very little say in that."

"No Charlie, it's different in Italy. The father has a big say in what his children do or shouldn't do."

"Yeah, but this is not Italy, this is Australia. Good luck and all that, but if you want my advice, I'd say expect nothing and you'll never be disappointed."

"Charlie, Charlie, you are too negative. Why should anything change?"

"Because change brings progress and we cannot stop progress."

"Well, perhaps we can agree to disagree. So tell me more about this dairy farm. You know how much I love cattle," and they chatted on well into the night.

Carmelo was about to experience first hand what Charlie Baldwin had warned him about. Until now he had been the ship's master in charge of his precious family and he navigated with an even keel even in turbulent waters. But the uncharted waters of a whole new generation who saw things differently from him still lay ahead; a generation which was not necessarily going to accept the codes of conduct that had always been inviolable in his father and his grandfather's time. Already, he had seen it in Vince and soon Vince's replacement would give Carmelo a glimpse of what this new generation, which included his own children, was about.

Carmelo's cousin on his mother's side, Antonio Scriffignano had four children and the youngest son was Salvatore. Salvatore's mother, Filippa Giannazzo had written regarding plans for Salvatore's future and Carmelo agreed to take him into his home and give him work until such time as he might venture out on his own in whatever vocation he chose to follow. As well, Carmelo was beginning to experience health issues of his own and he needed another man to help him on the farm. He was suffering from stomach ulcers and occasionally they would burst seeing him hospitalized for periods of up to one week. In fact, Rosario who had just entered his first year at Gatton Agricultural College west of Brisbane had to be recalled from his studies to help his father. It was Elena who was forced to write the letter.

3rd June 1953.

My dear son Rosario,
It is with great regret that I must inform you of the terrible situation your father finds himself in with regards to his health. As you know, he has been suffering from stomach ulcers these last couple of years. He has tried not to let them interfere with his work of running the farm, but lately his

condition has worsened markedly. Recently after one week in hospital when they operated on him for a burst stomach ulcer, he discharged himself without the doctor's permission. He needed to return to work with the gang, which had arrived and were ready to cut the next round on our farm. As you know, every man has to pull his weight including shifting portable rails or he can't cut in the gang. Your father, being the sort of man that he is, didn't tell them that he still had the stitches in from the operation. When it was his turn to carry the rails, his stitches burst and he had to be rushed to hospital with severe haemorrhaging.

Your father does not agree, but I insisted that you should return from college for a few months until such time as his cousin's son Salvatore arrives from Sicily.

I am enclosing a short letter to the Principal of Gatton College, which was written by Doctor Warnock explaining the situation so that you will be able to resume your studies as soon as Salvatore arrives. I am sending extra money to cover any unexpected expenses. Please come immediately.

I embrace you affectionately,
Your loving mother,
Elena xx

P.S. Your two brothers can't wait to see you.

Rosario returned home and the two youngest were so excited to see him. "You seem so grown up Ross," Abele remarked. "You must tell us everything there is to know about the big smoke."

"We missed you so much," said Davide as he hugged his leg. "I'm never going to let you go back to the big smoke again, Ross."

The next day, Rosario struggled across the paddock to carry the portable rails, which were laid across the cane field. The cane trucks were then positioned at intervals along the full length of the paddock in preparation for loading the cut cane. It was backbreaking toil and he had to run with grown men who were fit and who gave the gruelling work little thought. He couldn't wait for Salvatore to replace him.

Everyone in the family, but especially Ross who was only three years younger than Salvatore was excited about the prospect of another relative from the old country coming into their lives. Carmelo drove the old Dodge to the station and the three boys rushed to take their position on the platform to meet Salvatore.

"So, his name in Australia is Sam. He might as well start getting used to it now. Everyone clear on that?" checked Ross as the boys nodded.

The train squealed into the station and the moment Sam appeared out of the train the three boys couldn't believe how he was dressed.

"Get a load of that," gasped Rosario, "bell-bottomed trousers and pointed shoes!"

He was carrying a soccer ball and suddenly drove it into Rosario's midriff.

"Hey cousins, hope you guys like playing football in Australia. I bought you one to practice with, Rosario." He embraced him and Rosario looked around to check if there was someone around who might see him being embraced.

Sam patted Abele and Davide on the head and made a beeline for Carmelo.

"Hello, Zio. Nice to meet you. My uncles and aunts have told me all about you, so there are no secrets." Carmelo missed the humour and embraced him.

"Welcome to Australia, Toto. We'll talk once we get to the house. It's only a few minutes' drive from here."

The three boys launched themselves into the back of the truck.

"He's a lot younger than Uncle Vince," said Abele. "Seems like a lot of fun."

"Yeah, but he'll have to get out of those trousers and pointed shoes before he goes into town or the boys will grease him," said Ross.

"What does 'grease him' mean, Ross?" asked Davide.

"You wouldn't want to know," warned his big brother, "but I can tell you, they use axle grease."

At home, Sam began unpacking his suitcase. He had bought a beautiful silk scarf for Elena. For Davide he brought a little wind-up mule that bobbed up and down as it hobbled along on a front wheel that had the axle placed off-centre. For Abel, it was his dream come true; a miniature crystal set.

"Wow!" he screamed when he saw it. "Sam, I've always wanted a crystal set to listen to and study, so I can build my own."

The rest of the first evening belonged to the adults mainly inquiring after family in Sicily. There were also gifts from home, food and biscuits and photos. A pristine piece of Sicily had finally landed in their midst.

Chapter 35

Sam

Carmelo was actually Sam's second cousin but out of respect for the age difference, Sam always referred to him as 'Zio', which meant uncle. As far as attitude to work was concerned, Sam was utterly of Carmelo's ilk.

"You know Elena, that Salvatore is an incredible boy. He works harder than any man and he does everything willingly. He's a joy to have around and he's so energetic— he's like a grasshopper. He doesn't need to be told anything and even opens the gate for me."

"Yes, same with me; always wanting to help. He gets so embarrassed when I iron his shirts. He's so appreciative of everything we do for him. The boys adore him. Davide has taken it upon himself to teach Salvatore English. He's so cute the way he treats him just like a schoolboy. Abele follows him everywhere and Rosario has a good role model in Salvatore."

"He's certainly a good role model in terms of work but Rosario wants to do everything Salvatore does after work as well."

"He's not smoking, is he?"

"Not as far as I know but I wouldn't be surprised. His latest is that he doesn't want to return to Gatton Agricultural College. What can I do, Elena? I wanted him to have an education so that he wouldn't have to lead the life of a slave as I have. But he tells me he wants to be a farmer."

"I guess farming is different these days. With mechanization just around the corner, it's going to be a whole new industry with new opportunities. I don't think it's a bad thing that he wants to follow in the footsteps of his father."

"Sure Elena, but we've never seen eye to eye when it comes to farming. Rosario wants nothing to do with the horses, only tractors. He wants nothing to do with manual labour like chipping the cane or using the scythe to cut grass on the headlands. Everything has to be mechanical. When I talk to him about farming, he insists my methods are out-dated. Now he wants to buy a wheel tractor because they learned all about wheel tractors at Gatton College."

"Maybe, Meluzzo you should give him some encouragement. Consider buying a tractor and give him a chance to move with the times and show you what he can do."

At that point, Sam entered the room embarrassed he may have been interrupting.

"I've ironed your shirt for the Sugar Festival dance, Salvatore. Maybe you should eat before you put it on."

"There's no need, Zia. I'm too excited to eat. This is my first big night out in Australia and I can't wait to meet some of the girls." He leaned towards her, "What do you think of my aftershave?" he chuckled, serving a wry smile to her as he waited for her reply.

"I think those good mothers out there will soon learn to know better than to allow their daughters out on the streets now that a Scriffignano has come to town."

"It may not go down so well with the boys," added Carmelo. "They don't take too kindly to men who wear perfume, which is what they would call it. I see you're wearing your bell-bottomed trousers and those pointy shoes. I don't think they'll go down too well with the boys either."

"Come on, Zio. If I don't show them where the rest of the world is at with regards to fashion, how are they ever going to find out?"

"You don't understand, Toto. There's fashion and there's fashion. In Australia, fashion amounts to how short your short shorts are or whether you roll your sleeves halfway up the wrist, just below the elbow or right up under your armpit."

"You're not serious I hope, Zio! How could I roll up sleeves that have been so carefully and lovingly ironed by my favourite, Zia Elena here?"

Elena did a sign of the cross and exclaimed, "At this rate the daughters will be safe because all the mothers will want to go out with you Salvatore."

He gave her a peck on the cheek, "Thanks for ironing the shirt, Zia. See you later, Zio."

"You amuse me, Salvatore. You cannot speak a word of English, yet you go to the local dance dressed like Sammy Davis Junior. There'll be a lot of young people who have had a few drinks too many so be careful. If things don't look too good, I suggest you leave and come back here instead. We'll be down later to see the procession."

"Sure, I'll be careful, Zio. As for speaking English, dance is an international language, so who needs to speak any language at all? It's just like love, Zia Elena…you tell him!"

"Come on, you better go… otherwise I'll call you 'international language', that's what I'll call you."

Rosario stalked in, in one last attempt "Come on Papa, can't I go with Sam? He can't even speak English. Who knows what sort of trouble he might get into?"

"No Saro, I told you. You are not even out of school yet and you already want to go to the dance with all the adults. Maybe next year. We will all go down for a stroll later and you can accompany us."

Sam left and the family lined up to wash their hands in the bathroom and then sat down at the table for dinner.

"Pasta with beans… followed by grilled steak and salad," said Elena. "That's what's on the menu for tonight. The quicker we eat, the quicker we can go down town to watch the procession and the crowning of the Sugar Festival Queen for 1953."

The festival procession was one of the highlights of the social calendar in Babinda and everyone in town usually turned out to watch it. After the procession, the beauty queens would line up in the Memorial Hall and the judges would announce the best float in the procession and the new Sugar Festival Queen to the little rural community. The entire family was poised to spy Sam but they couldn't find him anywhere. Hardly anybody in town knew him so it was useless asking about him.

After the Queen had been crowned, Carmelo and the family surrendered the search of looking for Sam and were walking up Munro Street when someone broke away from the crowd and called to them, "Cottone, Cottone! Wait one moment! I need to talk to you."

They stopped and waited for him to catch up. It was Sam Catalano who lived in the house behind theirs.

"What is it, Sam?" asked Carmelo. "By the way, you haven't seen Salvatore by any chance have you?"

"That's what I wanted to talk to you about, Mr Cottone." He looked to Elena, "good evening, Signora." Then he looked back at Carmelo.

"Salvatore has been in a horrible fight. It was about an hour ago. He was dancing with the girls and they were all laughing and having a great time. I do mean girls, not girl. There were four or five of them at any one time. You know what it's like at these dances, the boys hardly ever dance with the girls until they get quite drunk and then the girls don't want to dance with them anyhow. So, one of the blokes, Bull Rogers, you know him he drives the locomotive. Well Bull starts yelling out across the dance floor… 'Hey coffee… what are you doing dancing with our girls in your poofy puffed trousers and pointy shoes?' He was drunk and he called out to him several times. 'Come on coffee… come outside and I'll teach you how to dance with your fists!' Salvatore must have asked one of the Italian girls to translate for him and when he understood what Bull was saying he turned to face him. Without another word, Bull rushed up and hit him with a haymaker of a punch to the head. Salvatore did two somersaults and landed on his back on the dance floor. He was stunned for a moment and Bull grabbed him by the scruff of the neck and dragged him outside the dance hall."

Sam Catalano drew a deep breath and turned to address Elena, "Signora, this Bull Rogers is thirty-one years old and three times Salvatore's size and he loves getting into fights when he's drunk."

"So what happened?"

"I ran outside and called out to Bull, 'You should be ashamed of yourself, Bull. You're thirty-one years old and three times his size.' Bull dropped Salvatore like a rag doll and took a couple of steps towards me but before I knew it, Salvatore jumped up off the ground and onto Bull's back. He punched and kicked and rode him around like a wild horse and Bull bucked and twisted and pulled at him until he finally flung him off. Then he proceeded to belt Salvatore up as he sat on him on the ground. Some of the others pulled Bull off the boy but as soon as Salvatore got back onto his feet, he charged at Bull with all his might and pushed him into the barbed-wire fence at the back of the hall. Bull was caught on the fence and Salvatore just kept laying into him with all his might. As soon as Bull freed himself from the fence, the crowd broke up the fight. Salvatore was pretty badly beaten up but he certainly gave out as much as he got."

"So, where's the poor boy now?" asked Elena.

"I went up to him after the fight and he recognized me," said Sam. "I told him I would take him home but he refused."

"Why?" asked Elena.

"He said he was ashamed that you and the children should all see him beaten up so badly. He asked me to tell you not to worry and that he would come home after he had cleaned himself up."

"So, where did he go Sam?"

"I don't know Mr Cottone," he just said not to worry.

Carmelo walked the family home and then rushed across the road to the hospital. Sam had not been there. Then he went to the ambulance and the police station but Sam had not been to either of those two places. He returned home and waited until midnight but Sam did not return. Around five o'clock the next morning, Carmelo woke and realized that Salvatore still had not returned home. He shook Elena gently.

"Elena, Salvatore still hasn't returned. The only place I think he could be is at the farmhouse. He must have gone there to clean himself up and decided to stay the night. I'm leaving now. I should have thought of this last night. I pray God he is all right."

As the farmhouse came into view, Carmelo was so relieved to

see the silhouette of Sam on the verandah. He looked so small, all crouched like a child on the large white cane chair. Carmelo parked the Dodge in the shed and by the time he reached the turnstile in the fence around the house, Sam was already there to meet him. At first, he turned away but then he looked back at Carmelo and gave him a huge cheesy grin.

"I got a hiding Zio but I sure made him pay for it. He'll be just as sore as me this morning and because there was a lot more of him, hopefully he'll be a whole lot more sore as well."

Carmelo treated Sam like his own son and Sam loved and respected him in return, working hard. After eighteen months as Rosario began to take more of a leading role in the operations of the farm, it was no longer economic to employ Sam and the young man knew he would earn more money elsewhere.

"I hope you don't feel bad about it Zio, but I think the time has come for me to look for work that is more remunerative. There is a great shortage of labour in the building industry and I need to accumulate capital so that I can eventually buy a farm of my own."

"Salvatore, you've been a great help to me and I'm going to miss you very much. I wish you every success as you venture out on your own and may your future be bright. You are worth so much more than I can afford to pay you."

"Thank you, Zio. I was hoping you would understand."

"The children will miss you. You have been such a great cousin to them all and they adore you," said Elena. "Remember, you always have a home here with us," and she embraced him.

He turned to Davide, "Thanks for teaching me how to speak English." Then to Abele, "Keep on working on those crystal sets." He embraced Ross, "Hey, cugino, don't forget I'm just up the road and this could lead to an even greater friendship. Any time you want to run away, you know you can come to me."

Sam remained close by for a couple of years. At first, he worked for a bricklayer and then for Zammit at Fishery Falls on a wage of fifteen pounds per week. But the big money was to be made picking tobacco so he went to Mareeba where he could earn more than double what he was earning at Zammit's. As well, he liked the idea of tobacco farming and it was still a fledgling industry and there would be opportunities there. Carmelo watched over him wherever he went and the family often talked about Sam at the dinner table.

"I am very concerned about the company Salvatore has been keeping, Elena. Young people around Australia are becoming more and more rebellious. They don't listen to their parents, they don't respect the law and they rebel against the system. Salvatore has become involved with one of these groups from Fishery Falls and I don't think he realizes these people are undesirables. Now he has bought a motorbike and they drive around in gangs on weekends. I'm worried where this is all leading to."

"The people he hangs around with are not bad people, Papa," said Ross. "I know many of them and they come from good families. They're just young and that's what young people do these days. Times have changed. This is the new age of machines, science and technology."

"So tell me more about this new age, Saro. Tell me because I am so ignorant that I can't see it coming," retorted Carmelo.

"He's not saying you're ignorant, Meluzzo. We just have to be more open-minded these days. As people become more educated, they ask more questions and they want answers that make sense to them," explained Elena.

"Oh they do, do they?" Carmelo challenged her, "How come you know so much about all this?"

"I read about it in my 'Psychology' magazines. Young people need to feel wanted and they need to be seen as free-thinking resourceful people."

"It's all about machines, Papa. The days of farming with horses are over. To survive in farming these days, you have to become more efficient. Horses are slow. Tractors save time and time is money."

"Oh, so that's what they taught you at Gatton College?"

"Yes Papa, that's what they taught us. They taught us about the use of fertilizer and more efficient cultivation practices and the importance of scientific research. That's what the Meringa Sugar Experiment Station is about. They are trying to breed new species of cane that will grow in poorer soils and have a higher sugar content than your conventional canes like Badilla and Clark Seedling, which require rich soil and lots of fertilizers."

"I don't need you to tell me what they do at the Meringa Sugar Experiment Station, Saro. You're still only a pup and you have so much to learn."

"Don't ridicule him, Carmelo. You ridicule him and he will lose his self-esteem. It's all about psychology."

"Ah psychology... stop it with that psychology, Elena... or I'll call you psychology, that's what I'll call you."

"Well, why don't we have a tractor if you know so much, Papa? And why aren't we planting the new varieties like Pinda, Q21, Q44, and Q57?"

"It's called being prudent, Saro and prudence is a virtue. But I suppose they didn't teach you that either at Gatton College. Before we go putting our whole farm under some new cane, it's prudent to wait and see how successful it is in the field. In fact Saro, I'm thinking about planting Pinda and Q57 this year where the badilla was in front of the barracks. In fact, those two canes have been proved to be more naturally resistant to the grubs and so that will cut back on our use of gammexane. See, I'm applying your efficiency principles and I only ever finished Grade Six in Italy. Experience Saro, that's what experience teaches you. So, if that meets with the approval of scientist Saro, then we shall plant Pinda and Q57."

"What about the tractor?" Rosario persisted. "Can't we at least look at some and talk to the salesmen from Williams Estate at the Cairns Show? All the latest equipment will be on display there."

"Come on tractor... you're still persisting with this tractor business. I should call you tractor, that's what I should call you."

"Well it wouldn't do any harm to look and talk to the salesmen, would it, Meluzzo?" asked Elena.

"What aspect of psychology is that suggestion drawn from Elena?"

"It's called common sense, Meluzzo." Elena stood indignantly and collected the plates with a little more clattering than usual until Carmelo understood her message.

"Okay… okay. Maybe we should have a look at the tractors," conceded Carmelo.

"And talk to the salesmen from Williams Estate?" added Elena.

"And talk to the salesmen from Williams Estate," agreed Carmelo.

"Now would you like a nice slice of pineapple tart, Carmelo? I made it especially for you."

"I would love a nice slice of pineapple tart that you made especially for me, thank you psychologia."

"See, psychology works. It's about stimulus, response and reward," Elena whispered quietly and smiled as she gently pressed the knife into the pineapple tart.

Chapter 36

Cash economy

Rosario had just turned sixteen when he received his first pay for working on the farm. He was finally on the payroll— now it was official. Carmelo was unhappy about it and he made it quite clear in his latest letter to Nino.

20th September, 1955.

My dear and beloved brother Nino,
I must confess, I am ashamed to have to tell you that today, I paid my own son a wage for working on the family farm. This is what the world is coming to. I am ashamed to have to tell you that today he paid board to live in the family house. Everyone is becoming obsessed with money. It obviates the need for trust and the obligation for reciprocity. Isn't my farm the farm of my children? Any work they do, isn't it for themselves that they do it in the long term? This has always been the logic of our fathers and our forefathers. Where am I going wrong with my thinking, dear brother?

Now my son has bought a motorbike. All of the young people are going crazy. On weekends, they want to 'do their own thing'. They stay out late, they are secretive, they are united against authority and they spend all the money they earn on having fun. This best friend of Rosario refers to his father as 'the old man'. How much lack of respect does this show?

In the industry, nobody wants to work with horses anymore. I too have been pressured into buying a wheel tractor. The majestic silence and peacefulness of the fields is broken by the roar of the tractor and motorbike. (Rosario even comes to work on his motorbike.) Young people have forgotten how to walk. Anyhow, I refuse to have anything to do with the wheel tractor. Rosario refuses to go anywhere near a horse, so I do all my work with the horses. Tractors just make a mess in the paddocks. When they get bogged, they rip out the stool and leave gaping holes and on the hills they rear up and could easily topple. They are so dangerous. This new age torments me, Nino, whereas before it was my debts that gave me stomach ulcers, now it is the way of the world that is giving them to me.

I have planted the paddock opposite the barracks with Pinda and Q57. They are two new varieties of cane that have been crossbred from conventional canes and the wild canes from New Guinea and Indonesia. At least all this science seems to be getting something right but I still don't trust it. Who knows what effect it might have on the industry in the long term?

All the family is well and the two younger boys are doing well at school. Thank God they are still manageable and they still do normal things like play with billy-carts, balls and swords and shanghais. They still have mandarin, guava and watermelon fights. Davide likes swimming in the creek and he sometimes rides out to the farm with his little friend after school. They go fishing and catch small bream and prawns and then cook them on an open fire. Ah… to be young again. Then again I don't think I would like to be young again in this new world. Abele spends a lot of time making little crystal radio sets and he tells me he has even been able to pick up broadcasts from the BBC.

Elena is always talking about psychology and studies magazines and books relentlessly. She drives me mad with psychology this and psychology that. All I want to do is live a peaceful life and everyone around me is venturing into other worlds. Elena says I am afraid of losing control over the family and that I am authoritarian. Is that such a bad thing, Nino? I don't want my children making mistakes they will regret. I want to protect them not dominate them. When the time comes for me to meet my maker, I want to be able to say I have been a good father and husband.

The other day, Rosario and I were pulling cane trucks with the horses along the portable rails. There is a very steep hill and the horses have to be harnessed up to the trucks so that the trucks can be lowered gently down the slope. Rosario's job was to carry an iron bar and in the event of a mishap, throw the bar into the spokes of the wheel of the end truck, jam the wheels and thereby act as a brake using friction. We lower three trucks at a time which when fully loaded with cane, weigh about ten tons. On that particular day it was the last three trucks of the rake. Anyhow, I had two of my best horses Bawly and Brutus on the job and they know exactly what to do as we have done this hundreds of times before. Something went wrong and I saw Brutus' front leg buckle from under him and he went down on one knee. Bawly's nostrils flared and his eyes almost burst out of their sockets as he took the full load of the trucks on his own. "Throw the sprag... throw the sprag into the wheel!" I called out to Rosario. "One of the horses is down... throw the sprag!" He took the iron bar but already the cane trucks were gaining momentum and as he threw in the sprag, the spokes spat it out.

Ah, my dear, Nino. He is an old horse now, but I knew Bawly was never going to give in. I called out, Hold Bawly...

Hold! *And screamed to Rosario to move to safety. I saw my beloved Bawly dig his heels in and I rushed to grab the discarded iron bar. His tail went up, his back legs bowed but didn't buckle and I feared his heart would burst. The only thing to do was to throw the sprag into the spokes and hold it there so that it couldn't be vibrated out. As soon as I rammed the sprag in, the wheel began bouncing on the line and to stop it being ejected, I held it hard. The bar came down again and again crushing my fingers against the ground nine or ten times but I held hard and slowly with Bawly straining against the harness, the trucks came to a halt. Brutus was all tangled in his harness but still managed to get up, which was fortunate because I was able to give the order to Bawly to ease up and slowly, with the sprag firmly in place, he eased up and the trucks slid to the bottom of the slope. My right index finger was badly crushed and I hid my hand under my shirt so that Rosario would not see it. Rosario took over and with me shouting commands to Bawly we got the trucks down to the points and added them to the rest of the rake. I left Rosario to record the numbers of the trucks in the truck book for the loco drivers to collect and walked to the farm house. It was the August school holidays and we were all staying there for a couple of weeks.*

I washed myself in the creek and Rosario met me just as I was climbing into the Dodge to go to the hospital. I told him to tell his mother what had happened and not to worry and that I would phone her from the hospital. There, they amputated my index finger, but thank God, it could have been much worse; the horses could have been killed and Rosario injured. This letter is so long, you will probably have to read it at two sittings. Sorry to burden you with my problems and sorrows but I'm sure you would want to know everything. Rest assured that everything else is fine and the good news is that the farm is beginning to pay for itself. In fact I am negotiating to purchase a house in Cairns as an investment so things are going well financially, thank God.

I embrace you and all the family my dear Nino and yearn to visit and be amongst you all again one day soon,

Carmelo

It wasn't long before Rosario tired of the motorbike. Sure, it was trendy and all, being a BSA but the novelty had worn off and it was more Sam's style than Ross'. A couple of his mates had bought Holdens and spent hours crouched under bonnets and talking about cars and sun-visors, mud-flaps, wheel spats, car radios, exhaust systems and every other car accessory known to man. When he broke the news that he was considering buying a sedan, Carmelo was scathing in his criticism of the idea.

"You've been working for one year and already you want to buy a car. Are you mad? How can you afford a car?"

"I'm thinking of getting one on hire purchase where you put down a deposit and providing you have a full time job, the Hire Purchase Company will lend you the rest."

"I'm quite aware of how hire purchase works, Saro and how they charge anything up to twenty per cent interest up front on a contract. That means you are still paying that ridiculously high interest rate even when you only have a few payments to go. They are worse than Ned Kelly those companies and they prey on the impulsiveness of young people."

Week after week, Rosario continued to pester his father about a Holden car. He must have desired his father's blessing because he could quite easily have gone out and bought one himself as his friends had done. There was nothing Rosario could say that would change Carmelo's mind. Then one day, he added, "Motorbikes aren't safe anyhow, Papa. Too many people have been getting badly hurt in motorbike accidents." This was a different Rosario talking now and Carmelo was not expecting it.

"Yes, well you are right there," and he thought about it. "Maybe I should talk to your mother about it."

Rosario was very excited by his change of heart. "I could sell my motorbike and put the proceeds towards the new car. Tell Mamma that. She doesn't like motorbikes and that would make her happy."

As it happened, it was no longer necessary to contemplate how dangerous motorbikes were; the hospital in Cairns phoned Carmelo to inform him that Sam had badly damaged his leg in a motorbike accident.

"There's a chance he might lose his leg," he was told. "As you are his legal guardian here in Australia, the hospital will need you to come to Cairns to sign the necessary permission papers in the event of an amputation being deemed necessary."

Carmelo went to Cairns and spoke to his doctor.

"Whatever it costs, I will pay for it. Just do everything you can to save his leg, please Doctor. Send him to Townsville or to Brisbane but don't take his leg!"

"Of course we will do everything to save his leg, Mr Cottone but both the knee and the leg have been severely crushed. We have operated and at this stage the best case scenario is that his leg will be shorter and his knee will be stiff," the doctor informed him.

Carmelo felt faint and flopped down in the surgery chair becoming very short of breath.

"Just relax, Mr Cottone and take deep breaths. You are in a state of shock." The doctor brought him a glass of water. "Salvatore has pins in his knee and in his leg. It's going to be months and maybe even years before he can go back to leading a normal lifestyle. He will need months of physiotherapy and will have to be admitted to a rehabilitation hospital. At this stage, we think it will be Greenslopes or one of the other places in Brisbane. I'm sorry, Mr Cottone but that's the way it is."

When Carmelo visited Sam he could not control his emotions.

"It was an accident, Zio. It just happened."

"Salvatore, Salvatore, what are we going to do? They may have to take you to Brisbane and we won't even be able to visit you. Your poor mother and father will be devastated… their youngest son. How shall I break the news to them? We pray God that He saves your leg. Salvatore, you must pray too. I will come to visit you every second day. In the meantime, if you need me, I will come. Do you need any money?"

"No Zio, I don't need money but I need some cigarettes."

Carmelo went off to buy cigarettes, biscuits and fruit for Sam. Upon his return, Sam lapsed off into sleep and once Carmelo was satisfied he had calmed down enough, he asked permission to leave.

"Do you think it's okay if I leave now, Salvatore? I would like to go home before dark and I shall return the day after tomorrow. Remember, phone if you need me and I shall come immediately."

"Yes Zio," he held his hand. "Thanks for coming. I'm so sorry I was so stupid."

"It's happened now, Salvatore. Where there is life there is hope. Keep your spirits up and have courage." He patted his hand and then pointed at him, "and pray. We will all pray for you."

Sam did not lose his leg, but he suffered from infections and ulcers and was overcome by pain most of the time. When he was able to travel, he was sent to Taringa in Brisbane. After the accident, Rosario was banned from riding his motorbike and the family discussed him buying a car.

"Mamma and I have been thinking about you buying a car. Would you consider buying a utility instead of a sedan?"

"No Papa, I want a sedan not a work car."

"Well, the Dodge is not suitable for our family anymore and I will need something to replace it. I was thinking maybe I will buy a utility and you can buy a sedan and if we need to go out as a family, we could always go with your car."

"Of course, Papa. But how should I buy it?"

"I can lend you the money through a bank loan and you can repay me a little at a time out of your wages. At least it's far better than hire purchase."

Rosario bought the newest model FC Holden, which was quite different in design and looked modern alongside the old FJ. It was a two-toned green.

"You should get a Holden too, Papa. They're built for Australian conditions. The FC Holden Ute is a top car."

"No Saro, I prefer to buy British. I will be buying a Vanguard made by the Standard Motor Company of Britain. Unfortunately there are none in stock, so I will have to wait a few weeks until one becomes available."

In the five years since the lifeline from the Agricultural Bank, Carmelo found himself riding the post-war economic boom as he too became embroiled in the new consumer economy. Elena now had a nice home in town and a new car and her next plan was to buy a television set, which she discussed with Mrs Kapor and Mrs Robinson over afternoon tea.

"It's a pity the reception is so bad in Babinda," said Mrs Kapor.

"The price is prohibitive anyhow," added Mrs Robinson.

"Elena wants a television, Mr Cottone," Mrs Kapor called out to Carmelo who was sitting on the back step reading the paper with a beer.

"Yes, well if she can find the money, there's nothing else stopping her, Mrs Kapor."

Elena cast an eye in the direction of the piano. Abele had not played a note on it since he finished lessons two years ago.

"Maybe if I can do some wheeling and dealing ladies, we could be watching television sooner than he thinks," whispered Elena from behind a devious grin.

Chapter 37

The new farm

Tom Carr had been a well-known and respected local identity for decades. He was a wise, righteous and honest man and he had the gift of the gab so he made a successful real estate agent. He was an entertaining, easy going, low pressure salesman and he achieved results. Everyone in Babinda knew Tom was a good family man and they trusted him. He knew every property in Babinda and if ever Tom put a price on a property, most people accepted it as fair value.

The thing about Tom that distinguished him from every other man was his weight. Nobody knew what it was because no ordinary scales had the capacity to measure it. Rumour did have it that he was weighed once on the weighbridge at the Babinda Central Mill and another rumour suggested it might have been the Babinda Railway Station but if ever and wherever the weight was recorded, it has always remained confidential. He drove around in an eight cylinder Ford Customline and the springs were so compacted on the driver's side that the vehicle was always at an angle of about twenty-five degrees to the horizontal.

Carmelo had been to see his accountant at Burnell, Barret and Walsh when he saw Tom sitting in his usual position on the public bench on the footpath outside his office.

"Hello, Tom my good friend," said Carmelo because it was the truth.

Tom swivelled his whole body towards the voice because he no longer possessed a neck.

"Oh… hello, Carmelo, how's the family?"

"Good Tom and yours?" They shook hands.

"You're not looking at the possibility of opening up another farm by any chance, are you?"

"I don't know. Maybe. Why, has something come up?"

"Yeah, old Arthur Cope owns about sixty acres there between Stager's and Pollard's place. Behind where the old dump used to be. Do you know it?"

"Behind the dump is mostly swamp, isn't it?"

"That's why it's going cheap, Carlo. Going for a song. Arthur's old, he's alone and he's sick. He doesn't want the land anymore. He just wants to keep the house. I reckon you could drain that swamp and the property would become prime sugar cane country just like Lloyd's, Pollard's and Stager's. On the southern side, Butler's farm and Steve Tuttle's farm, that's good country. Are you interested in having a look at it?"

"Maybe."

"Have you got half an hour to look at it now? Good, leave your car here and we'll go have a look at it. Now that you have Ross on the farm you need to be thinking about expanding."

They went to see the property and Carmelo liked what he saw.

"Yes Tom, if that swamp can be drained, I know I could turn it into a good farm."

"Well, I have just the right man who can give you an opinion on that and an idea of how much it would cost. My daughter's husband Arthur Stroud is a backhoe operator. He digs drains for a living. Why don't you have a talk to him and see what he has to say? That's if you're interested of course... "

Carmelo was interested and after talking to Arthur and getting a second opinion from Sam Gaviola who operated an excavator, he bought the farm. Four people drained that swamp and made a farm out of it; Stroud with his backhoe, Gaviola with his excavator, Phillips with his swamp dozer and Carmelo with his shovel. One day, Carmelo came home with six freshwater eels.

"I have never seen so many eels, Elena. With every bucket of mud in some places, they dig up three or four eels."

"Well don't look at me, I won't be cooking them," his wife muttered.

"Yuk," exclaimed Rosario as Carmelo hung them from a tree and proceeded to skin them. The slime was thick and sticky. "I won't be eating them, that's for sure."

"Me either," said Abele, while Davide stood in amazement.

"They're just like the ones that I sometimes see lurking under the pannikin grass in the creek, Papa."

"Same thing, only these are a smaller variety, Davide."

Carmelo cleaned the eels and cut them into chunks before stewing them slowly with garlic, onions, tomatoes, celery, black olives and potato. The meat when cooked was snow white and the meal smelt appetizing. Elena attempted a meagre helping but the two older boys refused. Davide claimed he had stomach ache and didn't want to eat anything. Carmelo insisted the meal was scrumptious but for whatever reason, he gave the rest of the eels away to the neighbours and never brought any home ever again.

After the new farm was cleared and drained, most of the work involved picking up roots and burning them, along with the piles of fallen scrub and palm trees. Some of the piles would burn for days. By the beginning of the next season, they had forty acres ready to plant and had built a shed to house the tractors, some of the implements and the fertilizer. The tractors were proving to be a Godsend and they had to purchase a second more powerful wheel tractor to do much of the heavier work. Because Carmelo refused to drive the wheel tractors, most of the work on the farm apart from the ploughing and the scarifying was done by Rosario. Soon, the new farm plus Happy Valley were becoming too much for him. Father and son began to quarrel because there weren't enough hours in the day to complete the countless tasks. Often, they would get home after dark and Rosario would be upset because he had arranged to go out with his mates and there wasn't even enough time to eat.

"Saro, eat the beautiful meal I made you," his mother would implore him.

"I haven't got time, Mamma. I have another life apart from work, you know." Sometimes, he would start eating it to appease her and then feed the rest to his pig-dog Terry who was his constant companion on the farm.

This went on night after night throughout the whole season and it would often be after two in the morning before he went to bed. So they quarrelled about rising in the morning as Carmelo wanted to be on the farm before dawn every day. Thus on some days, Rosario had to get by on less than three hours sleep.

Then one day, Rosario told his father and mother that he had found the girl he wanted to marry. The dilemma now was where they could live. The farm house had become quite dilapidated. It needed painting and there was a problem with white ants. As well, there was no electricity and his bride-to-be was a city girl from Cairns, so something had to be done about that. Times had changed and the wood stove, the kerosene and carbide lamps were things of the dim distant past. What was once the norm for farming families was now too ridiculous to contemplate. They repaired and painted the house as best they could and wired the house to DC current, which at least gave them lights. They used primuses for cooking but had to persevere with the kerosene fridge. Rosario used a water pump attached to the power take-off of the tractor to refill the tanks every week from the creek so that the washing could be done at the house. In Elena's time, most of the washing had been done in the creek.

On the third of October 1959, Rosario married Bini Dekker and they moved into the house at Happy Valley to start their new life together.

Sam, who had spent almost three years in rehabilitation in Brisbane, returned in time for the wedding and began working for Carmelo again. This time he cut cane because the money was far better than wages.

"I cannot understand how that man does it," Carmelo told Elena. "He has just come out of hospital after three years of operations and skin grafts and despite a short leg and a stiff knee, he still gets to the end of the row first every time. He has the heart of a lion."

"I worry that he might do some permanent damage if he keeps working at that pace," said Elena. "What can we do to help him?"

"Maybe we can buy a property together like Loiaconi's place and give him a start. We'll just have to take it one day at a time and let him make the decisions."

Sam finished the season cutting cane and went straight to Mareeba to pick and grade tobacco and with the money he saved went into partnership with Carmelo on Loiaconi's farm, which they bought for six hundred pounds.

As fate would have it, the farm was a great investment. Much of the value on a new farm was often recoverable through the timber on it. However, in Loiaconi's case, Carmelo and Sam were told most of the millable timber had already been removed. As well, Loiaconi had already sold the cane assignment on the place so it could not be used to grow sugar cane anymore. So in the end, they bought it cheaply as a cattle property. When Rosario, Sam and Jack Pontefract, a timber cutter, walked through the scrub to assess the quantity of timber left on it, to their surprise, they found that Loiaconi had been reading the map upside down. So all the timber Loiaconi thought he had taken off his property, had in fact been taken from Crown land. To add to their good fortune, Loiaconi's neighbour Rocco Cristiano had also been reading the map upside down and had planted cane on what was actually Loiaconi's property. Thus he paid them compensation to retain the land.

With the profits from the sale of the timber, the sale of his half share of Loiaconi's farm to Carmelo and the compensation from Cristiano, Sam went share farming on a tobacco crop at Emerald Creek with Phillip DeFelice and was finally self-employed. He had a solid grounding and Carmelo now had his herd of cattle, which had always been prominent in his dreams. Only it wasn't remotely near the size of the cattle station he had imagined. To him, they were like pets and his favourite was Jersey the house cow, who Carmelo retired to live her days out with the herd. He would see them every day and spent most of his time mending fences and spraying the cattle.

With Jim Lloyd, they built a state of the art cattle-yard and went to cattle sales to purchase prime Hereford cattle for breeding. Jim Lloyd had a sugar cane farm near the new farm but his true passion was cattle as well.

"Cattle farming is the way to go, Carlo. There's a huge demand for good quality meat now and that's why the Yanks have moved into the industry. 'Kings Ranch' is an American company and they have purchased huge tracts of land throughout North Queensland for cattle grazing."

"Yes, but I read they are having major problems with cattle-ticks and are moving over to Brahman breeds from India that are tick resistant."

"Sure, but that's only in the outlying areas where they have little contact with the cattle. Close in where they are planting improved pastures, it's all prime quality Australian Hereford beef."

As his cattle became accustomed to his routine, Carmelo could stand at the yard and call out to the herd. The whole valley was a caldera and his voice carried to every nook and cranny in the hills and soon they would assemble, walking single file back to the cattle yard with Jersey at the helm. There he would have their reward waiting for them; lashings of thick amber-black molasses spread over four separate troughs made out of halved forty-four gallon drums.

Rosario was settling into married life and had presented Carmelo with his first grandchild Malcolm Carl Anthony Cottone. Rosario could not be persuaded to follow tradition and name his son Carmelo after his father and his father would never ask him to do so. But he did include Carl for that very reason. Of course the name Anthony was insisted upon too because of his beloved brother and Carmelo would have fought hard to have that name included. Again Rosario gave him the English version, Anthony a wise decision as that too was Bini's father's name. Their second child, Denise Concettina gave Carmelo and Elena their first granddaughter thus Elena was ecstatic.

Abele had been at All Soul's School in Charters Towers for over a year and was progressing well in English, science and mathematics, but he was unhappy there. Elena had been too loving a mother and like Rosario once had, he missed home. He was quite popular with his housemates because Elena would send the best food parcels every month and after sporting prowess, the quality and size of food parcels was the second best determiner of peer acceptance.

What he objected to most was the brutality of the punishment meted out to students; often for very minor infringements of the rules. This included caning across the bare posterior and the use of the dreaded penny belt; a long leather pouch loaded with pennies to offer weight, which was used to belt the students. By telling Carmelo about this, he saved his younger brother Davide from the same fate as the younger of the two travelled by bus to the State's high school in Innisfail, thirty kilometres south of Babinda. Abele was forced to finish his Junior Certificate year of schooling at All Souls before joining Davide at the high school for his two Senior Certificate years of study, which would enable him to enter university.

Now that they no longer had access to Rosario's car, Elena approached Carmelo about buying a sedan.

"It needs to be automatic because I simply cannot drive a car with gears. I have tried so many times with the Vanguard and I simply cannot do it."

It didn't matter how many 'but Elena this' and 'but Elena thats' Carmelo put forward, Elena persisted until one day, for her birthday, Carmelo went to Williams Estate Cars and brought home a sage green SV1 Valiant.

"There you are, Elena it's automatic and it's all yours. It's even in your name. I didn't get the RV1 with the tyre imprint on the boot because I know you like everything modern. Happy birthday my love," and he kissed her.

Life was beginning to stagnate for Rosario's part. He had two children and he was struggling with an average wage. He knew he could earn more elsewhere and talked of putting his expertise to better use. Carmelo sensed it was time to act on improving Rosario's lot and considered making a handover of the Happy Valley farm to Rosario. He consulted Tom Carr on the matter.

"Tom, how can I arrive at a fair price on the Happy Valley Farm in order to sell it to Rosario?"

"I can tell you what that farm's worth. I can get you twenty thousand pounds for that farm within a week if you're in a hurry. Maybe a little bit more if you're not."

"Yes, that's what I think it is worth as well but I want to sell it to my son at a discount. How can he be sure he is getting a fair price?"

"Very easy, Carlo," said Tom. "To be fair, these deals have to be conducted at arm's length and then everything is above board and nobody can complain afterwards. Give me one week and I'll have an offer for your farm in writing for twenty thousand pounds. You go with this offer to Ross and you say, 'This is what I have been offered. From you, because you are my son, this is what I want... '."

"Thank you, Tom. Do your best my friend and contact me when you have something."

Within a week, Tom phoned Carmelo asking him to come to his office.

"Saffiotti has made a firm offer on your farm. I need you to come down to discuss it."

When Carmelo arrived, Tom presented him the letter.

"He's being a bit cagey, trying to get it cheap. He's offered nineteen thousand pounds in writing. I figured if your discount to Rosario brings the price to less than that, then we do not need to negotiate with Saffiotti any further," said Tom. "Will this letter suffice, Carlo?"

"This letter is perfect, Tom. I will be asking Rosario for only sixteen thousand pounds with some conditions. I am very much obliged to you for doing this for me."

"It's my pleasure. Hope it all goes well for you and young Ross. He's a good boy, that one. Other people should be so lucky." Then he tapped Carmelo on the shoulder three times and with the characteristic, "Eh... eh... eh... " and a wink, he added, "... and you're a pretty good dad. Other kids should be so lucky."

Carmelo hurried home to discuss the matter with Elena who was so happy for Rosario and Bini to be given this opportunity— to have their own farm. They decided to act immediately; it was Elena who drove.

Rosario and Bini accepted the farm at sixteen thousand pounds and the conditions were very reasonable. Rosario would continue working on the new farm until Carmelo could sell it. For his work, he would be paid a wage that would be deducted from the cost of the Happy Valley Farm. The equipment on the Happy Valley Farm would also be pooled for use on both farms until such time as the new farm was sold.

For Sam, on the other hand, life had become a living nightmare. Early one morning, Carmelo received a phone call from the Mareeba Hospital. Sam had been involved in an accident where his vehicle was sideswiped by an oncoming truck. His arm had been put in plaster but within twenty-four hours, it had become gangrened and he would lose his right arm. Carmelo was needed yet again to sign the relevant papers. When Carmelo arrived at Sam's bedside, his right arm had already been amputated above the elbow. Carmelo broke down and cried as Sam described the tragic course of events.

"Zio, the damage to my arm was nothing like the damage to my knee. The elbow was chipped and they put it in plaster because that's what they do. It was nothing out of the ordinary. The doctor they contacted was Flecker and he was sour as anything because he was off duty. He'd been drinking and he had a snarl on his face as he put the plaster on. I complained it was too tight. After about half an hour, I asked the nurse to tell him I was in pain. He was in a hurry to leave and he half looked at it and said, 'There's nothing wrong with it. You Italians are all the same; all you do is whinge.' They gave me something to make me sleep but in the middle of the night, I woke up with this tremendous pain in my arm. It was blue. The nurse was also worried when she saw it and she phoned Flecker to inform him. He told her to give me painkillers and that he would see me in the morning. This morning Zio, when he saw it, Flecker couldn't look me in the eye. It was too late and the arm had already become gangrened. I told them to phone you but they couldn't wait for fear it would spread to the rest of my body. Now I have lost my arm, Zio and that is the complete story."

"I am so sorry, Salvatore that I wasn't here last night after it happened. I could have done something."

"I didn't call you because it was not a major break. It was just a chip on my elbow. I was going to call you this morning."

"Make sure you get the name of the nurse on duty. We will certainly pursue this matter further. I will return to Babinda and arrange for Abele and Davide to come and help you on the farm as soon as the school holidays commence."

Sam was in the middle of harvesting his tobacco crop and the reports that filtered back from Abele and Davide were mind blowing.

"Sam acts as if he never lost his arm," said Abele.

"Yes, he never talks about it and he never complains or says things like 'Can you help me, I only have one arm'," added Davide.

"He picks tobacco with the other workers to set the pace. Nobody can keep up with him. He picks a handful and puts it down on the ground. Then every ten bundles or so he goes back and rams them under the stub of his arm, walks across the drills and deposits the pile onto the tobacco bags," was Abele's example.

"He asked me to climb up the chimney of the tobacco barn to release a vent that had jammed. Papa, you know me, I'm petrified of heights. 'I can't go up there Sam, I'm scared of heights I wouldn't go up there for quids,' I told him. He simply replied 'Okay' and proceeded to climb the ladder to the top. Don't ask me how he hung on and released the vent at the same time but he did," was Davide's example. "I was so ashamed of myself but Sam never said a word or mentioned it again. Papa, I will never forget that day and his courage."

"Not only that," added Abele, "one day he got into an argument with DeFelice who he's sharefarming with and DeFelice made the mistake of saying to him 'I don't want to get into an argument with you, you've only got one arm'. Well, Sam hit him three or four times with his left hand and as DeFelice ran away, Sam picked up a stick and chased him into the tobacco barn where he climbed out of Sam's reach and started calling out to his father for help."

"Sam's a legend, Papa."

It now fell upon Carmelo to have to write a letter to Sam's parents in Sicily. In their eyes, he was responsible for their son.

5th November, 1962

My dear cousins, Antonino and Philippina,
It is with a heavy, heavy heart that I have to inform you that your beloved son, Salvatore had another accident and this time it resulted in the loss of his right arm. If only I knew of any other way to tell you this, which might make the situation less tragic or less heart-breaking for you and your family, I would. He has infinite courage and any lesser man would never be able to cope with such misfortune. But Salvatore must be made of better mettle than most because he never gives up. Already he is back working on the farm and acts as if nothing has happened. He does not see himself as handicapped in any way and continues to live his life to the full. He is an inspiration to us all.

I thank God that he has blessed Salvatore with such a positive attitude to life and I know in my own heart that if Salvatore does not turn against God, then his reward like Job in the Bible, will come to him when God sees fit. I wish him every success and a long active life and I pray that God in the short term will grant him the opportunity to find a good wife and raise a family so that he will experience some joy in his life. Surely he deserves this after having had so much misfortune and disappointment in life to date. I pray for him every night and for God to comfort you both and his siblings Luigi, Teresina and Sara after such sad tidings. Rest assured that we will always be here for Salvatore who has always been one of us and more than that as someone we all respect and admire. Salvatore sends his undying love and loyalty to you all. May God bless you and help you through this dark chapter in your lives,

Carmelo

Chapter 38
The prodigal sons

The city was probably not such a good place for country boys like Abele and Davide; especially if they were to go there to study. Abele went to the University of Queensland to study Dentistry but his heart was never really in it because he claimed all he ever wanted to do was study Medicine. Davide went to the University of Queensland to study Law but his heart was never really in it either because he claimed all he ever wanted to do was to be a writer, a rock star or a school teacher if the other two preferences never came to pass.

The other characteristic they both shared was their love of the social life that university students enjoyed. Despite all of Carmelo's efforts and sacrifices for wanting only the best for his children, his ambitions were always thwarted by the fact that his children had a different view of what was best for them. They were young, they were foolish and they disappointed their parents terribly.

Abele left university unexpectedly and went to work as a labourer on a cane farm on the outskirts of Babinda as he couldn't find any other work half way through the year.

With what turned out to be a stroke of good fortune after the 'Bay of Pigs' incident with Cuba, America cancelled all of her sugar contracts with that country and looked to Australia to guarantee supply. The price of sugar skyrocketed and cane farmers were refurbishing their houses, upgrading their machinery and buying speedboats with the additional cash that was flowing into their coffers. Sugar mills were scrambling to issue new assignments to prospective farmers but the requirement stated that only new farmers could apply.

The main idea behind the regulation was to provide opportunities for the needy and not the greedy.

Abele seized the opportunity to acquire the land around Peter Accatino's farm which was next door to the Happy Valley home farm now owned by Rosario. To this he added Loiaconi's place which Carmelo owned and which adjoined both the home farm and Accatino's place.

His application for an assignment was successful and in a short period of time, he had readied the farm for planting. However, things did not go as well as had been anticipated in the industry. The 'Bay of Pigs' incident was over almost as soon as it had begun and the flow-on effect soon petered out. A world oversupply of sugar suddenly caused prices to plummet. Undeterred, Abele planted the farm with cane and worked very hard from dawn until dusk. Soon his debtors were writing threatening letters to him and all the bookwork was beginning to frustrate him.

"We can make this work, Abele," Elena assured him. "You worry about working the farm and I'll do all the worrying about the books."

She negotiated with each of his debtors and before long even with the poor prices, he was beginning to prevail. He also did extra work loading other farmers' cane under contract with a front-end loader to supplement his income. Like his father, hard work never fazed him.

Other assignees were not so fortunate and many were forced to sell. Abele's dogged determination had allowed him to rise to the challenge where many others had failed.

After two years of Law studies at the University of Queensland, Davide withdrew from his studies and went to work in the Commonwealth Bank in Brisbane and in Cairns. It provided an income and it was simplistic work. Carmelo had to accept his decision.

"Papa, I want to be a writer. I know you cannot make a living from writing so that is why I have to have a permanent job. Working in the bank is easy and secure. I can write in my spare time."

"But Davide, your Mamma and I have made all of these sacrifices so that you could have a good education."

"I may not have a good job, but I do have a good education, Papa and that will never be lost. You have given me the best start in life that any parent can hope to give his child. Now it's up to me as to what I do with it. I want to write. I promise you, I will not be remaining in the bank sitting in an office behind a desk doing mindless work. It is simply a means to an end."

Carmelo could not understand the rationale at all.

"What is the use of a good education if you can't get a good job?" he asked Elena.

Elena cajoled him, attempting to help him come to terms with Davide's decision.

"We must learn to let go, Meluzzo. This is his life to live and we have to accept the fact that we cannot live his life for him; just like we couldn't for Rosario or Abele. When our children are born, the doctor cuts the umbilical cord but we cling to them as children as if they are still attached to us. Now they are adults, we have to stop fooling ourselves that they are going to do what we want them to."

"But good children do what their parents want them to do. It's about respect, appreciation, obligation. It's about all of the things that keep families together, Elena."

"Exactly, Meluzzo and they were good children. But now they are adults. Rosario has two children of his own. He has already flown the nest. Abele and Davide flew the nest the day they left for university. We will always be here for them but this is the way of the world."

"I don't understand why it has to end like this. It brings me great disappointment. We don't deserve this. It's not 'the way of the world' that I have always known in my family. I have three children but I still love my siblings. I have never stopped writing to Nino. Why can't things stay the same for us too?"

"Carmelo, nothing's changed, it's just the next stage of their lives; just like it was for you and for me when we left our parents. We never even saw our parents alive again. At least, we still have our children nearby. How much luckier are we? It's not the end as you call it, it's just another beginning. It's not a disappointment. How could we be disappointed with what God gave us? We have three loving, healthy and intelligent children and two beautiful grandchildren. We have been blessed all our lives."

"I never gave up on anything," persisted Carmelo. "Even when I sold the new farm, I went in search of another property to develop. Now that dairy farm at Middlebrook is a showcase farm. I did it all for them and this is the thanks I get."

"Well, maybe this is a warning for us to start doing something for ourselves. We are not getting any younger, Meluzzo. You have already lost Teresa and only last year, your brother Angelino passed away. I lost my brother Liborio. Don't you think it's time we went back to visit those siblings you talk about before it's too late? After all, we promised we would."

Carmelo was moved by this and tears welled in his eyes as he contemplated the words and his loved ones.

"Yes Elena, you are right. It is time to honour our promise to our family in Italy. I will place the dairy farm on the market and as soon as it is sold we will go to see them."

"It's been almost thirty years, Meluzzo. We will have to go via America so you can visit Archangela there and we'll have to travel across Italy to find my remaining brothers and sisters. How I miss my Luisa and I wonder what my baby brother Giannino looks like now that he is a man. Then there are the children. We will see all of their children for the very first time."

Sam received a compensation payment of ten thousand pounds for the loss of his arm. He fell in love and married an Australian girl, Yvonne Norris and for their honeymoon, they went to Italy to meet Sam's family. They remained there for nine months and by the time they returned, Yvonne spoke Italian fluently. Both of Sam's sisters were school teachers and his brother Luigi was a university professor so she learned to speak 'proper' Italian. He returned to tobacco farming with Yvonne and share-farmed with Peter Cresta at Paddy's Green west of Mareeba on the road to Dimbulah.

Carmelo never gambled. However, for as long as everyone could remember he had bought Golden Casket tickets— a State lottery established to fund hospitals in Queensland.

"It goes to a good cause," he claimed. "it's not the same as gambling."

When the Sydney Opera House was under construction between 1959 and 1973, the New South Wales Government ran a lottery to help finance the cost. Carmelo subscribed to the purchase of one five pound ticket in every lottery drawn; the result of each draw was issued by mail. First prize was one hundred thousand pounds. After several years as a subscriber, the Opera House Lottery envelope arrived with the result slip as usual and Carmelo checked the contents to see whether he had won any minor prizes. To his surprise, instead of the standard result slip, there was a letter inside as well.

Dear Mr Cottone,

We are pleased to inform you that your ticket, Number 70132 has won you the Consolation Prize in the Sydney Opera House Lottery for being one number off the winning number 70133. (See result slip attached). The consolation prize is 1 500 pounds plus 1 500 pounds worth of tickets in the next Opera House Lottery Draw. A cheque for the sum of 1 500 pounds and 300 Opera House Lottery tickets will be forwarded to you by registered mail.
Congratulations and thank you for your continued support as a subscriber.

He assembled the family together to tell them the news.

"Wow!" said Rosario, "But for one ticket, we could have all retired."

"I don't know about retired but we certainly could have purchased a cattle station somewhere and at least you three boys would have been set up for life," added Carmelo.

"We've also had an offer from some New Zealand investors on the dairy farm at Middlebrook and I've accepted. Finally, Mamma and I are going to Italy and America to visit our relatives." The siblings were thrilled for them; but especially for Elena who had so dearly wanted to go for such a long time.

The free tickets won about another fifteen hundred pounds worth of minor prize money and at least some of this was soon put to good use by Elena who bought a set of fourteen matching suitcases.

Elena documented the entire journey in her diary and filmed parts of it using a Super Eight movie camera. They departed on the cruise ship SS *ORIANA* from Sydney and the first stage of the journey was to cross the Pacific Ocean through the Panama Canal and visit Carmelo's sister Archangela in Newark, New Jersey. They stayed there for an extended period of time and Carmelo developed a long-lasting jovial relationship with his niece Marie whom he adored and her husband Al DiMartino.

Then they crossed the Atlantic to Europe and disembarked in Naples, Italy on the 18th of June, 1968. First, they visited Elena's brother Mario and her sister Giulia and then Liborio's widow, Carmelina and her son Ettore. They visited Meluzzo's sister Adele and her husband Arimondo next before they travelled to Elena's home town of Enna where she paid her respects to her dearly departed mother, father and brother Liborio at the Tomba di Famiglia Coppola. This simple act gave her closure and she was thankful for it. Finally she was able to spend time with her beloved sister Luisa and they transformed into two young children again where nothing else in the world mattered and the world was their oyster. The more time passed, the more relaxed the whole family became with their presence and they simply blended in to the normal routine of daily life.

Carmelo would often wander the fields with his nephew Rosario and he would relay stories about the old days.

"So, you never got your licence to carry arms to protect the sheep from the bandits with Nonno's blunderbuss?" Carmelo joked.

"Well, for a start, the legendary Don Peppino never returned to Sicily and he was my ticket to that licence. Secondly, commonsense prevailed and I chose 'The Bible' over the rifle."

"A wise choice my dear, Rosario," acknowledged Carmelo.

"Whatever happened to Don Peppino? Did anyone eventually find out, Zio?"

"Yes, your father wrote to me when he discovered the truth many years ago but he always kept it a secret from Teresa who adored him. It would have broken her heart and he could not bring himself to inflict that heartache. He never did escape to Paris; he was captured and tortured by Mussolini's thugs, the Black Shirts. He had refused to cooperate and was clubbed to death in his cell. They say that throughout the ordeal, he relentlessly called 'Viva L'Italia': the very words of his father and my grandfather when they fought for the liberation of Italy in the 1860s. Ah… my dear Rosario, Don Peppino was truly a noble man and a gentleman in every sense of those words."

Soon it was Christmas. It would be their first in Italy since 1936. However, their biggest surprise was to discover that the domestic situation had entirely transformed in Australia. Carmelo who had received the phone call, sat down to explain it to Antonino and Elena.

"I cannot believe Rosario has sold the farm at Happy Valley," he told them outright.

"Rosario said he has had enough of farming for no profit and he wants to try something else." The report was met with silence as everyone in the room contemplated what could be said.

"The last three years have been dreadful," Elena finally spoke, trying to bolt on some justification to the decision. "They have been running the farm at a loss along with everybody else in the industry. Ross is in the unfortunate position of owing a lot of money to the bank. He even bought his own harvester so that he could cut his own cane and virtually bought himself a job while times were tough. I had hoped that with Davide leaving the bank and helping him for the season with the harvesting, Ross and Bini could survive."

"If they were running at a loss, why couldn't they simply close the farm down until things improved? Rosario could have gotten a job and at least, they would be ahead at the end of the year," suggested Antonio.

"The system in the industry today Nino, is that each farmer has an assignment or a right to deliver so many tons of cane to the mill. This assignment is recalculated every three years and adjusted to a figure, either up or down, which is the average of the tonnage over the last three years. If Rosario were to close the farm for three years, his assignment would revert to zero and he would not be allowed to grow cane anymore," replied Carmelo.

"Seems a bit unfair to me."

"It's the law of the jungle; survival of the fittest," said Elena.

"The mills would argue that it's not their problem. They have contracts to supply a certain amount of sugar to their customers so they need some guarantee of supply. That's where the assignment system originated," explained Carmelo.

"So, what will he do now?" asked Antonio.

"Apparently, the Australian Sugar Producers' Association had been approached by the West Indian Government about bringing over a foreign expert to advise on harvesting efficiency in their country. The position was advertised through their newsletter and Saro was interviewed by a panel at the Meringa Sugar Experiment Station near Cairns. He got the job and will be flying to the West Indies this coming February for three months.

He hopes to come to Italy with his wife at the end of the contract, so my dear Ninuzzo, at least you will get to meet my first born. After that, who knows what God has in store for him and his family."

For Easter they travelled to Rome, spending Easter with Giannino, Elena's baby brother, who was Commissioner of Police. After Easter, they returned to Sicily to be with Carmelo's family in his home town of Agira. There, they stayed with Rosario the priest and his sister Luisa, the two children of his brother Angelino. This was the old family home and Carmelo slept in the room where he had slept as a child. From there, they could visit Nino and his wife in Assaro where they lived in an apartment attached to his daughter Cettina's place.

In early May, after his contract with the West Indies had expired, Rosario and Bini arrived in Agira to meet the family. The festivities began all over again and the relaxed country atmosphere to which

Carmelo and Elena had become accustomed became bedlam again. Visits to all the families, to the cemeteries to pay respect to the dead and to all the places of interest became the new agenda and totally exhausted Carmelo and especially Elena who was developing mobility issues.

Carmelo did not discuss the sale of the farm with Rosario.

"What's done is done," was all he had to say on the matter.

"What else is happening in Australia? How's Abele coping with the downturn in the industry?"

"He just keeps plodding on, Papa. Just before I left, the Shire Council approached him about wanting to take the thirty-five acres of land, which belongs to him from the creek right up through the hills and including The Boulders for a National Park. They have offered him some ridiculously small amount of money for compensation but he refused. He managed to stall them by telling them he was waiting for you to return from Italy before making a decision."

"Good... and Davide?"

"After finishing the season with me, David went to Brisbane to continue working on the novel he was writing while living on the money he had saved. He finished the novel and the money ran out so he has since got a job with the ANZ bank this time. He is stationed in Home Hill, is heavily involved with putting on a production of *Summer of the Seventeenth Doll* and is going steady with a school teacher from Brisbane who is teaching in Home Hill."

"What will you be doing after you leave us, Saro?"

"Bini and I are going to visit her relatives in Holland. She was only thirteen when she emigrated so she is very excited about that. In Australia, until I decide what to do in the longer term, I have been offered a job driving the harvester for Jim Robinson in Babinda."

So Ross and Bini travelled to Holland. Carmelo and Elena embarked on the cruise ship SS GALILEO for their return journey to Australia via Malaga in Spain and Durban in South Africa and disembarked in Brisbane. Ironically, Elena did not have one day of sea-sickness for the entire ocean journey. This time she was returning home.

Chapter 39

Another day another battle

Carmelo returned to the fray where another battle was looming over the pending resumption of Abele's land involving thirty-five acres including the scenic spot known as The Boulders by the Council. Pritchard, a local businessman in Babinda had the timber rights to the property and was demanding compensation from the Mulgrave Shire Council. Carmelo made an offer on Abele's behalf to give the land to the Council for free in return for the right to purchase a special lease for land at East Russell on the other side of Babinda. The Shire Clerk Mr Forno agreed to Carmelo's generous offer and began making preparations to initiate the land resumption. Pritchard, however, would not accept the Council's figure for compensation and continued to flex his muscles over his timber entitlements until he received the desired compensation. Now that the land was being given to the Council for free, the money that Abele was entitled to was given to Pritchard and the Council acquired their land.

Abele purchased the Special Lease on the East Russell land and found that his access was blocked by a drain that the Winder brothers had dug on their property in order to drain their land into the Russell River. The brothers would not agree to build a bridge so Abele had to approach the Council to mediate in the matter. The Council decided that a bridge should be built and that each of the three parties including the Council should share the cost equally. The brothers refused to make any payment. Meanwhile, Abele needed access to his block so he decided to build a temporary crossing so that he could begin clearing the land. He brought all of the materials to the site but before the bridge could be built, the materials mysteriously vanished.

Carmelo decided the matter needed to be brought to the attention of a higher authority so he arranged for the Member for Mulgrave, Roy Armstrong to make an appointment for him to see the State Minister for Lands, Mr Sullivan. He then packed his cheese sandwiches like he did so many years earlier. Roy was at the station to meet him in Brisbane and together they met with Mr Sullivan.

Just like before, Carmelo meticulously explained all that had transpired in relation to the case from the Council's resumption of the thirty-five acres to the Pritchard saga and on to the threats and abuse Abele had received from the Winder brothers culminating in the eventual theft of the bridge building materials.

"What sort of cowboys are these in your electorate who seem to think they can ride roughshod over our system of law and order, Mr Armstrong?" asked the Minister. "Of course that is a rhetorical question Honourable Member for Mulgrave, but let me assure both you and Mr Cottone that this sort of behaviour will not be tolerated. I intend to approach the Police Minister personally about this matter and we'll see if we cannot sort this matter out for once and for all."

He addressed his secretary, "Please arrange for a letter to be sent immediately to the Police in Babinda stating that the matter regarding the theft of building materials on the Cottone property at East Russell has been brought to my attention and that I will be taking the matter up with the Police Minister in person. Request that they be particularly vigilant that such an event does not re-occur. As well, I want a copy of the letter to be sent to the Mulgrave Shire Clerk, Mr Forno and a separate letter thanking him for his diligence in this matter and asking him to begin construction of the said bridge post-haste and to refer any matters of concern to me directly."

Mr Armstrong was delighted with the expedience with which the issue was resolved.

"Come on, Carlo, let's celebrate this with a beer at the bar and a meal in the Parliamentary Refectory."

"Okay and thanks for organizing this Roy... my shout!"

"No need, Carlo. It's all on the house here."

"Yes Roy, I was joking. I've been here and done this before."

Carmelo returned to Babinda and there was no further trouble from that day forward at East Russell. In fact, the only troubles approaching were those associated with the onset of old age. First it was detached retinas and then cataracts in the eyes. One hip had to be replaced and then the other. After that, he began having trouble with his breathing and was diagnosed with emphysema. Elena had problems with her kidneys and hardening of the arteries. It seemed health issues were going to present the next battleground Carmelo was going to have to negotiate on his journey through this life.

But there were times of great happiness too; Davide married the school teacher, Elizabeth Rose Curnow and after one more year in the bank was accepted as a trainee teacher with the Department of External Territories at the Australian School of Pacific Administration in Sydney. He trained for two years and was appointed as a teacher in Rabaul, Papua New Guinea for four years where he enrolled in further studies by correspondence. From there, he moved to Brisbane and taught in high schools for Education Queensland. In his remaining spare time, he wrote poems, plays, musicals, short stories and two novels.

He had frequent contact with Carmelo because every time his parents were sick they would travel to Brisbane for medical treatment. He and Elizabeth had five children; Amatiz Elena Francesca, Antony Byron, Claire Elizabeth, Julia Rose and Louise Christine. With four girls, Elena was in her element whenever they were reunited. Every year without fail, Davide would bring his family north for Christmas and it was a joyous time and truly a time of peace.

Abele married another school teacher Laurel Shields and was a successful cane farmer. In his spare time, he studied iridology, acupuncture and herbal medicines and had measured success treating many patients to whom conventional medical practitioners had given little hope. He never accepted any payment from his patients. He had two children, a boy Carl Justin and a girl Kirsten Leigh.

Rosario bought a dairy farm and then a fuel depot and eventually returned to cane farming at Cowley, south of Babinda before retiring to Withcott near Toowoomba. Ross liked to refer to himself as 'The Pony from the Back Block', but intellectually at least he was always at the forefront of the phenomenal social, political, economic, religious and technological changes that swept the globe during his lifetime.

He embraced the mechanization of the sugar industry, was a highly skilled plant operator and within a short period of time was able to repair, strip and rebuild his machinery and equipment as well as being innovative and inventive in the area of mechanical harvesting.

With the advent of the technological era he faced those challenges passionately as well in spite of his advancing years and again in a very short time he was able to repair and rebuild his own computers. He taught himself highly advanced computer skills and utilized complex interactive financial tools and programs to trade in Derivatives, CFDs, Forex and Commodity Markets.

In his old age, Carmelo tended his vegetable garden and in his spare time read book after book. The more he read, the more he desired to read. One day, Davide went to the verandah where Carmelo was lying down reading. Always, when Davide came to sit with him, Carmelo would sit up in bed and put his book and glasses on the bedside table and erupt into conversation. He always had something interesting to chat about whether it was politics, the economy, religion, philosophy or one of the books he was reading. This particular day the book that he put down was by Plato.

"Plato!" exclaimed Davide when he saw the book, "Don't tell me you're reading Plato now, Papa?"

"Ah, Davide, now I can die happy."

"Why's that, Papa?"

"Have a quick look through the book and see all the parts I have underlined."

Davide flicked through the book and there were pencil marks throughout the entire book.

"You really have made a study of it. What did you read in particular that will allow you to die happy?"

"The part about women, Davide. Even Plato confesses he could not understand women. It has always worried me that women are so different from us men and I thought it must just be me so I have never discussed it. Even Plato gave up trying in the end. So now I can give up trying too and I can die happy."

"Papa you make me laugh," said Davide.

Elizabeth had sent him a copy of A.B. Facey's 'A Fortunate Life' and one Christmas holiday when Davide brought the family up to visit them, Carmelo mentioned it to him.

"What an incredible man Facey was. He was so accepting of his lot in life and thankful for what he had. I don't think I have ever enjoyed a book so much. You know, Davide I should get a biographer to write about my life. You have to admit, it has been an interesting life and it would be nice to be able to share it with someone else."

"You never speak about it, Papa. Both you and Mamma have always been so secretive about your lives. We hardly know anything about our family tree let alone your youth or experiences in Italy."

"What do you mean... what do you want to know?" asked Carmelo innocently as if it could all be done with the wave of a wand.

Davide happened to have a small spiral bound notebook in his pocket and thought he would at least attempt to have a piece of the family chart recorded. With his pen he sat poised.

"Okay, let's start with the family chart."

Carmelo obliged and meticulously scoured his memory offering answers to the hundreds of questions Davide put to him. His son wrote furiously and when he had done with the family chart, started on Carmelo's youth and then his experiences in Italy followed by his experiences in Australia.

In one session of about six hours, Davide learnt more about his father than he had learnt in a lifetime. It was all recorded in his little notebook.

The next day, Davide could not persuade Carmelo to contribute anything else. No matter how hard he cajoled and wooed him, it was clear Carmelo was simply not in the mood anymore.

"Papa, remember when you used to do the pay sheets for the canecutters?"

"Yes of course, Davide. Why do you ask?"

"Well, one of the things I remember most was how as we grew older, you used to ask us to check your additions. They usually involved several large numbers that had to be totalled at the bottom of the pay sheet."

"Yes, well it was important to get it right, that's why I asked you to check my additions."

"But Papa, in all the years that we checked your additions, you never got one wrong. When we thought you had made a mistake, you would say, 'Wait a minute, I'll do the proof check on it'. If the proof check said you were right, you were right."

"Ah, you mean 'La Prova'. Yes, I learned it at school in Italy. Do you want me to show it to you again?"

"Yes please, Papa. This time, I'm going to write it down, so I can pass it on for the rest of the world to marvel at how simple yet brilliant it is."

He penned a set of numbers and then proceeded to explain how to apply 'La Prova'.

Addition	Add L/R	Equals	Add L/R	Single Number
39	3+9	12	1+2	3
756177	7+5+6+1+7+7	33	3+3	6
425	4+2+5	11	1+1	2
36774	3+6+7+7+4	27	2+7	9
14	1+4	5	5	5
+_____				+ _____
793429	7+9+3+4+2+9	34		25
		3+4		2+5
		7	=	7

Therefore, the addition is correct!   **La Prova (The Proof)**

"That's so unbelievable," said Davide. "I must ask some mathematicians to explain why, I mean, according to what principles of mathematics it works."

"Be my guest and let me know what you find out. It's a pity that the things we do in life couldn't be subjected to something like 'La Prova' so that we could be sure our decisions and our actions or reactions were right. Sure, we apply religious principles and the thoughts of the great thinkers and philosophers to our behaviour, but nothing is infallible. Not like 'La Prova' is infallible."

"Of course, Papa that is the way of the world. Life is unpredictable, it's random, it's chaotic. Call it whatever you want but it will never be perfect and what you want is a perfect world, Papa."

"Why should we have to accept anything less?"

Chapter 40

Conversations on going home

One day in the back garden, Carmelo had just finished erecting the bamboo stakes for the climbing beans when he had one of his dizzy spells. He had experienced them a number of times before thus he wasn't concerned. He knew what to do: he went upstairs, had a shower, got dressed and told his Elena he was going across the road to the hospital for another needle to remedy the dizzy spell. It was a simple procedure. He would lie down on the bed and Dr Merlo would issue a needle. After a short while, when he came to, he would get up, follow the path across the road to his wife, they would have dinner, he would read, then he would sleep and the following day, he would fertilize the beans and the job would be finished.

"Hi Carlo, had another one of your dizzy spells?" asked Doctor Merlo.

"Yes Doctor, I was just putting some stakes up for the climbing beans. It's not hard work, and then I started getting that dizzy sensation so I came up here."

"You did the right thing, Carlo," he prepared himself to give the injection. "This will counter the effect of dizziness brought on by your emphysema." As the injection pricked his skin, he immediately felt a sense of well-being. "There, you'll be up and about and home before you know it, Carlo."

Those were the last words Carmelo heard as he drifted off only this time he simply didn't return. He was in his eighty-fourth year and his time had come.

But I was there for him. I wasn't going to desert him now. This was his hour of greatest need. I would prepare him for the cross-over. A moment later, as soon as he came to in my world, we spoke as if we had known each other all our lives. And indeed we had. After all, I was his younger brother. He looked as if he were searching for something in the distance that was coming towards him until I came into focus and then he relaxed.

Hey, I know you. Do I know you?

Sort of… like, I'm your kindred spirit… been with you since you were three. A sort of sotto ego… that's me. You see, when you were three, I was stillborn and our mother Concetta died. I was released into this world as a homeless kindred spirit of the Cottone clan. I chose to attach myself to you as you were the youngest in the family. You offered the best chance of me experiencing a full life. Pretty good choice as it turned out in the end. Met a lot of nice people, did a lot of things, saw a lot of places. So, after all these years, we finally get to meet each other.

A sotto ego in me. Well, well!! What an interesting concept? I'll call you Sotto. That's what I'll call you. Well Sotto, I've broken down. Those running repairs… they couldn't last forever. So, where are you going to go now that this body has bailed out on us?

It's been a bumpy ride. I reckon I could upgrade to something smoother… something more in touch with the times, but I like you the way you are. It's been a bit hairy mind you, like when you nearly died from smallpox. That would have been a real bummer for me. Or if Mussolini had shot you for not bowing to him, what a let-down that would have been. The list goes on. It was fun while it lasted.

You've been happy with my performance then, have you? You never considered jumping ship? Or attaching yourself to a female for example, did you?

Nah… Strange blokes, these women. You and me, we understand each other. Anyhow, time to get ready. You've got a deadline to meet.

I want to know where you come from and where I'm going to. Like, is there somewhere, a someone… a make-it-happen guy? Do I have a choice? Come on, that's not much to ask.

Hey Carmelo, stop pestering me. I have to get you ready. You've got things to do and places to go. You've got people to see.

You worry about being pestered? How do you think I feel? Not knowing where I'm going. The least you could do is tell me.

Well Carmelo, I can't do that. Someone could be listening to our conversation. You're just going to have to trust me.

Trust you? What are you, a politician or something? Hey Sotto... I've gone all stiff... I can't even move... I'm all seized up. Don't pick me up like that, I'll fall apart. What are you doing, Sotto?

I'm taking you home.

Home, to where? What's going to happen to you?

You want to know what could happen to me when you go? Well I could end up in Limbo.

Hey Sotto... come on... what Limbo? Why are you talking about Limbo? We got a deal you and me. You're my kindred spirit. We're in this together for the long haul you and me. All right... all right. I'll cooperate. What now? I mean where to from here? Am I ready yet? Sotto... Sotto! Why have you stopped talking to me? Sotto, you listening? Don't pretend you're not there. I can see stardust. Is that you? Or is that me? I'm losing it. Hello... Hello. Knock... Knock. Talk to me Sotto!

Elena entered as quietly as she sat. She held Carmelo's hand and stroked his forehead.

"Meluzzo, your time has come. May God have mercy on your soul," and she did the sign of the cross. "Together, we've raised three fine sons and they found us three wonderful daughters. We have many grandchildren and have never wanted for anything. God has been good to us." She wiped her eyes with the floral handkerchief she had decorated herself during the many lonely hours many years earlier as she sat by the hurricane lamp yearning to be with her siblings and her mother and father a lifetime away. She looked at him and continued to stroke his forehead. "Our children will look after me now that you're gone. Go and prepare a place for us, Meluzzo. You walk with God now." Elena stayed with him for an extended period of time and then, as quietly as she came, she left.

Sorry, had to stand back for the lady. I'm here now. It's time for us to make the cross-over, Carmelo. Get ready. It could be any minute now.

Ah, so you're talking to me again? I was wondering where you were. I can't see you Sotto. Keep talking to me at least while we're waiting.

Very well. Tell me, if the Heavenly Father asks you about your journey on this earth and grants you one wish to make it a better place, what would you ask for Carmelo?

I would ask for a perfect world... with guidelines for good people to follow... and a lifetime guarantee that the world would remain perfect if they stuck to the guidelines.

And what is your one regret? Something you feel would have made your journey on earth more worthwhile.

My one regret is that I've always wanted to tell my story. I used to tell my son Davide things. He's a writer but I only told him bits and pieces along the way.

Yeah, well I can tell your story.

How can you tell my story, if you're supposed to be coming with me?

Well, I'll simply pass on what I know to Davide... sotto ego to sotto ego. We're all linked, us kindred spirits. There might be a bit of static along the way, but eventually, it'll all get through to him and he can write it all out.

That would be nice. What would you ask for Sotto, if the Heavenly Father grants you one wish to make the world a better place?

I too would ask for a perfect world, Meluzzo, my dear brother. It certainly hasn't happened this time around!

And your one regret?

My one regret is I never really had my own body. I didn't even get your permission. It was like I was a stowaway.

Well Sotto, you'll have to try harder than that. What is mine has always been yours. So, are we ready yet?

Yeah, we're ready.

Well, there's a chamber in my heart that's just perfect for you. Come on, get in. We've got things to do and people to see and Teresa has prepared a place for you and for me.

oOo

How Green Was My Valley

"Welcome to Babinda"
Stand here by my side
Where I am buried
And gaze upon this wondrous land
My host Australia.

Then take a little stroll
Beyond the railway line and into town
Babinda was my home.

But further west against the hills
Huge boulders watch the garden that I grew
And the cattle that I kept.

Go there
Go see for yourself
How green was my valley
Happy Valley.

Carmelo Cottone: 23/12/1901 – 25/10/1985

Canecutter: Happy Valley, Babinda

oOo